"An interesting read that kept me captivated. Fantastic storytelling."

"His historical fiction novels are not only extremely well written, they remind me of the fact-filled and cleverly engaging style of Clancy or even Sir Arthur Conan Doyle."

"Feenstra is my new favorite author. I've read his Boundary, The Breath of God and For Want Of A Shilling, and now his Falls Ende short stories. I cannot get enough!"

"What a great read, 'Five stars!' This book caught me completely by surprise, is very well written."

"This is a great read. I am sure this is just the beginning of a great series."

Falls Ende - Primus
First published in 2018 by Mellester Press

ISBN 978-0-473-44108-1 Soft Cover
ISBN 978-0-473-44109-8 Hard Cover
ISBN 978-0-473-48113-1 epub

Published in New Zealand
A catalogue record of this book is available
from the National Library of New Zealand.
Kei te pātengi raraunga o Te Puna Mātauranga
o Aotearoa te whakarārangi o tēnei pukapuka

With heartfelt thanks.

Edited by Jill Davis
Cover Chris Largent

http://www.paulwfeenstra.com/
Falls Ende © 2017 Paul W. Feenstra
Falls Ende – The Oath © 2017 Paul W. Feenstra
Falls Ende – Courser © 2018 Paul W. Feenstra
Falls Ende – The king © 2018 Paul W. Feenstra

Published by
Mellester Press

Other books by
Paul W Feenstra
Published by Mellester Press

Boundary

The Breath of God (Book 1 in Moana Rangitira series)
For Want of a Shilling (Book 2 in Moana Rangitira series)

Falls Ende – Primus (Book 1)
Falls Ende – Secundus (Book 2)
Falls Ende – Tertium (Book 3)
Falls Ende – Quartus (Book 4)
Falls Ende – Quintus (Book 5)
Falls Ende – Sextus (Book 6)

Gunpowder Green (New Zealand Short Stories)

Leonard hardy Series
A Sinister Consequence
A Questionable Virtue

Into the Shade

A Gentleman at heart

FALLS ENDE

PRIMUS

Published by

Mellester Press

For

Roger, Sharon,

Troy, Solomon and Jasper.

CHAPTER ONE

Mellester Manor, Devonshire, England 1157 A.D.

Stained brown by recent heavy rains, dark, silted water cascaded over sizeable boulders to begin its clamorous and chaotic plunge. Worn smooth from erosion, gleaming wet rocks embedded into both sides of the narrow chasm increased its force and funnelled the river, propelling the turbulent water forward and down to collide with rocks in a continuous explosion of noise and spray. Caught by the prevailing breeze, even mild gusts whisked the spray up and back, where it descended like a gentle, soft rain.

The river's descent wasn't completely vertical; it was a naturally stepped decline that dropped about twenty–two feet over a distance of ten yards or so. The narrowest part of the falls was at the top, and the watercourse gradually widened until it formed into a deep pool at the bottom loosely ringed by even more boulders. A little farther downstream, tributaries joined, the distance between riverbanks widened, and the water flow slowed noticeably to meander sedately in a series of lazy curves through low-lying valleys, towards the coast, and eventually serenely drifted into an estuary.

Along the sheer sides of the waterfall, in cracks and crevices, clear from the tumult of passing water, moss and lichen thrived in munificence, their dull hues blending artfully into the background of dark, glistening stone and dirtied water. On the south side, a well-used narrow path, or riverwalk, ran parallel to the river and sometimes dangerously close to the river's edge. The trees and bushes growing on the forested hills grew all the way down towards the path and provided a home to abundant game and wildlife.

On the other bank, the north side of the waterfall, the land was dominated by cultivated farms that belonged to Mellester Manor. Tended by villeins[1] and freemen[2], well-maintained crops on strips of arable land consisted mostly of wheat and barley. In adjacent fields, separated by hedgerows and well-maintained wooden railed fences, cows and a flock of sheep grazed contentedly on thick, lush grass. It was a peaceful manor, free of rancour, but not without a little grizzling - if it had none, it wouldn't be natural.

Skywards, towards the west, high-lit by the early morning sun, remnants of the last weather front could still be seen, bringing rain and a bitter chill that lingered. Two figures squelched through a paddock from nearby Mellester village, which consisted of a small cluster of homes and buildings dominated by a church. They headed up the gently sloping field towards the waterfall. The larger figure pushed an oversized barrow that contained a pile of freshly hewn wood, all neatly dressed and trimmed, an assortment of tools, and wrapped in cloth, some bread, cheese and a few strips of dried pork they would eat later in the day.

The animated voice of a boy, his breath turning white from the cold, could be heard from a distance as he told his father how he would be a deierie[3] farmer when old enough. With childish naivety, he elaborated and described the herd of cows he would one day own and breed the finest

1　*A tenant farmer legally tied to a lord of the manor.*
2　*Freeman were workers not bound to the manor and paid rent in exchange for land and residence.*
3　*dairy*

deierie cows in all of England. The boy's father wasn't in a mind to explain to his exuberant son the harsh realities of life as a freeman in the manor.

The sound of a horn could be heard in the distance, disrupting the boy's exhortation. Its three haunting blasts were a signal that would invoke a chain of events destined to have a profound and lasting effect on Mellester Manor.

Almost immediately, it was followed by the frantic baying of hounds. The man stopped pushing the heavy barrow, carefully lowered it to the ground, turned his head slightly and listened. After a heartbeat or two, he pointed into the distance and explained to the boy how Edgar, the lord's huntsman, left the village before sunrise with his apprentice son and headed into the forest beyond the river to search for a sign of wild boar. Once he located the animal, with reasonable certainty, he would alert the lord's hunt party to the boar's location by blowing his horn. Immediately, the hounds would be released, and the lord, accompanied by a retinue of noblemen and knights on horseback, would set out after the ferocious beast. The huntsman and Seth, his apprentice, would follow on foot. The dogs would be secured once their quarry had been seen.

The hunt was expected to be exhilarating and challenging, providing its participants with a genuine element of danger to test their bravery and skill. A full-grown, grumpy wild boar intent on mating was certainly a worthy adversary when disturbed and one to be respected and even feared when angered.

Mindful of the tasks that needed to be completed that day, the man bent to pick up the barrow's handles and continued pushing it towards the River Eks near the waterfall. The boy lagged a step or two behind, all previous thoughts of fat deierie cows and farming temporarily forgotten as he contemplated with some seriousness the dangers a wild boar posed to himself and his defenceless father. His ruminations were interrupted as his father began issuing instructions on where he wanted the freshly milled timber to be taken and holes dug.

The constant moisture near the waterfall caused wood to deteriorate quickly. The ground was permanently saturated, and the existing fence had fallen in places, no doubt succumbing to rot, its condition aggravated by cows constantly leaning against it. Only recently, a grazing sheep stood near the edge, and though sheep were usually sure-footed, it slipped and tumbled into the waterfall, its sodden heavy wool causing it to drown in the pool. The value of a healthy sheep was almost incalculable, and the loss was of serious concern, so repairing the fence was a priority.

Sheep weren't the only victims of the waterfall. Over time, other animals lost their footing and fell, and some years earlier, a hunter walking close to the chasm slipped on moss and plummeted into the falls, hitting his head on rocks as he fell. After surviving the fall and being severely injured, he was unable to drag himself to safety. The unfortunate man eventually died as he clung to a protruding boulder at the base of the falls. Children searching for mushrooms discovered the grotesque sight of the decomposing body sometime later. Within Mellester village, out of earshot of the huntsman's grieving widow, speculation was rife as to how many days the poor fellow suffered, his tormented screams unheard before he eventually died.

While the waterfall may once have had a formal name bestowed upon it by a previous lord, it was now known by everyone, both near and afar, as Falls Ende.

With the morning's tranquillity disturbed by the sound of barking dogs, Godwin Read instructed his only son, eleven-year-old Odo, on where he wanted new fence post holes dug and within a short time, breathing heavily, each was enveloped in a white fog as both father and son diligently went about their work.

They were adequately and similarly dressed. Each wore a capuchin, a hood that extended over their heads and then went down and around the neck like a collar which draped over the shoulders. Beneath the capuchin, they wore a knee-length tunic, which, together with breeches made from coarse homespun wool, was secured by a belt at the waist. Godwin Read wore leather goatskin boots while Odo was barefoot. If he had cold feet, he didn't complain.

The fence they were repairing ran parallel to the river and about three feet from the precipitous edge. Hidden rocks buried beneath the soil made digging with wooden spades difficult. Even the metal foot, which prevented the wood from wearing out on the blade, was ineffectual. Warming up as he worked, Godwin removed his capuchin, and Odo, happy to emulate his father, was about to do the same.

Godwin could tell the hounds were drawing nearer from the sound of frantic barking. He paused in his digging and took a moment to listen. Seeing his father stop, young Odo gratefully rested, leaning on his spade as he waited for a hint of what was happening.

Godwin raised his arm and pointed in the direction of where he could hear the hounds. They watched and waited. Above the roar of cascading water, they could hear the clamour and the excited shouts of men on horseback as they came ever closer.

Suddenly, bushes near the track began moving, and a massive wild boar charged out. Standing over three feet in height and six feet in length, the immense animal slid to a halt on the narrow path, labouring for breath. It was coloured black and grey, and a raised line of coarse hair ran down the length of its back. Two curved tusks protruding from its snout drew attention to the business end of the dangerous and powerful beast.

Both Godwin and Odo, safely on the other side of the falls, stood transfixed as the boar turned its massive head to each side, deciding which direction to flee. Not wishing to be impaled by a hunter's spear and turned into a trophy, the boar, with its head down, rushed up the riverwalk and away. Godwin fervently hoped no one was walking further up the path, as they would surely be in grave peril.

More shouting immediately drew Godwin's attention to the tree line as a mounted knight carrying a spear broke free from the forest. Yanking hard on the reins, he expertly pulled the courser to a halt before it plummeted into the falls and looked in the direction of where his quarry fled. Godwin recognized the man immediately- Sir William Ainsley, Lord of Mellester Manor.

The lord saw the boar in the distance as it made good its escape. Accepting the challenge and baring his teeth in a smile, Sir William dug his spurs into the courser's sides, and the horse leapt forward to give chase. Before the courser had taken two steps, a hound shot out from the low bushes at the forest fringe and was almost trampled underfoot. Heedless of the effect its sudden appearance made on the horse, the young hound began gleefully pursuing the fleeing boar while ignoring yelled commands to return.

The courser hadn't expected the sudden encroachment on its space, and two things happened. The horse shied away from the dog and reared backwards. With one arm raised and grasping his spear, Sir William was caught completely by surprise and off–balance. As the courser lunged to the side and its front feet lifted from the ground, Sir William tumbled from the saddle, landing heavily on the thin border of wet grass that grew alongside the path and began to slide headfirst down and into the falls. With eyes wide and snorting, the horse regained its footing and began to trot away.

Although not in full armour, Sir William's mail and greaves added to his weight and did little to slow his momentum. Still clutching his spear, the lord unsuccessfully attempted to halt his advance by digging it into the soft, wet earth. His effort was wasted as the spear snapped when it caught on a buried rock. Sir William plunged into Falls Ende, somewhere just over halfway down.

Just before he vanished over the edge, two more mailed knights appeared from the forest and heard their lord's stricken cry. As one, they dismounted quickly while Godwin Read was already moving on the other side of the falls. He stepped close to the edge and saw Sir William Ainsley bounce from a boulder and rest partially submerged in the pool at the bottom. More noblemen began appearing, and Godwin, ignoring their questioned pleas, kicked off his boots and removed his tunic. In mere seconds, he stood barefoot at the edge of the falls, looking down. Sir William lay partly across a boulder and was about to slide into the pool – he wasn't moving. The weight of his armour would drag his limp body beneath the surface to drown, just like the sheep.

Odo ran up to stand beside his father just as he leapt. Godwin planned his jump carefully, and as he dropped, he contracted his body as much as possible lest an outstretched limb strike an object on the way down.

He hit the water with a tremendous splash just as the lord disappeared. Odo was relieved to see his father land safely. Godwin quickly found his footing at the pool's edge, reached into the frigid, silty water, grabbed Sir William's slack arm, and, with some difficulty, began pulling the spluttering man to safety. The lord was only submerged a few seconds before his head surfaced, and Godwin began checking him for injuries. Thankfully, he still lived.

Above, knights and noblemen peered over the edge and began shouting questions, enquiring about Sir William's condition. Some began removing their armour, preparing to come to Godwin's assistance. Within moments, Edgar, the huntsman's familiar face, appeared, and Godwin shouted over the noise of the waterfall, requesting a rope to hoist the lord up.

Blood flowed freely from a few lacerations on Sir William's head. The lord was most fortunate; he'd been wearing a *cervelliere*, a small metal skull cap, which probably saved his life. Now dented in at least two places, it was cast aside. His body armour appeared to have prevented further injury.

Somewhat dazed and confused, Sir William stirred, coughed a few times, and tried to struggle into a sitting position. Godwin spoke soothingly and respectfully, asking the lord to remain still until he could be pulled to safety.

Concerned knights and noblemen fawned over their injured lord and expressed no gratitude or acknowledgement to the man who bravely risked his own life to save him; Godwin was rudely shouldered aside. Shivering uncontrollably, Godwin began walking along the path to a bridge about a hundred and fifty yards away so he could return to the other side of the river and resume work. Seeing his father's state, Odo picked up his tunic and capuchin and ran alongside the river towards the bridge. Far in the distance, the muted and persistent baying of a solitary, disobedient hound could still be heard.

Sitting up, Sir William Ainsley regained his full faculties and was now being attended to by the huntsman. A few steps behind him, a group of four knights were discussing, their voices becoming increasingly louder. One young man, Sir William's only son, Sir Wystan, broke away from the group, stepped to his father and crouched at his side.

"Milord, I saw what happened, t'was the boy of the herdsman. He brandished his spade, causing yer horse to shy–"

Hearing the exchange, the three knights, all young men, approached the lord. "We saw it as well, Sir William; the boy's actions were deliberate and wanton," proclaimed one, lending support to the accusation.

The other two murmured in agreement with less conviction.

"I shall have the reeve[4]–" continued Sir Wystan, only to be interrupted

4   *Manager and overseer of a manor.*

again.

"Ye'll do no such thing!" bellowed the lord. The yelling caused him additional pain. He winced at the vocal exertion.

"The lad was irreverent and offered no respect, Milord," Sir Wystan appealed. "It was a deliberate act of insolence that cannot and must not go unpunished."

A supporting chorus of indiscernible mumbling from the three other knights added weight to the assertions.

"A wagon'll be here soon, sire," offered Edgar. "Take yer back to th' manor, it will."

Sir William's closed his eyes tightly. He took a deep breath and slowly exhaled. "Fetch m' horse, Sir Wystan. I'll not be trussed up in back of a Farandman's[5] wagon... So long as I live and breathe, I'll ride back."

Unhappy to be tasked with menial duties normally assigned to lessers, Wystan Ainsley prodded Edgar with his foot and inclined his head.

"Aye, Milord," Edgar bowed his head and backed away to retrieve Sir William's horse.

Sir Wystan's face was dark.

Across the river, Godwin and Odo were already hard at work. Steam rose from Godwin's wet breeches as father and son toiled in the cold morning air.

5   *Traveling merchant*

CHAPTER TWO

As far as manor houses were concerned, Mellester Manor wasn't particularly impressive. It wasn't constructed as a castle or built for defence. It was first and foremost a home to Lord and Lady Mellester and their only son, Sir Wystan. The manor house was built atop a low hill that overlooked Mellester Village and was accessed by a curving carriageway that swept up the hill from the road below.

The two–storied house was constructed from stone and contained two wings, much like the letter 'U'. The middle portion of the house faced outwards toward the village. Additional buildings were situated near the rear of the main house, behind a large open courtyard.

There was a particular room on the upper level of the manor house that the lord and lady used frequently, most often in the late afternoon. Because of its small size, it was easy to keep warm as the ageing knight and his wife became more sensitive to cold and dampness. The room offered a spectacular, expansive view of the countryside, and it was in this room that Sir William now sat. An old Irish wolfhound lay curled contentedly at his master's feet.

Although afflicted with no life-threatening injuries from his fall, Sir William suffered from severe bruising, mainly on his shoulders, arms, and legs. A bandage was wrapped around his head, causing his long grey hair to tuft up while a blanket draped over his legs. He held a goblet of heated, mulled wine.

Since the incident at Falls Ende four days ago, Sir William had been unusually quiet and reflective. The lady of the manor believed that the fall shook him badly and that he'd begun to question his own mortality. Today was the first day he had risen from his bed.

The stout, wooden door creaked open, and Sir Wystan stepped tentatively into the room. A quick glance ensured they were alone, and so emboldened, he walked towards his father and made to sit in the chair usually favoured by his mother.

"I did not invite you to be seated," growled the lord.

The abruptness of the remark almost made the young man jump.

Wystan's lips were suddenly dry, and he wished he had something to drink. He bowed his head in acknowledgement and respectively remained standing.

William Ainsley stroked his grey beard and felt saddened. Wystan, his only son and heir, was an abject disappointment. He'd realised that, at some point, he'd failed in his duty as a father to raise a son he could be proud of. He'd disciplined the lad and taught him everything he knew, just as his father had instructed him, but try as he might, he achieved nothing but suffered endless disappointments.

Sir William presided over Mellester Manor fairly and judiciously; his punishments were just and equitable when warranted. He supervised all aspects of farming, was decisive, and thanks to this, Mellester Manor thrived. Some would say the manor's affairs were even better now than when his father was lord. What would happen when God took him from this earth? How would Wystan, his heir, fare as lord and master?

He turned his head slightly and briefly looked up at his son. He felt thwarted, not by Wystan, but at himself and his shortcomings. When his time came, as it would soon, he would be judged before almighty God and answer for his failings. He slowly turned away in disgust and took a long pull on his wine.

Oblivious to the tension in the room, the old dog lifted a rear leg and pointed it up towards the heavens. It twisted around and shamelessly began to gnaw at something that crawled beneath its fur and over its skin.

Sir William pulled his gaze away from the hound and nodded. God had just given him a sign.

Sensing his father's agitation, Wystan nervously shifted his feet. The silence unsettled him.

Sir William reflected a moment longer.

When Wystan was a young lad, he'd been sent away to be schooled as a knight. It cost a small fortune, and the boy excelled only in carousing and rebellion. Certainly, he eventually became a knight, though the distinction did not come without a struggle. A relief to a father but of little consolation.

Again, the door creaked open, and without looking, Sir William knew his wife Constance entered. He allowed himself the briefest of smiles. Her timing was impeccable.

"Milord," she offered in greeting as she took her customary seat.

He gave her a smile. "Milady." Sir William twisted in his chair to look his son in the eye. "You defied me on the hunt. It nearly cost me my life, and an expensive hound was killed."

"Milord, I saw the herdsman's son–"

"You saw no such thing! You think me a fool?" interrupted the lord. "You think the knock to my head addled me?" he shook his head in displeasure.

"I know what I saw," continued Sir Wystan, somewhat less confidently.

"Enough of your lies!" Spittle flew from the lord's mouth, and his lower lip quivered in rage.

The wolfhound risked a look up at his master.

"I instructed you to keep the inexperienced hound tethered and not let it loose. Why did you flout me? Were my instructions not clear?"

Sir Wystan's eyes shifted around the room. A look of sympathy or understanding was not reflected in his mother's face. With defiance, he returned his father's piercing gaze and wisely thought it best to remain taciturn.

"I could have been killed!" Despite the injury, Sir William slowly shook his head. "I'm tired of all your falsehoods and lies, and I will have no more of them!" The room returned to silence as Sir William considered how to teach Wystan a lesson. He decided to mull it over for a day or two. "Begone from my sight, and while you ponder truthfulness, obedience and fealty, find another hound to replace the one that was killed – and pay for it from your purse."

Sir Wystan swallowed and bowed his head. "Milord, Milady." He spun and left the room, grateful he'd been spared a humiliating punishment.

Their son's continued abhorrent behaviour was a much-discussed topic by Sir William and Lady Constance. Over the years, they'd unsuccessfully tried to curtail his extravagances and indulgences. Their attempts to calm his temper, curtail his belligerence and instil a sense of morality and virtue into his life had all failed - as parents, they had failed. As the door closed, Sir William threw his goblet against the wall in frustration. Wine splattered everywhere, the empty goblet eventually settling beneath a tapestry. With a grunt, the Irish wolfhound slowly eased itself up, ambled to the wall and eagerly began lapping the ruby-coloured liquid.

It was half-light, neither day nor night, and young Odo had already turned the sheep, and the cows loose from their overnight shelter after milking. Attached to their home was another structure called a byre; it was used to house cattle and sheep during evenings and inclement weather and kept them safe from thieves and other predators. Grabbing a large rake, Odo began mucking out the dirtied straw as Godwin assembled the tools he needed to complete his tasks that day.

"Hail, Herdsman Godwin!" came a voice.

Not used to early morning visitors, Godwin turned in surprise and recognised the outline of the figure standing in the doorway. He smiled. "And good morn to ye, Reeve Norman."

The reeve entered the byre and watched young Odo, who suddenly had an extra spring in his step. The appearance of the manor's reeve was always a source of motivation.

Although a few years older, Reeve Norman Bloxham and Godwin grew up together and have remained close friends. Each man suffered the loss of a wife, and neither remarried. While Godwin was blessed with one son, Norman was childless. His wife died while giving birth to their first, a stillborn.

"Did yer come about th' leaky trough?"

Norman turned away from studying Odo. "Nay," he sighed. "Godwin, you'll need to come with me. Sir William wants to see ye."

"What fer?" Puzzled, Godwin placed the large mallet he carried into the barrow and turned to the reeve. This was highly unusual.

Norman shrugged. "I don't know. Sir William didn't feel the need to share his reasons with me." Norman knew something was going on and felt some concern for his friend.

Godwin scratched his head. "Has anyone complained–?"

"We need to go now, Godwin," interrupted the reeve.

"Let me give Odo some work to do."

"He's to come too. The lord asked for him."

Godwin looked up sharply. "He did?"

Both men came to the same conclusion and gave Odo a hard stare. Obvious to both men, the boy had been up to mischief again. It wasn't the first time he'd gotten himself into trouble.

"I'm sorry, Godwin, I have to do the lord's bidding." All traces of Norman's customary joviality disappeared.

"But why are we being summoned?" Godwin asked.

"I wish I knew, my friend," Reeve Norman shook his head in puzzlement.

"Odo!" Godwin called his son. "You heard Norman, lad. We must go."

Mellester Hall encompassed one entire wing of the manor house. It was an extensive room with benches and trestle tables strategically positioned along each wall, which left a free centre aisle, except for an enormous hearth in the middle of the hall. Upon a dais at the rear of the hall stood an ornate and solidly built chair from which Sir William adjudicated. It was padded and comfortable, and when seated, the lord exuded authority over his people and demesne[6]. Another smaller chair was reserved for the lady who frequently sat with him. On his left, at a roughly hewn desk, sat a steward who managed the finances of the manor and on the right side, half a dozen knights, along with Sir Wystan, stood in a group whispering. Some peasants waited in silence to have the lord settle a dispute, and a priest stood near the steward with hands clasped and head bowed.

A man-at-arms swung open the massive wooden door granting access to the Manor Hall. Reeve Norman entered first, followed by Odo, and lastly, Godwin, who took a big breath and mumbled a quick prayer before stepping inside. Outside, near the stables, a knight mounted his horse and rode away from the manor. Had anyone been outside watching, they would have been surprised to see the knight wore a white surcoat with a red cross emblazoned on the front.

This was the first time Odo had been in the great hall, and his head pivoted from side to side at all the unusual sights and accoutrements on display. Colourful pennants and tapestries hung from the walls, including hunting trophies, shields, and various weapons. A suit of armour lay propped up against a thick, wooden post. A few serfs scurried around, mainly young girls he recognised from the village doing various chores.

Norman, Godwin and Odo walked down the centre aisle, around the hearth and stopped ten paces from the dais. The lord, looking fully recovered from his accident over a week ago, quietly issued instructions to the steward.

6   *Land attached to a manor.*

Norman took a step backwards, leaving father and son to face Lord Mellester and whatever was in store for them.

From behind the dais, another figure emerged. Without speaking, Lady Constance walked behind the lord and took her seat. She turned to the new arrivals and silently assessed them. Godwin couldn't take his eyes off her; she was beautiful and a welcome distraction from his worry. He'd never been in such close proximity to her ladyship, and he was immediately taken with her. Despite her age, Lady Constance's face was smooth and free of wrinkles, and her figure was stately and proud. She truly was a sight to behold.

"Reeve Norman, what have ye fer me?" the lord asked, his voice clear, authoritative and loud.

Norman took a step forward. "I bring with me herdsman Godwin Read and his apprentice son Odo, Milord."

Sir William spared father and son a quick glance. "Sir Wystan, attend to me."

Godwin recognised the lord's son as he separated from the group of knights and confidently swaggered over to stand beside his father.

The lord, the lady, and Sir Wystan were now staring at him. Godwin felt very exposed and vulnerable. He raised his head and bravely looked at each in turn, lastly staring at Sir Wystan, who scowled.

"Ye were both in the common one week ago?" asked Sir William.

Godwin nodded. "Yea, Milord."

"Come closer, I can't hear ye."

Godwin and Odo each took two steps closer. Godwin cleared his throat. "Aye, Milord," he loudly repeated.

"Are these the two ye saw working on the fence?" Lord Mellester asked his son.

"They are, Milord," replied Sir Wystan with a slight bow of the head and a smirk.

Sir William turned to his wife and gave her a barely perceptible smile.

It did not go unnoticed. Something just passed between them, thought Godwin. He spared a quick look at the priest, who was staring at Odo.

"As a father, do you feel responsible for the actions of your son?" Sir William suddenly asked, surprising Godwin.

Oswald, the priest, looked up.

Godwin turned back to Sir William. "I do, Milord. I am responsible for my son."

"As am I … as am I," slowly repeated Sir William in a barely audible voice. He took a breath and spoke again with authority. "And your son, he is an apprentice herdsman?"

"He is Milord and a hard worker too."

"Have ye heard the charge against him of wilfully acting to endanger my life by recklessly brandishing a spade? I believe the word *wanton* was used?"

Godwin wasn't sure how to answer. He looked down at his feet. *This charge is ridiculous; surely, it is an error.* His mind was racing. He looked up to answer and saw Sir Wystan grinning. "I am not aware of any complaint made against Odo. He's a good lad, Milord."

Lord Mellester stroked his beard. "Sir Wystan, do ye wish to reconsider your accusations against the herdsman's son?"

The priest was watching the proceedings intently. His eyes narrowed, and he stepped towards the steward, bent over and whispered in his ear. Godwin saw the steward shrug his shoulders. What is going on? Even the steward and priest seem puzzled.

The smirk on Sir Wystan's face disappeared. All heads in the hall turned to him and waited for his response. Norman risked a glance at Godwin and silently mouthed his bafflement.

"Sir Wystan?" questioned the lord with his eyebrows raised.

Lady Mellester's face showed no emotion, although she, too, was looking intently at her son.

"I, uh, my accusation stands, Milord. I have witnesses–"

"Reeve Norman," stated the lord, interrupting Sir Wystan, "What say ye about the work of Herdsman Godwin and his son?"

Norman shuffled a step closer and stood beside Godwin and Odo. "I've never had to take issue with them. The herd prospers, and Godwin and the boy also lend their back willingly to other tasks, Milord."

Sir William turned to the priest. "Oswald, what say ye about Herdsman Godwin and the boy? Are their tithes met?"

The priest looked thoughtful and then flicked his eyes towards Godwin. He made brief eye contact and then looked at Odo for a moment. He turned back towards Mellester's lord and nodded solemnly. "Milord, the church has no quarrel with Herdsman Godwin, although the church is always in need–"

Lord Mellester waved his hand. He'd heard enough from the priest. "Steward Alard, is Herdsman Godwin in good standing? Has he accumulated debt? What say ye?"

Sir Wystan regained his confidence and was again staring at Odo.

"One moment, Milord, I need to, uh, find… ah, here it is. Milord, Herdsman Godwin is without debt, and I believe he never has been in debt, sire. He pays his taxes and rent in a timely manner."

Godwin saw another subtle look pass between the lord and lady.

Sir William shifted in his seat, "Herdsman Godwin, have you any words in defence of your son?"

Godwin didn't know how to respond. The lord was there one week ago, and he'd seen what had happened. Odo had done nothing wrong. Sir William knew this. Surely, he must. He felt anxiousness in the pit of his stomach. Beside him, he felt Norman stir. All eyes were again on him. He looked towards Sir Wystan and saw him sneer. Behind, the group of knights also stood with their eyes firmly fixed on him.

"Herdsman, are ye unable to speak?"

"Milord, it saddens me that I must defend my son when I know he's caused no harm. Last week, we was fix'n th' fence, that's all. We was workin' hard and had no interest in causing mischief. Odo couldn't have done anything, he was busy digging   I don't know what else to say, Milord."

Until now, Odo remained quiet and not spoken or moved, but now he began fidgeting and looking up at his father.

"It looks like your son is eager to speak, herdsman. What have ye to say, boy?"

Unbidden, Odo took two steps forward. Godwin went to haul him back by the ear, but the lord waved him away.

"Milord, my father says a man has his word, even when he has nothing else to give. He says his word is tethered to him like a calf to a cow. I can give you my word that I did no such thing as what ye said I done – that is all I have."

Godwin held his breath.

"Well spoken, lad. Tell me, will ye be a herdsman like your father?"

"I will have me own deierie herd one day, and make the finest milk in all England, Milord."

"And for this manor, I hope," said Lord Mellester. He didn't smile.

Odo nodded enthusiastically.

Others in the hall began laughing. The lord swivelled in his seat. "Silence!" he yelled. "I will not have anyone mock this proceeding. I do not jest, Herdsman Godwin and his son do not jest, and Sir Wystan does not jest." Sir William's eyes blazed. "Enough!"

Godwin pulled the back of Odo's tunic until he stood safely beside him.

"Someone bring me wine!" added the lord. His uncharacteristic anger simmered.

Lady Mellester knew enough of her husband to see the man was agitated. The cause of his foul mood was based on the seriousness of the business at hand and the unpleasantness that would follow. She looked towards her son and saw the dark look on his face as he stared at the boy.

No one spoke. The hall of Mellester Manor was deathly quiet. Even servants stopped work to listen. Other people, some knights, noblemen and residents, had silently entered the hall and now stood riveted, curious about the outcome of the unusual proceeding.

Godwin patted Odo on his back and whispered, "It'll be alright, you'll see."

A servant girl came quickly with a jug of wine and refilled the lord's goblet.

Lord Mellester sat back in his seat and stroked his beard. His eyes scanned the hall and studied his knights, men, peasants, and serfs. He may not have known them all by name, but he knew who they were and was acutely aware of his responsibilities towards them. Finally, he settled his gaze on the herdsman and his son. The boy's words unsettled him and drew attention to his own foibles.

"I have been shamed," began the lord, speaking in a more moderated tone. "It is obvious to me that the real issue is one of honesty. One son is telling the truth, and the other is telling a lie." Mellester's lord paused momentarily, brought the goblet to his mouth and took a hefty swallow. He wiped his mouth and beard with the back of his hand before continuing. "As a knight, Sir Wystan swore an oath; his word should be taken with the solemnity of the weight behind the oath and the status nobility affords. What happens if a knight lacks the desirable qualities he swore to uphold? After all, a knight holds a position elevated above that of common folk, so should we not take his word first and foremost before those of others?" The question was rhetorical, yet he paused and gazed around the hall as if waiting for an answer. "When faced with the decision of determining who has lied to me … and where I have the word of a knight challenging the word of a herdsman, just a mere boy … obviously I should honour the knight – and without question accept his word."

Heads nodded in supplicant agreement.

Lord Mellester placed his goblet on the armrest of his seat and stood. He pointed to both Godwin and Odo. "Come, stand before me."

Godwin was ready to grab Odo's hand and flee; he'd never been so frightened. He felt rivulets of sweat beginning to trickle down his back. He reached for his son's hand and took another tentative step towards the lord.

"How have ye shown loyalty to your lord, herdsman?" Sir William's voice grew louder through his impassioned oratory.

"I, uh –"

Without waiting for an answer, Lord Mellester turned to his son. "How have you shown loyalty to your lord, Sir Wystan?"

Sir Wystan raised his head proudly. "My oath and fealty, Milord."

Sir William turned away from his son to face Godwin and Odo. He glanced quickly at his wife, who smiled in encouragement.

"Steward Alard, Reeve Norman, make note of my judgement. Priest Oswald, see church records are also changed."

"Aye, Milord," they replied as one.

The priest took a small step closer.

"How many acres does the herdsman pay rent on?"

"Fifteen acres in total, Milord, which includes Falls Ende," squeaked Reeve Norman. He could hardly speak; such was the state of his nerves.

"Very well. From this day forward, title of the land currently farmed by Herdsman Godwin will be transferred to him in the name of Godwin Read. The land is his!"

In total surprise, people began talking, but the lord of the manor wasn't finished yet. "Silence!" he bellowed. "I also owe a debt of gratitude to this man. Without whose selfless bravery, I wouldn't be here today. He saved my life. Thank you, Herdsman Godwin." Sir William dipped his head in thanks and respect.

Godwin was in shock. He felt his friend Norman clap him on the back.

"Praise God," Norman said quietly to himself. He leaned towards Godwin and whispered, "Congratulations."

"Silence!"

Overwhelmed, Godwin was unable to speak. His heart pounded. It was almost too much to bear. He wiped his eyes and squeezed Odo's hand. He didn't understand why the lord granted him this gift. It made no sense.

Odo looked up at his father with tears running down his face. He saw Reeve Norman blinking rapidly.

"Milord!" appealed Sir Wystan.

"I have a gift for you too, Sir Wystan. Step forward."

Mollified, the knight relaxed a little as he took a step closer.

Sir William looked directly at his son, his expression grim. "As of this day, I release you of your oath of fealty."

Sir Wystan's mouth fell open.

The hall erupted. Knights, men–at–arms, and noblemen were all in shock. Some yelled.

"Silence!" again commanded Sir William, raising both his arms. "Quiet!"

He waited until things settled down and lowered his arms. The hard edge of his voice left no doubt about his feelings and mood. He eased himself upright and surveyed the room. "My son spoke falsely. When given the chance to reconsider, he chose not to." Sir William turned to face his son. "I can recall every moment of the accident at Falls Ende. I remember the young novice hound leaping before my horse after I insisted that *you* keep the animal tethered! Your disobedience nearly cost me my life. Instead of admitting your gaffe, you tried to blame an innocent boy.

The same boy who spoke to me in this hall and said, 'A man has his word, even when he has nothing else to give.' And he told me that was all *he* had to give!" Sir William returned to his chair, sat down and took another pull of wine. "I cannot have a knight in my service who does not uphold the oath of fealty he gave me – even if he is of my blood *and*... has plenty to give!"

Lady Constance's eyes flashed, and the corners of her mouth twitched. It lasted for a moment – it was doubtful anyone noticed.

Again, there was an upwelling of noise. Godwin cleared his throat and whispered to Reeve Norman. "Does that mean Sir Wystan is no longer heir to the manor?"

Reeve Norman scratched his head. "I believe he is still heir, just no longer a knight in the service of a lord; he has no master."

CHAPTER THREE

Mellester Manor, ten years later.

Oswald, the parish priest, continued his rant, extolling the virtues of the church in a litany of well-rehearsed utterances. As he did every Sunday morning, he stood before his congregation wearing a soiled and stained dalmatic tunic over his alb. He flapped his arms and decried unchristian–like behaviour and promised eternal damnation if tithes were not met and increased offerings weren't received.

"The church requires a new roof!" he exclaimed, raising both hands towards the heavens and a porous roof before looking up.

Only a few parishioners followed his example and lifted their faces towards the roof. Most believed the roof to be somewhat adequate and leaked only a little; some had their eyes closed, others snored. Odo looked at the back of Charlotte's head and had impure thoughts.

"God's house must be kept dry," intoned Oswald, suggesting parishioners could afford to bequeath a penny or two more to help pay for the new roof. Sadly, the village had little to spare.

Odo couldn't wait for the service to end and, independent of Priest Oswald's encouragement, silently mouthed his own prayer. Today was an important day.

Priest Oswald reluctantly concluded the service, and his congregation, the good folk of Mellester, exited the church as quickly as possible. Odo stood a little distance from the church and waited for Charlotte to emerge with her family.

Finally, he saw her tugging on the arm of her father. Her mother, carrying the baby, followed closely behind, and Odilia, her younger sister, brought up the rear.

"Hail, Herdsman Odo! Seems this Sunday morning has Charlotte in a tither," Gerald's eyes twinkled.

"Father!" admonished Charlotte. She gave Odo a smile and turned away in case her flushed cheeks provided fuel for a discussion she wanted no part of.

"Cheeseman Gerald, fare ye well?" Odo replied somewhat anxiously.

"I do, lad, that I do."

Charlotte gave her father a nudge.

"Oh, uh, yeah. Perhaps ye would care to join me for a cup of mead?"

Odo grinned, feeling some relief. "Thank ye, Gerald."

Rain began to fall, and neither Gerald nor Odo spared any thought to the church roof Oswald prattled about. They sat at a table inside Gerald's home, each with a tankard of mead in front of them.

Gerald and Agnes's home fronted the main village square, where they sold cheese that Gerald made in the shed attached to the rear of their house. Charlotte insisted to her mother that they allow her father and Odo to talk privately. She loitered near the curtain separating both rooms and, hidden from view, easily overheard every word as the two men spoke.

With every passing moment, she was becoming more frustrated. Odo wasn't sticking to the plan; instead, he talked about his cows and a bull he wanted. She resisted the urge to intrude and give Odo a subtle reminder. However, her patience was finally rewarded when Odo cleared his throat.

"Uh, Cheeseman Gerald, I have something I wish to discuss."

Gerald looked up, feigning surprise. "Then speak, lad."

Charlotte previously insisted that Odo recite, word for word, the phrase they'd practised.

"I have a fondness for Charlotte and would like yer permission to marry her."

Behind the curtain, Charlotte rolled her eyes and clenched her fists. *This is not what he was supposed to say!*

The request was unsurprising, and Gerald had been quietly looking forward to it. "I see," he said, nodding as though this was unexpected and serious news. He rubbed his chin as if in deep thought. "And as a father, I must ask, can ye provide fer her? Ye are young, and though I know that since the unfortunate passing of your father three year ago, ye have done well fer yerself, but can yer look after Charlotte and any kiddies ye may be blessed to have?" Gerald took his tankard and drained it. His little speech had taken some time to rehearse. He was proud of himself and thought he spoke well.

Odo's eyes were wide, and he nodded in agreement long before Gerald finished. "Aye, I can, Gerald," he said enthusiastically. "I have managed to save a bit, and Papa left me a little. Falls Ende is mine, and I'm goin' to buy more cows and produce even more milk so ye can make more cheese."

Gerald smiled, "That ye will, lad. And I say, as long as yer have the means to care for Charlotte, yer both have my blessing. Congratulations, Odo." Gerald was grinning.

Beside herself with joy and unable to restrain herself, Charlotte thrust aside the curtain and ran into the room to hug her father. She'd loved Odo since they were children. It was inconceivable for her to marry anyone else. She'd spurned many a boy and, later, any man who had shown interest in her.

Agnes was called, and it was quickly decided Odo and Charlotte would marry the following spring.

Oblivious to the rain and overwhelmed with joy and relief, Odo walked the short distance home without a care in the world. For a brief moment, he felt saddened that his father wasn't alive, but he knew Godwin would have been happy for him.

When Godwin became ill and bedridden, father and son talked for hours. Odo told his father of the depth of his love for Charlotte and his future plans, and although not surprised, Godwin encouraged him to save and make good sound decisions, and at the right time, he assured him Cheeseman Gerald would agree to the betrothal.

While Godwin prospered due to Sir William's decision to award him title on his lands, not everything had gone well. Sir William Ainsley, Lord of Mellester, passed away about four years ago, and Sir Wystan Ainsley, his heir, became Lord of Mellester.

Eager to prove himself and influence other lords and knights, the new lord began to hold regular feasts. He spent an enormous amount of coin to impress his guests and even hoped that word of his feasts and generosity would reach the ears of the king.

In fact, the king had heard about the goings-on at Mellester but not quite in the manner Sir Wystan envisioned. Rumours surfaced at court about lavish spending by the new lord of Mellester, and word went around that Sir Wystan incurred substantial debt while the manor failed to prosper.

Things hadn't gone well for the young man since that fateful day when Lord Mellester released Sir Wystan of his oath. His circle of close friends diminished, and he was no longer invited to events and gatherings of social importance. To compensate for his frivolous expenses, which the manor could ill afford, and against all wise counsel, Sir Wystan raised taxes and levies, and the people of Mellester suffered. Small businesses and merchants, dependent on a flourishing local economy, began to struggle. Many went hungry, and where jobs were once plentiful, now quite a few flag-fallen[7] beggars roamed the streets, and petty crime increased.

Reeve Norman tried unsuccessfully to change the ways of the young lord. As a reward for his diligence and years of dedicated service, he was replaced by Reeve Merick, a sycophant with far less experience in overseeing farming. Norman now lived in his cruck[8] house, selling a few eggs to help make ends meet. The childless Norman was like Odo's surrogate father, and as he advanced in years, he welcomed the relationship with the young man.

Odo's cows produced milk, which he sold to Gerald, who in turn made cheese – they were both dependent on each other. However, Odo intuitively knew that if he were to succeed, he would need customers beyond the borders of Mellester Manor and increase his milk production.

His milking cows were not large animals and thus produced a small

7   *Without work, unemployed.*
8   *A peasant's house*

amount of milk. He had an untested theory; if he cross-bred one of his cows with a larger bull from a different breed, he could end up with a bigger cow that produced more daily milk for a more extended period.

He knew of a local bull that would be adequate for testing this theory. It was stabled only a few miles away and owned by Mellester's lord. He approached the new reeve to ask about renting the bull to service his cows and was told he would need to take the matter up with Sir Wystan.

Since that memorable day in Mellester hall ten years ago, Odo had little interaction with the new lord. Sir Wystan seldom wandered his lands and chose not to involve himself in mundane and routine farming matters, preferring to hunt and host feasts instead. Odo decided it was time to seek permission to obtain the bull.

Rather than act rashly, Odo sought counsel from Norman and Gerald. Both supported his idea but reminded him it was an expensive gamble. He could end up with a larger cow that ate more grass and produced the same milk as the smaller breed. Charlotte, ever supportive, believed and shared in Odo's vision and encouraged him as much as possible. She was also the moderated voice of reason and insisted he be cautious.

Rain continued to fall, and the sky became bleak. There was no hope that the weather would improve anytime soon. The deluge beat down on Odo and Norman as they trudged up the carriageway towards Mellester hall, and by the time they were both granted admittance, they were soaked.

Understandably, Odo was a little nervous and unsure how the lord would react to his request and didn't know if there was any lingering animosity towards him. Norman and Charlotte urged care as Sir Wystan was notoriously unpredictable and fickle.

Their visit to the manor was short-lived, and by the end of his brief audience with the lord, Odo believed he should have stayed home. Sir Wystan slouched in his seat, drank wine and barely looked at him as he pleaded his argument for creating a crossbreed cow. It became obvious the lord wanted no part of it and offered no explanation for his decision. With an indifferent wave of his lordship's hand, Odo was dismissed, and he and Norman dejectedly sloshed home.

Charlotte insisted that the lord's rejection was, in fact, an opportunity to look for a better bull elsewhere and that Sir Wystan had actually done Odo a favour. Norman suggested that Odo should visit neighbouring Ridgley Manor. Herdsman Searl, he said, had access to a large bull.

CHAPTER FOUR

King Henry II was visiting his crowning glory, Dover Castle, and spending generously on renovations and improved defences. He'd invited several trusted lords whose counsel and wisdom he valued and asked them to visit with him. Sir Hyde Fortescue, lord of Ridgley Manor, was one of those closest to the king, and he now sat in private with him, discussing mutual concerns. Inevitably, Mellester Manor soon became the topic of conversation.

In exchange for lands, lords swore fealty to the king and provided soldiers and infrastructure when called upon. If a manor was experiencing difficulties, the king felt it was his duty to know why.

His Majesty wasn't tall, although his physique suggested he was strong. He kept his red hair cropped short, and freckles splattered his face. He wasn't delighted this evening, as his wife, Queen Eleanor, constantly bickered with him and found fault with everything he did. She was a confounding woman and the cause of much dolour.

The king cast aside involuntary thoughts of infidelity and looked to his dear and trusted friend, Sir Hyde' the wise' Fortescue.

"What say you, Fortescue, have you an opinion on Mellester?" asked the king as he paced his private chambers.

Sir Hyde took a deep breath and considered his reply. "I believe Sir Wystan's intentions are honourable, sire, but he has accumulated considerable debt."

"And the knights in his service?"

"They are young and eager to please."

The king scratched his neck. "And Sir Wystan has accrued debt to you?"

Lord Ridgley nodded. "Mostly from horses, sire."

"Can you send someone to the manor on my behalf and have them identify the nature of his pecuniary indiscretions? I'm told Mellester is a sorrowful place these days."

Sir Hyde couldn't disagree. "As you command, sire," the lord bowed his head.

King Henry II continued pacing, stopped at the hearth and stared into the dancing flames. "Perhaps you could share your wisdom with the man, like a father figure. Suggest ways to generate better income and manage the manor more effectively," The king waved his arm. "If things don't improve… I'd hate to have to take those lands away from him."

"I understand and will see to it immediately," confirmed Sir Hyde.

King Henry was silent as he continued to pace. After a time, he paused and turned to his friend. "You do realise there are problems in Ireland I may have to contend with and may need to marshal an army from all my lords, including your knights, Mellester's and from that irksome Wadenham Manor. Although I doubt Sir Warwick could field a decent moll, let alone any sober knights.

"Aye, I've heard rumours about Ireland, sire. Worry not; I am vested in seeing Mellester prosper and will attend to the matter with due urgency."

"Very well. Drink up, Fortescue. This night still has much to offer."

After much cajoling by Charlotte and Norman, Odo departed alone to find the highly touted legendary bull at Ridgley Manor. Privately, he was still quite disheartened and upset at Sir Wystan's unwillingness to consider his plea. Charlotte reminded him that the lord had no fondness for Godwin Read and his son and that it was best to avoid dealing with a man who allowed his emotions to interfere with common sense. As usual, Charlotte was right.

The weather had been miserable for days on end, but this morning dawned without rain, though the skies were grey and bleak. However, shortly after Odo set off, the heavens opened, and he was caught in a torrent of biblical proportions. There was little to do but forge on ahead as best he could. He wore a waxed, hooded, woollen cape to keep the rain out and helped somewhat, but water still found a way in, and his feet were soaked.

As he walked, Odo thought of Charlotte and how they would live together. She would make a fine mother to their children and a wonderful wife. She could be headstrong and obstinate at times, but that was because she was so clever – she challenged him intellectually, and that kept him on his toes.

Spring and marriage seemed a long way off, but even just thinking about Charlotte helped pass the time as he squelched towards Ridgley Manor. Despite heavy showers, there were times when Odo found himself smiling - such was the effect she had on him. Unsurprisingly, no one else was foolish enough to be out in this weather, and he didn't see another soul. He sloshed onwards, buoyed with thoughts of his sweetheart.

The first indication that there were other people about was when he heard raised voices. Alarmed, he paused and tried to identify the direction from where they came. Cautiously, he followed the muddy road which paralleled the River Eks and, after rounding a corner, saw the cause of the commotion.

A two-wheeled covered wagon with one of its wheels missing lay askew, blocking the road, and two men in some distress sat to the side. Aware this might be a ruse and be waylaid by bandits, Odo paused and watched closely for a heartbeat, and then he noticed a third person, a child. Deciding this wasn't an ambuscade, he yelled a greeting and quickly ran over to them.

One of the men, a man–at–arms, suffered from an injured leg, while the other man, in some pain, cradled his shoulder. The child, a little girl, was bleeding profusely from a severe gash to her arm.

"Hail, good fellow," came the reply through a clenched jaw. "My daughter, Ivy - can ye help her?" he pleaded.

Taking in the scene, Odo immediately went to the girl's aid. She looked to be about six or seven years old and required urgent care.

"The wheel, er, it just came off," said the man with the girl.

Odo quickly took in the scene and looked at the man-at-arms; his right leg lay in an unnatural position. The other man, Ivy's father, clearly suffered from a hurt shoulder and was in some pain. He could do little for either of them, but Ivy needed help quickly. The rain continued to fall heavily.

Using his knife, Odo quickly cut a long strip of fabric from the wagon and wrapped it around Ivy's arm, hoping to stem the blood flow. She was brave and didn't cry, but was bleeding excessively, and this was of some concern.

He stepped to her father. "I'm going to unharness the horse and take yer daughter to the parish church in Mellester. The priest, Oswald, will be able to see her. I will return with others to attend to ye as soon as possible. Ye will have to wait."

With rain streaming down his face, the man nodded. "I can pay for men to repair the cart."

"I will do what I can. Rest easy." Odo turned to the man–at–arms. "Can I do anything for ye before I return?"

The man shook his head, and water sprayed from his beard. Odo noticed how deathly pale he looked.

He moved the little girl so she could sit with her father while he unharnessed the horse from the wagon and removed all equipment that wasn't required. The horse was still a little skittish but calmed down after some soothing words. It was a gift he had with animals, and they inherently trusted him. Oblivious to the heavy rain, Odo worked as quickly as he could and hoped someone else would arrive to assist with the two injured men, but no one came; they were alone. Sparing a thought for Ivy's comfort, he found some cloth and folded it numerous times as a makeshift pillow for her to sit on.

She began to cry when Odo took her from her father. He lifted her onto the horse, then nimbly vaulted on behind her. He removed his cape, draped it over the child, and held her secure with one arm while his free hand gripped the reins as he rode off.

The horse was no destrier or courser; it was a simple workhorse, but with some coaxing when the road conditions permitted, managed to canter most of the four miles back to Mellester village. Occasionally, he looked at Ivy's arm and was horrified at the amount of blood he saw. She was a brave little girl and didn't complain throughout the entire journey.

On returning to Mellester Village, Odo found Priest Oswald, who immediately took Ivy into his care and began attending to her wound. Odo searched for Reeve Merick to arrange for men, tools, horses and a cart to help the two injured men and hopefully repair the cartwheel. He found Charlotte with her father in the shoppe and told them about the accident. Charlotte promised to check on the little girl. Within a relatively short time, a small group of men, braving the elements, headed to the site of the accident.

Once Odo spared a moment to think, he wondered why a man–at–arms was escorting the man and his daughter. They weren't nobles, but they must have been important. He put the thought out of his mind as they finally returned to the broken cart.

Both men remained in the same position as when he left them. The soldier was drifting in and out of consciousness, while Ivy's father was in better shape, although still in agony.

Blacksmith Neal immediately saw the problem with the man's shoulder. With a tug, a twist, and an agonising scream, the arm was repositioned. Although still in pain, the man was grateful and felt instant relief.

"Don't worry, Ivy is in good hands," Odo explained. "Oswald may be an irksome priest, but he can fix most things," he added with a smile of assurance.

"I'm most grateful to ye. I don't know what I would have done if ye hadn't come upon us," said the man. "Here, please accept payment fer yer trouble."

Odo shook his head. "A man should never take coin for helping another man and doin' what's right. Anyone would have helped ye. I'm just pleased I came by when I did."

"We need a helping hand here, herdsman!" yelled Blacksmith Neal to Odo as men began lifting the wagon to reattach the wheel.

It was early evening when Odo finally walked into the village of Ridgley Manor. He was exhausted, cold and wet and immediately sought an inn where he could rent a bed for the night.

Early the next morning and feeling better after a good night's rest, Odo was given directions to where he could find Herdsman Searl. Walking through the village, he was surprised to see its prosperity. The weather may have been cold and wet, but the people appeared content and well-fed.

It was easy to find the herdsman; he was in his byre, sharpening an axe.

"Hail, Herdsman Searl," offered Odo in greeting.

The herdsman returned his smile warmly as Odo introduced himself.

"I've heard o' ye," said Searl. "Hears ye doin' a fine job with yer cows, an' Cheesemaker Gerald is makin' some nice cheeses, too. People round here are talkin' 'bout it."

"Doin' our best, we are," replied Odo, pleased at the acknowledgement. "Good milk helps."

"Then ye be a fair distance from Mellester. What can I do fer yer?"

"I'm told ye have a bull, a breeding bull."

"Ahh, you'd be talkin' 'bout Blacky, he's a big 'un, he is. Would ye like to see him?"

Blacky was hard to miss. He was a massive beast with a thick, deep, muscular chest that tapered back to narrow hindquarters. On seeing the two men, he bellowed several times and walked a step or two closer but kept his distance.

"He's a gentle sod, this one is, Odo. Never had a problem with him, ever. If you need him for breedin', you'll be wanting him for a month or two?"

Odo nodded. "Two month."

"Guess we need to talk to the reeve then."

Reeve Peter Hardwick was a jovial man with a round, open, friendly face, and Odo took to him immediately.

"You'd be doin' us a favour, lad," said Reeve Peter. "Blacky's a big boy and eats plenty. We'd be more'n happy to rent him to ye for a while."

Odo asked to see some of the offspring Blacky produced and inspected them keenly. He asked questions, and both Herdsman Searl and Reeve Peter did their best to answer. In turn, they asked Odo questions, gauging his ability to care for such a valuable beast for a time.

"I will need to confirm the payment with Steward Baldric, but he ain't here right now. Lord Ridgley has sent him away on important matters, but the two shillings we discussed won't be challenged. My word will be honoured," said the reeve confidently.

Odo was impressed. He silently wished things worked as efficiently in

Mellester Manor.

They discussed details about transporting the big beast to and from Mellester. Another expense Odo was expected to pay for, but overall, the final cost of his experiment was slightly less than he'd anticipated. Once all the particulars were arranged, Odo shook hands with both men and began the long walk back to Mellester and Charlotte.

As he walked, he considered his life and how fortunate he'd been. He had Charlotte, his land and his cows. He was happy, more than he'd ever been in his entire life. The only thing missing was his father.

Godwin easily recognised Odo's good qualities. He nurtured them and taught him values and common sense. When taken ill and bedridden, both father and son spoke often. They'd spoken honestly about Godwin's sickness and impending death, as both men knew it was inevitable, and also of Odo's future and plans.

They'd lived frugally, so Godwin accrued some modest savings, a small amount of coin that could be used to invest in the land and the business when the time was right.

After his father's death, the land that he inherited continued to generate income from the sale of milk his cows produced. He charged a nominal fee or bartered for food in exchange for allowing villagers to graze their animals on his land. He hired an apprentice and sometimes additional labour when needed. While not rich, he moderately prospered.

His affection for Charlotte was deep, and his love was returned equally. From the day she first smiled at him, he'd always loved her, and they became inseparable.

For Odo, life was simple. He had Charlotte, and the thought of marrying her made him feel dizzy and joyful.

CHAPTER FIVE

"Why do we want a damned mill?" Sir Wystan's voice boomed across the empty hall.

"According to Sir Hyde's steward, a gristmill might be a more efficient way to process and grind corn or wheat. It was an idea he had, Milord. We could charge a nominal fee, and even other manors could bring their crops to us. It would generate more taxes and encourage growth in the village," patiently explained Reeve Merick.

"And where will the coin for the construction of this mill come from? Do tell." Sir Wystan waved his goblet dramatically in the air, slopping its contents.

"I believe Sir Hyde's steward suggested a partnership, Milord. Ridgley Manor has no place suitable for building a mill, and as we've been told, Mellester Manor has the perfect location."

Sir Wystan sneered as the effects of wine began to take hold. "And where is this marvellous place, Merick?"

"That would be Falls Ende, Milord."

Sir Wyston began to laugh. "Have you forgotten? My father saw fit to benefice[9] the land to Herdsman Godwin and his idiot son Odo, who now holds title."

"If I might venture to make a suggestion, Milord, perhaps you could offer to buy the land from him."

9 *A grant of land.*

Reeve Merick managed to duck as Sir Wystan threw his goblet.

The day arrived when a robust four-wheeled wagon pulled by two oxen entered Mellester Village carrying an unusual cargo. Curious by the sight, people came onto the streets to have a look; seldom had they seen such a beast. Blacky wasn't disturbed by the attention, nor was he offended when a couple of boys poked sticks into the wagon to annoy him. The bull ignored the taunts, swished his tail and slowly chewed his cud.

Odo was jubilant. This was a significant occasion, and he joyfully shared the moment with Charlotte, who'd ventured from the confines of the Cheese Shoppe to herald Blacky's arrival.

With her arm linked through his, she looked up and smiled proudly. She knew what this meant to him. Odo had been dreaming of this moment for years.

The oxen pulling the wagon rumbled through the village square and headed towards Odo's property without pausing. A ramp was placed on the rear of the wagon so that Blacky could easily step down, and with a gentle touch, Herdsman Searl guided the placid bull backwards and onto the ground. A rope was affixed around Blacky's head, much like a horse's bridle and the herdsman handed the rope to Odo.

"He's yer responsibility now, for a while at least, and I hopes he does a good job fer ye."

Odo grinned. "I hope so too and thank ye for delivering him. Let me give ye the money, and we'll be all set."

"As agreed, two shillings," said Herdsman Searl. "That's what was confirmed by the lord's steward."

"A fair price," said Odo, counting out the money. "We should celebrate; perhaps a visit to the inn would whet yer appetite?"

Herdsman Searl licked his lips.

Odo yelled for his apprentice to take the new arrival into the field and turn him loose. A small crowd gathered at the fence and watched as the cows saw the mighty bull for the first time. A few plodded over and stared at the virile beast; some resumed grazing, unfazed. Blacky lifted his massive head, stretched his neck and bellowed. "There ya go, big boy," laughed Odo.

"What have you there, Odo?"

Odo turned to see Reeve Merick standing with his hands on his hips. He didn't appear to share in Odo's joy.

"Did yer purchase a bull?" he asked.

"Nay. As Sir Wystan wouldn't allow me to rent his bull, I was able to find another. He'll be here briefly, then he goes back."

Merick stood silently for a moment. "I need a quiet word with ye, Odo,"

Leaving Searl with Charlotte, the two men walked outside. Odo turned to Merick and waited.

"Sir Wystan inquires if ye would be willing to sell yer land."

"And ye speak for the lord on this?" asked Odo incredulously.

"I do."

Odo thought carefully about how to reply. Many things came to mind, none of them pleasant. "I thank the lord for his interest, but I don't wish to sell."

"Ye haven't asked what the lord offers yet."

"Because I'm not interested, Reeve Merick," Odo's voice had an edge.

Merick gave Odo a cold, hard look and nodded. "Very well, if that's yer final word on the matter." He gave Herdsman Searl a long, ugly stare and went on his way.

Odo hadn't bothered introducing him to Herdsman Searl. "He's an unpleasant man and a poor reeve," he explained to Searl after ensuring Merick was no longer in earshot.

"What did he want?" asked Charlotte, concern creeping into her voice.

"He asked if I wanted to sell my land to Sir Wystan."

"Why would he want your land?" she asked, somewhat surprised.

Odo shook his head. "I have no idea," he said.

"No good will come of this, Odo," she cautioned. "I do not trust Reeve Merick." She looked around to make sure Herdsman Searl was far enough away and leaned closer to Odo, "… or Sir Wystan."

Spring was around the corner, and the incessant rain finally eased as the weather began to change. Blacky seemed comfortable enough in his temporary home. The healthy cows enjoyed the lush grass of the changing season and were rapidly gaining weight. Herdsman Searl would return in a month, and the big bull would be taken away. He would be missed.

All was well in Odo's and Charlotte's world. With spring only days away, they began making earnest plans for their wedding celebration. The two were well-liked in Mellester Village, and the feast that was being planned would be an event that would be talked about for years. Even Gerald, normally stoic and reserved, was excited and offered to lend a hand and relieve the burden a little.

Odo heard no more about the offer to buy his land and hoped it would remain that way.

Steward Baldric Bigge returned to Ridgley Manor and diligently reported to his lord what he'd discovered about the poor state of Mellester's affairs. Sir Hyde Fortescue was alarmed and genuinely concerned after learning of the accident that befell Baldric, his daughter Ivy, and the man-at-arms. The poor soldier would forever be a cripple, but neither Steward Baldric nor Ivy showed any lasting effects of their injury. Sir Hyde was genuinely fond of his steward and the little girl, and he expressed his apologies for insisting they visit Mellester in such foul weather.

"If it weren't for the good nature of a young local herdsman, I suspect Ivy may not have survived," Baldric told.

"Then I hope ye rewarded him," Sir Hyde said.

"Milord, the young herdsman, would not accept recompense."

"Then God worked through the young man, and we are fortunate to receive His blessings and have Ivy with us today," Sir Hyde concluded.

Steward Baldric continued with his assessment of Mellester and went to some lengths to describe the lack of available resources for making improvements which could generate additional revenue.

"Sir Wystan is overspending, and the people are overtaxed," tut-tutted Steward Baldric. "However, Milord, there is one opportunity at Mellester that could benefit Ridgley Manor and even other manors in the area."

Sir Hyde was curious. "Go on," he nodded.

"It is the River Eks, Milord. At a particular place, the river narrows and drops. It is a dangerous place for locals - in fact, the villagers told me that Sir William Ainsley almost perished there some years ago. They call it

Falls Ende, and it is a perfect location to build a gristmill."

Lord Ridgley was very interested, as he had no suitable land within his demesne where a mill could be built. Mellester, he knew, was a central location, and if such a mill were built, it would be advantageous to many. "I agree, and now I need to convince Sir Wystan of this."

"Milord," exclaimed Steward Baldric with some concern, "Sir Wystan has no money to build such a mill, and he is already indebted to ye."

"Worry not, Baldric, and allow me to dwell on this," offered Sir Hyde. "There may be a solution yet."

Deciding he needed a word with the young lord, Sir Hyde sent Steward Baldric back to Mellester Manor, inviting Sir Wystan to attend a small feast.

Pleasantly surprised by the invitation, Sir Wystan had no hesitation and eagerly agreed. It was seldom that he was invited to social gatherings by neighbouring lords. Perhaps things were finally looking up, or so he hoped.

In addition to delivering the invitation, Steward Baldric was required to learn more about Mellester's state of affairs and offer suggestions on reducing debt and curtailing unnecessary spending. Sir Wystan claimed that times were difficult and took no responsibility for his ill-advised and foolish squandering. One idea Steward Baldric formally put forth to improve the manor's revenue was constructing a gristmill. An idea he'd spoken to Reeve Merick about previously. "A local mill would generate substantial income and also be useful to other manors in the area," suggested Baldric to Sir Wystan. Steward Alard nodded in support.

Although he felt it was a good idea, Sir Wystan knew he didn't have the money for such an expensive venture. It was something he could ill afford. "I have no interest in a stupid mill," he told Steward Baldric with typical petulance. "Our villeins and freemen are lazy and unproductive. This is why Mellester is suffering through a difficult period, but it's only a temporary setback!" He grabbed his goblet from the table and stormed off, leaving his steward alone to discuss the manor's pecuniary matters with Steward Baldric.

On conclusion of his task at Mellester, Steward Baldric returned home to Ridgley Manor and reported all he'd learned. "Sir Wystan believes ye will understand that Mellester is faring rather well, uh, taking the difficult times into consideration, Milord," offered Steward Baldric, struggling to maintain a straight face.

"Is that so?" mocked Sir Hyde.

Accompanied by eight knights, Sir Wystan arrived at Ridgley Manor on a new destrier he purchased some months ago and was very eager to show it off.

The feast wasn't the ribald affair he expected. The wine was heavily watered, and only one other guest, a lowly lord from a manor to the north whom Sir Wystan found obnoxious. The food, however, was another matter, and he and his men ate well in their sobriety.

Sir Hyde was jovial and gracious as always, and after a few hours of feasting, with storytelling and entertainment provided by a troupe of minstrels, he invited Sir Wystan to walk a little.

"I have some important matters to discuss."

Understandably, Sir Wystan feared the lord would call in his debt. He remained unusually silent, allowing Sir Hyde to talk.

They walked around the exterior of the manor house with two men–at–arms following at a discrete distance. "Mellester Manor owes me considerable coin."

"Aye, and will honour that debt as promised," Sir Wystan responded quickly.

"Of course, and I expect nothing less from ye," Sir Hyde clapped the young lord on the back. "However, I have a proposition for ye that will change your fortune somewhat."

Sir Wystan stopped walking and looked at Sir Hyde.

"I want you to build a gristmill. I understand Falls Ende is the perfect–"

"How am I to build such a mi–" interrupted Sir Wystan.

Sir Hyde raised his hand. "Let me finish," he said

Sir Wystan nodded.

"I will pay to build the mill, but we will be partners and own half each. In turn, I will receive all the income the mill generates until I've recovered all the coin I have lent you. This way, your debt will decrease, and we will share equally in the profits once yer debt is paid."

"I understand, Sir Hyde," smiled Sir Wystan.

"No, you don't." Sir Hyde gave Sir Wystan a cold, hard stare.

Sir Wystan's mouth opened.

"Ye will provide the timber from your forest at your cost and the same for the stone. I will pay for the labour. There must be some incentive for me, don't ye say?"

Any thoughts of fleecing Sir Hyde by over-charging him on timber and stone from his small quarry were forgotten. "Very well."

"Good," Sir Hyde's look softened. "Steward Baldric will arrange the details with yer man, and we will discuss this again later. Now, let us return to the music and food."

Lord Mellester and his knights returned home four days later, and Sir Wystan immediately sent for Reeve Merick to talk about the logistics of building a mill.

"I asked Herdsman Odo to sell Falls Ende, Milord," Merick explained. "He said no, wasn't even interested to know how much ye would pay him."

"Could the man truly be such a fool?"

"He has a bull to service his cows. He needs that land," Merick offered.

"A bull? I told him I didn't want my bull servicing his damn cows!" yelled Sir Wystan in anger.

"This is someone else's bull, and he's a big one too, Milord," offered Merick.

"Then whose bull is it?"

Merick shrugged. "I didn't ask, Milord."

"Doesn't help me to obtain title, though - and that land should be mine anyway."

"I agree, Milord. If he was in debt or behind on his taxes, you could evict him from that land, but alas, he is not."

"That's what I need to do, Merick, remove him from that land," Sir Wystan began pacing. "Let me think on it. Meanwhile, go to him again and ask him his price!"

Reeve Merick nodded his head. "As you wish, Milord."

Merick knew Odo wouldn't sell his land, and he certainly wouldn't go to the man with hat in hand and beg him to sell, no matter what the lord demanded.

CHAPTER SIX

Her hair was the colour of summer wheat, her face smooth and soft, and when she smiled, little wrinkles around her eyes drew attention to them – green, deep and full of mystery. He marvelled at the length of her neck - it was the neck of a lady, slender and elegant, and it added to her height. She wasn't squat like other women. Her back was straight, and she carried herself with pride. She still had all her teeth, and when she smiled at him, it made him weak in the knees. Yet, as maidens fare, she was also smart. Oswald taught her to read Latin, although Odo believed the priest enjoyed her company for other reasons.

She laughed at something her father said, but Odo wasn't listening. He was intently studying his soon-to-be wife and marvelling at her beauty. Her happy voice made others smile; the sound of her angry voice made people listen.

Under the table, her foot rubbed against his leg. It was something they had always done, the unspoken words of the love they felt for each other.

"Odo? Odo!"

"Aye," Odo replied, snapping out of his reverie.

"How long before yer know if your experiment with Blacky worked?" asked Gerald.

"It won't be for a while yet. Firstly, we'll see if the calves are bigger, then I will have to wait until they mature and begin calving so we can get milk."

Gerald nodded, tore another strip of bread and added some cheese.

As he frequently did, Odo had an evening meal with Charlotte and her parents. They enjoyed his upbeat, positive attitude, and they looked forward to calling him their son–in–law. To them, he was already part of the family and had been for years.

Odo felt Charlotte kick him in the shin – a casual reminder. "Well, I suppose I should be leaving ye," he slid his chair back and stood. As always, he thanked Gerald and Agnes for their warm hospitality and for sharing their food with him.

"So soon?" asked Charlotte innocently. "Then I shall walk with ye."

The sky was clear of clouds, the stars bright, and the air had a biting chill.

Undeterred by the temperature, Charlotte held Odo's arm and pressed closely against him as they strolled through the village. Villagers didn't bother tongue–wagging anymore; Charlotte and Odo always walked like this, and long ago, people gave up gossiping about them. Instead, they quietly wondered how long this affection would last before the reality of a hard life as a peasant and marriage with children struck the smitten couple.

Odo believed the villagers were just jealous. He couldn't care less for gossip. Charlotte just laughed. If she had any thoughts on the matter, she kept them to herself.

They discussed wedding plans, changes to Odo's home, and a myriad of other details vital to them both. They said good night and kissed, then kissed again before she broke away with a laugh.

The news of Norman's death came as a gut-wrenching blow. Odo was repairing his fences, a task he was diligent about when he saw Cheeseman Gerald walk through the field to find him. The dour expression on his face gave Odo a sense of foreboding, but no advance warning was enough to ease the pain. Gerald didn't have much to say, only that Reeve Norman died alone in his bed during the night. Overwhelmed, Odo fell to his knees, overcome by grief.

Since Godwin's death, Norman and Odo grew closer, like father and son. Norman doted on Odo, loved Charlotte, and was a voice of reason and logic when Odo needed a guiding firm hand. They shared meals, laughed, and even cried together. For Odo, his death was unfathomable; he couldn't imagine a life without Norman.

It was entirely different when his father passed; he'd become ill and, soon after, bedridden. It was a gradual decline, and death was the expected and accepted outcome. He was emotionally prepared, and when Godwin finally died, it was almost a relief as he would suffer no more. But for Norman, his death was sudden and unexpected. Norman was big, larger than life and invincible. It was tragic.

The funeral service would be performed by Priest Oswald on Sunday, and even Mellester's lord was rumoured to attend.

As it turned out, Sir Wystan didn't come to the church. It was said the lord had overindulged and was feeling poorly.

Charlotte was heartbroken. She loved Norman too, but what distressed her the most was seeing Odo saddened and lifeless as he suffered through the loss. She did her best to raise his spirits, and although he did his best, it was not until a couple of weeks after the funeral that his mood finally returned to something resembling normalcy.

Within days, Reeve Merick assigned new tenants to Norman's cruck[10] house. With no regard or respect for the deceased, they threw out all his meagre belongings, kept the chickens, and moved in. The new occupants of the house were Charcoal-Burner Larkin and his woman.

Odo hardly knew Charcoal-Burner Larkin. He'd greeted him once or twice, and the man and his wife seemed genial. He'd not had any occasion to get to know the family as they'd only recently moved to Mellester Manor and previously lived on the village outskirts and were seldom seen. Word spread that the couple were very familiar with Reeve Merick and called him their friend; this was reason enough not to warm to the couple.

However, things worsened once Charcoal–Burner Larkin and his wife moved into Norman's house. The charcoal burner was not as kind anymore, nor did he offer a friendly salutation as he once did. Odo couldn't care less; he disliked the man anyway, most of all because he was living in Norman's home.

Daniel, the apprentice herdsman, and Odo were near Falls Ende, collecting cow manure, which Odo sold as fuel to the weavers who used it to bleach fabric. It was another cold, frosty morning, and they'd turned the cattle out early and trudged up the field with barrows when Daniel pointed out a figure on horseback riding towards them. It was only half-light, and as the horse approached, Odo recognised the figure of Reeve Merick. As Merick never idly passed by at this time of day, he could only surmise that

10   *A wooden framed peasant house plastered with wattle and daub.*

the reeve was the bearer of bad news. He felt a stab of anxiousness in his stomach.

Even from a distance, they could hear the reeve yelling: "Yer cursed cows and bull! Damn ye, Odo Read!"

Odo dropped his spade and began to run back down the field towards Merick.

"What do ye say? What happened?"

Merick pulled his horse to a stop and looked down, scowling at Odo. "Yer cows, they broke through the fence and were charging all through the crops. The bull has destroyed everything!"

"No, it can't be. The fences are all good. I often check them myself. Yer must be mistaken."

"You'll pay for this, Odo Read. I will have to inform the lord."

"Where are the cows?" Odo asked in disbelief.

Merick pointed to the southwest corner of the field; it was some distance away and still shrouded in the gloom of half-light.

Odo began to run with Daniel, following a step or two behind. They would have seen Merick astride his horse, grinning if they had bothered to look behind them.

Over time, Odo and Godwin had built a solid wooden fence that surrounded all the land they owned. Because they worked daily with cows, they needed to ensure their animals were kept safe inside their property. There was always some concern about the damage they could cause by eating and trampling crops if they escaped. Maintaining the fences was a priority, and through all the years of being a herdsman, neither Godwin nor

Odo ever allowed their cows to break free. What Reeve Merick described was Odo's worst fear.

As Odo and Daniel approached the fence, they saw the broken rails where cows pushed their way through. Odo saw peasants trying to herd his cows back through the gaping hole in the fence, but no Blacky.

Beyond the fence, the land was divided into long sections called *furlongs*, and each furlong was further divided into narrow strips called *selions*. These selions were distributed amongst the farmers, and in lieu of an early growing season, wheat and barley had been painstakingly planted. Only recently germinated from seed, the young crops were no more than a hand-breadth tall. The small, succulent leaves were a delicacy to the cows.

Odo scanned the ground and saw row upon row of trampled young plants. Thankfully, the cows hadn't travelled far, but the destruction of the small area they foraged on was complete.

Daniel ran off to help drive the cows back while Odo searched for the bull. It took but a moment to find him – he lay on the ground in a spreading pool of blood. His throat had been sliced open.

"Who did this?" he yelled. "Who killed the bull?"

A couple of the peasants came forward and removed their hats. "Hail, Herdsman Odo," said one. "We weren't here when it happened. It was Charcoal–Burner Larkin that first sees it, and it was him who did it. Says the bull was causing mischief, and he had to put 'im down, a shame really, to me, ol' Blacky was a kindly beast."

Odo hardly heard him. He was devastated. How would he explain the loss of the bull to Herdsman Searl? How would Sir Wystan react, and what would Lord Ridgley say? All of a sudden, the reality of what happened struck home. He was in big trouble. He buried his face in his hands. He didn't know what to do, and more than ever, he wished Norman were here to advise him.

And Herdsman Searl was due to arrive any day to return Blacky to Ridgley Manor.

Once all the cows were returned to his property and the fence repaired, Odo walked home lost in the hopeless situation. The farmers depended on the crops for their livelihood, and now they'd lost a portion of their potential yield and would be aggrieved. He knew they'd be angry; it was understandable, and he felt pity for them, but there was little he could offer other than some coin in recompense and a heartfelt apology.

He knew Reeve Merick would pay him a visit and summon him to appear before the lord to face the consequences. He imagined being flogged, first by Sir Wystan and then by the lord of Ridgley manor; whoever was second wouldn't get much.

As expected, and within a short time, Merick was at his door. "Sir Wyston will see ye at the end of the week. Steward Alard is determining the cost of the damage and will report back to the lord."

Odo nodded in understanding.

"Sir Wystan is displeased with ye, Odo. Don't ye go leaving Mellester, ye hear me?" Merick shook his head to highlight the seriousness of the offence. "He'll be expecting ye to make good, and so will I." He wagged a threatening finger.

Charlotte was livid. "Those fences are strong. There is no way the cows could have pushed their way through. Someone tore down the fence rails, Odo Read, and because of it, ye are now in trouble!"

"What can I do? Nothing, not a thing! I accepted responsibility for Blacky and will have to pay Ridgley's lord his worth. I hate to think of the cost."

"And the damage to the crops? Will that be a lot?" she asked.

"I don't know. The lord will likely have me pay for damages and levy a fine."

"Can't be much damage - how long were the cows loose?"

"We turned them out from the byre before dawn, and it was just about daybreak when Merick rode up."

Charlotte and Odo were sitting on a bench outside the Cheese Shoppe. Since Blacky's death, Odo had no zeal to work and mainly was worried about how Ridgley's lord would react. The thought of appearing before a lord he didn't know was frightening; anything could happen.

"Then someone tore the fence down during the night, waited for you to turn out the cows and chased them through the hole," she said.

"That's what I believe too."

"Oh, Odo, what will we do?"

It was mid-afternoon when Herdsman Searl arrived in Mellester, and a small crowd of onlookers expecting entertainment at Odo's expense followed the wagon to his home. Odo greeted him and led him into the empty byre.

Puzzled, Searl followed and wondered what was happening.

Odo invited Searl to sit while he stood fidgeting.

"What has happened, Odo? You look unwell. Have you taken ill?"

"I wish I were. I have some bad news. It's, uh, Blacky. He's dead."

Herdsman Searl took a big breath and exhaled slowly. The expression on his face was grim. "Tell me what happened."

Odo explained all he knew and spared no details. Searl listened, asked a few questions, and remained quiet until Odo finished his tale of woe.

"I've worked with cows me whole life, and they are not aggressive animals. What ye told me doesn't make sense. It means someone tore down yer fence and chased them through – simple. And Blacky wouldn't have been causing trouble. If the fence had come down in that short time, he would have grazed on the crops near where he crossed. Someone did this to ye, Odo."

"I believe that too, but I still owe Ridgley's lord a fair price for Blacky. He was my responsibility, and it is my duty to pay for him," he handed Searl a bag of coins. "This is all the money I have. I don't believe this is enough, but give it to the lord and explain what happened. I will pay him more when I sell some cows."

Searl hefted the bag of coin. "I will talk to Steward Baldric. He's a good man, Odo, and if something can be worked out, then… we can only try, eh."

CHAPTER SEVEN

Most of the inhabitants of Mellester village were walking towards Mellester hall. Amongst them was Odo, as today was the day he had to appear before Mellester's lord. A few people offered their sympathy, many said horrible things, and some even threw the small plants at him that his cows trampled. Resolutely, he walked up the carriageway, doing his best to ignore the taunts and avoid provoking anyone into violence.

Charlotte insisted she accompany him, but he refused, telling her that the villagers had every right to be angry with him. He couldn't predict what would happen and didn't want to see her come to any harm. She argued, but he was adamant. She stamped her foot in protest, folded her arms and gave him her no-nonsense look. It did her little good.

The walk towards the hall was slow and painful.

Not everyone was admitted to the hall. Many commoners waited outside, hoping for news of Odo's punishment, while nobles, freemen, and others with means were allowed in as spectators.

As Odo approached the man-at-arms guarding the door, a few people began jostling and pushing, and some began to spit. Gaining entry to Mellester Hall was almost a relief.

In the past, he was accompanied by his father or Norman, but today, he felt alone and uncertain. He wished Charlotte were with him, although after what he endured walking to the hall, he was pleased she listened and didn't come with him.

The hubbub quietened as he tentatively walked towards the front of the hall, sat, and wiped sputum from his face with his sleeve. He ignored the odd jeer and obscenities hurled at him. Some even offered kind words of support, but he didn't want to make eye contact with anyone and sat quietly, praying the ordeal would be over quickly.

Odo saw Merick standing near the dais. When the reeve noticed him, he winked. Odo looked at his feet and resisted the temptation to react. After a short while, the onlookers buzzed, and he looked up to see Steward Alard walking towards his desk. The priest, Oswald, followed, took his customary position near the steward, and stood as he always did, with his head bowed and hands clasped benignly in front. He didn't look happy. As usual, a few knights stood in the background and talked loudly amongst themselves. Some looked over at him and laughed, obviously looking forward to the spectacle.

Finally, Sir Wystan strolled casually in. Despite the lord's pretensions to dignity, Odo believed he was drunk.

From an early age, Godwin taught Odo to be responsible for his actions, avoid passing blame, admit wrongdoing, and face any outcome with honour.

His cows had trampled crops and caused damage, which was undeniably his responsibility. No proof could be offered at this moment to show that someone deliberately destroyed his fence and herded the animals into the fields. It was unlikely anyone would step forward in his defence and support his claim. If they did, it would be a matter of whose word the lord believed. Not for one moment did Odo think Mellester's lord had any sympathy for him - the outcome was assured to be harrowing. Determined to honour his father's memory, he lifted his head, squared his shoulders and waited.

"Herdsman Odo Read, come forward!" yelled Steward Alard.

A murmur rose around Odo and continued uninterrupted, rising to a crescendo. He stood and obediently stepped forward and waited. The crowd finally settled down, impatient to see punishment meted out.

"Ye come here before me yet again, herdsman," said the lord when Odo faced him.

Odo wasn't sure how to respond, so he chose to say nothing.

"Are ye aware of the charges against ye?" Sir Wystan questioned.

Odo shook his head. "Nay, Milord."

Behind him, some took the opportunity to heckle.

"Remind him, Steward Alard." Sir Wystan raised the goblet to his lips and took a gulp.

"Herdsman Odo Read, ye have been brought before Sir Wystan, Lord of Mellester, to face charges of negligence and wilful damage to the lord's crops!" stated the steward.

"What? No, no, there is more, Alard," spluttered Sir Wystan. "Tell him the rest, damn you."

Puzzled, Odo tore his eyes away from Sir Wystan and focused on the steward, who took a moment before replying.

Alard looked up briefly and made eye contact with him, his expression suddenly rueful. "And, uh, and theft."

Spectators began applauding.

Odo couldn't help himself. "Theft? What theft?" he blurted over the din.

In shock, Priest Oswald's mouth fell open.

"Enough!" Sir Wystan yelled, rising from his seat, his anger palpable. "You stole, herdsman… you stole crops!"

Odo shook his head in disbelief. "I did no such thing, Milord."

Feeling the effects of too much wine, Sir Wystan unsteadily lowered himself back into his seat and draped a leg casually over the armrest. "Do ye deny these charges, herdsman? Do ye have anything to say in yer defence?"

Odo's heart pounded, and he felt the blood rushing to his face. "I stole nothing. My cows ate the crops, but I knew nothing of it at the time, Milord."

"So say ye," Sir Wystan waved his arm disdainfully to emphasise his point.

"Someone tore down my fence and herded my cows into the crops, Milord. I didn't know this would happen," Odo turned to face the people behind him. "I can only apologise to the good men whose crops were trampled. I am so sorry."

People began jeering and yelling at him. Sir Wystan slouched, grinning and allowed the disruption to continue unabated. Finally, the lord continued when the spectators became bored with the catcalls. "Reeve Merick? What say ye?"

Reeve Merick took a step forward. "Herdsman Odo is lazy, Milord. This would never have happened if his fences were stout and in good repair."

"Milord!" Odo appealed.

"Be quiet, I've heard enough. I am growing weary of this. Herdsman Odo step closer. Steward Alard will inform ye of the amount of restitution."

A hush fell over Mellester Hall.

"Aye, Milord." Alard took a deep breath and began. "For wilful damage to the lord's crops… uh, five shillings."

Odo felt sick. This sum was almost beyond his means. There was no way he could pay so much money.

"For negligence – five shillings," added the steward.

Priest Oswald was shaking his head in disbelief.

"Don't forget the theft!" reminded Sir Wystan with a smirk.

"Of course, Milord. And as punishment for theft…" Again, there was a pause, and Steward Alard risked another quick apologetic glance at Odo.

"One day in pillory and five shillings."

The hall erupted in cheers and cries of glee as this was what many of them hoped for. Mellester Manor hadn't enjoyed a pillory in some time. Priest Oswald raised his hand to his mouth in astonishment; it was an exorbitant amount in damage payments and, overall, a severe punishment.

Odo was devastated and had no idea where he could obtain fifteen shillings. He shook his head in disbelief.

"Herdsman, you will make your payment to the steward by sunrise tomorrow and immediately submit to your pillory punishment until sunset."

Odo, overwhelmed, and incapable of speaking.

"Are you deaf?"

He looked up at the smirking lord.

"Do you understand the fines and punishment levied against you?" Sir

Wystan waved his goblet around.

"I can't pay that amount, Milord," said Odo quietly.

"I can't hear you, speak louder!"

"I'm unable to pay that amount, Milord," Odo spoke through clenched teeth.

Sir Wystan rose quickly from his seat, losing the grip on his goblet. It tumbled off the dais and onto the floor, splashing wine over a few people. The lord was oblivious.

"We do have a problem, then, don't we? How sad that ye can't pay… or is it that ye won't pay?"

Odo didn't respond.

"What will ye do, herdsman?"

He shrugged.

"Steward Alard, Priest Oswald, Reeve Merick, take note. If full payment has not been received at sunrise tomorrow morning, Herdsman Odo Read forfeits any rights and title to the land he currently occupies, and that title and all land will revert back to the manor."

The hall was deathly quiet. Everyone felt the seriousness of the punishment. It was one thing to have some wheat and barley plants trampled, but losing title on land over it was quite out of proportion.

Priest Oswald looked up in surprise at the declaration. His face clouded over.

A voice from the back of the hall shouted: "What of yer cows, Odo?"

Hearing the question, Sir Wystan responded. "Herdsman!" he shouted, "Your cows now belong to the manor."

"Milord?" queried Steward Alard. "Ye can't –"

"That's enough, Steward! It is my word – and it is so!" A servant handed the lord another goblet. "Have ye anything further to say, herdsman?"

Odo was staring at the wall behind Sir Wystan and wasn't listening. He wanted to run away and hide.

Unseen, Charlotte had quietly entered the hall and remained in the rear. She watched in despair as the man she loved was humiliated and lost everything he'd worked so hard for. She wanted to hold him and offer her support. But she couldn't. She had to watch as Sir Wystan took pleasure in humiliating and punishing him. Tears streamed down her face. Poor Odo.

The Lord of Mellester rose from his seat. "That is all! Now go back to your work!" he barked and strode unsteadily away.

Reeve Merick walked to Odo, who hadn't moved. "You're not thinking of leaving Mellester, are ye?"

Odo, still in shock, ignored him.

"I will see ye in the square on the morrow just before sunrise."

Charlotte pushed through the departing crowd and rushed into Odo's arms as the reeve stomped away.

The great hall of Ridgley Manor was similar to that of Mellester Manor, except larger and grander. When in residence, the Lord of Ridgley, Sir Hyde Fortescue, spent far more time conducting the manor's affairs with his advisors, reeve, bailiff and steward than his counterpart at Mellester. Most frequently, discussions were orderly and followed protocol, though sometimes there was a noted difference of opinion and subsequent argument. The lord approved this, feeling it promoted honesty and an expression of free thoughts and ideas. Whenever an exchange became heated and personal, he would step in, exert his authority and end it immediately. Later, at the conclusion of business, they would all share mead or wine and repair hurt feelings and bruised egos.

Steward Baldric Bigge invited Herdsman Searl to appear before the lord and his advisors and explain the unfortunate incident at Mellester where the lord's prized and much-loved bull, Blacky, perished.

Sir Hyde listened attentively as Herdsman Searl recounted all he knew.

"Was the young herdsman negligent?" asked Ridgley Manor's reeve, Peter Hardwick.

"I don't think so. Seems unlikely."

Sir Hyde turned to his herdsman. "You saw his fences, Searl. What do ye think?"

"His fences were sturdy, and I could see where repairs were made. From what I'd seen, Herdsman Odo knows his cows. I don't believe he was negligent, sire."

"How much was Blacky worth?" asked the bailiff.

"It is hard to say, perhaps seven shillings," replied Steward Baldric.

The bailiff whistled at the amount.

"How much did the herdsman give ye?" asked Sir Hyde.

"He gave me five shillings, Milord," replied Herdsman Searl.

Sir Hyde nodded. "I'm impressed that a herdsman had that much coin on hand."

"I've heard he is very astute, especially for a young fellow," offered the steward.

"Have ye spoken with him?" Sir Hyde asked.

"Nay, Milord, never met him."

The lord scratched the back of his neck. "How much was he to pay for the two months he had Blacky?"

"It was agreed to charge him two shillings, Milord," replied the steward. "He paid the full amount when I left Blacky with him. If ye insist Blacky was worth seven shillings, then he still owes you two shillings, Milord."

Lord Ridgley thought for a moment. "Thank ye all for coming. Please leave us. I need to discuss matters with Steward Baldric." He watched silently as his men left the hall.

Once the door to the great hall was closed and they were alone, the lord leaned forward in his seat. "I assume that Sir Wyston will penalise the herdsman. Knowing the state of Mellester's affairs, he will undoubtedly impose a heavy fine and recover all his damages and perhaps more." Sir Hyde gave Steward Baldric a steely look. "And he will do this before I can obtain compensation for my loss. I'm pleased it's only two shillings I am owed."

The lord sat back in his chair and resumed scratching his neck. Steward Baldric Bigge waited patiently, knowing that his lord, as he was apt to do, planned and thought two steps ahead. "Listen, Baldric, I want this mill to be built, and I promised Lord Mellester I would pay the cost. Your first visit to Mellester wasn't a pleasant experience, but it will be better this time, eh? I need you to go there again."

"As ye say, Milord," Steward Baldric nodded, groaning inwardly at the thought of returning to Mellester Manor.

CHAPTER EIGHT

Sleep eluded Odo, his mind in a state of turmoil, anxiety and angst. It would be the last time he would call this house home. This was where he'd grown and lived his entire life. Godwin told him this was where his mother gave birth to him in the very bed where he now lay, and years later, she died in it – as did his father. Perhaps this wasn't the estate of a wealthy merchant or nobleman, but it was home and held memories that were dear and important to him. It was to be the home of Charlotte and their children – his family. But no more. The house and fifteen acres of land, his cows, and even his dignity now belonged to Sir Wystan; it was all his.

With his stomach tied in knots, he eased himself from his bed. It was time to endure the humiliation of the pillory. Soon, the night would turn grey, and he was expected to present himself in the village square and submit to the lord's will.

A short time later, he hefted his bag and walked to the Cheese Shoppe, where Charlotte waited for him. Gerald promised to look after his things until he completed his punishment. Where he would go after that, he didn't know.

"Be strong, Odo. Remember, they can taunt and humiliate ye, but yer self-respect belongs to ye. They can't take it away unless ye allow it to happen," said Gerald at the door.

"Thank ye, Gerald, yer a fine friend."

Leaving the bag behind, Charlotte and Odo walked slowly to where the pillory, still shrouded in darkness, loomed like an evil heathen monument. They talked as young couples do and made promises neither could keep. The village was stirring and coming to life, and soon Reeve Merick would arrive to enforce the lord's judgement and demand payment.

"I don't want ye to watch, Charlotte. It will be difficult enough for me without seeing ye in tears, suffering at the hands of those who enjoy this. Please, just stay away," Odo begged. "Promise me."

"And a fine morn it is, too!" said Reeve Merick, interrupting them as he approached.

"Go, Charlotte, please, go," urged Odo quietly.

She looked up and kissed him on the cheek. "I love you, Odo Read." Then she hoisted her skirts and was gone.

"She's a fine one, that one is," said Merick, watching her leave.

"She is, and it's a good thing yer an ugly bastard 'cause she wants nothing to do with ye," snarled Odo.

Merick's smile disappeared. "Where's the money?" he snapped. "You heard Steward Alard, the lord wants fifteen shillings in restitution."

"I do not have the money the lord demands."

"Then ye have surrendered yer lands, assets and title to Lord Mellester. Ye may not return to where ye once lived, and all the house contents will be seized." Merick shoved Odo in the back and pushed him towards the pillory.

Assembled the previous afternoon, a thick upright post mounted vertically on a sizeable wooden base stood in the village square. A piece of wood was affixed across the top, parallel to the ground, much like the upper line of the letter 'T'. Another identical piece of wood lay across it. Each of the horizontal pieces of wood had nine half holes. Two small holes for each wrist to fit through and another larger hole for the neck. This pillory would accommodate only one person today, not three as it was designed for.

Merick pulled the metal pins from each end of the top cross portion, lifted the wood beam clear and instructed Odo to place his wrists and neck in the half holes. Odo turned to look behind him, and there was Charlotte, standing with hands clasped to her face. Cheeseman Gerald stepped up to stand beside her, placed his arm over her shoulder and led her away.

Taking advantage of dawn's first rays of light, a crowd began to gather. A few people yelled some unsavoury words, but most just watched curiously. Reluctantly, Odo did as he was told, and Merick placed the top cross piece over the lower part, trapping Odo's hands and neck. Lastly, the pins were inserted.

"Well, now, isn't this a lovely sight," grinned Merick. He stood before the pillory and crouched slightly so Odo could see his smiling face. "I'll be back later to check on ye. Have a good day."

A few people came to Odo to talk. Some even asked how it felt to be in the pillory and offered support and encouragement. It didn't take long for those who enjoyed these types of events to show up, and they began throwing a few things, mostly trampled barley plants that did no harm. Some young lads found cow dung, but it was difficult to throw, and from what Odo saw, they got more over themselves than he did.

By mid-morning, a fairly substantial crowd grew and bolstered by numbers; a few began throwing dirt clods. The dirt had stones mixed in with it, and they hurt. One hit Odo square on the forehead, and he saw a bright flash of light. Blood trickled down his face from cuts, and one eye was partly swollen shut, but so far, he was coping. He had no choice. People were frequently killed in the pillory, a fact Odo was acutely aware of.

Someone brought him water, he couldn't remember who, and it was most welcome. After that, the abuse and the variety of things hurled at him increased. Although he never saw what it was, he assumed someone had thrown rotten eggs because, almost at once, a vile, pungent smell permeated the air. Whoever tossed them did him a favour, as the fetid stench kept people from getting close. To the amusement of some, he vomited.

He prayed about a few things and called on God to give him strength. He also asked that Charlotte and her family be kept safe and that she wouldn't see him suffer. He had no way of knowing if she saw him because he couldn't see the Cheese Shoppe as he faced in the other direction. His neck hurt, as did his back and legs. His wrists were rubbed raw, and as the day wore on, the pain intensified, as did the attacks.

Later in the afternoon, he wasn't sure when, as he may have passed out, people grew bored of throwing things at him, and the insults stopped. He waited for them to continue – but they didn't. Someone tossed a bucket of clean water over him to wash the excrement, rotten egg, and other matter from his face. It enabled him to urinate, which he did with much relief.

He didn't know why the violence stopped and didn't care. He was relieved at the respite, but the punishment wasn't over. He still had hours to wait in agony – the degradation was almost unbearable.

Village folk he grew up with and spoke to every day, people he laughed with and shared mead with, people who had no reason to hate him, shouted and spat - and these were peasants who didn't have their crops trampled. Oddly enough, most of the farmers whose crops were damaged did not hurl abuse or throw things. They may not have been happy, but at least they were civil and decent.

Eventually, hours of endless insults and the foulness that dripped from him became too much and wore him down. As hard as he tried, he couldn't help himself, and tears ran down his face and splashed into the filth around him. He cried for his mother and unborn sister. He cried for his father, for Norman and other friends who'd passed away. His tears fell for the undeserved shame he felt and for having lost everything that meant so much to him. He wept for Charlotte because he had let her down, too. No woman deserved to see her man lose his dignity and everything he owned. He knew she'd been watching throughout the day because someone told him so, and he couldn't begin to think of how she felt. If Sir Wystan wanted to punish and humiliate him, he'd succeeded.

He lost all track of time and was unaware that the light was fading when he felt someone step up to the pillory. He tensed, expecting a vile concoction to be tipped over his head. Instead, he heard pins removed and the wooden cross section lifted away. He couldn't move, as his muscles had seized. Merick, or whoever it was, released him and, without saying a word, just walked away and left him to his shame and misery.

Appearing from nowhere, unseen gentle hands supported and helped free him from the dreadful apparatus. The relief was overwhelming, and Odo cried out in intolerable pain as he was half carried, half dragged away. When he finally had the courage, he pried his swollen eyes open and saw he was in the church rectory.

Charlotte was there, wiping the filth from his face. Standing above her was Gerald, and beside him was a neighbour and another. Each stood and looked at him with forlorn sadness and pity. His shame was consuming, and in a display of uncharacteristic emotion, he succumbed, broke down and wept. Overcome and unable to face those he loved and cared for, he buried his face in the pillow, and his shoulders heaved in total despair.

It was heartbreaking to watch.

Oswald firmly told everyone to leave, including Charlotte, who vigorously protested. She received a stern word and a harsh look, and eventually, she, too, left. She squeezed Odo's hand and quietly walked away, unable to hide her tears.

Oswald removed Odo's soiled clothes, wiped away the filth, bandaged his wrists and neck, and, with the utmost care, tended to his numerous wounds. Grace, Oswald's hearth wife, washed his garments and gave him something to wear. "Only as a loan", she reminded him with a wink.

Over the next few days, Oswald and Grace tended to his needs as best they could. They fed, cleaned and consoled him without complaint. Odo learned that Oswald had stood near the pillory during the late afternoon, his presence and disapproving scowl warning the rancorous away. This was a side of the priest Odo had never witnessed before, and when he remarked on it, Oswald replied philosophically: "I serve three masters – Almighty God, the Bishop and Lord of Mellester. So how do I keep them all happy, as I need all three?"

It was a reflective time for Odo, and he stayed inside the rectory while recovering physically and emotionally. The worst of his wounds were not visible, and it was through careful nurturing and love that he slowly began to heal.

Charlotte came as often as she could. Her visits were the highlight of his day, and surprisingly, Oswald and Grace allowed them some privacy. The priest seemed to know what Odo needed, and solitude wasn't amongst them.

He was beginning to feel a little better when Gerald came to see him. However, the look on his face surprised Odo, as the usually affable cheesemaker wore a grim expression normally reserved for funerals.

"How fare ye, Odo?"

"Much improved, thank ye."

Gerald nodded and remained silent, obviously unsure how to continue.

"I can see ye are troubled, Gerald. What ails ye?"

"What will ye do now, Odo? Do ye have somewhere to live, do ye have work?"

Odo shook his head. "I have nothing. Oswald says I can sleep in the church for a week or so, but tomorrow, I will go to the fields and help the farmers repair the damage to the crops. It's the least I can do."

"Have ye money for food?"

Odo looked around for Oswald and Grace. Not seeing them, he nodded. "I have some," he whispered."

Gerald took a deep breath. "Odo, I came here to talk. Ye are like a son to me; I've known ye almost yer entire life, and it pains me to have to tell ye this …"

Odo's heart began thumping furiously in his chest. He knew what Gerald was going to say.

"When ye asked me to give my blessing to ye and Charlotte marrying, well… I told yer, as long as you had the means to care for her… Ye can't take care of her now, Odo, you can't even care for yerself. I'm sorry, Odo, but the wedding is off. I can't allow ye to see Charlotte no more. It … it wouldn't be right." Gerald looked like he wanted to say more but didn't.

Odo looked down at his feet, the welling of emotion building up inside him again. Charlotte was all he had, and now… along with everything else that had been taken from him, he'd lost her too. "Does Charlotte know?"

"Yer a good man, Odo, and what happened wasn't yer fault, but it doesn't change the position yer in. Ye've been hard done by, and it's unfair, but ye can't take care of her."

"Does Charlotte know?" Odo repeated. He looked up at Gerald. "Let me see her, Gerald. Things might change for me. Maybe we can't marry just yet, but allow me to see her at least. I love her, and she loves me."

"I'm sorry, Odo. Reeve Merrick, he told me… uh… I, I wish yer well and hope ye can turn things around. When ye do, then we'll chat again, eh? Goodbye, Odo."

Odo was numb with disbelief. This couldn't be happening to him. "Gerald –"

Without another word, Gerald left Odo and walked home, where he would face Charlotte again. She had fought him tooth and nail, unrelentingly, and even Agnes was against his decision. But they didn't know – he had no choice.

Dogs had long ago picked through the scraps of food thrown at Odo. All that remained was the smell and some mysterious globs that were mostly unidentifiable. Even the pillory was dismantled and removed. Now free from its evil grasp and vile punishment, Odo could freely walk through the village. Those who scorned him, who had hurled obscenities and excrement at him, now looked away embarrassed. Some nodded in tempered greeting, preferring not to encourage more hostile feelings. Odo no longer cared what they thought or believed, although some in the village were compassionate and showed kindness. Now, he felt remorse for his unkind thoughts about them. Oswald was one such person, and if any good came from his punishment – if he learned any lesson, it was a simple one – do not judge.

The Cheese Shoppe was just ahead, and Odo slowed down, mentally preparing. He understood Gerald's position but couldn't accept his decision. If Charlotte's happiness mattered to her father, he should allow them to meet and talk.

He entered the Shoppe and immediately saw Charlotte. She looked sad and tired, but when she saw him, her face lit up and she smiled. "Oh, Odo!" She sprang from behind the counter and rushed into his arms. He could feel the wetness of her tears on his neck.

"I missed ye so much," she sobbed.

Odo saw Gerald standing in the doorway. He looked unhappy but said nothing, allowing Charlotte the time she needed. Eventually, he walked over and placed a hand on her shoulder.

"Go inside, Charlotte."

"Father, this is wrong, and you know it," Charlotte glared, challenging him.

"Gerald, please," appealed Odo.

"Odo, I'm sorry. I cannot agree to this betrothal until such time as ye can provide fer my daughter. Yer a dear friend, but…" He shook his head sadly.

"Why are you doing this?" she appealed.

"Charlotte, go inside!" ordered Gerald. The tone of his voice left no doubt that he was becoming angry.

Charlotte reluctantly tore herself away from Odo. "I love ye, Odo."

Gerald stepped forward and placed an arm over Odo's shoulder, steering him towards the door. "Time to leave."

"I thought ye were my family, Gerald," Odo looked at the Cheeseman and held his gaze.

Finally, Gerald turned away. He looked around to see who might be watching. "This isn't my decision, Odo," he whispered, "Ye need to understand. I have no choice."

In the background, he could hear Charlotte crying. Then the door was closed. Odo was devastated.

He made his way to the fields where his cows trampled through crops and began helping the peasants. If they were surprised to see him toiling alongside them, they didn't show it. In the early evening, they shared their food with him and at night, he wandered off and found a sheltered, comfortable place to sleep in the forest on the other side of Falls Ende.

Lost in a world of uncertainty and self-doubt, he began to withdraw, preferring his own company to that of others. He clung protectively to the only thing he knew to be absolute, his love for Charlotte. It kept him alive because he had nothing else except his promises to her.

Lacking confidence and humiliated, Odo stayed away from the village and tried to think how he could move on with his life without her. It was painful to think of, but what else could he do? Should despair rule his life? As a freeman, he was lucky enough to have the right to leave Mellester, but where could he go?

What would his father have told him? What would Norman have advised? Turn his back on Charlotte and his dreams, just walk away? The vision of both men standing over him gave him pause. Deep down in his heart, he knew he couldn't abandon everything. The more he thought of it, the more he realised he needed to hold true to his beliefs.

In fear of reprisal from Reeve Merick, the peasant farmers were reluctant to provide Odo with any clue who pulled the fence down and drove the cows across. However, one man whom Odo knew quite well whispered that he'd seen the new fellow, Charcoal–Burner Larkin, loitering in the area the night before it happened, but he would offer nothing more.

After finishing work in the fields for the day, Odo decided it was time to visit the charcoal burner. Perhaps he would also have a chance to see Charlotte.

Larkin wanted nothing to do with him and refused to speak, which was odd. What reason did Larkin have to not want to talk to him - unless he was guilty? Odo pleaded with the man to give him a few minutes but only succeeded in riling him, which ended with Larkin pushing him to the ground and loudly threatening him. A small crowd watched as Larkin stood over Odo with clenched fists and warned him to stay away.

This was excessively hostile behaviour, even for a small village where disputes were commonplace. Some villagers weren't particularly fond of Odo, but they liked Charcoal–Burner Larkin even less, and for good reason. Ahead of others and favoured by the reeve, Larkin was granted Norman's house before others and had no shortage of work either.

Odo realised he was out of luck and wisely decided not to push it with the charcoal burner. Feeling less than happy, he walked away from the village and headed towards the shelter he'd built in the forest. A couple of villagers pressed food into his hands and wished him well. He was touched by their generosity and thought that they might know of his efforts to help in the fields and wanted to make amends for the bad treatment he'd received. It was the first real change he had seen from the people who lived in Mellester, which gave him a little glimmer of hope. When he passed the Cheese Shoppe, he could hear Charlotte crying but could not see her, which broke his heart. He paused a moment, uncertain of what to do.

With a heavy weight upon his shoulders and with misery for company, he carried the gifts of food and walked to his forest shelter.

With the night sounds of the forest for company, wrapped in a threadbare dirty blanket, Odo lay on his bed of leaves and ate his meagre meal. He knew life couldn't become worse.

CHAPTER NINE

Sir Hyde sent an advance warning to Sir Wystan that he was sending Steward Baldric, accompanied by a few men-at-arms, to Mellester Manor along with a sizeable amount of coin to pay for construction of the mill so that work could begin as soon as possible.

Sir Wystan was ecstatic. A mill was to be built on the manor – a monumental achievement for Mellester and he immediately decided it was cause enough to celebrate and host another feast. Messengers were dispatched into the countryside with invitations, and preparations began.

Steward Baldric arrived safely at Mellester Manor, this time without any misadventures and met with Sir Wystan in the hall. After exchanging pleasantries with the lord, he inquired about the circumstances around Blacky's death and the fines levied on the herdsman.

"I wasn't aware ye did not have title on this land when Sir Hyde first spoke of building a mill at Falls Ende. I don't believe my lord knew of it," stated Steward Baldric with some apprehension.

Sir Wystan looked uncomfortable. "I'm sure you have more pressing matters to attend to, Baldric."

"Of course, Milord. It is encouraging to know that you now have title on the land, and we can proceed as planned. However, because of the severe fines imposed on the herdsman, Sir Hyde will not be able to receive full compensation for the loss of his bull, as the man is destitute. He suggests a fair compromise by dividing the value of the confiscated assets by half. Half for ye, Milord, and half for Lord Ridgley."

"Why would I want to do that, Steward?"

"Milord, I am only an emissary acting on behalf of Sir Hyde. However, it appears ye have taken everything of value from the herdsman, and Lord Hyde is still owed a sizeable portion. What is he to do?"

Steward Baldric suspected Sir Wystan already sold the herdsman's confiscated assets and probably squandered a significant amount of money on the upcoming feast he could ill afford. Judging from the peevish behaviour of Sir Wystan, the longer this conversation lasted, the more hostile he would become.

Sir Wystan gave Baldric a petulant look. He wasn't happy that a mere steward, not a lord or knight, was presuming to ask difficult questions.

Steward Baldric, looking thoughtful, decided to change the subject. "Where could I find the reeve, Milord? Sir Hyde is anxious for me to report back to him about Falls Ende, and I was hoping the reeve could spare some time to show me its location."

Sir Wystan shrugged. "Talk to Steward Alard."

"Of course, and once I have confirmed the suitability of the location, we can proceed with transferring the coin to ye, Milord. I'm sure ye are eager to see construction on the mill begin." Steward Baldric wasn't stupid and knew how to obtain a response from the querulous lord.

"Certainly, I will have Reeve Merick show you," replied Sir Wystan more enthusiastically. "Steward Alard will go with you. The man needs to be outside in the sun more often," he smirked.

A small group of men left Mellester Hall and proceeded down the carriageway, through the village, and onto the fields once owned by Odo Read.

Two of Sir Hyde Fortescue's men-at-arms followed Stewards Baldric and Alard, who were in deep conversation and trailed a step behind Reeve Merick. Eventually, they walked to where the falls began, and Merick explained where he thought the mill should be built by placing some sticks in the earth to show the actual location.

As Baldric discussed construction matters with the reeve, Steward Alard walked alongside the falls. He'd never been here before and thought it a pleasant place. He watched the river flow over the boulders at the top, then cascade down onto more rocks. Eventually, the water leapt over a ledge and fell the last few feet to splash over a body sprawled across a boulder at the base of the falls.

"Come, come quickly!" he yelled.

Steward Baldric and the men-at-arms ran over and stared at the body below. Merick, in no hurry, ambled up.

"Who is it?" asked Alard.

"Don't know," replied Merick grumpily.

"Looks like a man. I think we need to see if he's alive," Steward Baldric pointed to the two soldiers. "See if ye can climb down and find an easy way to bring him up."

Both men-at-arms began removing their chainmail.

"I will get rope," offered Merick, wandering away.

Both stewards watched from the top of the falls as both men-at-arms cautiously made their way down into the chasm. It took a while; the going was dangerous as the rocks were slippery and wet. On reaching the bottom, they checked the body, which lay in a tortured, unnatural position.

"Looks like his back is broken, Steward!" shouted one. "And he's alive. He breathes!"

Baldric turned and saw Merick some distance away, returning with men, a litter and rope.

"He's trying to talk!" yelled the soldier.

Steward Baldric watched as the man-at-arms bent over the injured man and placed his ear over his mouth. He couldn't see or hear what was being said, but from his position, it looked like they were communicating.

Merick eventually arrived and was quite surprised to learn the injured man was still alive. The rope was quickly lowered and tied beneath his arms, and once secured, they began hauling him up and out. The pain must have been excruciating because he screamed, then fell silent.

With assistance, the injured man was placed on the grass, a safe distance back from the edge.

"Looks like Charcoal-Burner Larkin," offered Steward Alard. "He's dead."

"Moving him must have been too much. I wonder what happened," said Merick. "He must have slipped. I guess we'll never know now."

Reeve Merick untied the rope around the body, and Steward Baldric noticed one or two deep scratches on the reeve's arms. Closer scrutiny revealed his face was also scratched, but his beard hid them well.

"Does he have family?" asked Steward Baldric.

Merick nodded, "He does."

Merick and his men placed the body on the litter and prepared to carry

Larkin back to the village. Steward Baldric stepped out of their way when one of his men-at-arms, still dripping wet, approached him.

"I need a word, Steward."

"What is it, John?" asked Steward Baldric.

The soldier turned his back on Merick and the others and whispered. "That man, he spoke before he died."

"And?"

"Well, at first, he says just the one word, 'Merick.' I told him Merick was here, getting rope so we could get him out. The man said, 'Merick did it. He pushed me.' and then says it again."

"Did he speak more?" Baldric asked.

"I says to him, why would the reeve push you? And he replies, 'cause of what he did to the fence and the cows.'"

"Cows?" Steward Baldric could only assume he was talking about the incident with Blacky. If so, this was important news to Sir Hyde. "John, do not breathe a word of this to anyone. Keep it quiet. Sir Hyde needs to know."

"Aye, very well, Steward Baldric."

Odo watched from a considerable distance as a group of men trudged over his land, or what used to be his land, and appeared to be carrying a litter. He found it puzzling, but it was of no concern to him anymore. He put it out of his mind and returned to tilling the ground and pulling weeds. The area which had been trampled no longer showed signs of the incident. The farmers, all peasants, continued to warm to him and appreciated his hard work and effort to help and make amends. Odo was not obligated to do so, but he felt it was the right thing to do.

The afternoon wore on, and Odo was looking forward to stopping work for the day when he saw Reeve Merick walking along the fence line with two of Sir Wystan's men-at-arms following a step or two behind. He was curious as to what they were up to.

Seeing Odo, Merick changed direction and walked towards him. *No doubt to offer more insults and to further torment me,* he thought.

Merick was grinning as he stepped up. He shook his head slowly from side to side and rested both hands on his hips. "Are ye a farmer now? Nothing like a good pillory to help a man find a new direction for his sorry life."

Odo turned his back on Merick and continued tilling the soil, hoping he would leave.

"Yer comin' with us, Odo. Ye went too far this time."

Odo turned and looked up in confusion. "What say ye?"

"Ye killed Charcoal-Burner Larkin."

One of the men-at-arms, carrying shackles, strode towards Odo. The other stepped behind and grabbed him firmly by the shoulders.

"What yer talkin' about, who was killed?"

"Ye killed poor Charcoal-Burner Larkin, pushed him into Falls Ende, ye did. What will his widow and wee ones do now? Sir Wystan should have taken your life when he had the chance."

"I did no such thing!" yelled Odo. "Why are ye doing this? Ye know I didn't do it!"

Merick laughed. "Sir Wystan will be the judge of that, as is his right."

Peasants stopped their work and watched as Odo's wrists were placed in shackles, and he was marched away. These were sad times for Mellester. They knew Odo and the sort of man he was and didn't for a moment think he killed Larkin, and they didn't believe in the justice of the Manorial Court, either. As uneducated people, the lowest rung of the social order, peasants and serfs knew that justice was reflected in the character of their lord and was often served without reason or logic. They didn't understand the politics or warrant behind the lord's decisions; they only knew their lives lay in his hands. They spared a thought for young Odo and hoped death, however, it was administered, was quick, for it would not be painless.

In full view of everyone, Odo was led through the village. People stopped to stare as if they hadn't seen enough of Herdsman Odo making a spectacle of himself. Hearing a commotion, Gerald, Agnes and Charlotte stepped out from the Cheese Shoppe to watch. Charlotte's hand flew to her mouth in shock. Gerald shook his head. Odo's dishevelled appearance only added to their surprise.

"Odo!" Charlotte cried as her father tried to pull her inside. She struggled against him, but he held her firmly. Against her wishes, she was taken into the shoppe, and the door was quickly closed.

Odo watched as Charlotte was dragged back inside the Cheese Shoppe. He wanted to help her but was powerless. There was nothing he could do.

Surprisingly, no one showed hostility or said unkind words. Instead, people were whispering to each other and speculating, sharing what little they knew as rumours spread quickly about Charcoal-Burner Larkin's unfortunate death. Priest Oswald stood at the steps of the church, and as Merick, the soldiers and Odo approached, he stepped out, causing everyone to halt.

"What have ye here, Reeve Merick?"

"Out of the way, priest, this is not church business but the lord's affair."

Oswald nodded but didn't move. "If this man has committed a crime, then let him be justly punished, but if this is trickery, then may God have mercy on your soul." Oswald glared at the reeve. After a brief moment, he stepped aside and furtively made eye contact with Odo. Nothing was said, but Odo understood the priest's words. Oswald would support him.

Merick pushed past Oswald, and Odo was shoved roughly forward to follow the reeve up the carriageway towards Mellester's manor.

One of the outbuildings behind the manor housed the gaol. Odo's shackles were removed, and he was tossed inside the cell. He would not be released until he was brought before the Manorial Court and judged.

As protocol demanded, Reeve Merick consulted with Steward Alard, and it was decided to wait a day or two before a decision was made on when Odo would stand before the lord. As a feast was planned, it was deemed most likely that Sir Wystan would be out of sorts and unwilling to want to deal with Odo. Although Merick agreed, his reason was considerably different. A public announcement of a punishment for murder would attract attention. Such a proceeding would bring many people to Mellester with coin in their purse for a day of entertainment and revelry.

The accused would wait in the gaol until such time as the lord decided to hold court. It mattered not to the manor and cost the lord nothing in food or drink; as was customary, the village fed the prisoner if they chose to do so.

CHAPTER TEN

Built from rock, the gaol of Mellester Manor was used frequently, mostly to offer some perspective to those who needed solitude and sobriety. It was never used to secure people for long periods of time, usually no longer than a day or two until the lord heard the plea in the manorial court or the accused's demeanour returned to a more temperate frame of mind. Punishment never amounted to gaol time, nor was any time spent incarcerated considered when contemplating a sentence. Floggings were popular; the pillory provided ample entertainment, and the death penalty was a noteworthy event that drew people from miles away.

Other than the family of the guilty, the entrepreneurial folk of Mellester Manor tended to see the bright side; an execution was healthy for the economy. So when the lord decided that the appropriate punishment for the accused was death, local merchants and innkeepers generally saw an upturn in business, and nearly everyone benefitted somehow.

Windowless, cold and dark, the gaol provided little comfort. Perhaps fifteen square feet in size, the stone floor may once have been covered in straw. Odo considered himself fortunate to have found a place to sit that seemed less filthy than the rest of the dank room.

Along one side of the cell, steel bars rose from the floor and disappeared into the ceiling. Everything else was made from rock. Beyond the bars was a larger room used for storage, and a large wooden door was the only entrance to the gaol. Light seeped through cracks in the door and allowed for a little illumination.

Alone with his thoughts, Odo was confused and depressed, knowing that he would again become the centre of attention in the village square, and most likely for the last time. Most perplexing was the reason why all this was happening to him. Was Sir Wystan unable to forget what had happened all those years ago? And Merick, what was his interest in seeing him punished? What was his motive, or was he just doing the lord's bidding? The thoughts kept circulating round and round in his head, and none of them made any sense and succeeded only in giving him a headache.

The large, wooden door creaked open, allowing sunlight to stream in. Blinking at the sudden change, Odo covered his eyes and heard Oswald's distinctive voice thanking the guard who remained outside. Once his eyes grew accustomed to the light, he saw Oswald standing before the bars, holding a bowl.

"I brought ye some food," said the priest coldly. He placed the bowl on the ground and slid it through a gap in the bars with his foot. When Odo was close enough to reach it, Oswald spoke quietly so the guard wouldn't overhear.

"I don't know what is going on, Odo, but I know ye didn't have it in ye to kill Larkin."

"Then why doesn't someone tell Merick, Steward Alard, or even better, the lord hisself?" pleaded Odo.

"This is a sensitive issue and requires some delicacy. Merick has the lord's ear. I don't."

Odo knew the priest was right. "And Steward Alard, can he help?"

"I will try to speak with him. He is a good man, Odo, but remember, he serves his master."

Odo looked intently at the kindly priest. "I understand… thank ye, Oswald."

"I will try to return in the morning with more food," Oswald turned to walk out of the gaol.

Odo was ravenous and picked up the bowl. The taste was very familiar and distinctive. "This food is from Cheesemaker Gerald, is it not?"

Oswald spoke over his shoulder. "It is, lad. Charlotte brought it to me."

For the first time all day, Odo smiled. He felt a little closer to her. Charlotte hadn't abandoned him.

Sir Hyde doubted Sir Wystan's ability to manage the manor. The more he learned, the more he realised His Majesty's concerns were valid and Mellester's lord was a problem. Building a mill was a sensible decision, and it was bound to pay off when it became productive. Sadly, Sir Hyde possessed little faith that Sir Wystan could be trusted to manage such a venture. He would likely squander the money if he received a single lump sum as payment and needed to be closely supervised.

Steward Baldric was a clever and trusted man. His wise counsel had proven itself time and time again, and sending him to Mellester Manor was the only option. This way, the steward would ensure that Sir Wystan would only receive small payments to cover the labour costs for work completed rather than give him a sizeable amount to fritter away.

Additionally, Sir Wystan was also indebted to him for a considerable amount of money, and Sir Hyde wanted that money repaid. King Henry II was petitioning his barons to help pay for improvements to Dover Castle and needed his lords to manage their manors productively and generate income. The more Sir Hyde heard about Mellester Manor, the more he realised how inept Sir Wystan was. As a trusted advisor to His Majesty, Sir Hyde was granted the privilege to deal with some issues within the realm, including Mellester Manor, while King Henry returned to Normandy to defend his lands from King Louis VII of Frankia.

Needless to say, the messenger sent by Steward Baldric gave Sir Hyde some disquieting news, namely the fact that Sir Wystan failed to mention he did not have title on the land when they first discussed building the mill at Falls Ende. However, he was pleased that the matter was now resolved… or was it? Steward Baldric added that the lord's constant inebriation, belligerence and unpredictable mood swings made communication rather difficult.

Steward Baldric was not born into nobility, and understandably, Sir Wystan found it difficult to discuss sensitive matters with a mere freeman. Sir Hyde could relate to that, but this was an issue young Wystan needed to come to grips with, or he'd be forever shackled by his self-serving attitude. Being born into nobility did not mean you were better than anyone else, though this point of view was not shared by all.

In response to Steward Baldric's message, Sir Hyde sent six more men-at-arms to Mellester along with Sir Gweir, a most capable knight, who would assist with any issues that might arise and speak with authority in his name.

"Herdsman Odo, stand before the lord!" cried Steward Alard.

Commonly, loud jeers filled the hall in such situations, but today, only a few spectators taunted Odo as he rose from the bench and took a few tentative steps forward.

Sir Wystan was slouched in his seat with a leg draped over the armrest, and he clutched a goblet of wine he was seldom seen without. Odo could see the man's eyes were bloodshot, and he looked unwell.

"You've been accused of killing Charcoal-Burner Larkin, and you now stand before me and almighty God to receive your punishment," said Sir Wystan.

"Beg'n your pardon, Milord, but I did not kill Charcoal-Burner Larkin," pleaded Odo. He was filthy, his hair was matted, his clothes soiled, and his wrists remained shackled.

"You have become a real problem for me, herdsman. Mellester Manor will be a far better place with ye gone."

"Odo didn't kill him!" someone shouted.

Another voice contributed: "Larkin was a sod!"

"That's enough!" Sir Wystan stood a bit too quickly and tottered for a moment. "I have decided that yer punishment –"

Priest Oswald took two steps towards Sir Wystan, interrupting him. "Milord," he said quickly, "Perhaps we should hear the evidence made against the herdsman?"

Unable to contradict the priest, Sir Wystan waved the goblet. "Very well, if ye wish, but it won't change my decision," he said, sitting back down.

"Reeve Merick, step forward and present the facts as ye know them!"
instructed Steward Alard.

Steward Baldric, accompanied by the newly arrived knight, Sir Gweir,
stood in the middle of the hall along the wall, watching with interest.

"Herdsman Odo threatened Charcoal-Burner Larkin outside his home,
Milord. Larkin defended hisself, and pushed the herdsman to the ground–"

"That's not true, Milord. I never threat–"

"Quiet, you'll speak when spoken to!" yelled Sir Wystan, spilling wine
over his tunic.

Odo, totally dispirited, looked down at his feet.

"Sometime early next morning, when Charcoal-Burner Larkin was
heading into the forest, he was attacked by Herdsman Odo in a most
cowardly way, Milord, and then thrown into Falls Ende, where I found
him," Reeve Merick smirked and looked at Odo.

A few friends of Larkin jeered angrily.

Odo reacted. "That's untrue, he lies–"

"I've had enough of you," spat Sir Wystan. He stared with malevolence
at Odo, who met his watery, bloodshot gaze.

"I love you, Odo!" came a cry.

Everyone in the hall stopped talking, all murmuring ceased, and even
Sir Wystan looked to where the voice had come.

Odo whipped his head around and saw her. "Charlotte!"

Steward Baldric saw Odo's head turn and, for the first time, briefly
glimpsed his filthy, muddied face.

"Silence!" yelled Steward Alard.

"I've had enough of this nonsense!" Sir Wystan glared. "I've made my decision, herdsman. You are sentenced to be flogged and caged until you die." He wouldn't look at Odo as he rose from his seat and stumbled away.

Many people in the hall began hissing, some yelled, and a few remained silent.

"No!" cried Charlotte. "He didn't kill anyone, and you all know it!"

"See her removed," said Sir Wystan over his shoulder.

A man-at-arms walked to Charlotte to lead her away. Odo heard her yell in protest. Some people laughed.

Steward Alard stood and waited for things to settle down before he spoke. When the hall was again quiet, Alard took a deep breath. "The lord has decreed that the punishment will be five days hence and take place in the village square."

Odo was again in the gaol, disconsolate. He would spend the last five days of his life in this filthy cell, then dragged to the village square, flogged, and hung by his arms in a cage, in full view of Mellester, until he died. All for a crime he didn't commit.

He heard voices outside the gaol and guessed Oswald was coming to see him. The door opened, and bright sunlight streamed in, causing him to shade his eyes. As he adjusted to the light, he saw a figure standing before him, and another remained at the door.

"Ye have found yerself in a bit of a pickle, have ye not?" said a voice.

Odo didn't recognise the man who spoke, and as he couldn't think of a response, he chose not to say anything.

The man moved so the light from the open door shone on his face. Odo recognised him at once. This was the same man he'd helped some time ago during the winter when his wagon lost a wheel.

"How is your arm and Ivy, how does she fair?" Odo asked, wondering why this man came to see him.

The man nodded. "She has a bad scar, but otherwise, she is well, and thanks to you, she is fortunate to be alive. My shoulder and arm still give me pain at times," he unconsciously flexed his shoulder a little.

"Who are ye? I never learned yer name."

"I am Steward Baldric Bigge from Ridgley Manor."

Odo had no idea. He was surprised at the revelation. "Ye are an important man."

Steward Baldric shrugged. "Perhaps to some."

Both men stood in silence for a moment.

"I never knew it was ye who wanted the bull from Sir Hyde. Had I known, I would have suggested a fairer price to the lord in thanks for what ye did for me and Ivy."

"I did nothing special. Any man would have done the same."

"Perhaps, perhaps not, but I am grateful either way. I am curious about a few things, though. Can ye explain what happened with the bull and this charge of murder?"

"I'd be glad to, but the guard at the door will not allow ye to stay here fer the time it would take to tell."

"The guard will not interrupt us. Continue, if ye will," said Steward Baldric, glancing at Sir Gweir, who remained standing at the door.

Odo had a natural distrust of knights and glanced nervously at Sir Gweir.

"You can speak freely in front of him," assured Steward Baldric, "he's one of Sir Hyde's liege men."

Steward Baldric and Sir Gweir left the gaol deep in discussion, and it was decided they would talk to Steward Alard as soon as possible. On entering Mellester hall, they found the steward in a heated argument with three men. Not wanting to interrupt, Baldric and Sir Gweir waited, and what they overheard was a little distressing. When the three men left the hall, both Baldric and Sir Gweir approached Steward Alard.

"We overheard the disagreement. Who were those men?" asked Steward Baldric.

Steward Alard looked a little frazzled. "The ginour, millwright, and the damster."

"Mill men, I thought as much," acknowledged Steward Baldric. "But why are they unhappy? They spoke of wages… But I made sure Sir Wystan could pay them for their work. I gave you enough coin."

Steward Alard nodded but didn't volunteer any information.

Sir Gweir stepped up to Steward Alard, his presence asserting authority. "What were those men complaining about?"

"I – I – I'm unable to tell ye. I apologise, Milord."

"Tell ye what?" Sir Wystan intruded upon the conversation.

All heads whipped round to face Lord Mellester.

Sir Hyde chose Sir Gweir to accompany Steward Baldric for reasons other than his status and fighting prowess as a knight. Sir Gweir was as quick with his tongue as he was with his sword. "I am trying to find out why the ginour, millwright and damster complained about not receiving their wages. Perhaps ye could explain, sir?"

Sir Wystan looked uncomfortable and gave Steward Alard a scathing look before answering. "I was unhappy with their work and decided to withhold half their pay. It is not of yer concern, and ye need not worry."

"But, Sir Wystan, it is my concern indeed. Sir Hyde has instructed both of us," he pointed to Steward Baldric, "to ensure his funds are used as intended. If there is a quandary or poor workmanship, then we need know of it."

"Sir Gweir, while ye remain here at Mellester Manor as my guest, let me remind you of your obligation to respect me as Lord of the Manor. I will not have ye intrude upon business matters that have nothing to do with ye."

Both stewards, Alard and Baldric, waited awkwardly. They preferred not to become involved in two knights having an argument.

"How ye choose to spend Sir Hyde's money is my concern, sir, regardless of yer position as lord. Have I made my position clear to you, Sir Wystan? I speak for Lord Ridgley in his absence."

Sir Wystan stared at the knight and wobbled slightly. "I will not be spoken to in such a manner. You are free to leave Mellester and are no longer welcome here as my guests. Both of ye be on your way," Sir Wystan waved his arm to dismiss them.

"Milord," responded Steward Alard, "Perhaps we should discuss this?"

"Steward Alard is right, Sir Wystan," Steward Baldric bravely added. "Perhaps we should discuss this when cooler heads prevail?"

"Be off, ye both. Sir Hyde can apologise to me personally rather than send me a couple of fish-fags to do the work of a lord. If he has something to say, let me hear it from his tongue," Sir Wystan stated with contempt before storming away.

CHAPTER ELEVEN

Sir Hyde did not feel like laughing when Sir Gweir and Steward Baldric returned to Ridgley Manor and explained what transpired at Mellester. He was deep in thought, pacing in front of the hearth. He turned towards his guests. "Fish-fags?"

Sir Gweir inclined his head.

"So, Lord Mellester is in need of coin and will rob the workers to get it. If he carries on like this, the mill will never be built. The workers will revolt and could spread to other manors, and that is the last thing King Henry needs."

"That is what I believe too, sire," answered Sir Gweir.

"What say ye, Baldric? Have ye any thoughts on this?"

"I do, and there is more."

"What now?" Sir Hyde was becoming visibly upset.

"Remember, Milord, last winter when the wagon lost a wheel and Ivy nearly died?"

"And ye hurt yer shoulder and arm. Of course, what of it?"

"It was a young herdsman with the name Odo Read who unselfishly came to our aid."

Sir Hyde turned to Steward Baldric. "Is he the same–"

"The same man who wouldn't accept payment for his good deed and proclaimed any man would have done as he did."

"I remember."

Sir Gweir listened intently.

"This was the very man whose father saved the life of Sir William, Sir Wystan's father when he fell into Falls Ende during a hunt…"

The fire in the hearth crackled and spat, and Sir Hyde continued to pace. "From what you've told me, it appears that this herdsman is nothing more than an innocent victim in the game Sir Wystan is playing – to exact revenge for losing his honour as a knight."

"I agree, Milord," said Steward Baldric. "This poor man has lost his land, home, cows, and even the woman he was to marry. He was pilloried, and now he's been sentenced to death. He only has his life to give."

"Good God! The poor fellow. Is there proof, has any man come forward to speak for the herdsman?"

"One man, a peasant farmer, said he saw the charcoal burner in the area where the fence was destroyed. The reeve had no interest in pursuing this claim."

"It seems to me that this reeve… what's his name?"

"Reeve Merick, Milord."

"That Reeve Merick is involved somehow, more than likely at the behest of Sir Wystan."

"We can't prove anything. There's no evidence other than mysterious scratches over his face and arms," said Sir Gweir.

"What can you do, sire?" asked Steward Baldric.

"I don't know."

"We have two days," added the steward.

"Perhaps I could have a little talk with the reeve. He might be willing to loosen his tongue for me," said Sir Gweir.

Sir Hyde stopped pacing and turned to the knight.

"You aren't welcome at Mellester Manor," the lord pointed out.

"If I could make a suggestion…" offered Steward Baldric.

Sir Hyde inclined his head.

"Perhaps talking to the charcoal burner's woman would be a good start."

A myriad of thoughts and emotions were swirling around Odo's head, namely, the fact that he would die in less than two full days. Oswald came to him every day and brought food and news. According to the priest, Charlotte's father kept a close eye on her, preventing her from leaving the house and coming to see him. Other than the steward and knight from Ridgley Manor, no one else had been permitted to visit.

Odo began to think about escaping. He examined the lock on the gaol door and realised he didn't have the tools or expertise to unlock it. He even fantasised someone would break him out, but that seemed more unlikely with each passing day.

When Odo paid five shillings to Lord Ridgley's herdsman, Searl, he kept two shillings and hid them in a pouch affixed to the inside of his breeches. This was all the money he had left. Two shillings was a considerable sum, and he considered offering the guard at the door a shilling to leave the gaol door unlocked. A shilling was more than a week's wages for the man and would certainly be tempting. Initially, this seemed silly, but now he wasn't so sure. The more he thought about it, the more he was convinced this was his only chance. What do I have to lose – a shilling for freedom?

he wondered.

He yelled repeatedly for the guard. At last, the door creaked open, and he stood at the entrance, saying nothing.

"I need to talk to yer, I needs a favour."

"What?"

"I have something to show you," Odo suggested.

"What ye got?" queried the sullen man-at-arms as he stepped closer to the cell.

Odo flicked the shilling into the air, making it flash in the light as it spun, then caught it and held it out for the guard to see.

"It's a shilling," he said.

"I can sees that."

"Ye want it?"

The guard looked at him suspiciously.

"Do ye want it?" repeated Odo. "It's yers."

The guard stepped closer and looked over his shoulder through the open door to ensure no one was watching. He turned back to Odo.

"All ye have to do is unlock the door and say nothing."

"Ye got more?" asked the guard.

Odo shook his head. "This is all I have."

"They'll know it was me, and the marshal will be angry. Anyways, I could just take it, couldn't I?"

"No, you won't, 'cause I know ye, and yer a good man," said Odo.

The guard was unsure.

Odo had an idea. "Unlock the door and wait until you are replaced, then cause a distraction so I can creep past him. That way, someone else will be blamed, not you."

"Could work," said the guard with a little more enthusiasm. "Let me think 'bout it."

The guard returned to his post outside, and Odo was left to wait. Time was dragging, and he was becoming increasingly nervous. For all he knew, the guard might decide to come into the cell and take his money anyway.

Day was turning to night, and the guard still hadn't responded. Odo was beginning to lose hope when the door swung open, and the guard quickly ran in.

"Where is the shilling?" he demanded.

"Unlock the door, and it's yours," he tapped the coin against a steel bar for the guard to hear.

"When the other guard comes to relieve me, I will begin to chat with the new guard. That is when you should run for it." The guard fumbled for the single key and unlocked the door but carefully left it closed.

"How do I know I can trust ye?" Odo asked.

"Ye don't," came the answer. "But I don't believe ye oughta be here. I think ye been stitched up."

Odo had no choice. With a big exhale, he handed the coin to the guard and waited. To his relief, the guard returned to his post outside. Escape seemed possible, and he knew this was his only chance.

At the same time Odo handed the shilling to the guard, a hooded man silently entered the house where Odo's dear friend Reeve Norman used to live. Charcoal-Burner Larkin's widow never heard the man enter, and when she discovered him standing in her home, she was too startled to scream.

She clutched her youngest child and backed into the corner as the man, armed with a sheathed sword, held a finger to his lips. Despite the flickering light of a candle, his face was completely shrouded in darkness.

"I won't hurt you," came the intruder's voice.

He took another step forward, and she recoiled in fright. Moving slowly and deliberately, he tossed a couple of pennies onto the table in the middle of the room.

"This is for you, and I have more."

He could see her eyes turn to the table and back to him again. "Do you want more?"

She nodded.

"Good, then perhaps you can help me. I need the truth; do you promise to tell me the truth? If you lie, I will find out and return."

"What ye need, Milord?" she finally croaked. From his mannerisms she determined the man was a noble and addressed him with fearful respect. It didn't go unnoticed, but it didn't matter – the widow would never recognise him anyway.

"Is about your husband, Charcoal–Burner Larkin. Was he responsible for pulling down the fence and driving the cows into the field?"

The widow's eyes returned to the coins.

"Tell me," he demanded.

The money was tempting. She nodded.

"Who told him to do it? Was It Reeve Merick?"

"He said he'd kill my baby if he finds out I talked," she cried. "He said not to tell anyone."

"He won't know. Your baby is safe. Did the reeve help him?"

"He did, Milord."

"And your husband slaughtered the bull on orders from the reeve?

"I think so. He wouldn't have done it otherwise. The reeve paid him and paid him well, too."

Sir Gweir asked a few more questions, tossed another coin or two on the table, and quickly left the house. Outside, dressed similarly, his friend Sir Kay stepped out of the shadows.

Inside, the widow walked over to the table and saw the money the intruder left behind. She began to cry; it was more money than she realised.

In anticipation of Odo's death, people began arriving by the dozens. Mellester Village was crowded, almost festive, and the mood buoyant. Jesters and minstrels wandered the narrow streets, drunkards lay where they fell and laughter and yelling filled the evening. Tomorrow would be exciting, and hopefully, the punishment imposed on the poor, guilty soul would be entertaining. No one wanted to see the man succumb too easily.

Two more strangers in the village attracted no unwanted attention, and after a couple of brief enquiries, Sir Gweir and Sir Kay learned where they could find the reeve.

At this time of the evening, he could always be found alone, sitting in his favourite corner of the local inn with a cup of mead. When two armed strangers entered the inn, Merick saw them instantly and raised his eyes in curiosity. His interest changed to apprehension when they pushed through the crowded inn and came towards him. A quiet word in the ear of two patrons saw them promptly vacate their seats, and the two knights sat down, facing him.

Merick said nothing and carefully appraised both men. By their air and appearance, he guessed they were knights, and he also knew they weren't Lord Mellester's liege men – which put him instantly on guard.

"Reeve Merick?" said one.

Merick knew lying was futile; these men wouldn't be sitting before him if they didn't know who he was. "I am."

"We have some news which we thought might interest you."

"Tell me, then, don't keep me waiting."

"Sir Hyde, Lord of Ridgley manor knows about your involvement in destroying the fence, driving the cows into the field and having Charcoal-Burner Larkin kill his bull."

Merick didn't respond. He was thinking how to rush past these men.

"He also knows ye killed Charcoal-Burner Larkin and threw him into Falls Ende."

The reeve had been in enough situations over the years to know when he was in deep trouble. Usually, he would rely on sheer strength to wrangle and bully his way out of any adversity, but when he felt a knife tip push firmly into his stomach beneath the table, he decided it probably wasn't such a good idea.

"Yer will come with us. Yer will slowly stand and walk after me out of the door. My friend will be behind ye. Do ye understand, Merick?"

The reeve swallowed. "I do."

"Come, then."

Sir Gweir stood, as did Merick and Sir Kay, and they shouldered their way out amidst curious stares. Again, the reeve was considering making a dash for it.

"I have men all over the village, Merick, and they have orders to kill you if you run."

Merick wiped his sweaty brow with a sleeve and nodded.

"Walk up to the manor," ordered Sir Gweir.

The three men set out and without another word spoken, headed towards the manor. Merick was relieved and needed no encouragement, as he knew that as soon as Sir Wystan saw what was happening, he'd be safe. They climbed up the carriageway and headed towards the hall, but then, as Merick turned to the hall, one of the knights grabbed his tunic, pulled him away, and continued past. Merick was totally puzzled and becoming increasingly frightened.

Odo heard the guard begin talking loudly; it was the signal. He opened the unlocked cell door at once and quietly eased his way towards the main door. It was partly open, just enough to squeeze through and peek around the corner. The guard he'd bribed was talking to the new guard and laughing at something the other man said. While the two guards were temporarily distracted, Odo carefully slipped through the door, stepped out into the darkness, and walked directly into Reeve Merick and two knights.

"What have we here?" said one of the knights.

Odo was stunned and deflated. *This can't be happening, not now.* He stopped. Hearing the voices, both guards rushed over. Only one guard was surprised to see Odo, but neither expected to see two strangers prodding Reeve Merick.

"I think you need to come with us, Odo," said Sir Gweir.

Odo desperately looked for a way out, a place to run and hide.

"Please, do not run. Do as we ask and trust us," said Sir Gweir kindly.

Merick was shoved in the back and propelled towards the gaol.

"Make sure these men are locked securely," said Sir Gweir to the men-at-arms.

Having little choice, both guards obediently followed. Odo and Merick were led inside the gaol. Merick began to protest again, which did little good, and Sir Gweir swung the heavy door shut, and the guard with the key turned the lock, securing both men inside. Sir Kay, who stood beside the guard, casually reached over and took the single large key from him. Odo, straining his eyes in the darkness, watched in total confusion.

Before either of the two men-at-arms could react, Sir Gweir commanded their attention and spoke with absolute authority. "Listen to me carefully. Both of these men are to remain in this cell until released tomorrow by Sir Hyde Fortescue, do ye understand?"

The guards looked at each other and nodded.

"Where is the spare key?"

"T'was lost years ago, Milord," replied a guard.

Sir Gweir nodded. "We will be watching, and both of ye will suffer Sir Hyde's wrath if anything happens to Odo or Reeve Merick." He turned to face the two prisoners. "Merick, yer owe some explanations to this young man, and ye have all night to do it. Make yer peace."

Odo's head swivelled from the stranger to the reeve and back again.

"Ye can't leave me here," griped Merick, "Sir Wystan will be furious."

Both Sir Gweir and Sir Kay quickly disappeared into the night and walked to the outskirts of Mellester village. A short time later, they were warmly greeted by their sergeants at their campsite.

CHAPTER TWELVE

The sun had barely risen, and already, a small crowd of knights, men-at-arms, and a few curious peasants stood in the area behind Mellester Hall near the gaol. Sir Wystan was incensed and demanded Sir Gweir brought before him, but no one had seen the knight since the evening before. He'd vanished. The blacksmith was called and given terse orders to force the gaol door open so Reeve Merick could be immediately released. This was easier said than done, and much to Odo's amusement, little progress was made. For the first time in five days, he hoped they wouldn't be able to unlock the cell door.

Steward Alard tried to mollify his lord, but it did little good. The enraged man had been up most of the night carousing and was quite put out to be woken so early to learn what transpired during the evening. The two guards who encountered both knights recounted their version of the events repeatedly, and the only conclusion anyone could arrive at was that Sir Gweir, or more likely, the lord of Ridgley manor, was behind this.

Reeve Merick said little other than to beg for his release, and Sir Wystan was becoming more agitated. The prospect of Sir Hyde arriving at Mellester left him feeling queasy... or was it the wine he'd drunk last night? For the first time in years, he was unsure of what to do. He returned to his chambers to think.

The first indication that something unusual was happening was the sound. To his immense displeasure, Sir Wystan was immediately called and reappeared outside the hall in a rage. What he saw stopped him hard in his tracks.

A double column of armed knights mounted on destriers snaked down the road heading towards the manor. It was an impressive sight, accompanied by the jingling of spurs, the clink of shiny armour and the sound of hooves on the hard-packed road. The unmistakable pennant of Sir Hyde Fortescue, Lord of Ridgley, flapped proudly by a standard bearer at the head of the column. But it was another flag that caught everyone's attention. Held proudly aloft, the distinguished Plantagenet pennant of King Henry II caused Sir Wystan's blood to run cold. Sir Hyde was here on His Majesty's business.

Someone yelled that there were twenty knights, which looked true enough. Another twenty sergeants followed, and then the column extended further back as spare horses brought up the rear, followed by aides and servants. This was a display of force intended for one purpose only – intimidation. Sir Wystan's marshal watched helplessly, his small force of knights unable to halt the advance. Sir Wystan felt the stirring of fear – there was nothing he could do but watch and wait.

At the very head of the column, directly in front of the standard bearers, proudly rode Sir Hyde. He turned up the carriageway, and the column obediently followed, the noise growing louder and the tension increasing. Sir Wystan's people began moving away, backing up to accommodate the mass of knights and horses. Most people hadn't witnessed such a display of power in years, and this unexpected event would be spoken of for some time to come. Even some of Sir Wystan's knights were smiling with pride at this grand display of power.

Each fully armed and mounted knight was a fearsome battle force by himself. Trained for years and years in all aspects of weapons, fighting, and horsemanship, these men dedicated their lives and swore a solemn oath to their liege, and when called upon, bravely stood shoulder to shoulder with their knightly brothers on bloodied battlefields. Even the mighty destriers were trained to kill; they could bite, kick and trample, and together, the horse and knight combination was formidable. Riding up the carriageway were twenty such men and their beasts of war. They rode proudly, heads held high and weapons ready – for Sir Hyde and King Henry.

Sir Hyde was the first to ride up to the manor, stopped in the open courtyard, and remained mounted. The standard bearers stopped behind him, and Sir Gweir and Sir Kay, not in armour but riding fine coursers, halted on either side of their lord.

The remainder of the knights rode up, encircling the area. The sergeants, arriving last, rode past their charges, dismounted quickly, and immediately ran to attend to their masters.

Sir Hyde removed his helm and, ignoring the gaping face of Sir Wystan cast a stern look around. Then, as one, all fifty knights dismounted. Sir Gweir and Sir Kay handed the reins of their horses to groomsmen and walked purposely past Lord Wystan, who was speechless, into the gaol, where they were relieved to find both prisoners still locked up. Without a word, Sir Kay produced the key and the cell door was quickly unlocked and opened. Reeve Merick and Odo, blinking in the sunlight, were brought into the open air just in time to see the impressive lord, his spurs jingling, stride into Mellester Hall.

"Bring Sir Wystan and the prisoners!" he called over his shoulder.

In obvious discomfort, Steward Baldric finally rode up and awkwardly dismounted. With relief, he handed the reins to a groomsman and followed his lord into the hall.

Odo was stunned; he'd never been this close to so many knights. It frightened him, and he had no idea what was happening. What he did know was that today was the day he would die.

Sir Hyde's knights were strategically positioned around Mellester Manor, clearly sending a clear message as to who was in control. Silent and aloof, they guarded doorways and entrances while Sir Wystan seethed in absolute fury. His knights were shepherded into the manor hall and left wondering what was happening.

When Odo and Merick entered the hall, they were ushered towards the front and told to stand quietly against the wall. In curiosity, villagers began arriving and were granted admission; the spectacle before them this day was very unusual. Quiet murmuring filled the hall, the hubbub of multiple conversations creating a feeling of expectancy and uncertainty. Some believed England was at war, and this meeting was a call to action. Others thought England was under threat of invasion.

Sir Hyde was speaking quietly to Steward Baldric as Sir Wystan entered.

Seeing Mellester's lord arrive, Sir Hyde broke off his conversation and climbed onto the dais. To the consternation of all in attendance and in a severe breach of protocol, he took the principal seat usually reserved for the Lord of the Manor. The murmuring came to an abrupt halt. The air was deathly quiet. Someone coughed - the sound seemed unusually loud.

Sir Wystan strode through the hall, his soiled tunic and deportment causing a few to shake their heads. He stopped in front of Sir Hyde. In contrast, Sir Hyde looked every part of a powerful knight and lord, while Sir Wystan appeared to be nothing more than a querulous drunkard.

"You have taken the seat of Lord Mellester," cried Sir Wystan in indignation.

Sir Hyde casually chewed his bottom lip and surveyed the people who sat in the hall. He took his time, offering additional insult to Sir Wystan by ignoring him. His grey eyes held the gaze of Mellester's nobles and knights, challenging them. Against the wall, he saw Sir Gweir and Sir Kay and, beside them, the dirty figure of a young man he presumed to be Odo, the herdsman. To the herdsman's credit, he did not flinch or look away. Beside him stood a larger, older man in shackles, and Sir Hyde believed this one to be the reeve. The man lowered his face when the lord's piercing gaze settled on him.

With a heavy sigh, Sir Hyde turned to Sir Wystan and looked at him in question, wondering how such a person could achieve power and status without God's gifts of reason and common sense. How could a man bereft of conscience and faith manage to survive?

Sir Hyde slowly stood, his presence commanding. "I stand before ye here today as proxy for King Henry II. Business of the realm sees him in Frankia. I speak for him. I am his voice!" He turned to the side and made eye contact with Steward Baldric.

Immediately, the steward handed a scroll to Steward Alard, who unrolled the document and read it quickly – he nodded and affirmed. "Sir Hyde indeed speaks for the king!"

A murmur filled Mellester Hall.

Sir Hyde raised an arm, and again, the hall fell into a hushed silence. He paused for effect and the significance of his surprise visit. "King Henry has decided to release Sir Wystan of his oath of fealty and take back all these lands under the demesne of Lord of Mellester."

The hall remained deathly still. Not a sound could be heard. No one spoke, and all eyes were fixed upon the back of Sir Wystan. It took moments for the import of Sir Hyde's words to sink in. Sir Wystan's reaction began with a subtle head shake and ended with a cry.

"No, NO! Mellester was bequeathed to me by my father, Sir William. As his only son and heir, I am entitled to these lands!"

"Only at the will and generosity of the king," continued Sir Hyde, ignoring Sir Wystan's protests. "Sir Gweir's presence is requested in Frankia so His Majesty may affirm his vow of fealty. Sir Gweir will be the new lord of Mellester!"

"I am Lord of Mellester!" yelled Sir Wystan.

Sir Hyde's intense grey eyes settled on Sir Wystan. His anger simmered. "Nay, ye have shamed the king and the good people who toil and work these fine lands. Ye are unworthy of such privilege and distinction and must find a new home. Ye are banished from here." If Sir Hyde was nervous, it was impossible to see. The steady rise and fall of his chest showed calmness. "I will speak to yer liege men after this. Be seated, Sir Wystan."

At once, Sir Wystan's knights began whispering among themselves.

Sir Gweir was grinning from ear to ear. King Henry promised him lands, but he had no idea it would be Mellester.

"However, another matter has been brought to my attention. It disturbs me greatly and must be dealt with promptly." Again, Sir Hyde made eye contact with Steward Baldric.

Baldric conferred briefly with Steward Alard, who nodded in agreement.

"Reeve Merick, step forward and stand before Sir Hyde, Lord of Ridgley," ordered Steward Alard.

The mood within the hall changed quickly, and a few brave voices began taunting the reeve.

"Ye have been charged with causing the death of the lord's bull… and the death of Charcoal-Burner Larkin," he added. "What say ye?"

"T'was him, Milord," Merick pointed with shackled hands to Sir Wystan, "He told me to do it."

People gasped. A quiet murmuring filled the hall.

Sir Gweir and Sir Kay turned to Odo, who was trembling. "All will be well," whispered Sir Gweir with a smile.

Sir Hyde's face showed his disgust. "You are declared guilty of these crimes. Your punishment will be decided in three days." He turned to a man-at-arms. "Take him back to the gaol."

"Herdsman Odo, step forward and stand before Sir Hyde, Lord of Ridgley!" ordered Steward Alard after further hushed instruction from Steward Baldric.

Odo, who wasn't wearing shackles, tentatively approached the dais.

"I love you, Odo!" came a voice. Odo stopped and turned. He saw Charlotte waving, as did every person in the hall. Some laughed, others mocked her words, and cries of "I love you, Odo!" spread throughout the hall.

Lord Hyde tried unsuccessfully to look stern and failed.

Odo stood before Lord Hyde, trembling. This was the day he was to be flogged and hung to suffer in a cage until he died. Was it true, would he be spared?

Lord Hyde raised his hand, and the room grew silent. "Young woman, are ye here alone?"

Charlotte didn't reply.

"Are ye now mute? Speak!"

"I am here with my father, Milord!" she answered, the tremor in her voice obvious.

"Who is your father? Have him speak!"

"I am Cheesemaker Gerald, Milord!"

"Do ye consent to having your daughter stand beside her man?"

"They are not betrothed, Milord."

"Will they marry?" asked Sir Hyde. He gave a subtle look to Odo, who was incredulous.

In a clear, loud voice, Cheesemaker Gerald answered: "If he's alive, Milord!"

People began to laugh. Sir Hyde again raised his hand for quiet. "Have yer daughter come and stand beside Odo. I fear he will collapse if she doesn't."

Charlotte didn't have to be asked twice and quickly made her way to the front of the hall. She wrapped her arm around Odo, and with her other hand, she grasped his trembling fingers. Both looked at the imposing lord who stood before them. Odo had never stood before a knight in full armour. It was intimidating

"Herdsman Odo's lands were unjustly confiscated. He was unfairly punished for a crime he did not commit, fined an unreasonable sum of money and lost his home, cows and even the woman he was to marry," Sir Hyde looked down at Charlotte and paused a heartbeat or two. "He is innocent of the accusations made against him. He has done no wrong and suffered as no man should with the penalty of death hanging over him." He turned to look at the faces of people gathered before him. He paused, allowing them to take in the gravity of what happened. "Reeve Merick and charcoal burner Larkin conspired to ruin your crops, not Odo. It even came to my attention that Cheesemaker Gerald was threatened and intimidated by the reeve so that he would not allow his daughter to see or wed Odo."

The priest, Oswald, unclasped his hands and edged closer to Sir Hyde to listen. The tension rose, and everyone in the hall held their breath.

Sir Hyde turned his attention to Odo. "Yer land, cows and home will be returned. Ye will be reimbursed fully for the fines and money ye paid to me and to Sir Wystan. On behalf of King Henry II, Mellester's new lord, Sir Gweir, and myself, we apologise."

Odo could barely speak. If it weren't for Charlotte clinging to him, he would have fallen. He took a breath, then another and couldn't find the proper words. After an uncomfortable moment of silence, he found the strength to speak. "Thank ye, Milord, but ye still need to be paid for Blacky's services and the value of his worth." Odo fought desperately to keep his composure and failed. His eyes welled up with the heartache and torment he'd suffered over the last six weeks. Charlotte held him tightly.

Sir Hyde nodded. "Indeed, I had not forgotten. Sir Wystan will pay the bulls worth, ye owe me nothing, ye already paid fer his service." He turned away from Odo and faced Sir Wystan. "Stand."

In a manner bordering on insolence, Sir Wystan slowly stood and made no effort to hide his feelings.

"Sir Wystan's personal assets will be sold until all debt is paid."

In contempt, Sir Wystan spat at the feet of Sir Hyde.

Sir Hyde ignored the insult. "Odo, I think ye have the right to speak to Sir Wystan. Have ye anything ye wish to say?"

Odo wiped his face with his sleeve, cleared his throat, and looked at the debased lord. "Milord, if ye wanted to build a mill at Falls Ende, all ye needed to do was ask. I would have been willing to see it done.

CHAPTER THIRTEEN

Three pairs of bloodshot eyes peered through the wet, leafy branches of low-growing bushes and into the near-darkness towards the treacherous waterfall known as Falls Ende. They lay in concealment, tired and still suffering from the effects of a night of excessive drinking, and none were in an agreeable mood. The brothers wore similar clothes: rough, woollen breeches, tunics, and capuchins covering their heads and shoulders. The only items they wore that separated them from the appearance of normal peasants were the rusty swords sheathed on their hips.

One brother, who fancied himself as an archer, who was worse for wear than the other two, carried a bow and half a dozen arrows in a quiver that had seen better days, but due to his inebriation, he had failed to protect the bowstring from moisture. It was now wet and useless. His contribution to their current task was further highlighted by the fact that even if he could string an arrow to his bow, he probably couldn't have hit a target more than three paces distant. Additionally, one of his brothers had to keep nudging him to keep awake. His brothers didn't care much if he slept; they were mostly concerned his obtrusive snoring would alert others to their presence. The persistent drizzle further dampened their enthusiasm and only added to their present and very foul disposition. They endured the unpleasantness because they were paid to do so.

It was neither night nor day; the inclement weather and heavy clouds delayed daybreak, but already the three men lying side-by-side, about fifty yards from Falls Ende, heard sounds alerting them of early morning activity near the falls at the construction site of the new mill. They were soon rewarded by the sound of talking, accompanied by the distinctive rumble of a wooden-wheeled handcart as two men approached in the bleak grey of a wet predawn.

The self-appointed leader of the trio removed his hood to listen and nudged the archer who'd annoyingly nodded off again. The archer woke with a start and quickly raised his head, disturbing the branches of the bush they lay beneath and causing a small shower of water to fall onto their heads. The leader silently cursed as cold water trickled down his neck and wisely resisted the urge to jam his elbow into the face of his compeer. With hand signals, he indicated for his brothers to slide backwards out of sight from the track, where they would move to a new position, more suitable for their attack.

Freemason Wouter Gurney and his seventeen-year-old apprentice son, Ralf, slowly trudged along the wide, broad path parallel to the River Eks. Recent heavy use by workmen carrying stone and timber had seen the narrow path usefully expand into more of a road. Closer to the mill near the highest point, the track wound perilously close to the edge of Falls Ende, and for the unwary, it was still extremely dangerous. Damp and slippery, it wouldn't take much to lose your footing and tumble onto the rocks far below – a fall very few people survived. On the other side of the track, trees and bushes grew to its very fringes, and it was unlikely the freemason and his son would have seen the outlaws lying in wait, even if they had been looking.

Wouter Gurney preferred Ralf to push the heavy cart laden with tools of his trade in the mornings, and later, when his arthritic and calloused hands were warmed, he would take a turn. He walked beside the cart and away from the ruts and puddles as his mind pondered the complexities of his next job. Occasionally, Ralf would ask a question, often having to repeat himself as his father was deep in thought and not paying attention.

Mason Gurney was expected at a neighbouring manor where he'd been contracted to build a bridge. For the first time in his lengthy career as a stone mason, he was to be the 'Master Mason,' a position that afforded him hard-earned respect from his peers and a fatter purse from his employer. This was a big job, and both father and son would enjoy gainful employment for quite some time. Having completed their small part in constructing the foundations of the Falls Ende gristmill, father and son were now headed to their new job at the manor.

Wouter and Ralf had no quarrel with the three men who waited in concealment for them; in fact, neither Wouter nor his son had ever met them. The three brigands lying in wait had mistaken Wouter for being Morel Mundy, the Master Mason responsible for the gristmill being constructed at Falls Ende. Had they known the man they now targeted was not Mundy, they would have allowed him to pass unmolested. But with swords unsheathed, each of the three brigands, now positioned behind large trees bordering the track, waited patiently for Wouter and Ralf to come alongside.

Not far away, on the other side of the river, was a sizeable plot of land farmed by a young freeman called Odo Read. The land was not owned by the Lord of the Manor as one would normally expect; a previous Lord had granted title to Odo's father some years earlier, and Odo inherited the land on his father's passing. His modest cruck home was situated at the outskirts of Mellester Village, and a large byre attached to the rear of his dwelling was used to shelter and protect his growing herd of cows, a small flock of sheep, and his workhorse during evenings and cold winter months.

Odo delayed releasing his cows and sheep from the byre this morning because Charlotte, his betrothed, had insisted the animals would trample the much sought-after St. George's mushrooms that had sprung up during the night. She was determined to harvest them as quickly as possible

Charlotte began picking the delicacies on the lower portion of the large field and systematically worked her way up towards the river and Falls Ende. She heard the voices of the freemason and his son as they began their journey down the track, but paid them no mind as she toiled to fill her basket so Odo could release the animals.

A panicked shout alerted her that something was amiss. Concerned, she stood upright, peered into the gloom, and, curious, walked up towards the river to see more.

To Mason Wouter's absolute astonishment, he saw three unkempt men brandishing swords leap from hiding and rush at him. With no weapons of his own, he was completely defenceless; there was little he could do other than instinctively raise an arm to ward off a descending blade.

Ralf shouted in alarm and tried to move out of the way, but his father, with a sword protruding from his back, collapsed against the handcart, toppling it over. Young Ralf slipped in the mud and fell heavily, sprawled amongst their tools now lying on the ground. Still on his back, Ralf grabbed the first tool he could find as the archer blindly lunged around the side of the upturned cart. The small handpick Ralf held had a sharp metal point; it was a lethal weapon, and the apprentice stonemason was a strong young man. He pulled his arm back as the archer approached and swung the pick as hard as possible. The pick glanced off the archer's rusty sword with a loud clang, causing it to drop, and although much of the force had dissipated, there was still enough energy to drive the point deep into the archer's thigh. With a scream of pain, the archer fell onto Ralf's legs, momentarily trapping him.

Without thought of consequence or pity, the brigand's leader, as he liked to call himself, pulled his sword free of Wouter Gurney's chest and unleashed his bloodlust with a series of wild and uncoordinated sword blows to his neck. It was a wasted effort as the dull blade did little more than create a nasty mess, and Wouter's heart had already stopped beating. With the realisation that his victim no longer breathed, the leader, still in a macabre fury, turned his attention toward the apprentice. Blood and bits of flesh fell from his sword as he stepped around the cart and saw the younger man trying to wriggle from beneath the much heavier and seriously wounded archer. Just as he'd done with the elder mason, the leader ran the sword tip through Ralf's chest, and just like his father, Ralf Gurney died at the hand of an unskilled and sadistic assailant, driven to kill in an alcohol-fueled frenzy.

The third brother glanced towards the field on the other side of the river. In the growing early morning light, he saw the figure of a woman watching them. Realising she had witnessed the hideous slayings and could probably identify them, he ran back into the trees to retrieve his horse. He now burst from the forest and quickly galloped up the track towards the bridge, where he could cross the river and kill or capture her.

Stunned by the violence she witnessed, Charlotte was frozen in horror. She saw the horse and rider appear from the forest, but the threat it posed had yet to register. With a growing awareness and alarm, she realised her dangerous predicament and dropped her basket, hoisted her skirts and ran for her life.

Herdsman Odo was taking advantage of daybreak and was inspecting his pregnant cows with Daniel, his young apprentice, when he again turned and looked over his shoulder, hoping to see Charlotte return with her basket full of mushrooms. It was becoming lighter, and the animals were unsettled, impatient to be let out to romp and feed in the field.

Odo climbed over the wooden rail inside the byre and stood in the doorway looking out through the open door over his land. "I don't know what's keepin' that woman. I swear she'd stay out there all day if I'd let her."

Daniel followed his master over the rail and sensibly chose not to comment. He knew better than to offer an opinion on Charlotte's behaviour and later, when Odo became mawkish and fussed over her, have to explain himself.

He stood with his hands on his hips and continued staring across the field. He saw no sign of Charlotte and knew she should have returned by now.

"Should we let them out?" inquired Daniel.

His question went unanswered.

"Odo, should I turn them out?"

"Oh … ahh, nay, not yet," Odo distractedly replied. "Stay here, I'm going to find her."

It was almost full light when he walked over his field and saw no sign of Charlotte. He decided to walk to the mill, as she might be talking to someone there. With growing unease, he quickly strode up the gentle incline and angled towards Falls Ende.

He'd walked his land thousands of times and knew every crevice, bump and depression in it; there wasn't an inch of ground he didn't know or wasn't familiar with. When his foot stepped onto an uneven piece of earth, he looked down and saw the sign immediately. The hair on his neck and arms stood on end, and his stomach turned in knots. He knew something horrible had happened.

Beneath Odo's feet were the clear indentations of hooves, where a horse had skidded to a stop and gouged the soft, damp earth. He could even see from what direction the horse had come and to where it headed – the unshod hoof prints led to the gate near the top of the field. He began to run.

"Charlotte, Charlotte!" His heartbeat raced as he passed the discarded basket of mushrooms, and then in the distance, he saw the open gate. His heart sank.

Someone was yelling at him. He looked towards the mill and saw Master Mason Morel Mundy, "Fetch the reeve, be quick about it!"

"Where is Charlotte?" he yelled as he shut the gate.

"Bring the reeve!"

Whatever the reason for Charlotte's disappearance, Stone Mason Mundy was also alarmed. Odo realised whatever had upset Mundy had something to do with Charlotte, and if he wanted the reeve, then it must be urgent. Odo sprinted down the field to find Mellester's new reeve, Petrus Bodkin.

Chapter fourteen

"Ye should've killed her!" angrily exclaimed the brigand leader. He paced backwards and forwards across the small campsite, safely hidden in the forest. His less-than-agile mind was only now coming to grips with the reality of what a prisoner meant to them. It wasn't part of the plan, and he was unsure what to do. "She ain't no good to us."

"Look at her, she's a lovely one, she is. I thought we'd have sport with her first," replied Charlotte's abductor as he wrapped a piece of cloth around his brother's bloody thigh. He twisted his head and leered at her. A sharp intake of breath warned he'd pulled the bandage too tight.

Charlotte sat against the trunk of a tree; her hands and ankles were bound tightly, a rag was stuffed in her mouth, and her head throbbed where she'd been struck. Since the brigand had snatched her from the field, she'd had no opportunity to escape, as she'd been knocked senseless. As far as she could tell, no one had even witnessed her kidnapping. Her eyes were wide in fear, muffled cries escaped through the gag, and tears streamed down her face.

"It be a mistake." The leader pulled his sword and inspected its dull and rusty blade. He wiped the remnants of blood and gore on his breeches and swung the blade heroically a few times, recalling the pleasure he'd felt as he slaughtered the two men only an hour earlier. He enjoyed the feeling of power, a sensation he was unfamiliar with. "We need to kill her," he said as he stepped towards her, the sword tip swinging in tiny circles around her chest.

Charlotte shook her head in panic. She could feel the primal hunger from the man who threatened her - his desire obvious. She pulled at the bonds that held her hands and legs, but the man who had tied her had done a good job. Perhaps one of the only things the three brothers had correctly done this morning.

The man bandaging the archer stood and faced out towards the forest and cocked his head. "Someone's comin'."

"Is it him, the lord?" asked the archer, more sober and alert than he was a short time earlier. He grimaced as he tried to stand unassisted.

The sound of horses and men's voices drifted to the campsite. The leader shrugged and turned away from his prisoner to listen. He still felt euphoric and cogent; normally, the expected arrival of his employer would make him nervous. He pushed those thoughts aside and embraced the vigour that coursed through his body.

"What will we do if he ain't gonna pay us?" asked one.

"Don't ye go a worryin', he'll pay. Or I'll take it," the leader replied with newfound bravado. He swished his sword confidently through the air again, relishing the extraordinary power he felt.

The approaching horsemen drew closer, and the unmistakable rattle and clink of metal confirmed they were knights. The brigand leader gave no thought to the expert fighting abilities of trained knights, his misguided confidence resulting from adrenaline, alcohol, and pure stupidity. He looked back over his shoulder at Charlotte and licked his lips. She was a beauty.

Three lightly-armoured knights, mounted on coursers, burst into the clearing. The three brigands nervously stepped back and crowded together, almost back-to-back, their bluster and confidence waning quickly. The knights pulled to a stop; their coursers, breathing hard, tossing their heads.

One of the knights, clearly the commander, casually leaned forward to rest his arms on the saddle's pommel, his anger simmering as he stared at the bound woman. The courser he rode, a nervous and large, black stallion with eyes wide, frightened the three brigands. The other two knights with swords unsheathed scrutinised the brigands warily.

"I'm unable to grasp why this wench is restrained and in yer camp." The knight turned and, for the first time, assessed the brigands. "Well, what say ye?"

The brigand leader swallowed. "Milord, she saw what we was doin'."

"Then why does she live?"

"I was just about to take care o' her, when you arrived, Milord."

"And ye thought ye'd have some pleasure first?" The knight turned back to Charlotte and laughed. His two friends joined in. He was clearly drunk. The knight unhooked a wine skin from his saddle and took a long pull, the silence broken by the occasional snort from a horse. "Am I correct, you killed the Falls Ende master mason?" The knight tore his gaze away from the woman and studied the brigand leader.

"Aye, I did. He'd be very dead," nodded the brigand with a toothless smile. "Just as ye wanted, Milord. If, ahh, ye gives us our purse, we'll be on our ways then."

"Don't travel far, I may have another task for ye." The knight untied a small purse from his waist and tossed it to the brigand. "And take care of the villein wench." The knight momentarily wobbled in his saddle.

"Aye, Milord, that we will."

"Keep yer mouths shut. If I hear ye've been talking about this, I'll hunt ye down and yer families."

Three heads nodded in supplicant agreement. The brothers felt it wasn't worth mentioning that their family were already dead.

The knight looked each man in the eyes to reinforce his threat.

Everyone turned to the prisoner as she began struggling and making noise. It was obvious she wanted to speak.

The knight commander laughed. "Let's hear what she has to say. Remove the cloth."

The high-spirited coursers stomped their feet and pulled at their reins, unhappy to be standing motionless. The knights, expert horsemen, spoke soothingly and stroked their horses' necks as Charlotte's gag was removed and water given. She was frightened; she knew who the knight commander was and feared him.

"What say ye, woman?"

"Release me, Milord. I know who you are, Sir Wystan. I have done nothing –"

"Put it back," ordered the knight, interrupting her plea.

"Wait!" she cried in desperation. "These men, they killed the wrong man!"

Sir Wystan's eyes narrowed, and he cast a quick sideways glance at the three brigands who looked at each other, stupefied.

Charlotte continued, "I don't know who they killed, but it wasn't the master mason. Master Mason Morel Mundy is a large, bald and portly man. The men they killed," Charlotte turned her head to look at the outlaws who now stood with their mouths agape, "were men with small builds and lots of hair. I speak the truth, Sir Wystan."

The knight commander cursed. "Does she tell the truth?" he bellowed. His hand slowly moved to grip the haft of his sword.

One of the brigands gave a subtle nod, but none of them had anything of value to say and, unable to meet the stare of Sir Wystan, looked away. He cursed, removed his hand from the sword and reached for the wine skin. After a healthy quaff, he wiped his mouth with the back of his hand and shook his head in disgust. "You know me?"

"Aye."

His eyes narrowed in comprehension. "You are the herdsman's woman!" he spat.

"Odo and I are betrothed," Charlotte proudly confirmed, raising her head and meeting his wrath with a cold stare of her own.

Her acknowledgement caused Sir Wystan's umbrage to surface. He leaned over, passed the reins to his friend and slid from his horse, his spurs jangling as he stomped towards her. "Not if I have a voice in the matter." He paused and glowered at her as an idea began to form.

Standing so close, Charlotte could see his bloodshot eyes and the pale, unhealthy pallor of his skin. She knew she was as close to death as she'd ever been. She turned away and fought desperately to control her fear.

"Shall I kill her now?" asked the brigand leader, now finding his courage and eager to atone for his error.

Sir Wystan, hawked, the spet coming to drip down her shoulder. "Nay, set her upon a horse." He delivered a hard kick to her side. "Trull!"

Charlotte cried out in pain and humiliation.

Unsure, no one moved.

"Now!" He spun impatiently and strode back to his horse and the wine skin.

"There are no spare horses, Milord."

Sir Wystan stopped. He stood frozen for a dozen heartbeats, then slowly turned to face the brigand leader and began to walk unsteadily towards him. His lips compressed into a thin, bloodless line.

"We, uh, we c-could lend ye one of ours," the leader stammered.

"Aye, that ye could," Sir Wystan replied. With unbelievable speed, he unsheathed his broadsword. Even in the dull forest light, the three-foot blade shimmered as Sir Wystan spun the five-pound sword effortlessly in his hands. Thousands of hours of endless practice at a pell had honed his skills. He may have been intoxicated, but when it came to close-quarter fighting with a broadsword, Sir Wystan was truly an expert.

Mesmerised by the twirling blade, the brigand leader failed to see the killing stroke. With apparent ease, Sir Wystan took a half step to the side of the brigand, and with all his body weight behind the swing, quickly pulled the sword backwards and up. The razor-sharp blade arced over the ground at unbelievable speed. Even Sir Wystan's two associates, both knights, marvelled at the accuracy and timing of the stroke. The brigand leader's head was cleanly separated from his neck as his heart continued to beat for a moment longer. Blood geysered upwards as the headless body remained unnaturally upright for a moment longer. The head came to rest on its side near Charlotte, and the unblinking eyes stared helplessly at her. The body crumpled and fell into a heap.

Charlotte screamed.

"Now ye have a spare horse." With indifference, Sir Wystan bent down and wiped his blade clean on the decapitated brigand leader's capuchin.

The archer could barely contain his rage and briefly thought about launching an arrow into the cold heart of Sir Wystan. The surviving brothers may not have been gifted with intelligence, but instinctively knew any retaliation would be fatal.

Mellester's new reeve, Petrus Bodkin, looked for somewhere to sit. Seeing a large collection of rocks, he eased his bulk towards them, his wooden staff helping him to navigate safely through the mill construction site at the top of Falls Ende.

Master Mason Morel Mundy followed a step or two behind, and Herdsman Odo Read anxiously trailed.

When Reeve Merick had been arrested for the murder of Charcoal Burner Larkin, and Sir Hyde Fortescue appointed Sir Gweir as Mellester's new lord, Sir Gweir had only one person in mind to assume the vacant reeve position. Without hesitation, he immediately asked Sir Hyde if he would release Petrus Bodkin from his service to become the new reeve. Hating to lose a good and trusted man, Sir Hyde reluctantly agreed.

Years earlier, Bodkin had been a sergeant and destined to become a knight when a destrier kicked him in the leg. His life would forever change; his dreams of knighthood shattered along with his leg. Despite a severe limp and limited mobility, Petrus was still a man to be respected and even feared by those who crossed him. His ability as a swordsman was renowned, and he'd successfully modified his fighting technique to accommodate his bad leg and extra weight he carried, for Petrus was not an insubstantial man.

Some say he was more skilled now than when he was younger, trim and healthy. He was intensely loyal to Sir Gweir and Sir Hyde Fortescue, lord of neighbouring Ridgley Manor.

Petrus Bodkin had come from a wealthy family with extensive lands. He knew almost as much about farming and cultivating crops as he did about military matters. If he didn't know the answer to a problem, he made it his business to find out. Although only in the job for a month, he'd already demonstrated fairness and honesty. Woe betide anyone who challenged his authority or sought harm to holdings or people within the bounds of his dominion, Mellester Manor.

Reeve Petrus didn't need to find a seat and rest, but although he knew that time was of the essence, he did want an opportunity to think. His mind worked furiously as he contemplated all he'd learned. He sat with a grunt as the master mason followed suit and lowered himself onto an adjacent large rock. Odo remained standing and impatiently waited for the reeve to make a decision. They'd just returned from inspecting the site where Mason Wouter Gurney and his son Ralf were slaughtered.

Petrus began to carve into the mud with his staff. He crudely drew a map and marked the location of the killings with a pebble and then another where Odo had discovered the hoof prints in the field. "Is this where Charlotte would have been?" he looked up at Odo for confirmation.

Odo nodded. With a small stick, he pointed. "Aye, and this was where I found her basket."

"I suspect she saw what was happening across the river, and then something occurred that made her run. What was it she saw?" Petrus stabbed at the ground with his staff. "The killers." He made sure both men were paying attention and then continued. "She dropped her basket and ran down the field. She hadn't gone far when she was overtaken by a man on a single horse."

"Knights!" said Master Mason Mundy with anger and a hint of contempt.

"No, they were not!" shot back the reeve defensively.

Both the master mason and Odo looked at Petrus with surprise. Generally, only knights wielded swords and rode horses. Banditry in and around Mellester and neighbouring manors was rare, perhaps a simple robbery or two and the weapon of choice was generally a knife. Ordinary peasants weren't normally armed.

"Knights didn't slay Mason Wouter and Ralf, and neither was it a knight who captured Charlotte. Whoever it was that killed 'em used a very blunt sword, probably an old discarded one they found or were given. They had no skill either. It was just butchery." The reeve shook his head. "The horse that took Charlotte wasn't a great horse, or courser, it was a hackney. It was unshod and small, 'bout fourteen hands high. I'd say they were commoners, and there were three of 'em. Judging from the blood, I'd say one was badly wounded, most likely from that small pick lying near." Petrus sat back. "Either o' you seen three commoners 'round here lately who don't belong?"

Master Mason and Odo shared a look. "No, we haven't," said the stone mason. "That's all very well, but where did they take Charlotte?" I needs to find her, Reeve Petrus," Odo responded in desperation.

Reeve Bodkin sighed. "Odo, they took her into the forest. You'll not find her today, but you can be certain of that."

"We can't do nothing–"

"And we won't, lad. We'll find their tracks and even the remains of their campsite; hopefully, there will be clues that will help us find her."

Odo looked crestfallen and stared out into the gloomy forest beyond the track.

"Tell me about Mason Wouter and Ralf. Were they good men? Why would anyone want to see them dead?" Petrus looked long and hard at Mundy. "What do ye know about them?"

"They were good men, worked hard, they did. We were only here a short time, Wouter had another job to go to."

Odo was impatient. Rescuing Charlotte was foremost on his mind, and he couldn't remain idle.

Petrus must have read his thoughts. "I will come with ye to visit Cheesemaker Gerald, and then I need to talk with the priest, Oswald." The reeve slowly stood. "And I suggest ye ask your men about Wouter and Ralf," he said to the master mason.

"Ye will inform the lord?" asked Mundy.

Reeve Petrus shifted his weight and turned to face the master mason. "Just talk with yer men and find out why someone would want to see Wouter dead. I will be back later to question them, and leave me to my work, understood, Master Mason Mundy?"

Mundy, an overbearing man who enjoyed his authority, nodded, "Aye, I will."

Odo and Reeve Petrus Bodkin slowly made their way towards the village and Cheesemaker Gerald's shoppe.

CHAPTER FIFTEEN

Branches lashed against Charlotte as they raced through the forest. Blindfolded and tied securely to the horse, she couldn't use her hands to protect herself, nor could she see. One of the knights had her horse tethered to him, and she had no choice but to turn and lower her head and try to avoid branches as they whipped against her. She knew her face and neck bled from scratches, and her body had also suffered as they rode quickly through narrow paths. They seemed to ride for an eternity, but where they were going, she had no idea. She was just grateful to be alive.

Finally, Sir Wystan called a halt, and they stopped. The horses were allowed water from a stream, and she was permitted to tend to her own needs. It was approaching nightfall, and instead of hurrying, the knights were content to tarry. From the snippets of overheard conversation, she learned Sir Wystan was waiting for darkness so that his prisoner wouldn't be seen when they rode exposed on open ground. She scratched at the soft, damp ground as the knights talked amongst themselves. It was all she could do to leave a mark, a clue she'd been here. She even managed to tear at the hem of her torn smock until she had a small fragment of cloth. Carefully, lest it be seen, she left it partly under a rock close to where she sat.

Odo was foremost on her mind. She knew he'd be distraught with worry, as would her family. Her father couldn't do much; he had the shoppe and other family members to consider. But Odo wouldn't rest until he found her. Such was the strength of their relationship. They were as close and inseparable as two people in love could be. Odo would come for her; she only hoped he would be in time.

Eventually, she was hoisted astride the horse again and retied so they could resume their journey. Once clear of the forest, the going became easier. She could tell they were approaching their destination as the horses began to quicken their pace, sensing the familiarity of home.

Charlotte was taken into an enclosure, and judging from the distinctive smell, she thought it was probably a stable for horses. The two knight accomplices tied her securely to a post, then pushed her to the ground.

"There's a guard outside. Be best not to move or try to get away. He'll kill ye if ye try," said a knight as he checked to ensure her blindfold was secure. The sound of their footsteps drifted away, leaving Charlotte cold, hungry and frightened.

Odo walked from the track and into the fringes of the forest. He paused briefly and looked back towards Falls Ende. The ever-present haze that rose like an inert cloud above the deep chasm blurred the beauty. From his vantage point, he could already see the progress the gildsmen had made on the foundations of the new mill and their indistinct shapes as they worked in dangerous, wet and slippery conditions. He turned to the forest, strode through low-growing bushes and followed a narrow path into the gloomy depths.

Once the path became overgrown and indistinct, he changed direction and began to angle back, roughly towards where the mason and his son had been butchered earlier that morning. He walked patiently in slow, silent, measured steps and looked for signs, anything, a clue to where Charlotte had gone.

The forest was familiar to Odo. As a child, he'd played here, gone hunting, and tracked animals with Seth, the apprentice and son of Edgar, the huntsman. This time, he didn't seek animals to hunt; he sought the tracks or any sign of the men who'd taken Charlotte and killed the masons.

He'd walked a good distance past where the slaughter took place and saw nothing of interest. Then he doubled back using a parallel route, but this time, deeper into the forest. He scoured the ground for footprints and eventually found them.

He wasn't skilled enough to determine how many men had walked here, only that the tracks were fresh. Odo was frightened, petrified, but the thought of what Charlotte's captors would do to her gave him the courage to continue.

Seth had shown Odo how to track animals. He learned to stay downwind, how to move deliberately and stealthily. "Don't step on twigs or fallen branches, be patient and take your time," Seth would say. Odo kept repeating his instructions like a mantra. Cautiously, he followed the footprints deeper into the forest and almost stumbled into the recently abandoned campsite and the headless corpse. He vomited.

The ashes of the fire were only just warm. It had burned out hours ago, and he saw where horses had been tied to a tree. Reeve Petrus Bodkin was correct. They were long gone.

He circled the campsite and found many sets of hoof prints. Again, he wasn't skilled enough to determine anything valuable from them, but he wanted to learn in which direction they'd gone. It didn't take him long to discover two sets of tracks, and each used a different route. Odo didn't know what to do and wished Seth was helping - he wanted to scream in frustration. With a calming exhale, he looked around, memorised the trees and landmarks where the campsite was located, and began to run back towards Falls Ende.

Odo ran out of the forest close to where he'd entered two hours previously, and almost collided with Reeve Bodkin, who sat astride an imposing courser. To his surprise, the reeve wore greaves and chainmail and a large broadsword swung from a belt at his waist. He looked more like a knight than a reeve and was accompanied by two other men, both sergeants, and all were similarly dressed.

Breathing hard from running, Odo slid to a stop and quickly stepped backwards to distance himself and the courser; the horse was extremely intimidating. Although not the heavy warhorses which knights preferred, coursers were high-spirited animals and could still be dangerous to the unwary. He spared the reeve's two friends a quick glance and could see they were hard, fighting men. In turn, they looked at him with disdain and annoyance as he burst out of the forest, eager to share his news.

"Odo, Odo, settle down, lad. Where—"

"Reeve," panted Odo, clearly winded as he interrupted. "I've found the campsite, and there's a body…"

Petrus gave his friends a quick look. Automatically, their hands dropped to their sword hafts.

"Take a moment, Odo, get yer breath. But why were ye even looking? I told ye I would do it."

"Cause I needed to do something, Reeve. They've got Charlotte!" appealed Odo.

Reeve Bodkin's expression softened. "Is a stroke of good fortune ye found us. We were about to go into the forest to search for the outlaws. Now, tell me, lad, what did ye find?"

"A man, his head chopped off, and horse tracks, lots o' them, but I can't make out where they went. We need Huntsman Seth."

"Do ye recognise him?"

Odo was bent over and breathing hard with his hands resting on his thighs. He shook his head.

"This headless man, uh, was it messy?"

Odo looked up at him, puzzled.

"Where the head used to be, was it messy where the killer had struck many a time, like with the masons?"

He shook his head. "Nay, I don't think so. I saw nothing like a mess; it was just blood."

The reeve's expression hardened, and again he gave his friends a look.

"Take us there, Odo."

"You'll need Seth to figure out the horse tracks."

"I can read signs, just do as the reeve asks," said one of the sergeants.

Odo looked to Reeve Petrus for confirmation.

He nodded.

Odo jogged back into the forest and took the most direct path possible. Behind him, the three lightly armoured men followed single file on horseback. It didn't take long before he stopped.

"It's just ahead," said Odo, pointing his arm.

Reeve Petrus dismounted awkwardly and unstrapped his staff from the saddle. He tied the reins securely to a branch while Odo caught his breath. The two other sergeants were also unmounted.

Odo stepped to the side and allowed the three armed men to enter the campsite first. They couldn't fail to see the headless corpse and immediately walked towards it.

With a grim expression, Reeve Petrus Bodkin stared at the body and where its head should've been.

He pointed with his staff at the neck. "Was a single stroke."

One of the sergeants cursed, then began looking into the gloom and unsheathed his sword. He looked worried.

Odo looked confused, unsure of what was going on. The sergeants didn't look like men who'd be easily frightened.

"Are ye sure ye don't know this man?" asked the reeve.

"Never seen him before," the herdsman replied.

The reeve looked thoughtful. "And where are the horse tracks, Odo?'

"Here." He carefully detoured around the corpse and headed to the far side of the campsite. Before he reached the end, he stopped and pointed to the soft ground.

One of the sergeants bent down and looked at the hoof prints. After a moment or two, he straightened, looked around, then walked a short way from the camp following the trail. A few moments later, he returned. "They'd be shod, Petrus. Is as you thought."

Odo looked from one face to the next. The reeve and both sergeants looked apprehensive.

"Where are the other tracks?" asked the sergeant. Ever vigilant, his eyes flicked from one tree to another.

"This way." Odo led the sergeant in a semicircle around the campsite and stopped at a tree with a large, low branch.

The reeve and the other sergeant were in a deep discussion.

"Horses were tied to that tree," Odo informed him.

The sergeant bent down and looked at the tracks, then, as he'd done previously, began walking away from the camp following the confusion of hoof prints. Ignoring Odo, he returned to the reeve. "Three horses were tied up, but only two went north. They were unshod. Likely hackneys."

Reeve Petrus walked to the remains of the fire and eased himself down on a log. He scratched at his beard.

"This isn't good, Petrus," said one of the sergeants.

The reeve made eye contact with the sergeant and nodded in agreement.

Both sergeants kept looking nervously beyond the campsite and into the trees.

Odo couldn't keep quiet any longer. "What is it, what did ye see?"

Reeve Petrus pointed to the corpse. "He wasn't killed by an outlaw; he was killed by a knight. Three knights were here, Odo. They killed him and took Charlotte on one of the hackneys."

"Then she lives!" exclaimed Odo. "Then we can go and find her, follow the tracks."

Petrus held up his hand. "Odo, Odo, knights are involved. We cannot go searching for knights. Even if we were lucky enough to find them, we would likely be killed if it came to a skirmish."

"But we can't leave Charlotte! We have to do something."

Reeve Petrus took a big breath. "I am going to do something, Odo."

Both sergeants turned to their friend, curious to see what he would say.

"I have to go to the lord of the manor, Sir Gweir. It becomes his decision now. Because if we have to face renegade knights, then we must do so with an equal or a stronger force."

"But Charlotte … she's in danger!"

"Aye, that she is, lad, but now it becomes Sir Gweir's problem."

"But … to which direction did they ride?" Odo asked the sergeant.

"The outlaws went north, and the knights, if they were knights, headed south, that way." The sergeant pointed his sword at a path.

Reeve Petrus rose from his seat. "Best we leave now."

Darkness was falling as Odo arrived at Cheesemaker Gerald's shoppe. Charlotte's mother, Agnes, greeted him at the door. She had been crying.

"Have ye word, Odo?" asked Gerald, forgoing a greeting.

"Nay, but she lives. I knows that much."

"What of the reeve, what will he do to get her back?"

Odo shook his head and explained what Reeve Petrus told him.

"Knights? What would knights want with Charlotte?

"Reeve Petrus says she saw the killing of the masons, that's all I know."

"But knights didn't kill the masons, it was outlaws, wasn't it?" asked Agnes.

"Aye, and now Sir Gweir must take issue with the knights and outlaws."

"I don't understand … poor Charlotte. Where is my girl, Odo?" Agnes began crying again.

"I will find her, worry not, I will do my best."

CHAPTER SIXTEEN

Herdsman Odo Read's business had moderately prospered since the death of his father, Godwin. He had invested heavily in crossbreeding productive milk cows and even purchased a horse and a saddle. Not a fine destrier or a courser like knights rode, but a simple workhorse. She was a healthy, good-tempered mare, and as always, Odo had plans to use her for breeding. He employed her mainly to transport animals or feed by hitching her to his wagon. As far as carthorses go, Sally was quite large at fifteen hand's breadth high to her withers. She had a powerful, deep chest; although she wasn't fast, she was strong, and he was immensely proud of her.

Daniel had just turned out the animals from the byre and was now busy elsewhere, while Odo tightened the saddle girth strap on the mare. The grey of dawn was only just yielding to what would be a glorious day.

Odo mounted Sally and plodded towards the bridge that would take him across the River Eks, just north of Falls Ende, where he would return to the outlaw campsite.

Now that he knew what to look for, it didn't take long to find the trail the sergeant had pointed out yesterday. Even though the hoof prints were now a day old, he began to see where horses had crashed through branches, breaking them. They were easy signs to track, and he and Sally followed the trail in a southerly direction.

Charlotte had spent an uncomfortably damp and chilly night in the stable and wriggled under straw for comfort and warmth. She hadn't eaten since the previous day, and hunger pangs had kept her awake for most of the night. This morning she was still cold, hungry and frightened.

The sun had not long risen when a man entered the stable. Without speaking, he untied her and led her outside and into an adjacent building. He didn't respond to her desperate pleas for food or answer her questions about where she was, and hadn't spoken a word when he removed the blindfold. Blinking in the subdued light, Charlotte saw she was in a room. It was a comfortable-looking room, actually, she thought it quite lovely, and had she been in a better mood and not frightened, she might have enjoyed its extravagant comforts.

"Sit," ordered the man, speaking for the first time.

When she was seated, he turned and left the room, leaving her alone.

Charlotte wiped away her tears and studied her surroundings. A comfortable bed with a horsehair mattress was positioned in the corner, and a clean blanket was folded at the foot of the bed. She sat on the only chair at a small table pushed against a wall. An old, worn tapestry hung from the ceiling to the floor from one wall, and a large chest sat against another. Shutters kept the room quite dark, although one smaller shutter was open and faced an inner courtyard, but there was nothing to see outside. The door squeaked open, and the man returned with a wooden bowl and ladle that contained gruel. He put it on the table before her, silently exited the room, and shut the door, leaving her alone once again.

Charlotte wasted no time devouring the meal. She was ravenous, the food was hot and tasty, and she finished everything. As she wiped the bowl clean with her finger, the door again creaked open, and a woman entered. She stood in the doorway with her hands clasped and silently appraised her.

She was tall and elegant, and even in her advanced years, she still carried herself with an awareness of her beauty. A few lines of age marked her otherwise flawless skin, and her fiery, red hair that swept back over her shoulders in thick, lush waves was tied with a simple ribbon.

Charlotte recognised her immediately; it was Lady Constance, Sir Wystan's mother. The widow of Sir William Ainsley, who was once lord of Mellester Manor.

With her present situation temporarily forgotten, Charlotte slid back the chair she sat on and stood respectfully. She held the gaze of Lady Constance without fear and scrutinised her in equal measure. There was something about the lady's emerald eyes - they looked devoid of life, almost dead, as if she was looking through and not at her - but then the lady inhaled deeply and seemed to focus on the present. Charlotte finally noticed a spark of vitality as she spoke.

"What have they done to ye, poor child. Yer clothes are torn, and yer face is scratched." She took a step closer and reached up, pulling a stem of straw from Charlotte's hair. Lady Constance sighed heavily and looked with pity at the dishevelled young woman standing before her. "I have something which may fit ye, and I will have someone look at the scratches."

"Lady Const–" began Charlotte, hoping for answers.

"Worry not, my dear, I will see to yer needs, yer in good hands now," interrupted the lady. "It was wrong of them to treat you like that." She gave her a warm, motherly smile. "Rest a while."

"But–"

With a swish of skirts, she gracefully turned and exited the room.

It was too late; Lady Constance had gone. Charlotte didn't understand what was happening to her and remained standing in total confusion. She was in an unusual situation and needed to let people know where she was. She didn't move as she considered her predicament.

She looked at her dress and tore off another small strip of cloth. She walked to the closed and locked shutters and, with care, fed the fabric between the shutter and sill and poked it through until it fell outside. It was all she could do.

Another clearing lay just ahead, and Odo coached Sally to a slower pace as he approached. He pulled her to a stop and dismounted. There were footprints everywhere. Knights had rested here; that much was obvious. A nearby stream offered water for the horses, and Odo took the mare for a drink.

There wasn't much else to see, and Odo hoisted himself back onto his horse. He was about to continue his search when a flash of colour caught his eye. He leapt down and scooped up the fabric partly concealed under the rock. "Charlotte," he whispered. It was a fragment of her dress. She was still alive. It gave him hope and renewed energy. He held the small cloth to his nose and breathed her in.

The trail continued for a mile further, and then the forest petered out and gave way to cultivated fields. Odo paused and wondered which direction to go. In the distance, there were cruck houses, similar to what he lived in, and he could see peasants toiling in fields. This was a small, insignificant collection of homes, a tiny hamlet, nothing more.

It was difficult to see much because an aged oak tree with great, gnarled branches blocked his view. Rather than ride through the fields and upset the villeins, Odo hobbled Sally, left her safely in the forest and began to walk carefully through the fields towards the old oak.

As he approached the tree, the countryside beyond became visible. Ahead was a large single-storied house constructed with stone and surrounded by a low wall bisected with a heavy gate. He surmised that if there were knights, then they would probably be at this structure. Considerably smaller than Mellester's fine manor, this building appeared similar to a manor house but without a great hall.

Warily, Odo approached. He walked as if he belonged and warmly greeted peasants he encountered, ignoring their curious stares and silent questions. He was an outsider, and peasants tended to be cautious with strangers in their midst. If asked, he'd say he was looking for work.

Odo hadn't decided what to do if the trail ran cold or if it led him to Charlotte. Fighting was out of the question, and he knew he would be killed if he faced a swordsman with any skill level, or even with none. Odo was a herdsman and never trained with weapons. As a youth, he'd certainly had his share of fisticuffs and could hold his own in a fight with an unarmed peasant, but that was it.

The sensible thing was to avoid confrontation and discovery by the knights. It was unlikely anyone here would recognise him, so he felt confident he could look around and not arouse suspicion. If he found clues to Charlotte's whereabouts, he would return to Mellester Manor immediately and inform Reeve Petrus.

Finding evidence that Charlotte was here would be difficult, and he wasn't even sure she was in this hamlet. He gave the dwelling a lingering look and decided to walk safely around the perimeter and keep his distance, rather than directly approach it.

As he slowly navigated around the property, he saw a small group of horses inside a fenced enclosure that backed up to a large detached stable. A narrow stream ran conveniently close to the stable and house, then wound through fields to the ocean not far away. Even from a distance, Odo could see the horses weren't rounceys, they were coursers, and only knights rode coursers.

Sir Wystan had enjoyed another long night of insobriety and was feeling its miserable effects. He'd woken late and with some prompting from his mother, decided to shake off the lethargy and ill-feeling with some solitary exertion. He walked into the yard between the stable and house, removed his tunic and stood bare-chested wearing only his breeches. Directly in front of him was a large post. It was partially buried and stood as tall as a man. The 'post', or 'pell', was used to train swordsmen, where they could practice technique and stroke combinations for hours by repeatedly attacking or striking it.

The only weapon Sir Wystan held was a wooden practice sword. It weighed twice as much as a regular sword, and its extra weight helped develop upper body strength and improve endurance. In comparison, a real sword would feel lighter, which would be advantageous in battle.

Before Sir Wystan could begin, he was interrupted.

"Sorry ta bother ye, sire."

Sir Wystan's bloodshot eyes glared at the peasant whose head was bowed. "What is it? Hurry, man, I'm busy."

"Thoughts ye oughta know, a stranger is prowling around, he'd be."

Sir Wystan's interest was suddenly piqued. "Where, where is he?"

"He'd be yonder, and was near the oak, sire."

"Leave it with me. Be on yer way."

The peasant stood subserviently in front of the knight but didn't move.

"Away with ye!"

"Beggin' your pardon, sire, but ye said … uh, we'd be paid."

Sir Wystan untied a purse from around his waist, fished for a coin and tossed it to the peasant. He was already looking beyond the confines of the wall, searching for the stranger as he retied the purse, the peasant completely forgotten.

With the wooden sword in hand, Sir Wystan stepped through the gate and began to walk around the perimeter of the buildings. It didn't take long before he came across the figure.

"What business have ye here!" yelled the knight.

Odo's head whipped around, startled by the man behind him. Although he was still some distance away and couldn't see features, he could see the man had a bare chest and carried a peculiar-looking sword. Odo felt his stomach tighten.

"Ye have nothing to say?" yelled Sir Wystan. "Speak, dammit!"

Odo began to slowly back away. The knight's voice was all too familiar. He knew the man with the sword was the disgraced ex-lord of Mellester Manor. The same man who'd wanted to see him dead. Odo was genuinely fearful. Now he knew it had been Sir Wystan who'd taken Charlotte. This is where she was, perhaps not far away, and probably in the large house. He gave the building another quick, searching look.

Sir Wystan stopped. Could this be a gift from God? He recognised the unmistakable features of the man he despised above all others. It was the herdsman Odo Read, the person responsible for his downfall and dishonour. The decision to bring his woman here had undoubtedly been a good one, and now here he was, the herdsman had come searching for her. The knight began to laugh.

He had lain awake for hours, hoping to exact revenge on those responsible for his disgrace. High on the list was the herdsman. Sir Gweir and Sir Fortescue were next, and they would suffer at his hand, just as the herdsman would. "Come for yer woman?" he yelled, taunting.

Hearing the knight laugh, Odo realised he was in deep trouble and turned to flee. He froze when he heard Sir Wystan yell about Charlotte. His thoughts about rescuing her were forgotten as Sir Wystan, waving his sword, suddenly stormed towards him.

Odo ran. He ran like he'd never run before. He headed towards the oak tree and the forest beyond. Already, he was outdistancing the angry knight. Odo didn't slow and kept going. One peasant tried to stop him, and Odo just charged into him and left the poor man sprawled and cursing over his felled cabbages.

Risking a look over his shoulder, Odo saw that the knight was no longer pursuing him and was now running back towards the house and stables. He knew what the knight would do. He would come on his horse and hunt him down.

Wystan was tiring quickly; he wasn't used to running and, with frustration, saw the herdsman begin to pull away. He angrily threw the wooden sword away and laboured back towards the stables. Such was his rage that it hadn't occurred to him that he couldn't kill Odo with the wooden practice sword when he first ran at him. But then again, he hadn't expected a foot chase either. It would take time to saddle his horse and put on his chainmail, but once mounted and armed, he knew he'd catch the herdsman, exact his revenge and finally kill him. With his groomsman away on an errand, the out-of-shape knight, sweating profusely, frantically sought to bridle and saddle his courser.

Sally had only moved a short distance when Odo rushed into the forest and found her. His thighs were burning from exertion, and he was spent and out of breath. He frantically removed the hobble from Sally, tightened the girth strap and with fatigued legs tried unsuccessfully to climb onto the saddle. After two attempts, he succeeded and immediately set off. Sally did her best, but she wasn't a high-spirited courser.

Odo tried to calculate how long it would take for Sir Wystan to come after him. He believed he had about two points[11] head start and didn't have enough distance to safely escape.

Unlike knights, Odo wore no greaves, no chainmail or head protection. Branches slashed at him, they whipped against his body, face and legs. He coaxed every bit of speed from his horse, and the faster they travelled, the

11   *Medieval unit of time measurement. 1 point = 15 minutes.*

more pain he felt. He knew that when Sir Wystan came for him, he'd be on a fast horse and wearing protection. The outcome didn't look good, and Odo spurred his horse to go faster. When the forest opened up, he urged Sally on; when the trees grew closer together, he tucked his arms into his sides, leaned low and turned his head away. He could do little about his legs.

After a while, he realised Sally couldn't maintain the breakneck pace and he slowed. The last thing he wanted was to be caught on foot in the forest. Odo needed the protection of Mellester and Reeve Petrus.

When Sir Wystan finally entered the forest, he did so at speed. His black stallion nimbly avoided obstacles and charged through low-growing bushes and branches. The chainmail protected the knight's body, although the occasional branch slashed against his face. He knew the herdsman was on horseback and had seen the tracks. For the moment, the herdsman even had a substantial lead. But it wouldn't last. Confidently, Sir Wystan pushed his horse to go faster, almost recklessly.

CHAPTER SEVENTEEN

Charlotte heard yelling and commotion from outside, but the closed shutters kept her from seeing anything. She tried to open the door, but it remained locked. With her fists, she hammered on it until her hands hurt, then the door suddenly opened, and the man appeared.

"Why am I held captive here?" she yelled. "Release me, please!"

The man stepped forward, his face expressionless, and struck her across the face. It was a hard, savage blow that knocked her to the floor. Without saying a word, he retreated, closing and locking the door behind him.

She remained on the floor in the clothes given to her by Lady Constance and wept. She didn't know how much time had passed or how long she'd lain there when the door opened again and the man reappeared. Without sparing her a second glance, he placed bread, cheese and water on the table and exited quietly.

Charlotte was famished, but she felt that eating the food would show her captors that she was weak. She left it untouched.

When the door opened again, Lady Constance entered. She saw the blood from Charlotte's nose where she'd been struck by the servant. "Oh, child, you're bleeding," she said with concern. She reached down, grasped Charlotte's arm, and gently helped her to the bed. She took her kerchief, dipped it in the goblet of water and tenderly dabbed at the dried blood from

Charlotte's nose. "Men are so brutal, are they not?"

"Why did that man hit me, and why am I being held here, Lady Constance?" Charlotte asked.

"Oh, dear," replied the Lady as if talking to a child. "Ye are not a prisoner. I am taking care of ye until you can go home."

"But the door is locked. I am a prisoner in this room."

"The door is locked to keep you safe, to prevent you from harm."

"That man beat me." Charlotte began to sob. "I want to go home. I wish to go home, now."

"Hush, I don't want to hear any more talk of this until you are better," admonished the lady in a quiet, soothing voice. "What you need is rest. You've had a difficult day."

Lady Constance rose from the chair and quietly left the room.

Charlotte, filled with despair, curled up on the bed with her eyes closed and soon fell asleep.

The landmarks became familiar to Odo, and he knew he was nearing the end of his perilous ride through the forest. At one time, he thought he heard the distant sound of a horse crashing through branches, but he wasn't sure. Sally was labouring; she was tired and had run her heart out for him. Seeing a large familiar tree, Odo turned Sally away from the path he followed and into dense bush. Slowing the horse to a walk, he guided her through the tangle of low-growing bush and after a few minutes they appeared on the track that ran parallel to the River Eks, although still some distance from Fall Ende.

Sally was exhausted and could run no more. He slid from the saddle, quickly loosened the girth, knotted the reins over her head, and began jogging along the track, leaving Sally behind.

It was late afternoon, and the sun was casting long shadows. Odo, although tired, maintained a steady pace. Again, he heard a horse crashing through the trees and knew Sir Wystan almost had him. He picked up the pace and ran harder, hoping to reach the foot bridge first.

Falls Ende was just ahead and around the next corner, the bridge. He ran on.It was no surprise that Sir Wystan was waiting for him in the woods near Falls Ende and darted from concealment just in time to cut him off and prevent him from escaping. Odo could see the knight's face bled; he too had suffered cuts from thick branches. He wondered for a fleeting moment how his own must look.

The immense, and impressive black courser stood between him and safety. With its nostrils flared and breathing hard, Odo knew the horse wasn't in much better shape than his sweet Sally. It pranced and kicked out its front legs, as Sir Wystan fought control of the skittish animal with one hand and his knees. He was brutal and yanked hard on the reins. His cruelty extended to mistreating animals as well. With his free hand, he wielded a lethal-looking broadsword and waved it threateningly. Odo tried to keep his distance and pretended to scoot to his left. Suddenly, the horse moved to block his path, and Odo sidestepped to his right. There was a small gap, and he took it. He heard Sir Wystan curse behind him as he struggled to dominate his horse. Odo shot through the gap and ran; Falls Ende was only yards away. He didn't risk looking behind. Based on the sound of thunderous hooves, Odo knew the courser must finally be under control and bearing down on him again. Sir Wystan was screaming incoherently, his tirade a profanity-laced torrent of vile abuse.

There was nowhere to run. Odo was trapped, and he knew Sir Wystan knew it.

Wystan cruelly yanked the reins, and the horse slid to a stop. He had him. He swung his offside leg forward over the high saddle pommel and skilfully slid to the ground. His eyes never left Odo and were locked onto him in a crazed stare.

Masons from the Falls Ende mill stopped working to watch the spectacle as Sir Wystan stalked towards him.

Odo looked to the mill, but no help was coming, and no mason would endanger his own life by challenging a knight. He backed up a step and felt the mushy, saturated earth at the precipice of the falls.

Sir Wystan sneered and pretended to lunge at Odo. He was tormenting him, viciously delaying the moment when he would finish him off with a series of wounds that would result in a painful and lingering death. The sword swept upward with remarkable speed, and Odo swayed backwards to avoid the flashing blade. He almost lost his footing but regained his balance before falling. Sir Wystan moved into a better position to begin his killing ritual and laughed manically.

Odo turned away from the knight and looked down into the depths of Falls Ende. The cascading water beckoned.

Remembering what his father, Godwin, had told him all those years ago, Odo judged the distances carefully and made up his mind. He wouldn't die at the hand of Sir Wystan, and before the knight could react and prevent him, he turned and with a leap of faith jumped into Falls Ende. As his father explained to him all those years ago when he had leapt into the falls to save Mellester's lord, he had tucked his arms to his sides and kept his legs straight to avoid striking a jutting rock and prayed.

For Odo, there was no room for error, and his body dropped into the narrow chasm. Immense protruding boulders flashed by, missing him by a whisker.

He couldn't bear to look and kept his eyes tightly closed as he waited for the impact when he'd strike a boulder on the way down. It seemed an eternity when his legs finally entered the cold water of the deep pool, and in reflex, he extended his arms for balance. One arm glanced from a rock, although not hard, but enough to cause incredible pain.

Sir Wystan screamed in rage and sprang forward, and just as quickly, his cry ended. An arrow had inconceivably pierced his chainmail and embedded into the back of his thigh. Unable to bear the weight of his body and armour, the damaged leg gave way. Powerless to stop his forward momentum, he pitched forward, and shortly after Odo splashed into the pool at the bottom, Sir Wystan followed head-first, in an uncoordinated tangle of waving arms and legs.

Wystan was mostly unaware of his fall. His head struck a rock near the top, snapping his neck and killing him instantly. The sickening sound of his body colliding with granite as he bounced from boulder to boulder carried down to Odo, who scrambled away to avoid being hit by the falling knight. Misshapen and almost unrecognisable, and with his sword still clutched firmly in his right hand, Sir Wystan, with a sickening thud, landed on top of an outsized rock at the base of the falls. His sword fell near him with a useless clatter and slid into the water.

Sensing movement from above, Odo looked up, and through the haze of pain and spray, saw two men he didn't know staring down at him.

The archer and his brother confirmed the knight was dead, and then their heads disappeared. They quietly crept away and returned to the forest. They had exacted their revenge for the death of their oldest brother.

Like sure-footed goats, stone masons were already scrambling down the rocks of Falls Ende. Odo lay on his back, closed his eyes and waited for them to arrive.

The wooden staff of Reeve Petrus Bodkin was stout. Its end, the part that touched the ground when he walked, was three fingers thick and black where it had once been fire-hardened. Odo knew these minor details with clarity as the end of the staff repeatedly jabbed him in the chest.

The reeve was angry. His face glowed red, not from good health and vitality but pure rage. Odo wished he was still soaked at the bottom of Falls Ende, where it was safe, instead of on dry ground beside the mill with a furious reeve attacking him.

"I warned ye, I told ye, but ye wouldn't listen, and ye almost got yerself killed. What would ye have said to yer woman if that had happened, eh?" The staff poked him again.

"An' ye thought ye could challenge a knight, outsmart him, and succeed?" The reeve bellowed with mock laughter. "I thought I'd seen it all, I did, but Odo Read, ye are either dumb as one o' yer sheep, or a brave, fearless soul!"

Odo wisely thought to remain silent.

The reeve poised to poke him again when Oswald arrived. Never had

Odo been so pleased to see the priest. Oswald managed to shoulder aside the reeve's staff and bent down to assess Odo's injuries.

A short time later, Odo was back home and seated at the table. Reeve Petrus was with him, and thankfully, his face had returned to its normal colour. Oswald also sat with them and dourly nursed a mug of mead.

"And what can we do?" asked Odo during a brief pause between the reeve's numerous questions. His bandaged arm was still painful, but according to Oswald, only intused. The water from Falls Ende had washed away the blood from the scratches he'd received on his face, and other than a few other minor aches and pains, he had fared rather well. One of the apprentice masons had retrieved Sally and returned her to the byre, and Daniel was rubbing her down, as the reeve continued to pepper him with questions. With some difficulty, Sir Wystan's courser was also secured inside the byre, and Oswald had the corpse of Sir Wystan in his care at the church.

"I've sent word to Sir Gweir. Since his return from Frankia, he's been with Sir Hyde. I suspect he will arrive here in a few days."

"Then we can get Charlotte?" Odo pressed.

Reeve Petrus sighed.

Sensing the volatile mood of the reeve, Oswald put his near-empty tankard on the table. "Odo, it isn't quite so simple. Lady Constance is the widow of a respected lord of the manor. While her son may have been mercurial, we still have to offer her the respect she's due."

"We can't just barge into her home and accuse her of a crime, Odo," added the reeve. "We need to make sure the lord supports us. It must be his decision."

"What about Sir Wystan, will ye not hand over the body?"

The reeve turned to Oswald for his opinion.

"The church believes he deserves a Christian burial, and his family has the right to see it happen."

Odo gave the moment some thought. "Then what is to stop yer from going there and ask her nice, like? 'Scuse me, Lady Constance, have you seen Charlotte, Gerald the Cheesemaker's daughter? And by the way, your son is dead, his corpse is on the wagon."

"Hold yer tongue, Odo!" admonished Oswald, "Ye will show respect."

"He never gave me any," Odo replied under his breath. "But ye can still go to her, respectfully, in sorrowful mourning, of course?"

Oswald turned to Reeve Petrus, who was scratching at something in his beard. "I, uh, I suppose that wouldn't offend anyone, would it? Odo is right, you do need to inform her that her son is dead."

Oswald shrugged.

"Ye said ye knew of this hamlet and house?

"I do, I visited with the lady not long after she took residence there," offered Oswald.

"Good, then we can leave on the morrow," said Odo happily.

"No!" both men replied in unison.

"Ye ain't comin' Odo, ye'll remain here," informed the reeve with finality.

CHAPTER EIGHTEEN

Charlotte cowered in the corner as the man entered her room to remove the dishes. As he walked past her, he lashed out and gave a sadistic kick to her side. She cried out in pain and remained unmoving long after the door was closed and locked.

Why does he do this? Lady Constance had shown nothing but warmth and kindness, maybe too much, and yet her manservant was brutal. Was she not aware of his inhuman cruelty? Of course, if she was aware, why didn't she stop it?

Time seemed to crawl. From time to time, she heard noises, voices, and at one point, there was some sort of argument. Even with her ear pressed against the door, she could not hear any words clearly.

Later in the afternoon, Lady Constance arrived and sat on the bed. She'd brought a brush with her and insisted Charlotte sit while she brushed her hair. She talked of trivial, insignificant things, and then, when the subject turned to Odo, Charlotte noticed the lady was less gentle and tugged a little too hard. Charlotte gasped. Immediately, the lady settled down and continued to brush with more care.

"Lady Constance, ye've made me feel very welcome by allowing me to stay here. I'm grateful to ye, but I have imposed enough and think it is time I returned home to Mellester."

"Nonsense, ye are my guest, and I won't hear of it. Ye aren't in any condition to travel all that way, besides, I'm enjoying your company."

A quick knock on the door interrupted further discussion, and the manservant appeared. In reflex, Charlotte recoiled; however, this time she was ignored. If the lady saw Charlotte's reaction, she gave no indication. She looked questioningly at the man.

"Milady, two strangers approach with a wagon."

"Not Sir Wystan?" asked Lady Constance with hope.

"Nay, milady."

Lady Constance stood and, without another word, left the room. The man closed the door after her.

The behaviour of the lady puzzled Charlotte. Her warmth and kindness were nothing more than cruel and sadistic. Charlotte wasn't fooled by the lady's duplicity, but it did frighten her to the lengths she would go. To what purpose, she didn't know, but the lady unnerved her.

Suddenly, the door flew open, and the servant entered and quickly lunged for her. Before Charlotte could cry out, the man hauled her to her feet, grabbed her from behind and walked towards the wall, forcing her ahead of him. Holding her securely in one arm, he pulled the hanging tapestry to the side, revealing a large, solid door she hadn't seen before. He pushed it open and propelled her forward and down steep, unstable stairs into the dankness. The only light source was from the door they entered, and it grew progressively darker as they descended. Charlotte had no option but to obey and cautiously navigated her way into an underground room. It was cold and smelled foul.

On reaching the bottom, he shoved her roughly to the ground and silently climbed the stairs, shutting and locking the door behind him. The basement room was windowless and dark. The only way out was up the stairs. Charlotte had never felt such loneliness or fear.

Reeve Petrus Bodkin rode his fine horse, and Oswald drove a borrowed wagon pulled by a borrowed hackney. The battered corpse of Sir Wystan, wrapped in cloth, lay in the wagon's rear. They travelled on a well-used road that wound around the forest outskirts in a southerly direction. Eventually, they spotted a solitary oak tree surrounded by fields a short distance from the forest. According to the priest, Oswald, this was the place.

As they drew near, they saw two knights outside the main manor house. Each was armed, and their weapons remained sheathed. Under their watchful gaze, a peasant swung open the bulky gate, which allowed the reeve and Oswald to enter the compound. He led them to a horse trough near a good-sized stable where they were allowed water. The peasant, obviously a groomsman, offered to look after the horses while they tended to matters in the house. The knights hadn't moved; one stared curiously, the other with open hostility.

Reeve Petrus dismounted and untied his staff, and together, he and Oswald walked towards the main entrance to the house; the hostile knight blocked their path.

"What business have ye?" he demanded in challenge.

As previously agreed, Oswald spoke for them both. "I am the priest, Oswald, from Mellester, and have church business to discuss with Lady Constance. He silently appraised the knight and his weapons.

"And who are ye?" The knight turned to the reeve.

"I am Reeve of Mellester, Petrus Bodkin.

Oswald went to walk around the knight.

"Wait," he commanded.

One of the knights walked to the central doorway and disappeared inside. The remaining knight looked over the reeve with a practised eye. The sword at his hip didn't go unnoticed. Within moments, the other knight returned and whispered to his associate. He flicked his eyes towards the reeve's sword.

With a heavy sigh, the reeve reluctantly unbuckled the lethal blade and handed it to the knight. The staff was given a cursory glance, and only then were they allowed to continue.

They were met at the door by a manservant and led inside to a spacious room. A couple of tables filled the centre space, a few of Lord William's colourful pennants graced the walls, and a sturdy hearth was built into a far wall. At one end was a solid chair, and beside it another slightly smaller one. They were almost like thrones.

Reeve Petrus was momentarily stunned by the sight of the woman who sat in the smaller of the two great chairs. She was a sight to behold, such was her beauty. Reeve Petrus took an involuntary breath and almost coughed. Oswald gave him a scowl.

She, in turn, watched both men indifferently as they walked towards her and then stopped at a respectful distance.

"Hail to ye, Oswald," she said quietly.

Oswald shuffled a step or two closer and bowed his head in courtly mindfulness. "Lady Constance, this is Mellester's new reeve, Petrus Bodkin."

Petrus nodded.

Her eyes appraised him but she turned back to Oswald in question.

"It is a pleasure to set eyes upon ye, although this day I wish I could be here with worthier tidings."

Reeve Petrus stood to Oswald's side and slightly behind. He studied the urbane woman intently.

Her expression never faltered, although she flicked her eyes behind her visitors towards the door where the reeve suspected the two knights observed.

"I see ye are healthy and still generously fed. The church provides ye well." She smirked, then inclined her head slightly. "Have ye an epistle?"

Oswald ignored the jibe. "Nay, Milady."

She shifted nervously in her chair. "Then what have ye?"

Oswald unconsciously reached for the cross that hung from his neck and grasped it firmly, its weight offering spiritual strength. He felt a trickle of sweat run down his back. "With wretchedness … uh, Milady, we bring to ye the body of yer son," he finally managed to say.

Her hands flew to her face as her mouth opened. Doubting his sincerity, her eyes flicked to the reeve, hoping this was nothing more than a whimsical jest. She was momentarily speechless.

Oswald shifted his feet nervously, and Reeve Petrus risked a quick look over his shoulder as he heard a movement at the room's rear. One of the knights had taken a step closer, his hand resting on the haft of his broadsword. They weren't pleased.

The priest allowed her a few moments longer to compose herself, then continued with a practised conciliatory averment. "His spirit has returned to God; he is in good hands now."

Understandably, she was distressed, although not overcome as one would expect. She cleared her throat and bravely faced Oswald, then the reeve. "Tell me, what happened?"

"He was ambushed at Falls Ende and shot by an arrow, Milady," responded the reeve. "The arrow entered his thigh, his leg flopped, and he tumbled into the falls." Reeve Petrus swallowed thickly. "He, uh, he was dead when he landed at the bottom."

The room was quiet; no one spoke. Lady Constance rose slowly from her chair and paced backwards and forwards as the reeve and Oswald stood awkwardly and waited. After a few moments, she wiped her eyes and sat back down. Reeve Petrus noticed she was now sitting in the larger of the two chairs.

She again looked first at Oswald, then at the reeve. "Was the herdsman involved in this?" Her expression was hard, her eyes cold.

Oswald opened his mouth to speak, but Reeve Petrus spoke first.

"If ye mean Herdsman Odo Read, Milady, then nay, he was not involved, nor did he cause the death of yer son."

"But he was there?"

"Aye, he was there, Lady Constance, but did not cause his death," reaffirmed the reeve.

The lady seemed to accept his answer. "The man who shot the arrow…"

"The archer?"

She nodded.

"We have not spoken to him or his accomplice. They appear to be brigands and were responsible for the murder of a stone mason and his son a day or so ago. They fled into the forest near Falls Ende."

"Then ye have them not?"

"Nay, Milady."

"Milady, we have brought yer son with us. He lies in the wagon," informed Oswald, hoping to change the direction of the conversation.

Lady Constance looked towards the room's rear and gestured with her head. Immediately, both knights exited the room.

"Thank ye both for coming. I will see ye have some food and drink before ye leave." She stood from the chair. A signal that the meeting was over. "I have matters to attend."

"Perhaps we should pray, Milady?" offered Oswald.

"Nay!"

Oswald looked offended.

"Ah, Milady, there is one other thing ye could help us with," said Reeve Petrus quickly.

Lady Constance paused and turned to face him. Her face, her expression, was void of feeling. She waited impatiently for the reeve to continue.

If she had been beautiful when he first saw her, now she looked heinous. The transformation was astonishing. Recessed into dark sockets, her unblinking eyes bored into his own. The skin over her face seemed unusually tight, drawing attention to her pallor and bloodless lips. "We are searching for a young peasant woman called Charlotte, Cheeseman Gerald's daughter. Do ye know of her whereabouts, have ye seen her?"

"Why would ye ask me?"

"She was seen in the area, Milady. Are ye positive ye haven't set eyes upon her?" Reeve Petrus pressed.

"She's not here!" she snapped. "You may look around. Feel free to walk and search for her, I will see ye are not molested." Lady Constance walked to the door and was gone.

Reeve Petrus exhaled a long, drawn-out breath. "Come, Oswald, let's do as she says."

The manservant appeared and offered them food and water, then gave them a tour through the house. They entered every room, and there was no sign of Charlotte or hint of another woman.

Both men thanked the servant and stepped outside. Reeve Petrus was handed his sword by a knight, and after buckling the belt, he and Oswald decided they would walk the perimeter of the house before they departed. As the lady promised, they were left alone.

There wasn't much to see. Reeve Petrus walked on ahead, and Oswald was lost in the perplexities of church affairs and the ambivalence of Lady Constance's reaction to the news that her son was dead. They had almost circumvented the house when Oswald noticed a shred of cloth lying on the grass. He vacuously picked it up, looked at it once and called to the reeve. Reeve Petrus gave no indication he heard, so Oswald pocketed the cloth rather than shout and draw attention to himself. He spared no more thought to his find.

After their walk, they returned to the wagon and saw that Sir Wystan's body had been removed. Both knights stood nearby and continued to watch Mellester's priest and reeve.

Reeve Petrus leaned close to Oswald so his words would not be overheard. "Odo claims Charlotte is here, but I think he might be mistaken. Why would the lady lie to us? I see no reason, do you?"

"Perhaps a reason isn't necessary," suggested the priest.

"Ye believe Charlotte is here?"

Oswald looked at the reeve, "I tend to believe Odo, and the lady is aberrant."

"Lady Constance is indeed peculiar," mumbled the reeve in agreement.

A knight swaggered over and stopped in front of the reeve. With disdain, he looked him up and down, then took another step closer so they were almost nose to nose. "The lady didn't ask, so I will ... were ye involved in the death of Sir Wystan?"

If the reeve was frightened, he didn't show it. He didn't move, returned the maleficent stare, and spoke slowly and clearly. "I did not witness his death and recounted to the lady only what I learned from observers."

The knight nodded once. "We will avenge the death of Sir Wystan, of that ye can be sure." He spun and walked away, his spurs rattling in synchronous time.

"Your name, sir?" asked the reeve.

"I am Sir Borin," he said over his shoulder.

Oswald released the stranglehold on his cross and breathed out slowly. It was times like these he longed to feel the weight of a sword again.

Within a short time, both men were on the road back to Mellester Manor, each man perplexed as to the whereabouts of Cheesemaker Gerald's daughter. Their first stop would be to tell Odo the bad news.

CHAPTER NINETEEN

The manservant roughly pushed Charlotte through the doorway and returned her to the familiarity of her temporary room. He never spoke, and luckily, she was spared a beating. The time she'd spent in the dark, damp room was terrifying. She still shook.

Not long after the secret door was closed and she was locked in the underground keep, she heard the scurrying of small creatures – rats, and then as they grew bolder and more curious, they came for her. She felt them run over her feet, and she screamed. One rat tried to climb up her leg under her clothes. She pulled up her dress, grabbed the rat by the tail, and before it could twist and bite her, flung it hard against the wall. For a short while, they left her alone, and then the rodents hunted for her again.

In the blackness, she found the rickety stairs and, with her hands, felt her way to the top where she waited. Occasionally, she kicked at a rat as she heard it bravely climb up towards her. The incessant drip of water was the only other sound she heard.

Eventually, the door at the top of the stairs opened, and as light speared the darkness, the rats fled.

She was so frightened; her body convulsed from fear. She lay on the comfortable bed with the thick mattress and had the blanket pulled up over her head. She wept for Odo, she wept for herself, and she wept for the unknown.

She never heard the door open, nor did she feel the presence of Lady Constance as she stood silently observing her, and she never saw the cruel smile on the lady's face. Charlotte jumped when she felt someone sit on the bed.

"Poor little thing," Lady Constance whispered. She pulled the blanket covering Charlotte's face and stroked her hair. "Ye have nothing to fret about."

Charlotte kept her eyes tightly closed and sobbed as the lady comforted her.

On returning to Mellester, Reeve Petrus and Oswald informed Odo what they had learned from their visit to Lady Constance. As the reeve explained, there was no evidence to suggest Charlotte was at her home or had ever been there. Odo was furious, but as the Reeve explained, there was little he could do until he had spoken with Mellester's lord, Sir Gweir. The reeve and the priest departed, leaving Odo angry and unsatisfied with their explanation.

Once home, Petrus couldn't relax. He had questions and wanted answers. He had a naturally inquisitive mind, and the more he thought about it, the more he believed his initial reaction was wrong and somehow Lady Constance was involved.

He was tired after his long day, but there was one more thing he wanted to do before he turned in for the night. Coming to a decision, he immediately set out for the tavern and purchased a small cask of mead.

Seated at the table in the comfort and solitude of his home, Odo stared listlessly into the dying embers of the fire when a knock on his door disturbed his reverie. With a grunt, he eased himself upright and felt a stab of pain from his arm as he straightened. He limped to the door, the unfamiliar ache of a battered body an unkind reminder of the previous day he'd had. In the flickering light of a candle, he saw Reeve Petrus standing in the doorway.

"Thought ye might need some company," smiled the reeve.

Reeve Petrus wiped his mouth and beard with the back of his hand, thumped the tankard on the table and belched. "I've heard many a tale from locals about the bad blood between Herdsman Odo Read and Sir Wystan, but I think it's time I heard from ye. From the beginning, lad, from the beginning."

Odo sighed. "Are ye sure?"

"I am, and hurry will ye, don't have all night," replied Reeve Petrus.

Odo nodded and eased into a more comfortable position, and began to recount all he could. From that unforgettable day, all those years ago, when he and his father had been digging fence post holes and Sir William Ainsley fell from his horse and into Falls Ende. He spared no detail, and Reeve Petrus listened.

One of the horses in the byre nickered, interrupting Odo's recollections, which set off a chain reaction and soon a chorus of grunts, snorts, and baaing could be heard. Odo looked puzzled and, with a heavy candlestick, walked to the rear door and looked into the byre. All the doors appeared to be secured, and within a short time, the animals settled down.

"A dog?" asked the reeve.

"Perhaps," replied Odo with some measure of doubt. He waited for a dozen heartbeats, listening. "All seems quiet now." He closed the door, returned to his seat, and continued his story until nothing was left to say.

The flames of the fire held the gaze of both men as they sat in companionable silence, staring into the crackling hearth.

The reeve sighed, drained his tankard, and refilled it. "Ye know Odo, I think ye are in a spot of bother."

Odo looked from the fire at the reeve. "Ye don't say."

"Everything that has happened to ye is a result of what happened that day at Falls Ende. Today, when I laid eyes on that woman, I was taken with her beauty. Then I saw her for who she really is, and she is pure evil, Odo. She's the one behind this." The reeve shook his head, looked at the table, and saw a salt dish. He reached across, grabbed a small handful and threw it into the fire.

He turned to Odo with one eyebrow raised and waited. With a sigh, Odo did the same. The flames flickered, almost extinguished, then slowly licked hungrily at the logs again. The old pagan ritual for warding off evil spirits had worked in the past for the reeve. As he often told people, he'd be long dead if it hadn't.

"Sir Gweir returns on the morrow; ye will have to come with me to see him, Odo."

Odo didn't reply, his head cocked at an angle, listening. He heard a metallic sound, a muted clunk from the byre.

Reeve Petrus also heard it. He bent close to Odo and whispered. "Keep talking." The reeve stood, reached for his staff, and as quietly as he could, walked to the rear door that led to the byre. His sword sat on his table at home, and besides the staff, he was defenceless. Meanwhile, Odo continued talking about Charlotte as the reeve edged closer to the door and waited.

Both men knew someone was in the byre. The sound they heard was not made by an animal; it was man-made. Odo began to talk about his cows. To anyone listening, the measured timbre of his voice sounded normal, but his pounding heart threatened to leap from his chest.

Reeve Petrus held his staff vertically as he stood with his back to the wall beside the door and waited. His knuckles were white as he fiercely gripped his only weapon.

Suddenly and without warning, the door crashed open and slammed into the wall with an ungodly clatter. A knight in chainmail charged in with his sword aggressively extended. He never saw Reeve Petrus or the staff as it swung upwards with unbelievable speed and force. It struck the knight on the underside of his forearm just behind the wrist. There was no mistaking the sickening sound of bone breaking. With a cry of pain and unable to grasp the heavy weapon with a shattered arm, the knight dropped the sword. In response to the unexpected counter-attack, he took a defensive step backwards and collided with another knight who followed closely behind with his sword extended. Both men tumbled backwards onto the hard-packed earth of the byre.

Odo watched in horror as the reeve spun on his only good leg, placed his bad leg in front of him and launched another vicious strike. With all his considerable weight behind him, the end of the staff impacted the chest of the fallen knight with a resounding thump.

Had there not been a man behind the knight with his sword drawn, he may have lived and suffered only a fractured forearm and a couple of broken ribs in addition to the humiliation of being bested by an ex-sergeant with a stick. However, the downward force of the staff aided the sword tip that pressed into the back of the knight. The tip tore through the chainmail and protruded from the knight's chest in a gush of crimson blood.

Protected from the angry reeve by his fallen associate, the remaining knight scrambled to stand to his feet and struggled to pull the blade from the back of his comrade. The reeve gave a mighty jab, thrusting his staff downwards towards the face of the surviving knight, but missed. The sword came free, and the knight warily retreated into the blackness.

The byre had been extended three times to accommodate Odo's growing herd, and it was quite substantial. A narrow walkway ran the full length of the enclosure, while the other side was divided into pens. Sheep and a few goats filled one pen, another much larger enclosure contained cows, and at the end, there was a stable for Sally and normally, an empty stall for another horse. That space was presently occupied by Sir Wystan's courser, the black stallion.

All the animals were unsettled. Normally placid and unflappable, even Sally was agitated, while the courser, with its eyes wide, was also disturbed. The only available light spilt through the doorway, and then from a candle as Odo moved to stand in the entryway to watch the reeve attempt to disable the retreating knight.

A knight wielding a sword on the battlefield is a terrifying force to behold. Trained in all aspects of close-quarter combat and use of weapons, knights were formidable opponents, either on foot or mounted, and they were feared for good reason. But in the close confines of the byre, the surviving knight was disadvantaged and not in his natural fighting environment. Reeve Petrus was well aware of this and used it to his full advantage. Anticipating what the knight would do, Petrus tried to position himself to prevent the knight from escaping, while his staff moved in a blur as it poked and jabbed relentlessly in the poor light.

Petrus was forcing the knight backwards into the wooden rails of the stable, the extended reach of the staff proving to be a handful for the knight, who could do little more than swipe ineffectually at it.

Knowing that his luck wouldn't hold, and one well-timed slash could snap the staff and change the situation dramatically, Reeve Petrus yelled. "Get his sword!"

Odo had taken a step over the dead knight and now turned back to retrieve it as ordered. He bent down to pick it up, and immediately the byre was shrouded in darkness as he lowered the candle.

Sensing opportunity, the knight used the darkness and quickly flung himself over the rail and into the stable. He sought to charge through the stable and escape through the door where he and his dead comrade originally entered.

The staff slashed into empty space. Unable to see and unaware that the knight was in the stable, Reeve Petrus took a step backwards and began a series of defensive strokes to protect himself.

"Odo, the light!" he screamed.

With the sword in hand, Odo straightened and turned. Immediately, the area was bathed by the soft, flickering, orange glow of candlelight, and the reeve could see again. He was just in time to see Sir Wystan's skittish courser sidestep, swing its hindquarters around, and launch a brutal kick with both rear hooves at the retreating knight. One hoof connected with his head, the other on the hip. With a thud, the knight collapsed.

Both Odo and the reeve watched as the frightened stallion pranced in the limited confines of the enclosure and continued to lash out, its powerful rear legs driving into the inert body of the fallen knight.

Without thinking, Odo passed the candle to the reeve, climbed the rail into the stable, and spoke soothingly to the distressed animal.

"Wh-Wh-what are ye doin?" questioned the reeve at Odo's foolish move. "It'll kill ye!"

Ignoring the question, Odo continued to talk to the frightened horse. With a calm, controlled voice and not displaying the fear he felt, he tried to gain the horse's attention and trust. Both the courser's ears lay flat against its head, but as Odo spoke, one ear swivelled in the direction of the sound, and it turned slightly to face him. It snorted and stamped its feet as Odo edged closer. It lashed out one last time at the knight. Odo didn't react or move.

Reeve Petrus heard the sound and winced; it sounded like a rock hitting a pumpkin.

Unnerved, Odo cautiously held his hand out. The horse snorted, its eyes wide in fear. Slowly, Odo came within reach, and rather than grab the rope halter attached to the stallion's head, he stroked its neck, speaking softly and soothingly the entire time.

"Odo, get away from there," hissed the reeve.

On hearing Odo's calming voice, Sally had settled and watched curiously at her high-strung, overwrought neighbour.

Odo petted the neck and withers and could feel the tension of the quivering stallion. Slowly, its breathing returned to normal, and it began to relax.

"Odo," he repeated.

Odo risked a look behind and could see the knight hadn't moved. He lay in a growing pool of blood and gore.

Only when the stallion's ears were turned and focused entirely on him did Odo slowly grab the halter and reattach the rope. He continued to rub along its neck, withers and finally its back. The courser was no longer panicked.

"By all that's holy," exclaimed the reeve in amazement, "I don't know who is crazier, ye or that horse – he could've killed yer."

Chapter Twenty

Odo again found himself in the great hall of Mellester Manor. His past visits here had been less than enjoyable, and he was understandably nervous anytime he stood before the lord. This time, the Lord of Mellester Manor, Sir Gweir, was not seated on the large chair typically favoured by lords; he sat on a bench at a roughly hewn wood table in the great hall. Beside the lord sat Oswald, and opposite him sat Mellester's reeve, Petrus Bodkin. Odo sat next to the reeve. A tankard of mead sat before each man, and while Reeve Petrus had met with Sir Gweir earlier and briefed him on Charlotte's disappearance, for everyone's benefit, he again summarised all that had transpired. He began with the death of the stone mason and his son, and ended with the death of two unknown knights last evening in Odo's byre. Steward Alard sat at his customary seat behind his desk, a short distance away. No one else was in the hall.

Sir Gweir was still coming to grips with his new status as lord of the manor and the unfamiliar responsibilities the position required of him. As requested by Sir Hyde Fortescue, Lord of Ridgley Manor, who acted as a proxy for the king on local matters, he was ordered to visit Frankia and swear fealty to King Henry II. He returned to Mellester exhausted a week or so ago, and without time to rest, immediately set off to visit his friend and mentor, Sir Hyde, to update him on the latest developments in Aquitaine. He wasn't happy to be recalled to Mellester before he had time to conclude his business and had impetuously vented his displeasure at anyone and everyone, including the reeve. However, after hearing the full explanation, he realised Reeve Petrus had acted prudently.

Appeased somewhat by a nuance of guilt and a ministration of mead, he looked closely at the face of each man who sat with him and felt paternal affection for them all. He was still trying to comprehend the grumpy, learned priest, Oswald. Beneath the gruff exterior, the priest had a heart of gold and a generous disposition, although he had an element of mystery. Although a mite over-pious, he was a good and wise man, thought the lord.

Then, of course, there was Petrus, good old Petrus. Dependable, loyal and trustworthy. A shame he was never able to take the oath and become a knight. He would have made a perfect knight and an even finer lord. He felt fortunate that Petrus had accepted his offer to become Mellester's reeve, and even more so now with the revelations of ongoing turmoil during his absence.

And finally, the herdsman, the enigma. Here was a man, only a few years younger than himself, whose ambition and intelligence were surpassed only by his honesty. Yet he was content to live a simple life with simple dreams. He was almost envious. Odo had land, a thriving farm and a beautiful, fine woman he would marry. Now she had disappeared, presumably at the hands of nobility. Although still unproven, he reminded himself.

Sir Gweir studied the herdsman a moment longer, perplexed by the obvious. Freeman Odo Read sat at this table with men above his social station, yet they all accepted and respected him as an equal. The poor fellow had received his share of bad fortune -- been unjustly imprisoned, pilloried, and faced death at the hand of a knight and still he survived. He knew the young herdsman had never fought with a sword, faced battle or been taught the finer points of weaponry and horsemanship, yet he even managed to impress Petrus. That was an accomplishment if nothing else. Sir Gweir smiled. He was fortunate and wouldn't underestimate or take the trusted men before him for granted.

He turned to the priest and saw him observing Odo. He suspected Oswald had something to do with Odo's education and upbringing. But why? Had the priest seen something special in him?

With a long, drawn-out exhalation, Sir Gweir downed his mead and turned to the herdsman. "Ye've taken some foolish risks and are lucky to be alive, Odo. I can't say I approve, but I suppose if I were in yer position, then I may have done the same."

Oswald's head bobbed up and down in agreement while the reeve just watched impassively.

"Reeve Petrus tells me you believe Charlotte is held at the home of Lady Constance," continued Sir Gweir. "Why, what evidence have ye?"

Odo leaned forward and looked directly at the lord. His eyes never wavered. "I followed the tracks, Milord. They led me through the forest until I came upon the manor house. There was nowhere else for them to take her, and t'was there I came upon Sir Wystan."

"How did ye know that Charlotte was with them?" He didn't wait for an answer and thumped his hand on the table to emphasise his viewpoint. "Here is my problem." He turned to each of the men to ensure they listened. "Lady Constance is nobility; I can't just go in and accuse her of wrongdoing without proof. I need something. Offer me evidence!"

Steward Alard looked up from his work at the outburst.

The men at the table were silent.

"The two knights who were killed last evening–" Sir Gweir turned to Reeve Petrus. "Could you identify them as the same knights at Lady Constance's home? Has anyone seen them previously with Sir Wystan?"

The reeve shook his head. "Never seen 'em b'fore."

Odo fished in the pocket of his tunic. "I found this when I followed the tracks. 'Tis a piece of Charlotte's dress." He placed it on the table for everyone to see. "This proves I was following Charlotte, does it not?"

Sir Gweir nodded, "Aye, that it does."

Oswald moved with a start, causing all heads to turn to him. His hand appeared from beneath the table and placed an almost identical, but larger, piece of cloth on the table. "I, uh, I forgot I had this." His face turned a rosy shade of red.

"Where did you find it?" Odo cried. "This is from Charlotte!"

"It lay on the ground, outside the manor house of Lady Constance. I forgot I had it until I saw the piece Odo found." He was clearly embarrassed by his forgetfulness.

"Why did ye not tell me?" asked the reeve.

"When I picked it up, I spoke to ye, but ye were deaf to me," replied Oswald.

"Ye should–"

"It matters not," interrupted Sir Gweir. "Ye found it where exactly, Oswald?"

"T'was on far side of the manor house, Milord. On the ground, only a step from the manor."

"How did it get there?" questioned Odo.

"Could it have been dropped or thrown from a window?" asked Sir Gweir.

"Aye, now that I think about it, where else could it have come from but a window?" offered Oswald.

"What more evidence do ye need, Milord. That cloth proves Charlotte is there," pleaded Odo, his voice rising in frustration. He got up from the table and started to pace.

Sir Gweir turned to Odo, his eyes briefly flashed in anger at the tone and action of the herdsman. He was about to rebuke him when he remembered what he'd gone through. He knew Odo wasn't being disrespectful. His expression softened. "I agree with ye, Odo. I cannot think of another reason, can any of you?"

"That means you can find her there," Odo suggested. Odo placed his hands on the table and leaned towards Sir Gweir.

"Wait, not so fast, Odo." Reeve Petrus turned to the lord. "Oswald and I looked through the entire house; we found nary a sign of Charlotte. We need to make a more thorough search."

"And I can't see Lady Constance agreeing to that," added Sir Gweir. "Going in by force to the home of an uncooperative noble will have repercussions."

The sound of a chair scraping on the wooden floor disturbed the discussion. Steward Alard ambled over and bowed his head apologetically to Sir Gweir. "Milord, if I may be so bold?"

Sir Gweir nodded for the steward to continue.

"Perhaps if Milord invited Lady Constance to attend an inquire into the death of Sir Wystan. Of course, ye will host this inquire here at Mellester.

She would be obliged to attend, and I'm sure the lady will take with her a retinue of knights, leaving her manor largely unprotected–"

"And while she's here," added the reeve, "her manor could be searched. I like it," he smiled.

"If we find Charlotte, then Lady Constance will be here at Mellester, and we can delay her departure until Sir Hyde advises me what to do with her," Sir Gweir added. "Aye, that could work. Well done, Alard."

The steward bowed his head and returned to his desk, somewhat pleased with himself.

"Am I to stand in judgement again?" asked Odo with a worried look.

Sir Gweir laughed, "No, Odo, this inquire will confirm the brigands were responsible for the death of Sir Wystan."

"And absolve ye, Odo," Oswald added.

Odo looked relieved, then his expression clouded over. "Milord, how long will this take? Charlotte is in danger."

"I think if the lady wanted Charlotte dead, then it would already be so. She is probably still alive, and I believe the lady intends to keep her that way," suggested Reeve Petrus, offering some hope to Odo.

Sir Gweir leaned over towards Odo. "Ye will not, I repeat, ye will not leave Mellester and attempt to rescue Charlotte or do anything to interfere with our plans. Ye promise me, Odo?"

There was a hint of a smile on the lord's face, but Odo knew the trouble he would be in if he disobeyed Sir Gweir.

"Aye, Milord, perfectly." Odo returned the smile as the lord patted him on the back.

"Steward?" Sir Gweir shouted.

"Aye, Milord?"

"See to it a message is sent to Lady Constance requesting her presence ... ah ... five days hence, for the inquire?" He looked to the reeve for confirmation.

Reeve Petrus nodded.

"Make it so, Alard."

"As ye wish, Milord."

Sir Gweir rose from the bench. "Now I must take my leave and return to consult with Sir Hyde. And Petrus, if ye can locate and bring in those brigands, it would help with the inquire."

"Of course, Milord, I've been working on that."

Odo and the reeve walked down the carriageway from Mellester Manor towards the village.

"Reeve, I have a question."

"Aye, lad."

"Why can't the lord assemble a group of knights and just go to Lady Constance's manor and just ..."

"Force their way in and search?"

"Aye, it seems so simple," replied Odo, somewhat perplexed.

"I'll tells ye why. 'Cause Lady Constance was the wife of a fine lord. Sir William Ainsley was well respected and had many friends, including the king," added the reeve. "Regardless of the behaviour of her wayward son, it has not been proven the lady has done anything wrong. Remember, Sir Gweir is a young and new lord of a small manor. If the lady were to protest, Sir Hyde could petition the king, or even act upon hisself and remove Sir

Gweir as lord. Sir Gweir now has evidence that a search is warranted, and he will explain that to Sir Hyde. So if the good lady were to protest, Sir Gweir has his vulnerable backside protected."

"But then, why not just go to her in force and demand to search her manor with Sir Hyde's blessing?" Odo pushed the point, still not grasping the complexities.

"Odo, Odo, you still have much to learn," tut-tutted the reeve, "The manor or house of Lady Constance doesn't fall into the demesne of Mellester Manor. And if we sent knights and demanded to search, we'd be out of order, and she has every right to refuse us entry. During the delay, they would likely hide Charlotte, and we probably wouldn't find her. Remember, lad, Oswald and I already searched and found nothing. It will take a lot of time to be thorough. With the Lady in Mellester, we will have that time."

"I want to come with ye when ye search."

Reeve Petrus stopped walking and turned to face the young herdsman.

"I'd love to see ye come, but ye can't. There may be some unpleasantness and ye've no skills to defend yerself. Ye haven't even a horse to keep up with us. We will be riding very quickly, Odo. Yer dear old nag Sally wouldn't last." He laughed at the thought of seeing little Sally trying to keep up with five mounted knights, and himself, all riding coursers.

Odo looked thoughtful and spoke no more about it.

"Remember what the lord said, Odo?"

"Aye, I know reeve."

"Good, now I have brigands to find."

CHAPTER TWENTY-ONE

There were rents in clothing to repair, dresses to be hung and a slew of other household tasks that required attention. Charlotte held her ground and firmly refused to perform the assigned duties.

"I am not a claviger[12] and will not be treated like one. I am born to a freeman," she insisted with a measure of force. "My father is Gerald, the cheesemaker in Mellester. Ask anyone!" Her hands remained on her hips as she glared defiantly at the servant.

The manservant waited patiently until she had finished her outburst, then, without warning, drove his fist into her head.

Charlotte fell to the floor, clutching her face. Ignoring her plight, the man dropped a bundle of clothing on a table and walked away. "See to it."

"I want to go home," she sobbed.

The manservant had hit her squarely on the eye, and she could already feel it becoming inflamed and swollen. She remained where she lay and wept.

Sometime later, Charlotte heard some bellowing and shrieking outside. The manservant barged through the door, hauled her roughly to her feet and forcibly led her by the arm back to her room. He locked the door and left her alone. She tried to see outside through a small gap in the shutters, but saw nothing but some of the lady's knights standing together. Her eye was painful, and turned blue and black. It affected her sight; even her nose

12 *Servant*

hurt. She promised herself he wouldn't hit her again without receiving one in return.

A short time later, she heard the lady yell angrily, but had no notion of its cause. She kept her good eye pressed against the shutter and, through her narrowing field of vision, saw a solitary horseman riding away in the distance. Someone delivered bad tidings, she thought. Despite the hurt, Charlotte managed a smile. She knew Odo would come for her.

Lady Constance was seething. She stormed through the house and faced the knight who stood stiffly before her. "Why, tell me why, two knights failed to kill a simple herdsman!" she screamed at Sir Borin. Spittle flew from her mouth, and her eyes blazed.

The knight stared at a fixed point on the far wall and dared not meet her eyes. "T'was Mellester's new reeve, milady."

She spun and marched to the far side of the room, where she turned and again glared at the knight. "What of the three brigands, where are they? No doubt spending my coin, drunk and lying between the legs of some village wench." She clenched her fists and strode purposely back towards him.

"I know where they'd be, and there are only two. One was killed–"

"Then find them!" she snapped back at him. "And have them take care of the herdsman once and for all – I want him dead!" She bared her teeth in a feral snarl. "Then have them finish the job they fouled. I want the Falls Ende master mason killed." She stepped closer to the knight, only inches away from his face. "I paid them to do a job, and they will finish it. That mill will never be completed. Never! Do you hear me!" Her pale skin was drawn tightly back over her jaw and cheekbones, emphasising hollow cheeks and deep sunken eyes.

She turned away from the knight and returned to her chair, the anger evaporating quickly. Colour returned to her face, and her eyes once again sparkled. She flicked her hair over her shoulder. "Hurry back, we depart for Mellester in four days. See to it that everything is ready," she added in a more temperate tone.

The knight looked at her in puzzlement. "Mellester, Milady?"

"That meddlesome new lord is holding an inquire into the death of Sir Wystan. I have no idea why…" Her voice trailed off as she was lost in thought.

"Very well, Milady, if that is all?" He was eager to leave.

She waved her hand, dismissing him.

Daniel was sent out into the field as Odo nursed his injuries. Although feeling better, he was careful to rest his shoulder as he wanted it to heal as quickly as possible. He was in the stable talking quietly to Sir Wystan's courser, and with his good arm, rubbed him down with a brush. The horse stood placidly and responded to Odo's words with twitching ears and an occasional snort. There were no lingering effects of the violence of four nights ago.

"And ye talk to yer women that way, eh?" asked Reeve Petrus as he leaned against the doorway to the byre, his large body filling the space. His unexpected visit caught Odo by surprise.

"Ye should try it, reeve, you may find ye'll spend less lonely nights in yer bed," Odo replied with a grin.

"I don't think a horse will fit in my bed, Odo."

Both men laughed.

"I was thinking 'bout what ye told me th' other night..." began the reeve. He walked outside into the sunshine.

Odo gave the courser a final pat and slid his hand down its back onto its rump as he followed the reeve. It never occurred to him that the animal could lash out at him with its deadly and powerful legs.

"...and I think ye need to be careful. After everything that's happened." The reeve shook his head. "And if Lady Constance is behind it all, as ye believe, then she won't rest until yer dead."

Odo said nothing and looked at the reeve. He noticed the sword that now swung from his hip.

"What? Nothing to say?"

"Ye think I don't know that? I go to sleep at night on the floor, in fear someone will stab me in my bed. I look over m'shoulder wherever I go, scared a knight will come charging at me with his sword out."

"That would be having his sword drawn, Odo."

"Ye know what I mean."

Reeve Petrus stroked his beard. "Would yer consider learn'n how to fight? Sir Gweir asked if you'd want to learn. Then ye could protect yerself and yer lovely woman."

Odo looked thoughtful and kicked at a stone on the ground. "Took ye a while to learn how to fight, didn't it? I mean, you spent years learn'n all the ways to kill a man with a sword and yer stick."

"Aye, and ye never stop learn'n."

"And that's my point, Reeve. I'd never be good enough to prevent a knight or an outlaw with a weapon from killin' me. Best thing I have is my head."

"Think about it, Odo."

"I have."

The reeve grunted. "Suit yerself," he said and looked out across the distant fields. He could see the distant figures of men working. "I should be out there, supervising them, Odo, not looking for a captured woman or searching for outlaws." Reeve Petrus looked reflective. Odo waited to let him speak. "I want the grass cut early this season. We may get more rain, and I think we can have a second harvest of hay if we cut the first crop early"

"Aye, the weather has been good fer growing," Odo replied distractedly. He didn't want to talk about farming.

"We'll need yer wagon and nag for harvesting." The reeve sighed.

"And when will ye be leav'n for Lady Constance's home?" Odo asked, wanting to return to the subject that occupied his thoughts.

Reeve Petrus turned away from farming and looked at the young herdsman. "She arrives on the morrow, so we shall leave at sunrise and wait for her to pass us. Then we go to her manor."

Odo nodded. "Can I go? I'll stay out th' way, I promise."

"Nay, ye can't Odo."

The dimly lit tavern wasn't part of a manor; it was completely isolated and sat on a low rise at a major crossroads between a sprinkling of small hamlets. It was convenient and suitable for travellers and outlaws alike, as the amenities provided a handful of useful services to its discerning patrons. Attached to the tavern was a rooming house, and guests could rent a room for privacy or, for a thriftier option, sleep in a larger dormitory with others. A handful of ladies with sullied reputations called this place home and plied their craft with practised skill and jaded enthusiasm.

Behind the tavern, and beside the rooming house, was another amenity much valued by clientele - stables. About a dozen and a half horses were currently quartered beneath the large lean-to, and an ageing ostler[13] was tending to a couple of hackneys that had been here for two days while their owners took advantage of the hospitality inside the adjoining buildings. Just as he completed his duties and sat down, the sound of an approaching horse made him turn to look at the adjacent road.

The man who rode the impressive horse did so with subtle commands from his legs and heels, leaving his hands free. From years of experience, the keen-eyed ostler noticed this detail immediately and determined the man, although dressed in normal attire, was a knight. Only knights rode in that style, and his expensive, highly-trained courser was unaffordable to anyone except the wealthy.

Sir Borin pulled the courser to a stop, dismounted quickly and spoke to the horse before giving it an apple. The ostler, perched on his three-legged stool, just watched. Knights were particular when it came to a stranger handling their horses. He'd wait.

The man led his horse towards the stable and pointed to an empty stall.

The ostler nodded, spat, and remained seated, leaning forward with his elbows on his knees.

The man loosened the saddle but didn't remove it. "Don't touch him. Just see he gets water and some feed, will ye." He threw a coin at the ostler,

13   *A person who looks after horses at an inn.*

who rose from his chair in time to snatch it from the air.

The knight adjusted his sword and slowly approached the tavern's entrance. "I won't be long."

The ostler hawked again and decided to give the courser water and feed as the customer requested. He didn't approach the horse from the rear and moved slowly towards it from the side. He deliberately spoke softly the entire time so as not to spook the beast. He didn't trust the horses knights rode. While the heavier and stronger destriers were trained to kill and maim, the lighter coursers often were trained similarly. No smart man who wished to reach old age fully trusted such an animal.

The knight opened the door, stepped into the gloom and waited for his eyes to adjust.

The room was reasonably full. About twenty to twenty-five men nursed drinks in solitude, or drank noisily with friends. A couple of ladies chatted by themselves, a few were clinging to men, as were the two whores sitting on the laps of the two brigands he'd come to find.

The knight slowly walked towards them to the far side of the room. Customers moved aside, allowing him to pass, and slowly, conversation subsided. Everyone stared, and if he was uncomfortable or nervous at the attention he received, he didn't show it.

The two brigand brothers were each busy with their guests and reluctantly removed their faces from the ample cleavage that held their interest. Sir Borin stopped, one hand resting on the haft of his sheathed broadsword, the other hooked on his belt. He said nothing.

"Clear off," said the archer to his new fiancée.

The other whore gave the knight a thorough up–and–down look and wisely decided to leave with her friend. She heaved her bulk from the brigand's lap and followed her friend, who had waddled away to find a new husband. She gave the stranger a wink as she passed.

The other brigand watched the whore walk away, eventually tore his eyes from her swaying form and focused his bloodshot eyes on the knight. "Must be important if ye came all this way t' see us." Both brigands remembered the knight. He had been with Sir Wystan in the forest. They were nervous and expected to be killed for their revenge attack on Sir Wystan.

The archer laughed nervously. His hand had moved beneath the table and gripped his rusty sword. His brother had a smaller, lethal Ballock knife hidden in the folds of his capuchin. When the opportunity arose, he would leap from his seat and drive the blade between the knight's ribs. He tensed.

The knight spoke in a measured tone. "Outside, now." He turned his back on both outlaws and retraced his steps, returning to the stable where he waited.

The brothers turned to each other in mute surprise, shrugged, and followed the knight. Moments later, they stumbled outside, squinting in the light.

"Wots this all 'bout, then?" the archer asked suspiciously, looking around in fear that other knights waited.

Sir Borin noticed the archer's bandaged and bloodied leg. "Ye were paid to kill the master mason at the Falls Ende mill. Ye killed the wrong man."

"Only 'cause we were given wrong information," replied the older brother. "We would've killed–"

The knight held up his hand to stop him from talking further. "You will return to Falls Ende and kill the right man this time. Do you understand?

"But the reeve be lookin' for us in Mellester," appealed the archer.

"It's a job ye've already been paid for," added the knight with a slight edge to his voice. He spoke slowly, his threat unsaid but implied.

The outlaws turned to each other for mutual support. Seeing they had little option, they both nodded. "Aye, if that's what yer wish," replied the archer.

"I have another task fer ye."

The archer raised an eyebrow suspiciously.

"Are ye familiar with herdsman Odo from Mellester?"

The brothers nodded. They remembered him from seeing him at the falls; he'd jumped in to flee the lord. "Wot of 'im?"

"I want him killed."

The brothers were quite happy and smiled, showing rotting teeth. This was an easy job. "Ow much?" the archer asked.

"Same as last time, half now and half later." The knight untied a small bag of coin and tossed it to the archer.

No mention was made of the attack on Sir Wystan. The two outlaws believed the knight knew nothing of the incident.

However, Sir Borin did know, and had certainly not forgotten. On instructions from Lady Constance, he'd brutally slay both men once they'd performed his bidding.

The ostler sat on his stool and leaned against the wall. His scrawny arms were folded, and his chin rested comfortably on his narrow chest, rising and falling in time to a rasping, rhythmic cadence. He heard every word and knew better than to alert the knight that he was awake. He fought the urge to swipe at a fly that crawled over his face, kept his eyes tightly closed, and pretended to sleep.

"I will know when the job is done and will meet ye in the forest at yer old campsite. Wait there fer me," instructed the knight.

With a bag full of coin, the archer was already planning how to spend them as soon as the knight departed. In anticipation, he looked over his shoulder at the door to the tavern.

"Be gone. Leave now and do not return here, ye hear me?" The knight's voice rose, for the first time displaying the contempt he felt for the brigands. "Best make yer move on the master mason tomorrow, be less people around as there's an inquire in Mellester's hall."

"We, uh, have unfinished business here," appealed the archer. His brother nodded in complete agreement.

"Ye'll have unfinished lives if ye don't make yer way." The knight took a threatening step closer.

Both brigands glared with hostility at the knight, each assessing how they could kill him. While not gifted with acumen, they both realised they'd never overpower the knight, let alone kill him. "Aye, best we leave then," said the archer morosely, resigned to missing out on another evening of frolic and fun.

In the tree line less than half a furlong away, Sir Borin's sergeant watched as his master instructed the outlaws. He was adequately armed and sat astride a courser. In the event he was needed, the knight would signal with a prearranged gesture.

"Ostler! Ostler!" the archer yelled.

The wizened old man slowly stirred, scratched his face, and turned to the voice.

"See to our horses, an' hurry, dam ye," yelled the archer.

The ostler spat, rose from his stool, and creaked towards the two hackneys.

The knight followed the ostler, quickly stepped beside him and lowered his head. "Breathe one word of what ye heard, an' I'll come for ye, and yer family," he hissed.

The ostler swallowed and nodded. He wouldn't be telling his daughter, who lived in Mellester, what he'd overheard. "As ye wish, sire." He bowed his head in supplication.

CHAPTER TWENTY-TWO

Distant clouds showed a hint of pink as the grey of dawn broke over Mellester Manor. Reeve Petrus Bodkin looked skyward towards the east and, with a grimace, reluctantly acknowledged the clouds and changing weather. He didn't want rain, not yet, not until the hay had all been harvested. He hoped this business with the missing girl would end today so he could focus on the manor's farming needs. His courser, impatient to be in motion, skittered sideways as ten more mounted men arrived. Five knights and five sergeants would leave Mellester this morning, and Reeve Petrus would accompany them.

Sir Dain, one of Mellester's most experienced and senior knights, would be in command. He pulled up beside the reeve. "Ye may lead the way until we enter the forest and wait fer the lady to pass. Petrus, if yer content we'll follow ye."

The reeve nodded.

The knights were not expecting to fight this day and believed intimidation alone would grant them access inside the holdings of Lady Constance. They didn't fly pennants, carry shields, or wear standard armour, preferring basic chainmail and leg greaves. Otherwise, they were fully armed, as were the five sergeants who would complete the detachment.

Reeve Petrus lightly squeezed his horse with his legs, and without encouragement, the courser shot forward. Beside him rode Sir Dain. Four other knights rode two abreast as they cantered down the road. The sergeants brought up the rear, emulating their masters by riding side by side, and had no difficulty keeping pace as they also rode expensive coursers. Anyone using the road would be expected to move aside as the small force headed south.

The sound of eleven warhorses travelling at speed was considerable, and if the reeve and Sir Dain hoped their departure would go unnoticed, they were mistaken. Peasants already toiling in the fields raised their heads to stare into the half-light as they passed. No one waved. Peasants were wary, and even frightened of knights. The principles of chivalry were lost to many, and they disapproved of the privileged and often extreme lives knights led. While war, killing and violence were part of a knight's life, most peasants never came into contact with a knight and believed them to be violent, ruthless and pampered. Nonetheless, the thunderous sound and spectacle were magnificent, and anyone who recognised Reeve Petrus Bodkin leading the knights was impressed, if not puzzled by the reason.

It was essential to arrive at the forest where they could rest and wait undetected as quickly as possible. They didn't want to meet Lady Constance on the road and arouse suspicion about their destination or purpose.

Even ex-sergeant Reeve Petrus felt exhilarated. He'd never ridden at the head of a column of knights before, and his courser, a legacy from his time as a sergeant, was enjoying the thrill of being in front and leading.

The small column slowed briefly as they navigated through some windy roads that snaked over the low hills, when a sergeant rode up beside Sir Dain and pointed behind them. The knight and the reeve looked back over their shoulders and could see a man on horseback, riding fast and intent on catching them.

Sir Dain indicated that the column should halt as they waited for the horseman to arrive. The reeve's eyes turned to narrow slits as he recognised the horse and form of the rider.

"Is that who I think it is?" asked Sir Dain incredulously.

"Aye, sire, that it is. Is Odo on Sir Wystan's horse."

The knight laughed. "Who taught him to ride?"

"When I find the man who did, I'll kill him, I will," hissed the reeve.

"Perhaps he brings a message," said a knight behind him.

"Nay, I doubt it," replied Reeve Petrus with a sigh.

All eleven men were watching the horse and rider approach. The pure, black stallion was a beautiful animal, the depth of its colour unique amongst so many other fine beasts. The reeve had to give Odo credit. It took guts to mount an animal he hadn't even trained or ever ridden, and yet, surprisingly, the courser appeared totally at ease and relaxed, as did Odo. This sentiment was apparently shared by all the knights and sergeants who watched with interest as the high-stepping stallion strutted past. None of the men had ever seen a peasant ride a courser before, and probably never would again.

Odo self-consciously rode down the column of men and stopped in front of Sir Dain and Reeve Petrus. "Hail, Sir Dain," Odo greeted the knight formally and dipped his head in respect. He turned to the reeve with equal seriousness, "Hail, Reeve Petrus."

The reeve's initial anger had dissolved into amusement, and he fought hard not to smile.

"Bring ye a message?" asked Sir Dain.

Odo's eyes flicked to the reeve.

"Sire, Odo wants to ride with us. He feels he can assist us and help with his woman."

The knight glowered at Odo. "I see ye are comfortable on a borrowed horse," his expression stern. He paused a heartbeat or two, then made up his mind. "Ye will remain at the rear, and not pass any rider in front. Understood?"

"Aye, sire," nodded Odo, grinning from ear to ear.

"If ye fall from yer horse, which is very likely, we will not stop. Petrus, we need to press on."

Odo waited as the reeve headed out, and the column began to move.

Sir Dain, alongside the reeve and out of sight from the herdsman, was smiling broadly. He couldn't wait to tell this story to Sir Gweir upon returning. As each knight and sergeant passed Odo, they turned and acknowledged him with a nod of respect. Each man knew the difficulties of riding and controlling a high-spirited courser. But the black stallion was not just being ridden well; it was showing off.

Odo and his mount fell into step behind the column, and the small contingent of men quickly ate up the miles. Odo loved it and thoroughly enjoyed the feeling, the soreness of his shoulder long forgotten.

A lengthy rope was tied between two trees, and each horse was tied to the rope. The sergeants tended to their own horses and to those of their master's. Odo ministered to the black stallion and whispered words of encouragement for a job well done. The animal nickered and nuzzled Odo's pocket for a carrot it knew to be there.

With the aid of his staff, Reeve Petrus limped towards Odo. He made eye contact and then walked on. His meaning clear. Odo gave the stallion a final pat and followed. Once out of earshot from others, the reeve stopped and faced the young herdsman, his expression grim.

The reeve had rehearsed what he would say and intended to give Odo a severe tongue-lashing. Odo had disobeyed him and fully deserved to be verbally flayed.

But he couldn't. Seeing the naïve young man standing before him, he could only admire his tenacity, resourcefulness and guts. He stepped towards him and placed a hand on his shoulder. His eyes crinkled into a warm smile. "Next time ye decide to do something foolish, talk to me first, Odo. It will save embarrassment for us both."

Odo guiltily looked down at the ground as he thought about his planned defensive response. Something he'd practised in his mind over and over again for when he knew the reeve would yell at him. But he didn't raise his voice. Finally, he looked up and met the reeve's gaze. "What was I to do, Reeve? I had no choice."

"I understand, Odo. And yer lucky that Sir Dain is a fair and pleasant fellow. Ye may not have met with such a favourable welcome from another."

They walked back towards the horses. Neither spoke.

The knights gathered on a slightly elevated piece of ground and, through the forest, could clearly see the road and the surrounding countryside. Reeve Petrus and Odo weren't invited to join them, so they lingered behind and waited.

"When did ye learn to ride like that? Yer riding like a natural."

"I was never taught. Is just that after the other night, I knew if I had any chance of coming with yer today, then I needed to be able to ride Sir

Wystan's horse. I was scared at first, but then I thinks to me self, let the horse do the work. Don't fight him, respect him. So I talked and talked with him, fed and brushed him, and we became friends. Then at night, when no one was watching, I saddled him and he let me climb up. We rode around the paddock each evening for quite a while, and I learned if I wanted the horse to do something, I just had to sort of, um, think it."

Reeve Petrus chuckled.

"I'd seen enough knights riding around and watched them. I'd seen how they hold a sword and shield and use their legs to control the horse. So if they can do it, then I can too. And that's what I did. Was easy. I used to practice on Sally when no one was watching."

"Just be careful, Odo. Am warning yer. Sir Wystan's horse is a fierce stallion and was badly treated. He'll kill ye as easily as look at ye."

A sergeant posted as lookout further up the road came running back through the trees. "Lady Constance comes, sire. She brings only two knights and two pack horses."

"Only two?" Sir Dain scratched his beard. "And no sergeants?"

The sergeant shook his head, "Nay, sire."

"She rides on a litter?"

"On a horse."

"That's odd," he shrugged. "Everyone out of sight, the lady comes."

Reeve Petrus and Odo could not see the road from where they waited and watched the knights hide themselves from view. It didn't take long before the sound of horses could be heard. The lady and her escort rode past the hidden detachment of knights and continued towards Mellester.

The archer and his brother spent the night in the forest at their old campsite. Neither was surprised that the remains of their oldest brother were nowhere to be seen. It didn't bother them much either way. It wasn't because they had forgotten about him or didn't care; it was just that he was dead and of little use to them now.

As the sun rose in the east, they left their hackneys at the camp and made their way to the forest's edge, creeping as close to the mill at Falls Ende as they dared. They chewed on some dried meat and watched the activity below them.

"Which one is the master mason, then?" asked the younger brother.

The archer shrugged, "Don't know."

"Shouldn't we find who he is so we can kill him?"

The younger brother had a point conceded the archer. "Well, he don't go walkin' round with a sign round his neck, does he."

The younger brother gave the matter some thought, and his brow furrowed with the effort of concentration. "Should we go down and ask someone? Might be easier."

"What … they'll ask why, won't they? What am I gonna tell 'em?"

"Yer could say we be lookin' fer work, tell 'em we're stone masons."

The archer tore his gaze away from the mill and faced his brother; again, he'd made another good suggestion. "You go, m'leg is sore and someone may remember me."

After discussing exactly what to say, the younger brigand disappeared into the forest, reappeared down the track beside the falls and casually strolled up towards the mill. The archer watched from concealment.

The young brigand paused directly opposite the mill and yelled across the falls to a crew of men positioning a large boulder. "Hail!"

The masons paused, looked in question, searching for the source of the sound.

"I'd be a mason!"

One man, presumably the crew leader, stood slowly and rubbed his back as he eyed the stranger. "What did yer say?" he yelled back at the brigand."I'm a mason! Who is the master mason here?"

The mason scratched the back of his head at the man who stood across from him. He wasn't dressed like a stone mason and had no tools that he could see. A couple of minor details that the archer and his brother had forgotten about. He looked familiar. Instantly suspicious, the mason shouted back. "Ye need to talk to Master Mason Morel Mundy!"

"What?" yelled the brigand.

"Master Mason Morel Mundy, he'd be the man you seek!"

"Where he'd be?"

"At the manor, but be back soon!"

The young brigand gave the matter due thought. He waved in thanks, turned around and headed back down the path.

Stonemason Arter observed the stranger walking away and came to a decision. "I'm going t' the manor t' find Mason Mundy. Get that stone in place and locked in. I'll be back soon."

A man-at-arms granted Stonemason Arter access to Mellester's great hall. Inside was a hive of activity as servants prepared for the inquire which was to be held the following day. Arter immediately saw Sir Gweir,

Steward Alard, and Master Mason Morel Mundy deep in discussion and headed towards them.

Mundy looked up and saw one of his masons walking cautiously through the hall. He excused himself from the lord and walked towards him, anxious about why he was not working. Mason Arter explained the purpose of his visit, and with Arter at his side, Mundy approached the lord.

"Beggin' yer pardon Milord, I have information ye might be interested in."

Sir Gweir looked up at Mundy and then at the stonemason. "Oh?"

Steward Alard listened intently but appeared to be engrossed in his work. "Is about the warn'n ye gave us about brigands.""What of it?" questioned Sir Gweir as his eyes narrowed and focused on Mason Arter. Master Mason Mundy explained what had happened earlier, and Mason Arter nodded frequently.

"Could be the same man who shot at Sir Wystan?" asked Sir Gweir.

"Aye, could be," replied Mason Arter. "He sort of looked familiar."

"Return to yer work and thank ye for coming to me. Say nothing and continue as normal."

"As ye wish, Milord," replied Mason Arter, who nodded at the master mason and walked quickly out of the hall.

Sir Gweir turned his attention to Mundy. "I don't want yer near Falls Ende; remain here where ye are free of harm.""Aye Milord."

Sir Gweir turned to the steward, "Alard, find Sir Matheu and send him to me immediately. I think we may have found the brigand who killed the mason and his son, and probably shot Sir Wystan."

"Milord, why do you suspect the stranger? He could be anyone."

"Because, Alard," grinned Sir Gweir, "whoever shot the stone mason and his boy made a mistake. Killing them served no purpose. They wanted the Falls Ende Mill master mason. They killed the wrong mason, and now they want to finish the job."

The lord could see Alard wasn't convinced.

"Look, one of the brigands was killed by the hand of a knight; he was beheaded by a sword wielded by a knight. Who was that knight, Alard?"

The steward shrugged.

"Who is the person who doesn't want to see the mill completed?"

"Uh, Sir Wystan? I can think of no one else, sire."

"Aye, Sir Wystan! And would he kill the master mason himself?" He didn't wait for an answer. "Nay, he would hire outlaws, would he not?"

Alard nodded.

"The outlaws killed the wrong mason, and Sir Wystan and other knights were in the forest at the campsite of the brigands. We found their tracks. I suspect the brigand was beheaded because of their error. So now they've been told to finish the job."

"But sire, Sir Wystan is dead."

Sir Gweir sighed. "Alard, Sir Wystan wasn't clever enough to conceive and implement a plot. Nay, the person who is behind this is Lady Constance. She is the one. I know it."

"Can ye be sure, Milord?"

"The day Sir William fell into Falls Ende changed the fortunes and lives of his wife, Lady Constance, his son Sir Wystan, and altered his own life as well. A life of shame and disgrace, where Sir Wystan was forever banished from the place where he was once lord of this manor. To now live in a small hamlet with a few knights they can ill afford. How would you feel? No, I cannot prove Lady Constance is behind all this. Sir Hyde believes she is a conniving witch with a muddled mind. Mark my words, above anything else, she despises Falls Ende and the Herdsman Odo Read." Sir Gweir wagged a finger at Steward Alard, "The kidnapping of his woman was a boon for Lady Constance, and she can strike at the heart of the person who she believes ruined her life–"

"Odo!" exclaimed Alard.

"Aye, poor Odo."

CHAPTER TWENTY-THREE

Odo was told to wait at the old oak. The instructions were quite clear. He wasn't to approach Lady Constance's house unless called on. Ahead, Reeve Petrus and Sir Dain still rode at the head of the column towards the gate that allowed them access into the courtyard, stables and the manor house. From his vantage point, Odo could see a couple of knights running through the yard and heading towards the gate.

He had dismounted beneath the oak and held the reins to the stallion that stood impatiently behind him. The mischievous beast kept pushing him with its nose in the middle of the back, causing to him to pitch forward.

Out of curiosity, peasants working on their crops stood to stare at the unfolding drama. A couple ambled over to Odo, keeping a wary eye on the stallion and ensuring they kept their distance.

"Hail," greeted an aging serf.

Odo politely nodded and focused his attention on the knights at the gate.

"Yer with them, lad?"

"Aye, sort of. From Mellester Manor," said Odo as if that explained everything.

"Oh…." The old man turned to his friend. "He says he'd be from Mellester.

The other man said nothing and focused on what was happening at the gated entrance.

"Halt, go no further," yelled one of Lady Constance's knights with a nervous edge to his voice. Another knight, a short distance away, looked uncomfortable as he surveyed eleven armed men.

The column halted, and Sir Dain continued to advance towards the two knights. "I am Sir Dain, and I am here at the request of my liege, Sir Gweir, Lord of Mellester Manor."

Both knights exchanged a look. "The lady has already departed for Mellester; ye missed her," the leader informed Sir Dain.

"I am not here to escort the good lady. I seek access here to search for a woman. Please open the gate and allow us entry," appealed Sir Dain pleasantly.

Both knights spoke briefly to each other, trying to decide what to do. "Ye have no authority here. Nay, we cannot grant this request without the word of Lady Constance."

"Who is it I am addressing?" queried Sir Dain.

"I am Sir Marden of York, he is Sir Renier de Pierrepont." Sir Marden's eyes flicked past Sir Dain and fell on the reeve. "Why is he here again? He was here some days ago."

Sir Dain was losing patience. "He is here on behalf of our lord. Now, stand aside and allow us entry, sir," demanded the knight commander. His voice had hardened, but he had yet to draw his sword or make a threatening gesture and fervently hoped he wouldn't need to.

Both of Lady Constance's knights drew their swords. Sir Dain wasn't easily intimidated and casually used his hand that rested on his thigh to make a subtle signal. Immediately, his knights dismounted, handing reins to waiting sergeants who led the horses away.

"Ye may not pass," Sir Marden reiterated.

"And ye can't stop us," Sir Dain added. "Stop this foolishness."

"I'm prepared to die for my liege and will take some of ye with me," warned Sir Marden.

Sir Dain's knights had spread out and were waiting for command to leap over the low wall.

"Aye, as is yer right," Sir Dain said with a sigh and dismounted. He handed the reins to his sergeant, who'd been waiting.

"Open the gate!" Sir Dain's voice had taken an authoritative tone. None of his men had drawn their swords, yet the two knights who stood in defence of their Lady's property were steadfast, if not frightened.

The knight who called himself Sir Marden was probably not well-trained, and his chainmail was dirty and needed repairs. The other French knight wore expensive chain link armour, but Sir Dain looked into the man's eyes and saw he had no fight. It pained him to shed blood here today. These two knights were undoubtedly good and loyal men and only did what was expected of them.

Sensing the situation was escalating, Reeve Petrus awkwardly dismounted, untied his staff and limped towards the commander, stopping slightly behind and to his side.

The two knights were becoming desperate. They couldn't defend the entire wall, and they knew it.

Sir Dain nodded, and four knights spread out and scrambled over the wall. Sir Dain took another step and slowly reached across to unhook the gate when Sir Marden sprang forward with his sword raised and pointed directly at the commander. He was quick, and the move unexpected, especially when challenging another knight who had yet to draw his own weapon. Not an honourable gesture.

Before Sir Dain could defend himself or step back out of reach, the point of the broadsword pierced his chainmail and drove deeply into his shoulder joint. Sir Dain howled in pain and leapt back, clutching the wound. With a quizzical look, he stared at the knight as if to ask, What have you done?

Reeve Petrus, the closest person to Sir Marden, stepped forward and, before the knight could react, reached over, opened the gate, and entered the compound.

Pulling his gaze away from the injured knight from Mellester, Sir Marden saw the reeve enter and immediately challenged him with another powerful overhand thrust. It was a well-timed move designed to kill, but Sir Marden had never encountered Reeve Petrus Bodkin before. The reeve was ready for it and, seemingly without effort, just batted the sword away with his staff.

Two of Sir Dain's knights came to defend their commander as blood began to stream from his wound, while the other two raised their swords to attack Sir Renier. It wasn't necessary. The Frankian knight turned his sword and drove it into the ground. He removed his right gauntlet, offering it to the nearest knight. "*Merci*," he said, going down on one knee. "*Je me rend!*"

Sir Dain's knights, as did most European and English knights, knew the Frankish language. It was the language of court, and they knew Sir Renier had said 'I give myself' and surrendered by offering his gauntlet.

Reeve Petrus had his hands full, and he knew it. He feinted a lunge forward, tossed the staff to the ground and stepped back, drawing his sword and adopting the unusual fighting stance he'd developed by standing with his feet close together. He blocked the knight's powerful, downward slash with ease, then made a clever little move designed to flick his blade away so the attacker could strike at his heart.

Sir Marden was unsure. A look of uncertainty crossed his face at seeing his associate yield without a fight, and now he faced the unorthodox technique of the big man who stood skilfully before him. He was intensely loyal to Lady Constance, and while common sense and logic suggested he yield just like Sir Renier, he knew it was impossible. He was vastly outnumbered by hostile knights, yet the man before him had a bad leg, was overweight, and wasn't even a knight. Yet he was an expert with a sword and more so than any other he'd ever faced. He had no choice but to strike quickly.

Sir Marden had his body in perfect position. He stood side–on to his opponent, one foot in front of the other, and his left arm was behind and out of harm's way. He began a series of quick strokes, each designed to force the defender to overreact and overextend.

The swords clashed, and with each move, the reeve countered and blocked. Slowly, Petrus advanced by taking short, quick steps, his strength and agility forcing the knight back a step, then another.

Sir Dain and the other knights watched spellbound at the reeve's mastery. They could have come to his assistance, but could see it wasn't necessary.

Realising his ploy wasn't working, Sir Marden ducked beneath the reeve's swishing blade and swung upwards in a desperate move. He never expected to see his opponent pirouette, nor did he foresee that by striking upwards, he'd just exposed his side to the reeve when he'd completed his spin.

Reeve Petrus held back slightly, but the force of his blow still tore through Sir Marden's chainmail and into his side. The knight staggered with the force of the strike. It wasn't a killing stroke and was implemented to injure the knight and end the fight. The reeve took a step backwards, his voice boomed across the compound. "Enough!"

Sir Marden knew he'd been bested and glared at his opponent. After an age, he lowered his sword as sharp stabs of pain set in. Suddenly, Reeve Petrus stepped forward and thrust the tip of his sword into the knight's chest. "That was cowardly to strike an unarmed knight, a brother unable to defend himself. Ye bring shame upon the brotherhood." He tensed in preparation for a final thrust.

"Wait!"

Sir Dain stepped forward and into the compound, cradling his injured shoulder as blood dripped onto the ground. "Leave him, Petrus. He had no choice, and I have no ill feelings. He could easily have killed me, and he chose not to. It was my stupidity that caused me to be injured."

The reeve was breathing hard, his body tensed. He was furious, but his sword never wavered. Petrus Bodkin had spent years training to become a knight; his father had paid a fortune for horses, weapons and armour. He'd suffered punishments and hardship, he'd trained in the cold when his hands and feet were numbed, when sick and feverish, and above all he'd been taught about chivalry and honour. These two virtues became his life, and though injury had taken his dream away from him, he still valued them above all else. He looked at the knight with contempt; this man had it all, except he didn't have what he'd been trained to uphold – honour.

"Petrus."

He steeled himself to take the life of the knight.

"Petrus!" Sir Dain touched his arm. "Relax, my friend. You fought well, like a knight. It's over."

The haze of red dissolved into clarity, and Petrus saw the man before him as he really was, a poor knight defending his liege. He exhaled slowly, lowered his sword and stepped back. "As you wish, sire."

Odo was almost beside himself. He was too far away to see details, but the sound of clanging swords drifted up towards him, and he saw enough of flashing blades to know the reeve could easily have been killed. With relief, he saw him step back. No one had died. He waited for a signal that would allow him to ride down to the manor house. It never came.

An unseen voice yelled for the two peasants standing with Odo to return to their work, and with a shrug, they reluctantly walked away. Already, Odo could see the wounded knight being seen to by a sergeant, and despite being hurt, Sir Dain, Reeve Petrus and the four knights began a search of the stable.

The great stallion munched on grass as Odo watched impatiently from beneath the oak. After an eternity, he saw them all emerge from the stable, and with both Lady Constance's knights leading the way, they entered the house. Two sergeants remained with the horses, and another stood on guard by the doorway to the manor.

He was tempted to ride down and wait in the courtyard, but Sir Dain had been insistent. He was told not to come down until signalled. He kept his eyes on the door, willing Charlotte to step out.

Odo heard a shout and turned. The ageing peasant who had come to see what the fuss was about earlier shouted again. The old man stood in the field and pointed. Odo squinted and followed the direction of his arm. He saw it. A man was running away from the manor. He'd hurdled over the low wall and was headed into the fields. Obviously, no one in the house had seen him because there was no shout of alarm. Without thinking, Odo leapt upon the stallion, slid his feet into the stirrups and squeezed tightly with his legs. Needing no second urging, the courser leapt forward with a surprising amount of speed. Odo leaned forward, low over the horse's neck as they galloped towards the fleeing man. He was some distance away, and Odo guided the powerful stallion down a pathway between crops. In fear of being trampled, peasants dove out of the way as the massive horse exploded past.

The courser had seen the fleeing man, and through training, knew exactly what his master wanted. With his ears pointed forward, the courser bore down on him.

The manservant found running on the crops difficult. The soft earth hindered his speed, and once he found the hardened ground of the pathway carved between rows, he turned and ran along them, hoping to put as much distance from the manor house as fast as he could.

When he first saw the knights approach the manor, he'd stuffed a gag into the young woman's mouth, tied her hands and struck her hard on the side of the head. She'd collapsed into his arms, and he threw her into the darkened underground room. He raised the wooden stairs with a rope and a pulley until they were far beyond her reach. He knew with certainty she could never leave the room unless the stairs were lowered. Then, when he saw Lady Constance's two knights surrender, he felt the first knot of genuine fear in his stomach – it was time to save himself. With the sound of armed men entering the manor, he ran to an empty room on the far side of the house. He opened a shutter, leapt through, closed it again behind him, and ran for his life.

Odo had yet to experience the full power and speed of the courser, and he found it exhilarating. The animal had truly come alive and was obviously enjoying the chase. Ahead, the running man was only now becoming aware that a courser was charging him down, and he panicked.

When Odo leapt on the back of the courser, he had not spared a single thought of what he would do when he caught the man. It mattered not to the stallion; he had the situation in hand, and as he had been taught, would please his new master.

As they approached the fleeing man, Odo slowly pulled on the reins and leaned back. Using the stirrups for leverage, he gently pulled the reins to slow and stop the galloping horse. But the stallion wasn't having any of it. Ignoring the command to stop, it powered on regardless.

Again, Odo pulled on the reins, then tried to guide the galloping horse away from the man. Immediately, it dawned on him what would happen. In horror, he tightly grasped the saddle's pommel and held on as best he could. Without slowing, the swiftly moving courser ploughed into the servant. The horrendous impact propelled the man forward to land in a heap at the feet of the charging stallion.

The powerful horse slowed as it trampled over him. As he passed by, and as taught, he lashed out with both hind legs and delivered a bone-crushing kick with each of his legs. As the courser's hindquarters rose to kick, Odo almost pitched forward, and he hung on for dear life. The stallion slid to a stop, and Odo turned to look back at the carnage. There was no point in dismounting; the man was dead.

A few peasants, who had hidden in fear, risked looking. Odo saw them standing with their hands to their mouths at the bloodied gore that had once been a living, breathing man.

Odo knew he was in big trouble. He'd just killed someone, and this would take some explaining.

CHAPTER TWENTY-FOUR

Two scullery maids were being questioned by Sir Dain while a sergeant saw to the deep gash in his shoulder. The maids weren't talking and provided no information about Charlotte's whereabouts. The angrier he became, the less they spoke. It was frustrating. Another servant girl was tending to Sir Marden's side, and when questioned, she wouldn't talk either.

Sir Renier had readily agreed to parole when offered to him, and he understood his future now lay at the whim of Mellester's lord. His sword and gauntlet were returned, and he sat on a chair in the corner and silently watched. When spoken to by Sir Dain, he admitted that Lady Constance begged him to stay a few days, as he'd only been travelling through the hamlet. As expected, he knew nothing of value.

Knights and sergeants had been paired into teams, and they began to systematically search each room. Reeve Petrus wandered around on his own, carefully walking from room to room, but like the others, he found nothing. Something wasn't right, but he couldn't put his finger on it.

Everyone met in the large kitchen and discussed what to do. The reeve was insistent that Charlotte was in the house, and again went to search for her. As he entered each room, he yelled her name and listened. Nothing. In frustration, he returned to the kitchen, hoping for a clue to her whereabouts.

"Is there a cellar?" one of Sir Dain's knights asked. "Places like this often have a keep or cellar," he added.

The reeve was studying the face of Sir Marden, who sat sullenly against the wall. When the idea of a keep or dungeon was suggested, Petrus saw a flicker of reaction from the knight. He eyed him suspiciously.

"No towers," answered Sir Dain in response to the question.

"Some smaller manors have 'em underground," the knight added.

Reeve Petrus limped towards Sir Marden. The knight saw him approach and looked uncomfortable. "*Oubliette*! It's an *oubliette* isn't it? Where is it?" His uncharacteristic outburst caught everyone by surprise.

All heads turned to the reeve. A couple of knights edged closer to Sir Marden, equally displeased that the innocent young woman they sought might be hidden in such an evil place as an *oubliette*. The disgust was evident in everyone's face, and Sir Marden looked worried.

"Well? Speak, sir!" Sir Dain shouted.

All men in the room knew what an *oubliette* was. It was a room, a secret dungeon in which the only exit was through a doorway or trapdoor in the ceiling. Escape was impossible.

With a grunt, Sir Dain eased himself from his seat and strode towards Sir Marden. "If ye have any honour, any chivalry left in ye, then speak now." He spoke slowly and quietly. "If ye don't, we'll tear this place apart, stone by stone, until we find her." He leaned forward until he was a handbreadth away from the knight's face. "When we do, we'll leave ye to rot in it."

Suddenly, Sir Marden charged Sir Dain, knocking him down. He would have made it to the door if it hadn't been for the staff belonging to Reeve Petrus, which collided against the side of his head. He dropped like a stone.

When Sir Marden could focus his eyes, he stared up at five angry knights and Reeve Petrus, whom he feared the most. A sword was being pushed into his stomach. "In the…" He swallowed. "In the small chamber, behind the tapestry."

The reeve's sword didn't move and continued to press down.

Everyone except Reeve Petrus and Sir Dain ran for the other room. Sir Renier watched with a look of disgust on his face. He, too, knew what an *oubliette* was. They waited.

"We found her!" came the cry. "She's here!"

Sir Dain looked into Petrus's eyes and nodded. Without a further word, the reeve, with all his weight and strength, pushed down. The sword tore through the chainmail and into the knight's stomach. With a further wrench, he pulled upwards into the torso, eviscerating him. The knight died without another sound.

The servant girls wept and turned away, all three huddled together.

"Soon as we learn of her condition, we can return to Mellester. I'm sure Sir Gweir is anxious to hear how we fared," said Sir Dain, turning away from the body. His wound was painful, and he returned gingerly to his seat.

"Aye, and we can return to our lives," added the reeve.

"*Où est le bâtard?*" spat Renier.

"*Quelle?*" asked Sir Dain.

"What bastard? What is he talking about?" asked the reeve. All of a sudden, he remembered what had bothered him.

One of the sergeants ran into the kitchen. "Sire, the young woman is hurt; she's been beaten badly about her face. She did manage to tell us about the servant who did it to her."

"*Oui, oui, le bâtard,*" exclaimed Sir Renier.

Sir Dain turned to the scullery maids, his fury evident. "Who is this servant and where is he?"

"He was here when Oswald and I first searched the house. I haven't seen him. Where is he?" said the reeve.

Now that Sir Marden was dead, they feared no retribution. "Milord, ain't seen 'im since ye came. He was 'ere." The other two maids nodded in support.

"What's his name? His name!" yelled Sir Dain.

"We only knows him as Duncan, Milord, that's wot the lady calls 'im."

"Look outside," ordered Sir Dain, "Find that man, and when you do, I will personally execute him!" He was beside himself in anger.

Reeve Petrus was also furious. He went to look at Charlotte and wished he hadn't. She lay unconscious on the bed, and a sergeant was gently dabbing her swollen face with a wet cloth. The reeve stood over her, his fury barely containable. In addition to some minor cuts that crisscrossed her face, she was black and blue from bruising and her right eye had almost swollen shut. He stormed out of the room as fast as he could and returned to the kitchen. "Get off yer lazy arses and tend to her, so help me!"

Fearful of their lives, the three maids ran from the room. Without another word, the reeve went outside, determined to kill the man who had done this to Charlotte. Then he remembered Odo, poor Odo! He looked toward the oak tree, but he wasn't there.

"Where is Odo?" he asked. No one had seen him. Concerned for the young herdsman's safety, the reeve walked around the side of the manor and in the distance saw the unmistakable form of the courser, Odo, at his side. The reeve put his fingers to his mouth and gave a shrill whistle, and when Odo looked up, he waved. Within moments, he saw the herdsman mount up and quickly ride towards the compound. The reeve returned inside to speak to Sir Dain.

None of the knights or sergeants had seen the manservant. "He couldn't disappear, he must be here somewhere! Look again, find that whoreson!" Sir Dain was livid.

Odo cautiously entered the kitchen, and all heads turned to face him.

"Charlotte is alive and safe, Odo, but she is hurt," said Sir Dain.

Odo's face changed from nervousness to relief and back to nervousness in a heartbeat.

Reeve Petrus put a hand on Odo's shoulder to lead him to her.

"How bad?" Odo looked with concern at the reeve.

"Come."

Odo gasped when he saw her and fell to his knees beside the bed.

The reeve quietly pointed to the door, and the three servant girls quickly withdrew from the room. He heard Odo's sob as he shut the door.

Sir Dain was issuing orders to his men. Already, a sergeant was heading out the door to return to Mellester with haste to report to Sir Gweir. The remaining sergeants were building a litter to carry Charlotte. Two long poles would be attached at each end between two horses, and Charlotte would lie between the poles on blankets. It would be a slow journey back to Mellester, but Charlotte would be comfortable and arrive safely.

Once the sergeants had departed to the stable, Sir Dain began to map out a search plan. He was determined to find the servant and wouldn't give up until the man had been executed. His outrage extended to Lady Constance, who would have known and even supported the beatings and cruel treatment of the innocent young woman. However, that was the lord's concern, not his; his immediate need was to find the errant servant. His plan was interrupted when Odo entered the kitchen. Again, all heads turned to him; this time, every face showed pity.

"Sire, I have to–"

"Not now, Odo, speak to me later," said Sir Dain.

"I want ye to search the area I described–"

"Sire, I killed a man!" Odo interrupted.

"Yer what?" exclaimed Sir Dain.

Everyone started talking at once. "Silence!" Sir Dain turned to Odo. "Speak."

Odo looked at his feet. "A man ran from th' manor, sire. No one saw him but me. I didn't mean to kill him, 'twas an accident. I'm sorry."

"From this manor?" asked the commander.

"Aye, came from round th' back, jumped the wall and ran like blazes."

Sir Dain nodded, his expression serious. "How did you kill him, Odo."

Odo wasn't sure what to say. He didn't want to put the blame on the courser.

"Go on, tell Sir Dain, Odo," the reeve encouraged him.

"I climbed on the horse, and we chased after him. When we got close, well, the horse wouldn't stop. I tried to stop him, but he wouldn't listen, sire. The horse hit him hard, sir, real hard, and he went flyin'. Then the horse … well, then the horse…"

"Kicked him?" Sir Dain added.

"Aye."

Sir Dain began to laugh, and so did another knight. Soon, everyone was laughing, including Reeve Petrus. The tension immediately drained from the room, and Odo, not understanding, became angry.

He couldn't help himself and spoke without thinking. "I just killed a man, and you laugh at me!" Odo's face turned scarlet with rage, and he glared in outrage at each knight in the room, including the reeve. He went to leave the room and return to Charlotte, but when Sir Dain slowly stood, clutching the wound to his shoulder, he stopped and waited.

Sir Dain chewed his bottom lip thoughtfully for a moment. Deciding how to reprimand the peasant for his disrespect, he sighed and grimaced as his wound continued to cause him pain. He acknowledged to himself that the young man had a valid point. A man, even a cruel, despicable man, had knowingly hurt a young woman and had then died horrifically and most unimaginably, and including himself, all had laughed.

He saw the young man staring at him, not out of insolence or disrespect, but out of dignified curiosity, almost naivety. He felt ashamed. "The borrowed horse you rode here this day was owned by the knight, Sir Wystan. It's a courser. Most knights train their coursers to kill. A fleeing man on foot is a target, and when you chased after the man, the courser did only what it was trained to do." Sir Dain paused. "What you don't know is the man the courser killed is the same man who hurt yer woman. He was the one who beat her. Ye've done no wrong, Odo, ye did well," the knight smiled. "Now we can leave. Let's get that litter finished and take Charlotte home to Mellester."

For Odo, the relief was overwhelming.

The reeve smiled and clapped Odo on the back. "We'll make a knight out of yer yet."

This time, everyone did laugh.

CHAPTER TWENTY-FIVE

Lady Constance arrived at Mellester Manor, and Sir Gweir was trying hard to evade any contact with her. It was proving to be nigh on impossible, and through constant messages, she continued to voice her displeasure at the continual delay of the inquire. Unable to avoid her any longer, he came to see her. They greeted each other coolly and spoke politely of the weather and crops.

She sat as a guest in his dayroom. It was small and comfortable and had always been her favourite room when she lived here. With the shutters open, it afforded a pleasant view across the countryside, over the village, and in the distance, Falls Ende and the wooded hills beyond. Sir Gweir stood at the open window with his hands clasped behind his back and looked over his demesne. She sat comfortably in a chair and watched the new lord with barely concealed bitterness.

Thankfully, a sergeant had arrived only a short time before and delivered a message to him that provided detailed information and an update on how Sir Dain and his detachment were faring. Sir Gweir was pleased and relieved they had found the young woman, and equally as important, he was very distressed to learn that it implicated the woman who sat in this very room. Now, more than ever, he needed to keep her at the manor and ensure she remained unaware of what was happening. Since arriving in Mellester, she had sought an explanation and demanded to know why the inquire was delayed. Finally, he could offer her a plausible and reasonable explanation, albeit not quite the truth.

Coming to a decision, he turned from the window and looked at her across the room. For a brief moment, he was captivated by her beauty. Her fiery, red hair, flawless skin and elegance were a sight seldom seen. Even her shape, which he couldn't overlook, was enhanced by her dress. Her head was slightly inclined as she stared at him quizzically, waiting for him to speak.

"Lady Constance, I have just received information, and I can now share with ye the reason for this unfortunate delay." He shook his head disapprovingly as if he too was unhappy.

In response, she shifted her position slightly and raised her hand, laying a single finger alongside her cheek.

"The herdsman, Odo Read, has vanished…"

The lady didn't move, but Sir Gweir noticed her eyes flashed.

"…I have sent men to find him and return him here to face the inquire."

She repositioned herself again and removed the finger from her cheek. "When do ye expect to find him? Soon? This day, or next week?"

He ignored her mild sarcasm. "We have him now, and he'll be here this afternoon, milady, and I will keep ye informed. Now if there is anything ye need, please ask, as I have servants at yer disposal."

"Please send for Sir Borin, I wish to speak with him."

"As ye wish." Sir Gweir exited the room and breathed out a sigh of relief. He knew her hatred was for Odo, and the only thing she wanted more was to see him suffer. Using Odo as an excuse was convenient, especially because he had gone missing. Again, there was relief that he had ended up with Sir Dain. He didn't know how the herdsman managed that, but he'd find out later.

Directly across from Mellester Manor, and still lying in the fringes of the forest, the two brigand brothers waited for the Falls Ende master mason to make an appearance.

"We could come back, maybe look for the herdsman instead," suggested the younger brother.

The archer felt this complex question required some thought and absentmindedly picked at a scab on his arm as his mind muddled over the problem. "Aye, that we could, but that means having to come back, doesn't it?"

His brother grunted.

They were silent, watching the gildsmen positioning a large stone to complete the mill's foundations. It looked like slow, tedious work with lots of yelling and shouting. Neither of the brigands was thinking of a career in stone masonry.

"Where should we go when we be done 'ere?" asked the younger. "Frankia?"

"Takes time to get there, have to go by boat. I hear it takes months, sometimes years b'fore ye arrive," advised the all-knowing archer.

Before the younger brigand could ask another question, the bushes behind them moved. Both men turned simultaneously, their heads twisted at impossible angles, and they stared with mouths agape at the highly polished swords wielded confidently by two of Mellester's knights.

Now mounted astride their hackneys with hands tied, the brigand brothers were led around the village and eventually up a seldom-used, narrow path that would deposit them to the rear of Mellester Manor. The two knights led the small procession, trailing the group were two sergeants.

On orders from Mellester's lord, the knights were instructed to take the prisoners directly to the small gaol housed inside a larger building set back, well behind the manor. Their orders were to do it with minimal fuss and hopefully out of sight from villagers and any of Lady Constance's knights.

It didn't take long before Sir Gweir was informed, and he hurried down to the gaol to question the outlaws.

It was dark inside the room, and to see more clearly, the large door was kept open. Sir Gweir strode in and stopped in front of the cell. He scrutinised his guests and quickly arrived at a conclusion as to the nature of the two sorrowful men now locked up.

"What are ye called?" asked the lord.

"I is Samuel Brooker, Milord," said the archer respectfully, "and he'd be Tedric, me brother."

"What brings you to Mellester, and why were you skulking at the forest edge?"

As the older and therefore the more intelligent of the brothers, the archer believed he should answer the question. "Was lookin' for work, we was."

"Stone masons?"

"Aye, Milord," nodded the archer enthusiastically.

"Is that how ye became injured?" Sir Gweir pointed to the archer's thigh.

"Aye Milord, dangerous work."

Show me your hands," ordered Sir Gweir

The archer hesitated, while the younger, Tedric, moved first with both palms faced down.

"Turn them."

Tedric obliged.

As he suspected, Tedric's hands were not calloused like a mason's.

"And yer tools, are they in the forest?"

Tedric nodded. "They are Milord."

"Yer both liars. "Sir Gweir turned to the two knights who found the brigands. "We may as well take their heads."

Fully aware of the lord's strategy, the knights nodded solemnly. "In the morning, sire, or now?"

"Oh, no, not in the morn, methinks now is better," answered Sir Gweir, turning to leave.

Both Samuel and Tedric were exchanging silent looks of horror. "We ain't masons, Milord!"

Sir Gweir stopped, his back to the cell and the prisoners. If not for the seriousness of the circumstance, he would have found this amusing. "Why were ye in the forest?"

Both the archer and his brother tried to talk at once.

"Stop!" Sir Gweir turned to face the prisoners and looked at the archer. "Ye," he pointed, "why are ye here?"

"Milord, we was hired for our skill…"

Sir Gweir raised his eyebrows and remained silent. *Skill?*

"…Mercenaries, we is. Trained to kill."

"Kill who?"

"Oh, that be the master mason, Milord, and the herdsman, Odo."

The lord looked down at his feet and shook his head. "Who is yer employer?"

The archer and Tedric looked unsure.

"Who hired you?"

"Ah, Milord, aye, that was Sir Wystan."

"Where did ye meet Sir Wystan?"

"In the forest, but never him alone, he was always with two others. They'd be knights, Milord."

"Do ye know their names?"

The archer and his brother Tedric shook their heads.

"If you saw them again, would you recognise them?"

The archer nodded. Tedric was puzzled.

"Did ye kill the stone mason and his son at Falls Ende?

"No, Milord, that was Bert."

"Who is Bert?"

"Sir Wystan killed him, he did. He was our brother."

"And ye shot Sir Wystan with yer bow?"

The archer nodded, "I did, Milord, was revenge," he said proudly.

Sir Gweir had heard enough and asked the two knights to follow him. He had an idea.

CHAPTER TWENTY-SIX

When villagers and noblemen were finally admitted into Mellester's great hall, they did so impatiently. Many had been anxiously waiting for some time, and grizzled and grumbled as they found a place to stand. A few fortunate people even found a seat. Noblemen and knights were given their customary seating towards the front.

For many, the last time they had been in the great hall, they had seen Sir Hyde Fortescue assert himself as proxy for King Henry II, and release Sir Wystan as Mellester's lord and replace him with the unknown, Sir Gweir. Some ardent supporters of Sir Wystan still found it difficult to accept the new, unproven lord and favoured the presence of the beautiful Lady Constance.

Word had quickly spread of the inquire, and when it was heard that the lady would be present, so did the desire to attend, even if the inquire was nothing more than a series of statements of facts.

Sir Gweir kindly allowed Lady Constance to sit with him on the raised dais as a courtesy. Another chair had been positioned beside the lord's larger seat, and everyone waited impatiently for the principals to arrive.

Steward Alard was seated at his desk and studiously reviewing his notes. He would play an important part in the inquire. The priest, Oswald, stood close to the steward and to the astonishment of many, mostly his parishioners, they observed that his vestments had been laundered. He stood piously with his tonsured head bowed and his hands clasped benignly in front. He, too, would play a part in the afternoon's proceedings.

Closer to the front, and against the walls, many of Sir Gweir's knights and sergeants stood. Anyone paying particular attention would have remarked how their positioning was not normal. This was by design and strategic. In a shadowed corner behind the dais, and partially hidden by pennants, stood the archer, Samuel. Behind him stood two concealed knights. The archer scanned the crowd, looking for the familiar faces of the knights who had accompanied Sir Wystan to their campsite in the forest.

"Do you see them?" asked a knight.

"Nay, sire," replied the archer.

"Keep looking."

Suddenly, all heads turned to the rear of the hall, back towards the entrance. Flanked by her two knights, Lady Constance made her grand appearance. She wore a flowing, green silk dress with a yellow sash tied to her waist, and there wasn't a person in the hall who didn't admire her beauty and grace. The women in attendance were envious, and the men sighed, wishing their wives were as beautiful. On entering the hall, she paused briefly but focused her attention on her seat. People respectfully parted and moved aside to allow her through, and she walked slowly and gracefully down the length of Mellester's great hall. Her two armed escorts looked impressive; each walked slightly behind and to her side. At least one hundred and threescore pairs of eyes followed her every step.

"That be them," said the archer excitedly.

"The two knights with the lady?" whispered a knight.

"Aye, them both," confirmed the archer.

With a yank, the archer was pulled backwards and was forcibly taken from the hall through a small door lest he be seen. One knight frantically went to find Sir Gweir and inform him that the archer had identified Sir Wystan's accomplices.

Lady Constance made a deliberate and dramatic show of her entrance. She intended to eventually resume her rightful position as Lady of Mellester, and no one would, or could, stand in her way. Discrediting Mellester's new lord was foremost on her mind. A small smile played across her face as she approached the dais. A few people watching commented how she seemed to glide when she walked. The lady wanted people to remember her, and as in a pantomime, her appearance and mannerisms were carefully planned.

With the chivalrous aid of Sir Borin, she climbed the low step to her seat while Sir Borin and Sir Kasos stood in the only available place, between Sir Gweir's knights against the wall.

As soon as she was seated, Reeve Petrus Bodkin and Odo appeared. The reeve had to push and fight through the crowded hall while Odo followed closely in his wake. They reached the front and sat on a bench, directly in front of the lord's chair. Lady Constance glared at Odo with open hatred the entire time. Oswald looked up and made brief eye contact. The corners of his mouth twitched, which Odo took for a smile.

The great hall had always impressed Odo. This was where the Lord of Mellester Manor ruled; his decisions could have far-reaching consequences and result in a new lease on life for the blessed, or even death for those less fortunate.

He looked around him and saw many faces he recognised. The four knights with whom he had travelled to Lady Constance's manor stood against the wall and flanked both the lady's knights. Even the paroled knight, Sir Renier, stood against the wall. At the request of Sir Gweir, Renier wore a cloth around his face to hide his identity. According to the reeve, Sir Dain was poorly and would not attend. His wound and subsequent loss of blood had taken its toll.

His thoughts returned to Charlotte. How he wept when he saw her! Her face was bloodied, scratched, and swollen badly. According to Oswald, her head suffered from too many blows, and her brain had swelled. He kindly reassured Odo and her father, Cheeseman Gerald, who'd been summoned, that Charlotte would recover quickly, and rest was all she needed.

The journey from Lady Constance's manor had been slow. Charlotte rode in a litter, cleverly attached to a horse in front and another behind. She had drifted in and out of sleep, and Odo had ridden at her side the entire way. At one point, the procession paused, and Odo's courser turned its massive head, nuzzled Charlotte's hand, and licked it. Even the horse was concerned for her, he believed.

On arriving back at Mellester, they had quietly ridden through the rear entrance to the manor grounds and remained out of sight. With the help of a sergeant, Oswald attended to Charlotte while Sir Gweir, in a growing rage, listened to Sir Dain explain all that had happened. Sir Gweir upheld the parole offered to Sir Renier, and he was allowed to retain his weapons, but not use them against anyone in the lord's service, or leave the manor without permission.

Odo hoped that this inquire would end quickly so he could be with Charlotte. He ached to be near her and missed her terribly. His eyes filmed over and he gave them a wipe.

Finally, Sir Gweir entered the hall through a private side entrance near the dais and strode briskly to his chair, taking his seat without fuss. He wore breeches and a simple shortened surcoat worn over his clothes, forgoing chainmail and weapons for comfort. If he was nervous, it didn't show; he looked relaxed and calm. However, inwardly the lord's stomach was in absolute turmoil, and he was seething with ire. Uncharacteristically, he neither acknowledged Lady Constance nor offered a greeting.

The priest, Oswald, stepped forward and cleared his throat. "Most beloved brethren…"

The chatter in the hall continued.

He coughed loudly, and slowly the noise subsided. He waited a heartbeat longer, the displeasure on his face obvious.

"Most beloved brethren, urged by necessity, the will of the church and his Royal Highness King Henry II, we gather here this day before almighty God, and all of us stand in witness to what we shall hear!" Oswald raised his arms and looked reverently up. After a moment, he lowered his hands and surveyed the crowded hall. "Let no man perjure himself or offer untruths, lest He condemn ye and drive ye from His loving presence – or ye shall suffer at His will and hand!"

The hall was deathly quiet. To the serfs and freemen, such threats were to be taken very seriously.

"In God's name, this inquire will determine and accept the truth around the circumstances of the death of Sir Wystan."

Odo glanced at Lady Constance. Her expression hardened, and she shifted in her seat. Sir Gweir was staring into nothingness.

Reeve Petrus nudged Odo and bent his head down to whisper. "Ye'd have made a fine priest. With a tonsure, ye almost look like him."

Odo raised his head and quietly suggested the reeve needed to question his own lineage.

On instructions from the lord, Oswald was told to keep the introduction short and to the point, and no, he wasn't to appeal for more coin to replace the church roof.

Having completed his opening address, he returned to his customary position.

Steward Alard turned slightly towards the lord and looked apprehensive.

Sir Gweir gave a subtle nod of encouragement, urging him to proceed.

"In the late afternoon on the day in question, Sir Wystan arrived at Falls Ende after a hurried ride through the forest. His face showed minor cuts from branches. It was at Falls Ende where he confronted Herdsman Odo Read. In fear, and to preserve his life, the herdsman leapt voluntarily into the falls."

A few spectators had not been aware of Odo's heroics, if not his foolhardy leap, and gasped.

"That's a lie!"

Everyone in the hall shifted their gaze from the steward to Lady Constance.

Steward Alard was about to interrupt the lady, but Sir Gweir waved him off. This was what he wanted.

The lady continued. "The herdsman had come to my home!" She looked at the faces of people to evoke sympathy. "He came to my home as an outlaw and attempted to steal from me and my son." She spoke passionately, her voice carrying to the furthest corners of the hall.

A few spectators growled, unhappy at the revelation.

"He was caught and then managed to flee. Not knowing the danger he was in, my son, Sir Wystan, risked his life to apprehend him!" She raised an arm and pointed at Odo.

About to protest, Odo felt the reeve's hand clamp down on his arm. He shook his head. "Wait," he whispered.

Odo fought the impulse to speak out.

"My son chased him to Falls Ende. It was there at Falls Ende where the herdsman pushed my son to his death." A *foulard* magically appeared, and the Lady delicately dabbed at her eyes.

"The herdsman," she spat, "is a murderer!"

There was an immediate uproar, and Sir Gweir stood. "Silence!"

He turned to the lady, "How have you arrived at this conclusion? What facts do you have?" He fought to keep his voice moderate as everyone in attendance needed to see him as being fair and just. He sat down, feigned disinterest, cupped his chin with his hand and allowed her to continue.

"My knights saw this. They witnessed his death and could do little about it. They were too late," she sobbed. The *foulard* reappeared.

Odo fumed, almost silently.

"Easy, Odo, easy," reassured Reeve Petrus.

"Lady Constance, to uphold the truth, bring forward yer witnesses." Steward Alard, once again in control, asked.

"Sir Borin and Sir Kasos, there." She pointed at the two knights.

"Step forward, sirs," the steward asked. "What have ye to say?"

"Is as the lady says, we saw the herdsman push Sir Wystan into the falls. We were too far away to prevent it," Sir Borin said.

"Sir Kasos?" asked Steward Alard.

"Aye, that's what happened." the knight's dark eyes shifted around the room uneasily.

"The masons think otherwise, Milady," offered the steward, "as they witnessed the leap by Odo and the fall by Sir Wystan after he was struck by an arrow. Have you a rebuttal to their account?"

"The masons are under the employ of the Lord of the Manor. Of course, they would support anything he says," she scoffed.

Sir Gweir fought to control his own anger and bit the inside of his mouth.

The knights returned uneasily to their place against the wall.

"Have you more to say, Milady?" asked the steward.

She slowly stood and dabbed her eyes. "Ever since he was pilloried, the herdsman has held rancour against my son. Remember, Odo Read owed Sir Wystan coin; he was in debt and never forgot the punishment." She glared at Odo with loathing.

People were nodding in agreement, of course, they remembered. Odo had been pilloried not long ago, and how could they forget, after all, a good pillory was a superior source of entertainment. The beautiful Lady Constance looked stunning as she stood on the dais. People were enamoured with her looks, style and social standing and wanted nothing more than to believe her. Why would she lie? Odo Read, most conceded, was a likeable fellow, but he was only a herdsman and certainly had every reason to hold a grudge, and therefore probably did kill Sir Wystan as she claimed. The lady confidently returned to her seat as the buzzing of multiple conversations began. She was pleased. She had tugged at the pliable heartstrings of those assembled and had successfully manipulated them – and now they stirred.

CHAPTER TWENTY-SEVEN

The upwelling of anger grew in intensity. They wanted blood, and Odo was becoming more anxious. He knew what Sir Gweir intended to do. Earlier, he had discussed his plan with everyone, but sitting still and not saying anything in his defence was difficult.

Steward Alard received another subtle signal from Sir Gweir, and so emboldened, stood. "There remain–"

"Can't hear ye!" shouted someone.

The room settled down as people began to focus on the steward. He wasn't used to performing this role and having all the attention thrust upon him. He regretted opening his mouth and suggesting to the lord that he hold an inquire. He would have thought of an alternative if he had known he would become pivotal in this proceeding.

"There remain some unanswered questions," he repeated.

Lady Constance nodded in agreement, and Sir Gweir sat unmoving. No one noticed that most of Sir Gweir's knights had tensed; none of them looked at ease.

"Herdsman Odo Read has been accused of murder by Lady Constance, and she would have us believe that is the truth." Alard risked a look at the priest, Oswald, who looked very unhappy.

Lady Constance shifted nervously in her seat. Her ever-present smile had vanished, as had her *foulard*.

"Let us go back a little, before Sir Wystan's death and recall some important events." The steward was warming to his new role.

"Out with it, Alard, don't keep us in suspense," came the unknown voice. A few people laughed.

"Earlier that same unforgettable day, in the morning as the sun came up, a stone mason and his apprentice son were brutally slain on the track at Falls Ende."

Heads nodded in agreement. Many knew the mason and his son and had been shocked by their deaths.

"They were killed by an outlaw named Bert Brooker."

The hall fell silent. This was a new development that no one had previously heard.

"Three brigands, all brothers, were hired to kill Falls Ende Master Mason Mundy and unknowingly killed the wrong man!" Alard spoke with emphasis, his voice growing louder as he became more confident. "Instead, they mistakenly killed Freemason Wouter Gurney and his seventeen-year-old son, Ralf."

"That is a lie," Lady Constance scoffed.

The steward gave a hand signal, and a pennant moved behind the lord. A knight and a ruffian appeared, and prompted by the knight, the archer tentatively walked with a noticeable limp and paused at the side of the dais.

"What are ye called?" asked the Steward.

The archer looked frightened and remained silent.

"Who is this vagabond? Why is he here?" ridiculed the lady.

Sir Gweir sighed heavily, rose, and stepped toward the brigand. It was time to take matters into his own hands. "What is yer name?"

"I, I am Samuel Brooker, Milord." The archer's voice had a tremor, and his hands shook.

The priest's face darkened.

"Who killed the stone mason and his son?"

"T'was Bert, Milord, as I told ye b'fore."

"How do ye know this?"

"Me and Tedric were there, we was hired to kill the master mason."

"Who hired ye?"

"This is nonsense," cried Lady Constance, rising from her seat. "These men are outlaws, dishonest men with no values."

"Let him finish, Milady," Sir Gweir shot back. "Answer the question, Samuel."

"Sir Wystan told us to kill the Falls Ende master mason, and he gave us information, but t'was wrong. We didn't mean to kill the other one, Milord, we—"

"Yer a liar!" exclaimed the lady. She sat down, twisting away from the brigand with her arms folded across her chest.

"Someone saw what ye did, didn't they?" asked the lord, ignoring her outburst.

The archer nodded, "Aye, there was a lass in the field across the river."

"Do ye know her name?"

Odo sat straighter, staring at the man.

"Nay, Milord," the archer shook his head.

"It was Charlotte, Cheesemaker Gerald's daughter."

Samuel shrugged.

"What did you do with Charlotte?"

"We captured her and we bringed her to our campsite. Sir Wystan came with two other knights and they takes her away, Milord."

Lady Constance waved her arm, as if the statement was fallacious.

"Do you see those knights here?" asked Sir Gweir.

"Aye, Milord, that be them," without pause, the archer raised his arm and pointed directly to Sir Borin and Sir Kasos against the wall.

Before any of Sir Gweir's knights could prevent him, Sir Borin broke from his position against the wall, drew his sword and suddenly sprinted towards the dais directly towards Sir Gweir. In response, Reeve Petrus bolted upright, his staff ready to defend his lord, while Steward Alard scrambled quickly out of harm's way. Other knights, while quick to react, were a step behind. From somewhere, a woman shrieked.

One of Sir Gweir's knights, with his face partially masked by a cloth, was quicker than the rest, and in a surprising turn of speed, leapt forward with his sword drawn. Before Sir Borin could advance, he was cut down; a sword protruded from his chest. He fell heavily in a growing pool of blood, almost directly in front of Odo.

People screamed, and some hurriedly ran for the door to leave.

With the cloth around his face, the mystery knight extracted his sword, wiped the blade on the fallen knight's surcoat, and sheathed it. To everyone's amazement, he turned to Sir Gweir and bowed deeply, then straightened and returned to the wall. People yelled in fear, some women wept, others loudly questioned the identity of the mystery knight, and many were shocked into silence. Seldom had they seen death at such close quarters. It was violent, messy and upsetting. Sir Gweir appealed to everyone to return to their places and calm down.

Lady Constance's face was emotionless. She showed no reaction to the brutal death of her knight. The only sign of agitation was from her hand, which fidgeted with the sash tied around her waist.

Sir Borin's body was carried away, and order was restored to the hall, although the atmosphere was still charged.

The inquire resumed.

Sir Gweir returned to the archer with a final question. "Where did Sir Wystan, Sir Borin and Sir Kasos take Charlotte?"

"They takes her to th' lady's manor, Milord."

Lady Constance stood angrily with her fists clenched, her face scarlet with rage. "How dare ye speak such lies and show me disrespect!"

"Return to yer seat!" bellowed Sir Gweir. All pretence of civility was gone. He glared at her, daring her, wishing she would disobey.

In the hall, people were mute in astonishment. This was unheard of, scurrilous.

Slowly, Lady Constance sat down, and Odo noticed her fidgeting with her sash again. Her face had drained of colour, and she looked haggard, he thought. Then realised the priest, Oswald, had disappeared.

Steward Alard had sufficiently regained his courage and again took the floor. He swallowed nervously. "Uh, it seems that some may doubt the sincerity and honesty of Samuel Brooker."

Someone laughed nervously.

The steward inclined his head as if he too doubted the words of the brigand. "Where did Sir Wystan and his accomplices take Charlotte?"

The hall had returned to a deathly cold silence. If Steward Alard intended to create drama, it worked.

"Where did they take Charlotte?" he shouted.

"They took me to the manor of Lady Constance, where I was beaten," came the soft, frail voice of Charlotte.

Odo launched to his feet and immediately felt the reeve's unbreakable grip on his arm. "Sit, Odo, has to be this way, lad. Sit."

She stood with a knight on one side, and Oswald on the other, and appeared from the same doorway Sir Gweir had entered from earlier.

The bruising and swelling were evident for everyone to see, and she looked fragile and weak. There were gasps, and again another woman began to weep. People were confused, and everyone started talking at once. Charlotte was well known and liked, and what had happened to her was unthinkable.

Odo and Charlotte made eye contact. He wanted to go to her and hold her close. But he couldn't, he wasn't allowed.

With the reeve pulling his arm, Odo slowly sat and felt the grip loosen.

Lady Constance's mouth opened, and she was stunned. Her eyes flickered from Charlotte to Sir Gweir in confusion. Final realisation dawned on her face. She looked infuriated.

All heads were turned towards Charlotte, except for Odo, who had shifted his gaze and stared at the lady in revulsion. Her hand returned to her sash, and then he saw the darkness of a handle – the handle of a knife. She had a knife hidden in her sash! Before the thought had fully registered, he saw her leap from her seat and pull from concealment a *misericorde*, a slim, lethal knife frequently used to deliver a deathstroke. It was a weapon of an assassin.

Odo was two large strides from Lady Constance, and she was separated from Sir Gweir by only a single step. She was halfway to Sir Gweir when he freed himself from the reeve's loose grip and launched forward. He saw her arm and the knife slowly extend outwards; it was aimed at the exposed neck of Sir Gweir, who still had his head turned looking at Charlotte.

Charlotte had been watching Odo, and she saw what was happening. "Odo!" she cried. Her voice was too frail to be heard. Her hands flew to her mouth.

"Sir Gweir!" Oswald yelled in alarm.

The warning was too late for the lord to defend himself or even move, as he was looking directly at Charlotte.

Odo desperately flung himself at the lady and stretched for her knife. He managed to strike her wrist with his hand, and at the same time, he drove into her body with his shoulder. The knife remained firmly in her grasp, but her hand holding it was deflected away. Instead of severing the arteries in Sir Gweir's neck as she intended, it sliced through the thin fabric of his surcoat and undergarments and into his upper chest, carving a long, deep line across his shoulder. Blood immediately welled, creating a darkening crimson red line as Odo and Lady Constance tumbled onto the dais, his momentum and speed carrying him past her and safely out of her reach.

Winded and with his shoulder reinjured, Odo could only watch as she rose to her knees. Sir Gweir looked down at the spreading stain, unaware that the demented woman would strike again.

The imposing figure of Reeve Petrus Bodkin loomed over her, his broadsword moving with a flash of polished, hardened steel. She screamed a feral cry of unconstrained hatred and loathing as she pounced again, a last desperate attempt to kill Mellester's lord.

Knights were scrambling forward, running to the aid of their liege. They were too far away to offer protection, but they tried desperately to reach him. Not a single person in Mellester's great hall failed to see the reeve's killing stroke.

Her body position lent itself perfectly to the savage and fatal downward slash of the reeve's knife-edged sword. She was on her knees, one arm extended forward and reaching, exposing her long, elegant neck. The reeve didn't miss, and the sword didn't falter. The downward motion, powered by muscle and weight, cleanly separated her head from her body. Her scream, cut unnaturally short, ended with her life.

Odo scrambled to reach Charlotte, who had sunk to her knees. Ignoring the pain from his shoulder, he rushed towards her, enveloping her in his arms and burying his head in her hair. It had been too much for them both.

CHAPTER TWENTY-EIGHT

Reeve Petrus Bodkin found Odo as he was leaving Cheesemaker Gerald's shoppe. Immediately, the reeve noticed how tired and exhausted he looked.

"And how does she fare?" asked the reeve as he limped towards him.

"She had a bad night but is gaining strength and is asleep now. Oswald insists she'll be her normal self in a day or two. But he says the damage is inside her head and isn't physical."

The reeve nodded sympathetically. "She needs yer love, Odo."

"Aye, she has that," he sighed.

Reeve Petrus waited a moment. "Come, we've been summoned by his lordship."

Odo looked up, "Am I in trouble? I disobeyed Sir Gweir, and–"

"Odo, Odo, calm down, relax. All is well, I am sure of it. Let us go and see what ails him, shall we?" He threw an arm around Odo's shoulder, and together they walked through the village and up the carriageway towards Mellester Manor's great hall.

The man-at-arms indicated that the lord was expecting them, but not in the great hall. They were to go to the lord's dayroom inside the manor. Odo had never been inside the manor and was surprised and impressed with what he saw. A far cry from his simple cruck house. His head swivelled at the tapestries, the finely crafted wood and stonework. Even the floor was made from wood. It felt odd to walk upon it.

"Pick yer feet up lad, the lord awaits," admonished the reeve.

A servant girl led them through the manor, and it seemed an eternity before they arrived at a massive, wooden door set into a stone wall. With her fist, she banged on the door, then opened it and stepped aside, allowing first the reeve to enter and finally Odo.

The room was crowded, and Odo was surprised to see the Lord of Ridgley Manor, Sir Hyde Fortescue, seated beside Sir Gweir, and on the other side of Mellester's lord, sat Sir Dain. Oswald stood in the far corner with his arms folded, leaning against the wall. He nodded and offered Odo a rare smile, and beside him sat the stoic and learned Steward Alard. The biggest surprise was seeing Sir Renier. He looked relaxed and comfortable in distinguished company, and while Odo normally didn't receive many acknowledgements from knights, Sir Renier smiled warmly at him too. Odo was instantly on guard.

Sir Gweir kicked a seat towards the reeve. "Sit yerself down, Petrus, b'fore yer fall."

Sir Hyde laughed. "I release yer to Sir Gweir as his reeve, and yer can't stay out of mischief. Things will never change." Most laughed, except Odo. He was feeling very self-conscious. His social status as a lowly freeman was far removed from the company he was now in.

"At least he still maintained his sword," added Sir Gweir, which only caused more laughter.

Odo noticed Sir Gweir's knife wound was causing him pain, and he moved stiffly. Sir Dain looked remarkably well, considering the injury he'd received. Rest had done both men a world of good.

Odo felt Sir Hyde's steel grey eyes settle on him. Remembering what his father had always told him, Odo looked up and met the gaze with silent curiosity. No one spoke; the men in the room were quiet.

After what seemed an age, Sir Hyde turned to Sir Gweir. "Are all yer freemen like him?

"Thank heavens, no," said Sir Gweir without pause.

The room erupted in laughter, and Odo felt his face flush. Sir Gweir stopped laughing suddenly and held his chest. The pain too much.

"Odo, I never thought we would meet again, and most certainly not like this," began Sir Hyde. His voice was deep and resonant. "I am pleased that finally we can put to rest this bad blood between ye and Sir Wystan. I admit this has been a worry, and I have yet to explain to the King what happened. Despite what Sir Wystan and Lady Constance did, they had powerful friends and, King Henry's ear. However, for ye and yer fair maiden, it's over."

Sir Hyde again silently appraised the young herdsman.

"Ye acquitted yourself bravely on many accounts. Dare I say it; few people I have ever met have been capable of taking initiative and at great peril to themselves without training and experience as ye have." Sir Hyde shook his head, and his gaze softened. "Ye saved the life of my dear friend. I am eternally grateful and in yer debt," he said quietly. His gaze on Odo never wavered. "Thank ye."

"Wouldn't any man do as I did?" replied Odo.

"No, Odo, and one day, I'm sorry to say, ye will accept that all men are not born equal."

To Odo's astonishment, Sir Hyde rose from his seat and stepped towards him with his hand extended. They clasped hands and shook. This was the first time Odo had ever shaken the hand of a knight and lord. He found the gesture sincere; he was moved and felt a lump in his throat.

Odo risked a glance at Oswald and noticed he was grinning.

Sir Renier rose, walked across and reached out with his hand. "I hear ye are the finest herdsman in *du sud Angleterre*?"

Odo looked at Oswald in question.

"Southern England."

"No, no," Odo shook his head, "all England." He grabbed Sir Renier's hand and shook.

Again, there was an uproar as the knights laughed. Sir Gweir was trying hard not to and failed. One by one, each man shook Odo's hand, all except Oswald. He shuffled over and enveloped him with his arms and gave a hug. To Odo, the priest felt cold and clammy. Perhaps he's unwell, he thought.

"When are ye going to marry that fine maiden of yers, Odo," asked Sir Hyde. His grey eyes sparkled.

"Soon as she is better, Milord."

"I hope ye invite me."

"And me too," responded Sir Gweir. He stood again, "Thank ye for all you've done, Odo and fer saving my life."

Odo nodded. He had a question. "Milord, what will happen to the two outlaws who captured Charlotte?"

"As I understand it, we will have a pillory, Odo."

Sir Gweir saw Odo's reaction. "I know ye suffered unfairly when pilloried, and I'm sure the memories are still fresh. But in this case, the crime warrants the punishment."

"Aye, Milord," Odo replied quietly.

"Now if you'll excuse us, Odo, we need to discuss Sir Renier's responsibilities and his new demesne.

Odo looked surprised.

"Sir Renier has sworn fealty to me, and I have granted him Lady Constance's manor. You'll be seeing a lot more of him," volunteered Sir Gweir.

Odo turned to the knight, "Congratulations, Milord. Then, like Sir Gweir, you will go to Frankia and swear an oath to the king?"

Sir Renier offered another warm smile and dipped his head in acknowledgement. "I will."

There was genuineness to the French knight, and Odo liked him. He turned to face Sir Hyde and Sir Gweir. It was time to leave. These men were busy and had things to discuss. "Good day, Milords," Odo respectfully bowed his head and walked to the door.

"Ah, Odo?"

He turned to Sir Gweir, "Milord?" He felt everyone staring at him.

"Please remove your nag from my stables. He's already kicked two groomsmen and a sergeant and won't settle down. If you don't take him, we'll butcher him for meat," said Sir Gweir with a straight face.

Odo furrowed his eyebrows in question. "My horse is in pasture as we speak, Milord."

"The courser, Odo," said the reeve, "Not that sway-backed nag ye call Sally."

Odo's face split into the biggest smile. "Do you jest, Milord?" he asked.

"No, Odo, he is my gift to you," replied Sir Gweir.

No one saw Priest Oswald wipe dust from his eyes.

The door slammed shut as Odo ran from the Sir Gweir's day-room to the manor's stables. A short time later, the immense, black courser thundered down the carriageway, scattering a handful of surprised scullery maids as Odo, leaning over the stallion's neck, held on for dear life. "Charlotte!"

CHAPTER TWENTY-NINE

Mellester Manor, Devonshire, England 1167 A.D.

With skirts hoisted, Charlotte ran. She swerved deftly around merchants selling wares from hand carts, dodged tables stacked with vegetables, and scattered a small herd of goats after narrowly avoiding barrelling into them. A rather large billy took exception to her antics and gave her a long, hard look. By the time the goat-herder had mustered and regained control of his agitated animals, she was gone. It was too late to yell or shake a stick at the fleet-footed young woman.

Now she was attracting curious stares from villagers who had no choice but to step out of her way or risk being run into. She didn't stop to greet, wave, or offer an apology, and skillfully manoeuvred around any obstacles or people that impeded her. A couple of lusty drunkards watched and debated following her, but both were having trouble standing, let alone running and soon gave up on the idea.

She spared a cursory glance at the pillory as she ran by. It was being assembled for the two brothers who'd kidnapped her a fortnight ago. For some, the sight of a beautiful, flaxen-haired maiden running through Mellester's village gave them pause; however, Charlotte was no stranger to Mellester, and most knew or guessed her destination.

On arriving at Odo's cruck house, she opened the door and charged in. It came as no surprise to her that the house was empty. She didn't stop and continued to the door at the far end of the house that led directly to the byre. Without a thought, she flung it open and in the blink of an eye saw he wasn't there either. She dashed through the byre and into the large, open field and thankfully saw him in the distance. "Odo! Odo!" she yelled and rushed towards him.

On hearing her alarmed cries, Odo looked worried. He knew her well enough to know something was wrong. He dropped the tools he carried and ran towards her, looking for a threat or looming peril.

"Odo, it's Oswald, he's dying and asked for ye!" Charlotte's face was flushed; she was breathing hard as she ran to him.

Odo was relieved it wasn't something more serious. "Nay, can't be, I saw him this morn, he looked hale and hearty. Did one of his parishioners finally have a go at him? T'was bound to happen? I knew it would."

"He's dying, Odo, is his heart or something, he wants to talk to ye, come, ye can't dally here."

"His heart … why does he want to see me?"

"He didn't say," Charlotte grabbed Odo's hand and pulled him. "Come quickly, Odo, we can't waste time."

Even before they reached the priory, they could hear Grace, Oswald's hearth wife, wailing in despair. Charlotte led the way inside and discovered they were too late; Oswald was dead. Odo looked indifferently at the lifeless body of the priest for a few moments, then signalled to Charlotte, who was consoling the distraught woman, that he would return home.

Alerted to the sound of Grace's howls of anguish, a few people began gathering outside, and a couple of women were about to enter the priory when Odo stepped out.

"What happened, Odo?" asked a curious onlooker

"Is Oswald, he passed." He ignored further questions and shrugged his shoulders in response as he pushed by them and began to walk home.

He had known Oswald his entire life and had never warmed to him as a person until recently. As a priest, he was pious and angry, and perhaps that is what a good priest needs to be, but he had always singled him out when he was just a boy. If there was trouble and Odo was involved, the priest would always make a spectacle of him. He was convinced Oswald never liked him. Normally, he was gruff and scowled disapprovingly at anything he did. It wasn't until a month or so ago, when he was being pilloried, that the priest demonstrated any overt kindness towards him.

Odo felt a little ashamed. Maybe Oswald deserved better from him. After all, he had nursed him for days after being humiliated and injured in the pillory until he was physically healthy again. He stood all afternoon near that evil apparatus and, at great risk to himself, warned people away. He grimaced at the recollection. Whatever it was he wanted to tell him, he'd never know. He felt the sadness and feeling of loss. Odo stopped and thought about returning. If nothing more, he owed the cantankerous old priest a modicum of respect. Just over a week ago, Oswald hugged him when he was called to the manor house to receive thanks from Sir Gweir for saving his life – certainly that was an unusual, if not a kind gesture.

"Yer lost something?" Mellester's reeve, Petrus Bodkin, yelled.

Even from a distance, Odo could see his broad grin. He hadn't seen much of the reeve in the last week since the excitement in the great hall with Lady Constance. He'd been busy with the harvest. "Is Oswald, he's dead," Odo informed him, as the reeve with his ever-present staff limped towards him.

"Oh, do tell, what happened?" he looked concerned.

"Just now, Charlotte came and told me something about his heart. She's with Grace now."

Reeve Petrus pondered the matter. "Poor Oswald… I expect I should notify the bishop." He looked at Odo carefully and could see his conflicted emotions. "He was a good man, Odo. I only wish more clergy were like him."

Odo's face showed a measure of doubt.

"I ain't been here in Mellester long, but I can tells yer, the priest had a soft spot for ye, he did."

"And if yer had been here longer, then yer would've known the man tormented me for years," Odo replied sourly.

The reeve laughed and looked back towards the church and priory. "I s'pose I should go over and have a gander and offer condolences to Grace."

A Bishop could not leave a thriving manor without a parish priest, and with some urgency, Bishop Immers immediately dispatched Durwin Babcock as Mellester Manor's new priest. His selection wasn't based on Durwin's ability or piety, but rather for pecuniary reasons. For a bishop, a major consideration when considering a bestowal of fine grazing lands, the Church received as a healthy emolument.

Many years earlier, and on behalf of the Church, a young Bishop Immers gratefully received title on gifted lands, and in exchange, promised the benefactor, Durwin Babcock, the elder, that he would ensure his son,

Durwin Babcock, the younger, received a proper ecclesiastical education. The bishop vowed he would personally preside over the boy's auspicious future.

After many a year of dolour, the boy finally became a priest. Truth be told, the bishop was quite happy to be rid of the irksome young man and Mellester Manor was far enough removed from the sacrosanct expanse of his cathedral for Durwin to be bothersome.

On arrival at Mellester Manor, Priest Durwin quickly made himself home in the priory and asked Grace to stay on and take care of his domestic duties. Having settled in, the priest set about meeting the locals and gathering stock of his congregation. He walked the village, chatted and reminded villagers that failure to attend church services was a personal affront to God and retribution would be swift. For a young man from a wealthy family, Priest Durwin Babcock wasn't endearing himself to Mellester Manor's fine inhabitants.

It was a surprise to Odo to hear a knock early one evening, only to discover the gangly young priest at the door.

"Hail, Herdsman Odo. Grace and peace to you from God, the Father, and the Lord Jesus Christ," offered the priest as he sized up the herdsman. "It is God's will that I, Durwin Babcock, now minister to His flock in this fine parish, and I, too, am deeply saddened by the passing of Oswald." Durwin managed to look suitably penitent. "He is with God and can now rest peacefully. God rest his soul." The priest bowed his head as if he were about to pray.

Odo was thinking about his pregnant cows and wasn't paying attention to the priest's prattle.

"It is the Church's desire that I introduce myself to the congregation–"

Odo noticed the priest seemed uncomfortable maintaining eye contact with him – there was something about the man that he found disquieting. "Er, how can I help yer?" he asked quickly. He already missed Oswald.

"I have a matter to discuss with ye. We should chat inside?" suggested Durwin.

Odo raised his eyebrows in question and remained silent.

Seeing he wasn't to be invited in and share a cup or two of mead, the priest continued on regardless. "Church records indicate yer tithes have been met, but to minister God's word is an expensive undertaking, and it is the Church's–"

"Aye, it is. And I already pay the Church more than a 10th of my income. I have given more to help the wretched as well, is that not enough?"

"The Church is grateful for what ye have done, but ye are successful and virtuous and could offer more." Priest Durwin gave him a stern look and was debating whether he should recite some scripture to solicit some feelings of guilt.

Now it was Odo's turn to take measure of the man who darkened his doorway. He saw the fine cloth of the belted alb, the large jewel-encrusted cross that swung from his neck. Even the priest's sandals looked expensive. In comparison, Oswald always dressed as a peasant when out in the village, not in the fancy vestments of a well-to-do clergyman. No doubt, Grace would also be cooking him a fine meal this evening. This priest wouldn't be without want. "Perhaps when ye have something of import to discuss with me, then I will listen. I am busy and in need of all my time. Good day to ye." Without waiting for a response, Odo closed the door and returned to the byre, shaking his head at the audacity of the priest.

Priest Durwin wasn't impressed with the herdsman and the lack of respect he demonstrated towards the church, and walked back to the priory angry and disillusioned. He wanted to impress the bishop by generating a higher income from Mellester, and so far, he'd only been met with apathy and disrespect by the villagers. It was becoming quite clear to the priest that Oswald had not put the Church first and foremost. That would soon change.

After Grace provided him with a very satisfying meal, Priest Durwin sat down to continue to look over Oswald's affairs. With Grace's help, and over the next few days, they managed to wade through a lifetime of chattels, books, writings and more. She answered questions and filled in details as he slowly learned about the dead priest and the parish.

"What is this?" Durwin asked, holding up a thick, wax-sealed letter he found beneath a stack of scrolls. "Why is this addressed simply, 'Odo'?"

Grace looked at it but could offer no explanation. "I have never seen this before, master, I will see he receives it," she offered to take it.

"Methinks not, yer will do no such thing," he barked, snatching it away from her outstretched hand. "It is no good to him, anyway; peasants don't read."

"Oh, master, Oswald taught Odo to read a little. But Charlotte is the one, she reads very well, even Latin," Grace volunteered.

"Charlotte, the herdsman's betrothed, she can read Latin?"

"Aye, she's a fine lass, master."

"Is heresy for a peasant woman to read Latin." Durwin waved the letter in the air as he thought about Charlotte and Odo. "Nay … nay, I don't think this will do him any good." He slid his fingernail beneath the wax, broke the seal, carefully unfolded the document and began to read.

It took but a dozen heartbeats before he realised what the letter contained. "Leave me," he waved his hand dismissively, "I wish to be alone." He continued to read. Once finished, he reread it, then again. This was extraordinary.

The following morning, Priest Durwin, clutching Oswald's letter, exited the priory and made his way up the carriageway to Sir Gweir's great hall, where he would speak to Steward Alard.

CHAPTER THIRTY

A short time after his surprise meeting with Steward Alard, Priest Durwin Babcock, in his newly purchased wagon and horse, departed Mellester to visit Bishop Immers. He told Grace he would return in three or four days.

With the priest out of town, Steward Alard spoke to Sir Gweir about his visit with Priest Durwin and what he'd learned. Sir Gweir was incensed. He paced backwards and forwards inside the great hall, trying to decide what to do. This new priest was meddlesome; he'd been here only briefly and was already causing trouble. "Damn him!" yelled Sir Gweir.

With this revelation, he knew Sir Hyde Fortescue needed to be informed. This latest development could have a far-reaching impact on Falls Ende, especially for Odo Read.

"Yer know Odo best, Alard, how should I speak to him about this?"

Steward Alard placed two fingers across the bridge of his nose and squeezed gently, and sighed. "Milord, I suggest ye do this..."

Reeve Petrus Bodkin visited Cheesemaker Gerald's shoppe and asked Gerald if he could spare Charlotte for the afternoon.

"Has she done wrong, Reeve Petrus?" Gerald was anxious.

"Nay, of course not, I need her help. I have a task for her to do. Is important and I'm sure she'll tell yer all about it when she returns, Gerald."

Even the reeve had no idea why he'd been ordered to summon Charlotte and Odo and then escort them both to the manor. He wasn't happy about it and was quite put out – he needed to be in the fields supervising the harvest, not playing wet nurse to two children, well, maybe they weren't children, he admitted. But still…

With Charlotte hounding him for answers, Reeve Petrus remained resolute and didn't answer her questions.

They found Odo easily enough, and the reeve explained to him all he knew.

"It's about the pillory, isn't it?" asked Odo.

The reeve shook his head, "I doubt it, and like I told yer, I really don't know."

Charlotte, Odo, and Reeve Petrus walked up towards Mellester's manor house, and instead of continuing towards the entrance to the great hall, Reeve Petrus turned away to another door. Both Odo and Charlotte were surprised.

"Not to the hall?" Odo asked

"Come," replied the reeve, ignoring the question.

It was the same room where Odo last saw Sir Gweir, the room the lord called his day-room. After knocking, Petrus held the door open and Charlotte entered, followed closely by Odo.

"If that will be all, Milord, I'll return to the harvest," informed the reeve, still holding the door open.

Sir Gweir sat in his customary place, with Steward Alard beside him. "I'd like ye to stay, Petrus. Close the door and be seated." Sir Gweir gave Charlotte a warm smile before turning to Odo, "It pleases me to see you both." He waved his arm at the empty chairs.

do could feel the uneasy sensation of his chest tightening. This was not a regular occurrence. The Lord of the Manor did not invite freemen to the manor house for an afternoon of chit-chat and social pleasantries. He looked at Reeve Petrus; he, too, was equally puzzled. Extra chairs had earlier been brought in. There were enough seats for everyone, and the only available chair for Odo was directly in front of Sir Gweir.

Charlotte was also looking worried and reached out for Odo's hand.

"Is good to see yer have almost healed," said Sir Gweir to Charlotte.

"Aye, Milord, every day sees an improvement," she replied nervously, touching her hand to a discoloured and lingering facial bruise. "Thank ye."

Odo glanced at Steward Alard, but his face was impassive. The only person missing was the priest, Oswald. Then he remembered the man was dead. Again, he felt the pang of sadness. He realised then that Oswald had always been close to him when something important was happening. He missed his presence.

Other than Alard, all faces were turned to Sir Gweir in question. The chairs were positioned such that three chairs faced the lord; Charlotte sat at one end, Odo in the middle, and Reeve Petrus closest to the door.

"I'm sure yer all wondering why ye are here," began Sir Gweir.

Odo felt Charlotte squeeze his hand reassuringly.

"Uh, there is a matter of importance, but first there is one other thing … Alard, if you please."

Steward Alard reached behind him and grabbed a light and lengthy bundle wrapped in cloth. Odo noticed it was quite long and narrow but wasn't heavy.

If Odo bothered to look towards the reeve, he would have seen a smile forming. In return, Sir Gweir saw his reaction and gave a little nod of acknowledgement.

"In three days, both Samuel and Tedric Brooker will be pilloried. It gives me no pleasure to do this, and I find the practice barbaric. However, an example must be made of them." He turned to Charlotte. "What these men did was wrong, and you could easily have been killed."

Four heads nodded.

"Samuel Brooker, the archer, believes he will not survive the pillory, but to his credit, will face his punishment honourably. He also understands the pain it has caused you and how you almost died." Sir Gweir gave Charlotte a sympathetic look, then turned to face Odo. "He also realised that you were unable to defend yourself, and almost perished as a result. While Samuel Brooker is not blessed with a nimble mind, he is remorseful and offers ye an endowment."

Steward Alard awkwardly handed the bundle to the outstretched hands of Sir Gweir. With care, he reverently laid it on the floor and unwrapped the gift.

Charlotte and Odo were puzzled, and Reeve Petrus was grinning.

It was the archer's bow and quiver full of arrows.

"I had our Fletcher make some arrows, ye have a new bowstring, and ye will see the quiver has been repaired. I understand this is a Welsh longbow made from a yew tree.

Odo's mouth hung open.

"What say ye?" asked Sir Gweir.

"Why would Samuel Brooker give this to me?" Odo asked. "This is a beautiful bow, but…"

"No buts, Odo. Yer will accept this gift," Reeve Petrus interjected. "A fine bow like this is hard to come by and by the Gods ye will learn to use it without causing harm to yerself," he laughed.

"I don't know what to say. I am grateful to ye Milord and Samuel Brooker," Odo added.

"Very well, now that is taken care of, I have another matter to discuss," Sir Gweir shifted in his seat, impatient to return to the topic and the reason he summoned Odo.

The bow was quickly wrapped in the blanket and placed against the wall. All smiles vanished as four faces again turned to Mellester's Lord.

"I never expected that becoming lord would require such strength, strength I never knew I possessed. I can fight for my liege and defend our lands, but another part of the responsibility of being lord is far more difficult." Sir Gweir took a deep breath. "It is the human part, I am responsible for those who serve me. Ye serve me, Odo, and ye have done so in a way that proves to me yer loyalty, spirit and the strength of yer character."

Sir Gweir held Odo's gaze.

"Perhaps what I am about to say now is the hardest thing I have ever had to do. I wish there was another way." Sir Gweir rose, walked to the open shutter, and stared across his lands.

Everyone twisted in their seats to look and waited for him to continue.

"But there isn't." He walked back and took his seat. "Odo, you must trust me."

Odo swallowed, and Charlotte again held his hand. Petrus was scratching at his beard, puzzled about where this was all leading.

"Oswald passed just over a couple of weeks ago, and due to the efficient nature of the Church, a replacement priest was sent here by the bishop. I'm sure yer have all met Priest Durwin Babcock."

"Aye, and a weasel he'd be," suggested the reeve with a scowl.

"I'm sure we'll grow accustomed to him," Sir Gweir added. "However, in the course of his duties, and tidying of Oswald's affairs, Priest Durwin discovered a missive, which was addressed to Odo."

Odo's brow furrowed. "To me?"

"Aye, to ye."

"Then why have I not received it?"

"Because Priest Durwin decided not to deliver it to ye but to open and read it. Once he had done so, he visited Steward Alard to confirm some facts. The priest immediately left Mellester in great haste. We think he has gone to see Bishop Immers."

The room was quiet, the questions unspoken.

Sir Gweir took another breath. "The priest allowed Steward Alard to read the letter, and in it, I have learned Oswald has made a rather astonishing claim."

Odo was leaning forward, elbows resting on his knees and staring at the floor as the lord spoke. He slowly lifted his head to look at Sir Gweir.

Sir Gweir paused, "Odo, Oswald has written that Godwin Read is, uh, not your father."

"No, this can't be," Odo shot to his feet. "Why would he say that?"

Sir Gweir continued. "Oswald was not always a priest, he'd once been an … archer," he quickly looked at the Welsh bow leaning against the wall and shook his head at the irony and coincidence. "He was married and once had a family. It appears a lord intent on revenge came to where Oswald and his woman lived and killed his wife and two of their three children. One child, a newborn son, survived, as did Oswald, who was absent at the time."

Odo was shaking his head. *This can't be true, Godwin was his papa.*

Charlotte reached for Odo, pulled him back down to his seat, and then scooted her chair closer to hold him.

"According to the missive, Oswald was consumed by hate and intent on retribution. He hunted the lord and eventually slew him and all the men involved in the death of his family. The missive is a little unclear, but Oswald was plagued by guilt and grief and turned to the church for solace and spiritual guidance. He decided to become a priest, but couldn't care for the baby. He knew he'd never be a good father, so he asked a young married couple he met, if they would take the boy. That couple was Herdsman Godwin and Hetti Read."

Odo covered his face with his hands. "Nay, this can't be true." He pulled his hands away and looked up at Sir Gweir. Tears ran down his face as he tried to make sense of it all. "On yer word as a knight and lord, is what you tell me the truth?"

Sir Gweir nodded. "Aye, Odo, yer have my word, what I have told yer all comes from Oswald's letter.

Odo turned to Steward Alard in question.

"Odo, ye have known me yer entire life, I wouldn't speak untruths. When I read Oswald's letter, I was as puzzled as ye, but some things began to make sense. When yer have time to think on it, ye will see."

"For heaven's sake, Odo, yer even look like Oswald," volunteered the reeve.

Odo had many questions, but his mind was trying to understand this absurd revelation.

Charlotte quietly wept for Odo and held him tightly; she was glad to be with him and understood why the reeve brought her here.

"There is much to ponder, Milord; I have many questions that need answers. But why did that priest need to see Steward Alard and the bishop? Surely, Oswald's claim is only about a priest and a herdsman, and a bishop need not concern himself with such a banal matter."

"Aye, ye are right, Odo, here comes the other part." Sir Gweir slid his chair closer to Odo. "You see, Durwin Babcock is no fool. He checked with Alard to verify how you came to hold title on your land."

It dawned on Reeve Petrus what this was all about, and he lowered his head in despair. *Poor Odo.*

"Yes, I inherited the land when my fath– Godwin, passed away. I don't understand. Why is this a concern?"

"Do you remember how he did this?" asked Steward Alard.

"Of course," Odo wiped his eyes, "He had a paper that you created for him. It said he wanted the land passed on to his son when he died."

Everyone was quiet as Odo began to see the picture.

"Durwin believes that the land was given to ye in error. Because ye are not Godwin's son, ye should never have received the land. Therefore, the land is unclaimed, and the Church now feels it should possess it through dereliction. I can only think of one reason why Priest Durwin has gone to the bishop, and that is to plead his argument. If the bishop agrees with Durwin, then Odo, I expect you will have to pay a substantial levy for rent from the day Godwin died.”

“That means the land the mill sits on at Falls End could be owned by the Church, and they will likely charge a heavy fee,” stated the reeve.

Sir Gweir nodded, “Exactly.”

“Would the Church do such a thing?” Charlotte asked.

“Greedy buggers, th’ lot o’ them,” stated the reeve in disgust.

“This means I will lose my land.” Odo had his face buried in his hands again. “Why is this happening to me?”

Reeve Petrus and Sir Gweir shared a look. Neither man was smiling; the severity of this situation was obvious to them all.

“Could Oswald’s letter be wrong?” Charlotte asked.

“How can it be proved that the letter is incorrect?” replied Steward Alard, “The Church will cling to it like a holy relic because that land will fill their coffers with gold, especially when the Falls Ende mill is completed.”

“Can Sir Hyde influence the bishop?” asked the reeve.

“That is what I wonder too,” stated Sir Gweir. “I will ride out to Ridgley Manor in the morn and speak with him.

Odo was obviously shaken. Sir Gweir rose from his chair and requested that they provide the couple privacy. The three men exited the room and walked outside.

“I can’t believe this … the bastard!” exclaimed Reeve Petrus when out of earshot.

“I feel the same, Petrus. There is little I can do, and I wish this were different. I feel for Odo. He has endured so much already, and now to find out his father is not his father, and he may lose his lands. It doesn’t bear thinking about.”

"And of the king, can he rule on this?" Steward Alard asked.

"Aye, that he could, but will he? This matter must first go to Sir Hyde, as the king's proxy in local affairs, it will make him look ineffective if he cannot resolve the issue."

Steward Alard was mulling it over. "But this is more about the Church, is it not? Sir Hyde has no real power to wield against the Church; it is a battle he cannot win–"

"–and King Henry does have the power." Sir Gweir interjected. "If Sir Hyde chooses not to petition the king, as I suspect, then who is the most persuasive person to petition the king?"

"The ways I see it, if this land is taken by the Church, then Mellester will never benefit from the coin the gristmill will produce. All income will go to the Church in levies."

"We all have a vested interest in ensuring Odo retains this land," said Sir Gweir.

Chapter Thirty-One

It was early evening when Sir Gweir arrived at Ridgley Manor, much to the surprise and delight of its lord, Sir Hyde Fortescue.

"Yer can't keep away, can yer?"

"If only yer knew the half of it," exclaimed Sir Gweir.

Both men embraced and retired to Sir Hyde's private chambers, where they could talk.

"Is fortunate I am here, I was at the iron mine and returned early."

Oh, and how does the mine fare? Is it productive?"

"Aye, but I'd like to see more iron. The king needs it badly."

Sir Gweir nodded.

Sir Hyde saw the look of apprehension on Sir Gweir's face. "And what brings ye back, more trouble at Mellester?"

Sir Hyde listened attentively as Sir Gweir detailed all he knew about Falls Ende and the death of Priest Oswald. When finished, Sir Hyde remained silent and stroked his beard. He rose from his seat, walked to the hearth and began prodding at it in frustration with a poker. In anger, he threw the metal poker down and returned to his seat. He composed himself and was quiet for a few heartbeats. "How is Odo faring? I can't imagine the lad is taking this well."

"He's struggling at the moment, but his biggest fear is losing his land."

Sir Hyde nodded. Again, he remained silent as he contemplated the issue. "I know Bishop Immers, I have met him a few times, and find him to be a slimy, scurrilous fellow. I do not see the man turning away from any opportunity that puts coin in his soft hands. He'll take Odo's land, and yer right, he'll also add back rent. If young Odo can't pay, he'll take Odo's fine stock as payment. He'll ruin him, and then the Bishop will start on us. In the beginning, he'll charge us a nominal rent for the Falls Ende mill land, then once it begins production, he'll steadily increase the levy."

A log in the hearth shifted and looked in danger of rolling out. Sir Gweir rose from his seat, walked over, and in a shower of sparks, pushed it back in with his foot. "What can we do?"

"I can talk to the bishop, explain the circumstance, and hope the man has a conscience and a heart. Beyond that, nothing," offered Sir Hyde.

"What of the king, can we petition him?"

"And what will the king say to the bishop? 'You've upset a herdsman in a tiny manor in Devonshire and you must not take his land.' King Henry will scoff! This is why he has vassals like me to resolve these petty disputes. Except this time, I'm fighting the Church, which is really Pope Alexander III and not some hoggish English nobleman whom I can influence. The king wants closer ties with the Church; he's made this very clear, so the last thing he wants is to enter into a dispute with His Holiness." Sir Hyde saw the expression on the young lord's face. "Going to the king is a fool's errand and a wasted effort. He has enough to deal with. The Irish need placating, and last I heard, King Henry will continue to wage war on Frankia and Louis VII. No, he has no stomach or time for this."

Sir Gweir had an idea. "Perhaps if I returned to Frankia and–"

"Ye will do no such thing," Sir Hyde interrupted.

"Then what do you ye suggest I tell Odo?"

"Wait until I have spoken to Bishop Immers. First, let us see what he says. But remember, a lord must be resourceful." Sir Hyde tapped his head, "It's our biggest weapon, we can outsmart him."

"You think the bishop will come?" asked Sir Gweir.

"Oh, indeed."

It was late morning when a servant informed Sir Hyde that he had a guest. Bishop Immers wasted no time arriving at Ridgley Manor and requested to meet with the lord at his earliest convenience.

Both Sir Hyde and Sir Gweir went to the great hall to greet the bishop and found him surrounded by a gaggle of clergymen, including Ridgley Manor's ageing priest, Kirby, Priest Durwin of Mellester and three more clerics who were unfamiliar to them.

Bishop Immers wasn't in an agreeable mood. He detested travelling and hated waiting for a bleary-eyed, obtuse lord to drag himself from slumber and attempt intelligent discourse. In his venerated and highly educated opinion, knights were vulgar and frequently godless heathens. More so, contributing to his ill temper was the fact that Durwin Babcock unexpectedly returned and disrupted his sanctity and busy schedule. The insufferable man had only been away for less than a fortnight. He was like a recurring bad dream. However, the young priest's information could significantly benefit the Church in several ways. When completed, it was well known that the Falls Ende gristmill would be an asset that the Church could rejoice in. Even the pope would likely acknowledge the acquisition.

"Hail, Your Grace, Bishop Immers, it is a pleasure to see ye again." Sir Hyde bowed his head in respect. "Have you met Sir Gweir, Lord of Mellester Manor?"

Bishop Immers smiled warmly and held out his right hand. As required, Sir Hyde bent low, kissed the episcopal ring on his fourth finger, and stepped back. The hand remained generously extended.

 "Yer Grace." Sir Gweir squared his shoulders and reluctantly followed suit, almost cutting his lip on another large ring on the same finger. He stepped back, resisting the urge to spit and wipe his mouth.

The bishop studied the young lord carefully for a moment.

"Sir Hyde, I find travelling so wearying these days, but God's work knows no bounds, and I find myself constantly in need to minister to the indigent and wretched. Thus, for the first time I find myself seeking yer generous hospitality." He smiled with practised ease and turned to face the young lord. "I have heard much about ye, Sir Gweir. Your new parish priest, Durwin Babcock, has been telling me all about yer quaint little hamlet." The Bishop offered another copy of his smile. "Sir Hyde, I understand ye have yet to meet Durwin Babcock, Mellester Manor's new parish priest."

Priest Durwin took a step forward and bowed his head. "Milord."

Sir Hyde nodded at the lanky priest with hooded eyes. He felt an immediate dislike for the young man; he turned away and looked again at the bishop. "Forgive me for my rudeness, had I known we would be blessed with yer presence, I would have made preparations," offered Sir Hyde with equal silkiness.

"I am but a simple man of God and require nothing more than shelter, refreshments and a quiet place for worship, Milord." Bishop Immers dipped his head in pious humility.

Sir Gweir fought to control his reaction.

"My servants will attend to yer needs. If ye require more, please, let me know."

"Thank ye, however, I will not be here long. I have some urgent business west of here and thought I would visit the deaneries in the area as I pass through. Just church affairs, Milord, just routine."

Sir Hyde inclined his head. "Yer Grace. I will come to say farewell before ye leave. If ye will excuse me, I have some urgent concerns to attend to." Sir Hyde made brief eye contact with Sir Gweir and turned to leave.

The bishop raised his finger, "Ah, Milord, there is one small matter."

Sir Hyde froze, then slowly turned to face the bishop, his saintly expression rivalling that of his prodigal guest.

"A small matter hardly worthy of yer time ... the Church recognises that there is some derelict land in..." He looked over his shoulder, and a cleric secretary whispered in his ear. "...ahh yes, Mellester Manor, I believe. That would lie in yer demesne, Sir Gweir." The bishop nodded acknowledgement to the young lord and continued. "It would be negligent for this land to be inadequately managed, and the Church understands the land in question should be turned over."

"Oh, what land is this that ye speak of?" asked Sir Hyde innocently. He knew full well that the bishop knew all the pertinent details.

Ridgley's priest, Kirby, looked uncomfortable and turned his attention to an object on the floor.

Bishop Immers was again being given information by a secretary.

Priest Durwin licked his lips. He was enjoying this.

The bishop nodded once and faced Sir Hyde. "The land previously titled to Godwin Read, Milord. I believe it is more commonly known as Falls Ende."

Two could pay this game, thought Sir Hyde. "Oh? What do ye know of this, Sir Gweir?"

"That land was bestowed by Godwin Read to Odo Read. He has prospered on this land, and Mellester Manor and the Church benefit greatly by his hand."

The bishop pulled a face and looked troubled. "Aye, although I understand Odo is not the son of Godwin Read, therefore the land is without a title holder."

"I am truly blessed by yer visit today, Yer Grace, and bringing this minor matter to my attention. I will look into this immediately." Sir Hyde concluded the matter with a benign smile.

"The Church would like to see title transfer soon. It has been derelict for some time."

"And of Herdsman Odo, what will become of him?" asked Sir Gweir.

Bishop Immers waved his hand dismissively. "He can tenant on it. I have no quarrel with that." He clasped his hands together and laughed. "I don't think a lowly herdsman should stand in the way of Church affairs."

Sir Hyde took a calming breath. "Thank ye kindly, Yer Grace, as I said, I will investigate this thoroughly."

The bishop again dipped his head, acknowledging the lord. "The Church expects to receive this title in seven days." His smile vanished.

"Yer Grace, I have a lot of land in my demesne, and local affairs of the king to adjudicate. Far be it from me to act without due consideration; that would be negligent. Yer will hear from me, at least by month's end. If there is nothing further, Bishop Immers?" Sir Hyde looked at the bishop and smiled. His eyes challenged.

The bishop glared at Ridgley's lord. "One month." He spun and began to walk from the great hall, his retinue following closely behind. Priest Kirby, the last to leave, looked over his shoulder at the two lords and shrugged his shoulders in mute apology.

CHAPTER THIRTY-TWO

It was a difficult and sleepless night for Odo, and the day wasn't any better. His mind was consumed with thoughts of Oswald and his father, or as he had to correct himself, Godwin. He tried to rationalise the facts, and yet his heart felt sorrow for them both.

Godwin, because he could never tell the truth about not being his birth father, and Oswald because he could never enjoy his son and relish in the experience of being a father. He came to think of it as having two fathers – but the priest, Oswald, as his father? He shook his head in confusion and anger. Why didn't they tell me?

Sir Gweir told Odo not to fret about his land until after he had spoken and sought counsel from Sir Hyde. How could he not worry? The more he thought about it the more anxious he became.

He stood in his field. All this land was his and soon the Church would claim it. He remembered how he felt only a short time ago when Sir Wystan managed to take his land away. He'd rather die than experience it all over again. He looked at his cows grazing happily in the distance, the few sheep he had, and then his gift, the mighty black stallion that was prancing around him playfully and tossing its head.

"Odo!"

And there was his beautiful Charlotte; all he wanted to do was marry her. But how could he do that when he had nothing to offer to her? He waved, and she began walking cautiously towards him. He could see she was nervous about the courser and didn't want to be charged. "He won't hurt yer, he knows yer don't mean him harm!" Odo yelled.

Charlotte quickened her pace, and the big horse stepped around her snorting.

"He's playful today," he said as she walked up to him.

"I've never seen such a beautiful and mighty horse, and I can see he likes ye. I think ye have a friend," she said wrapping her arms tightly around him.

"Is days like this when I need friends," Odo said despondently.

"Then that is the name for him."

Odo twisted his head so he could see her face. "What name?"

"Amica."

"Amica," he repeated. "Is that Latin?"

"Aye, and it means friend," she said with a laugh.

"Amica!" he yelled.

The big stallion bucked, kicking its rear legs out then then stopped to face them.

"Amica!" Odo yelled again.

In response it snorted, and began to trot towards them. Then it cantered, kicking its front legs forward. Charlotte was frightened; it seemed the big horse was charging for them.

"Keep still, he won't hurt us, ye have to trust him."

Charlotte was ready to run, but Odo stood his ground and watched. She clutched him tightly behind his back.

At the last second the stallion locked its front legs and slid to stop directly in front of them. It nuzzled Odo searching for a carrot it knew he had. Odo dug for the treat. "Here, give it to him," he suggested and handed her the treat.

Charlotte tentatively held her hand out with the carrot. Within moments the horse was crunching away and Odo stroked its neck. "I will call you Amica. That is your name."

Amica began searching for another carrot.

Odo and Charlotte began to walk back to the byre and Amica followed a step behind, occasionally nudging Odo or Charlotte in the back.

The couple were lost in conversation, discussing Oswald and Godwin and failed to see the figure of a man leaning against the byre watching them.

"*Bonjour*!"

Odo and Charlotte both looked up in surprise to see Sir Renier de Pierrepont grinning at them.

They dipped her heads in unison, "Milord," they said together.

"You have a fine horse," offered Sir Renier, pronouncing horse like orse.

"Are ye lost?" asked Odo searching for a reason why a knight would be leaning against his byre.

"*Non, non*, I came to see Sir Gweir, but he is not in Mellester. I think to come and see ye and yer beautiful lady while I wait." His smile vanished and he turned to Charlotte. "I am happy to see yer look better, *mademoiselle*. I am sorry for what happened." He bowed dramatically.

Charlotte felt her cheeks flush, and suddenly conscious of the way she looked. "Thank ye, Milord. Odo, I must go, I will return soon." She dipped her head, gathered her skirts and rushed off.

"I think she was embarrassed."

Sir Renier laughed.

Amica wandered off to eat grass.

"You both must be happy to have these problems over, *oui*?"

Odo turned away from watching the stallion and faced Sir Renier. "If ye only knew what has been happening."

The Frankian knight feigned a look of surprise.

Odo felt awkward. "Would yer like a mead?"

The knight smiled, "But of course."

Sir Renier sat comfortably in Odo's cruck house, and each nursed a tankard of mead. Odo told the knight of Oswald's death and Sir Gweir's theory as to what the priest Durwin would do.

"I see you are sad to learn about who your father is."

"Aye, it bothers me."

"Was he a good man, this Godwin?"

"When growing up I loved him as any son would a father."

"Then now, ye still love him as a son would?"

"Of course."

"Then what has changed?"

Odo stared at the wall for a moment. He smiled. "Nothing."

"Now ye must find room in yer heart for the love a birth father has for his son."

"Yes, I must."

"So, what is this sadness then?" Now it was Sir Renier's turn to smile.

Odo had no answer. He was warming to this friendly, unassuming knight.

"But your land is a worry, *oui*?"

"Other than Charlotte, the land is what I care about the most."

Sir Renier twisted in his chair and spotted the long bow against the wall. He said nothing.

"What will I do if the bishop feels the Church is entitled to take my land?"

Sir Renier tapped his fingers against the tankard he held. "Ye can't go to the pope, he has enough problems at the moment. But, er, you could appeal to the king, *oui*?"

"Why would the Church overrule the bishop's decision just because the king tells them to do it?" Odo asked. He was clearly frustrated.

Sir Renier laughed. "Because the pope needs support to return to Rome. He seeks allies and he's currently hiding from those who do not want him as pope. He will not wish to make the English king unhappy in fear of losing his support, *oui*."

"Then Sir Gweir could do this for me, or even Sir Hyde?"

"Perhaps, but ye must wait, just like me, for Sir Gweir to return before ye have an answer."

Odo felt a little better.

"There is another reason why I came to see yer," Sir Renier added.

Odo turned to look at him.

I was granted land by Sir Gweir, you know this?"

"I was there."

"*Oui*, you were. I wish to raise cows for milk. I want to make cheese. I am told ye are the best."

Odo was grinning. "I am the best."

Sir Renier laughed. "But I have no one that can, er, advise me to do this. I will pay if ye will help me."

"Competition?" Odo eyed him warily.

"*Non, non*, only for me, but if I have more milk, then I can sell it to ye, *oui?*"

"I'd be honoured to help ye, Sir Renier. Thank ye."

"And, I can arrange, as, er, part payment, for my squire to show you how to use that long bow."

"Like lessons?"

"*Oui.*"

The thought of actually learning how to use the bow wasn't something Odo devoted any time to. But in light of everything that happened he was very interested. "I would like that."

"I will send someone to show you this bow. Yer first lesson," smiled Sir Renier.

"I am pleased. Thank ye, Milord."

"*Non, non*, I am most grateful to you, Odo." He rose from his seat. "Now I must return to Mellester Manor and await the return of Sir Gweir. I have to swear fealty to the king, and Sir Gweir will give me instructions."

"Ye have t' go to Frankia?" Odo asked.

"*Oui*, but it is not difficult. A ship will leave from South Hamtun[14]. Is easy for me."

Odo nodded.

"You have been most kind, Odo."

14   *South Hampton*

Reeve Petrus found Odo. "Come lad, Sir Gweir is back and wants to see yer.

As before, Odo stood before Mellester's lord in his day room. As soon as he entered, he felt the knot of fear twist at his insides. Steward Alard was seated beside the lord and looked very serious. Reeve Petrus remained standing.

"Be seated," Sir Gweir instructed without pleasantries.

Odo sat, leaned forward and studied the face of Sir Gweir, and found nothing reassuring in his expression. The steward was looking at the reeve.

"As we thought, Bishop Immers and Priest Durwin went to Ridgley Manor and spoke with Sir Hyde. The Church has every intention to claim Falls Ende, Odo."

"Nay, they can't, it isn't their land to take! It belonged to my father and he bequeathed it to me."

Sir Gweir raised a hand to silence him. "Odo, both Sir Hyde and I agree with ye. The bishop challenges that, as ye are not the son of Godwin Read ye are not entitled to the land."

Odo was heartbroken.

Sir Gweir looked to the reeve for help, but he too looked as dismal as Odo.

"Can the king help?" Odo asked.

"Sir Hyde does not think … Sir Hyde believes it would reflect badly on him, or me, if either one of us were to approach the king with such a trivial matter."

Odo's mouth opened. "Trivial! Milord, this is my life and my land!"

"No decision has been made yet. Sir Hyde managed to convince the bishop to wait a month. He hopes that a solution will present itself."

"Does Sir Hyde have any ideas?" asked the reeve.

"Nay, and neither do I," said the lord.

"What are the chances that Bishop Immers will change his mind?" Steward Alard asked.

"From what I saw, he is already counting coin. I don't think he will change anything," added Sir Gweir.

Odo looked at Mellester's lord, "So I have only a month, one month before the Church claims my land?"

Sir Gweir nodded, "Aye, Odo, one month."

"One month!" Charlotte yelled. She stomped through Odo's home in anger. Odo sat morosely at the table.

"One month! If I lay my hands on that priest, I'll choke him, I will," she added with vehemence.

Odo had never seen Charlotte so angry.

"Odo Read!"

Odo looked up at her and waited for the next outburst.

She stared at him, her eyes blazed in fury. "Then so be it. Ye will go to Frankia and plead to the king yerself, if the mighty lords of this shire are too weak-kneed to stand up fer what's right, then ye will have to do it."

Odo launched from his seat, stepped in front of Charlotte and held her by the shoulders. "Charlotte, I don't know the first thing about traveling across the ocean, let alone how to get the king's ear and then have him listen me. I'm a herdsman, not a noble."

"Yer a man, Odo Read and ye will do what is right. That's what Godwin always told ye."

"Aye, he did."

"Yer told me Sir Renier is traveling to Frankia – go with him," she urged.

"He couldn't allow it as it would go against what his liege lord wants."

Charlotte wrapped her arms around Odo and held him tightly.

Odo placed his chin on her head and thought. *Sir Gweir never said I couldn't go to speak to the king.*

CHAPTER THIRTY-THREE

Led by Mother Rosa, local women were hired to milk Odo's cows each day and early mornings were always a busy time. Daniel supervised the task, and when completed, Odo and Daniel took the milk to Cheesemaker Gerald's and he would begin the complex process of making cheese and selling Odo's surplus milk.

Originally, Cheesemaker Gerald sold his fine cheeses in small amounts only to residents of Mellester. Word spread, and soon people from neighbouring manors came to purchase from him. Cheesemaker Gerald's cheeses were now much sought-after and sold all he could make.

In addition to his own land Odo also rented additional land from Mellester's lord where he grazed his growing herd of cows. Odo had a theory, and once put into practice proved to be invaluable. He believed that large pastures for cows were inefficient and that placing more cows in smaller fields saw them eat more grass. Other fields were left empty which allowed the clover rich grass to grow. When the lush grass was a sufficient height he moved the cows to the new pasture and let the grass grow in the newly vacated field. This constant rotation meant his cows always ate the best grass, never had to scrounge for food and became more productive. As a result, he was always able to provide Cheesemaker Gerald with all the milk he needed and both Herdsman Odo and Cheesemaker Gerald prospered.

Odo and Daniel just departed Cheesemaker Gerald's shoppe after delivering the morning's milk and were heading out to move his cows to new pastures when Daniel spied a man trudging through the field towards them. Odo stopped to watch. As he drew near, Odo saw the man was in fact rather muscular looking and judging from his surcoat, looked to be a sergeant to a knight.

Odo instructed Daniel to continue without him, and he waited for the stranger to approach.

"Hail. Herdsman Odo?" inquired the sergeant with a friendly smile.

"Aye, and greetings," replied Odo, curious as to the reason for the visit.

"I'm told yer have a longbow."

"Aye, I do," replied Odo with suspicion.

The sergeant seemed to relax. "That would be fine then. Sir Renier asks that I spend some time to instruct yer on how to use it."

"Oh. He did he. What are ye called?"

"Thomas Roundtree."

"And ye'd know something about archery?"

"Aye, a little," smiled the sergeant.

Odo had work to do but in light of the worry and anxiety he felt, perhaps a distraction for a few hours wouldn't be a bad thing. "C'mon then, Thomas."

They walked back across the field towards Odo's home.

"How fares Sir Renier, is he at Mellester?"

"Nay, Sir Renier asked me to tell ye, and he apologises he can't be here to watch, but had to leave earlier for Frankia."

"He's gone already?"

"Aye, left this morn for South Hamtun, which is where I am to meet him and from there to the port of Herosfloth[15] in Frankia."

"Is that where King Henry is?"

"Oh, nay, the king is in Chaumont-sur-Epte, not far away from Herosfloth."

Odo was thoughtful and remained quiet for a few steps. "He left earlier than expected, didn't he?"

"Sir Gweir wanted Sir Renier to see a man in Herosfloth when he first arrives, this will delay his journey by two days."

They walked in silence until they arrived at Odo's home. Thomas waited outside while he retrieved the bow and unwrapped it before handing it to him.

"It is a fine bow, this is. Did ye know it's a Welsh long bow. See the yew in between the other wood?"

Odo looked carefully and could see the different layers of wood bonded together to make the bow.

Thomas spent time detailing how to take care of and maintain the bow, and then how to string it. No easy feat as Odo discovered. Once strung, he explained the proper body and foot stance, then showed him how to notch an arrow, and finally the correct arm and finger position. Odo was impressed with himself and thought he showed remarkable talent in learning all about the bow. He couldn't wait to tell Charlotte.

Thomas walked twenty paces from the side of the byre and stopped. "Now Odo, doing everything what I told yer, I want yer to hit the byre with an arrow."

15   *Harfleur, Normandy, Frankia.*

"Is only a little distance away. I've heard about these bows, and an arrow from a Welsh long bow will pierce the armour of a knight at great distance. If I shoot at the byre from here, the arrow will go clean through. It could hit someone outside."

"A tankard of mead says ye can't hit yer byre from here," laughed Thomas.

Odo gave Thomas the evil eye before turning to the serious matter at hand. He notched an arrow, checked his stance just as Thomas instructed and began to draw the bowstring back. He found it difficult, more than he believed possible. He gathered himself and pulled the bowstring back as hard as he could, yet the arrow hadn't moved much. Grunting with effort, he let the string slip from his fingertips. The arrow flew straight for about eighteen paces and clattered to the ground, short of the byre wall.

"Well then, that is yer lesson fer the day," informed Thomas with a grin and began to walk away. "I'll have the mead on my next visit."

"That's it?" asked Odo. "Is the lesson over?"

Thomas stopped and turned around. "Now ye need to develop strength. It will take yer a while, I reckon, maybe two years or so to be moderately good. When yer ready, let me know and we'll have the next lesson."

Not far away, but far enough not to be observed, Reeve Petrus Bodkin stifled a laugh and watched. When he saw the squire leave, the reeve slipped away and returned to the manor.

Charlotte howled with laughter when Odo told her about his very short archery lesson. Tears ran from her face as Odo looked on, trying desperately to appear indignant and hurt. When she calmed down and wiped her eyes he told her what Thomas told her about Sir Renier leaving for Frankia.

"Thomas seemed quite willing to tell ye all about Sir Renier's plans. He was very helpful, wasn't he?"

"T'was what I was thinking."

"Yer could find Sir Renier in Herosfloth. He'll be there two days. Then ride together to the king."

"If he agrees… that's the risk I take."

"And what other choice do ye have?"

The inside of Odo's home was quiet. Each of them lost to their own thoughts and fears.

Charlotte broke the silence. "Odo, yer must go. Ye know this don't yer?"

He looked at her and said nothing. He saw the deep, liquid pools of her eyes and felt the love from her. Their bond was strong; they were inseparable and had always loved each other. She felt it too and reached for his hands, she pulled them to her chest and returned his gaze. He felt her warmth, even their heartbeats were in sync. He breathed in her scent and it gave him hope. She gave him life and he wanted nothing more than to make her happy.

"Aye, Charlotte, I must go to Frankia to speak with King Henry." He felt wetness on his hands, she was weeping. "I will leave early first thing in the morn."

From the light of candles, Odo brushed Amica. He talked to him as he would to a friend. Amica's ears rotated as he listened to Odo and enjoyed the attention.

Odo gave Daniel and Charlotte instructions, and in response they both told him that they would take care of things in his absence. They reminded him he should focus on seeing the king and not to worry. Afterwards, he went in search of Reeve Petrus but was told he was busy with Sir Gweir at the Manor.

The next few days would be difficult. It would take two days of hard riding to reach South Hamtun, and he was pleased he had a horse as fine as Amica to ride. On advice from Charlotte, Odo divided his money into small purses. He kept one attached to his belt, and three more purses were hidden in other creative places. If he were robbed, they might steal one purse, but not all four. Charlotte suggested with a deadpan expression that Odo could take his longbow with him for defence. But she was unable to maintain a straight face and began laughing. Odo joined in which eased the tension and the heartache of his departure.

Amica was saddled and ready. Daniel and Mother Rosa arrived to begin work and soon the rest of the women would arrive and begin milking.

"Good luck Odo," Daniel said. "Be careful, and I look forward to yer stories of adventure when yer return."

He clapped Daniel on the back and couldn't avoid a bear hug from Mother Rosa before he led Amica from the byre and onto the darkened street. He slowly walked to Cheeseman Gerald's shoppe where Charlotte waited. They hugged. There wasn't much to say that they hadn't said already. What Odo was doing was extremely dangerous for an unarmed man who'd never travelled far from home.

Charlotte pulled Odo's head down and whispered softly into his ear.

He swallowed thickly and held her face in his hands; words didn't seem to be enough. With sadness he climbed onto Amica.

He felt Charlotte's hand on his thigh. "I love ye Odo Read."

"And I love ye too, Charlotte Cheeseman."

The grey of dawn made it easier to see the road. A few peasants were out, and they respectfully made way for the stallion. It was too dangerous to travel at a speed greater than a walk until it became lighter, and with a heavy heart Odo and Amica began their long journey to Frankia.

CHAPTER THIRTY-FOUR

Odo was well past Mellester's lands when an imposing figure on a sizeable horse stepped from concealment onto the road. Warily, he eased Amica to a walk as he decided what to do. Brigands were numerous in these parts and although he was still some distance from the man and couldn't make out his features or intentions, he still felt some apprehension. Cautiously Amica brought him closer.

Sensing his anxiety, the stallion became skittish. He spoke soothingly and patted his neck as they came nearer. Odo had a plan, and the moment the figure ahead showed any hostility, he would urge Amica into a gallop and race past. He doubted there was another horse ridden by an outlaw that could outpace his.

Shadows from tall trees made it difficult to see the man, who remained unmoving.

"Hail!" Odo yelled in greeting.

There was no reply. They walked closer for a few more steps.

"What took yer so long? I've been waitin' here since daybreak when I should be helping with harvest!" came the sound of a familiar voice.

"Reeve Petrus?"

"Thought yer could skulk off and not say farewell?"

Odo didn't know what to say.

"C'mon then, we can't tarry 'round here." He dug his heels into his courser and they shot off. The staff tied securely to his saddle looked like a wobbly flag pole.

Mellester is in the other direction, he thought, why is the reeve heading towards South Hamtun?

With no urging required, Amica lunged forward and soon they caught the reeve who slowed to a moderate canter.

The reeve turned to look at Odo who rode alongside and grinned.

People they encountered stared at them and moved away in fear as Petrus Bodkin and Odo Read rode quickly through the undulating countryside. They passed small hamlets, cultivated fields and rich, golden pastures. Both men were dressed similarly; with capuchins and breeches they looked like peasants, yet peasants didn't ride expensive horses and certainly weren't armed. The reeve carried his broadsword on his hip, and so it was easy to mistake them as outlaws. No wonder people didn't wave as they thundered past.

They stopped to water and rest the horses beside a stream, and both men sat beneath the shade of an oak watching the animals eat lush grass.

Reeve Petrus was waiting for Odo to question why he was riding with him, and he didn't disappoint.

"Why do ye ride with me, do ye even know where I'm bound?"

"I'd like to think yer headed for South Hamtun, and then take a ship to Herosfloth where Sir Renier waits, and then ride to Chaumont-sur-epte where we will find King Henry," Petrus said with a laugh.

"How do yer know this?"

Petrus was still laughing. "Odo, do yer think Thomas Roundtree volunteered the information to ye from the goodness of his heart?

Odo's mouth fell open. "I did."

The reeve finally stopped his cackling. "Sir Hyde said he or Sir Gweir couldn't and wouldn't petition the king. It didn't mean that ye couldn't. Sir Gweir was concerned that if ye decided to go to Frankia alone, then ye would likely come a foul of brigands or someone and either be killed or never return. He made sure Sir Renier planted a seed then Thomas gave ye the details. Going to Frankia had to be yer decision. Sir Gweir decided I should go with ye – alone, ye wouldn't survive."

"Does Charlotte know?"

"Nay, although by now Steward Alard would've told her. Oh, speakin' of…" The reeve fished around under his tunic, pulled out a document and handed it over.

"What this be?"

"Can yer read it?"

Odo began to read very slowly. He couldn't make out every word, but soon figured out what it was. "A warrant for a black stallion, issued by the Lord of Mellester Manor. Why?"

"I sometimes wonder how ye even manage t' wake in the morn." The reeve shook his head in mock disgust. "How many people who aren't nobles ride coursers? Not many, eh? If someone challenges you and asks where yer got the horse, what will yer say? They could call ye a thief. Then what will ye do? Now ye can prove ye own him."

Odo felt like a half-wit, he hadn't thought of that.

"And yer can thank Steward Alard for that when we return."

Odo thought a moment longer. "Then Sir Renier knows we are coming?"

"Aye, he does. He was the one who came up with the notion, yer can thank him as well," said Reeve Petrus grumpily. "At least ye had the sense to leave yer bow behind." He began to laugh, the vivid memory of Odo's archery lesson still a source of mirth. "Is alright Odo, I had a wee wager on ye, but I lost. I had to buy Thomas a tankard of mead." He wiped his eyes. "I thought yer would at least hit the byre." He continued to laugh as he struggled upright and with the aid of his staff, limped to his horse.

Petrus was still laughing hysterically when both men rode away. "Yer should've seen yer face when that arrow flopped onto the ground!" shouted the reeve. Tears ran down his cheeks and blew away in the wind as they cantered onwards.

Odo joined in. It felt good to laugh. It registered on him, as he turned to look at the reeve, he was also risking his life for him.

They didn't push the horses too hard, and it was late afternoon when the two weary, saddle-sore men entered the small market town of Dorn-Gweir[16]. Odo's head swivelled from side to side as he took in the unusual sights and spectacle of a new town. They found an Inn near the river that the reeve said was affordable and took both horses to the stable at the rear of the building. The stable was more of a lean-to constructed of earthen walls with a thatched roof. The Inn wasn't much different and a wooden fence and rickety gate offered security. The ostler was delighted when his two new guests chose to groom their own horses and he prepared a bucket of feed and water.

Odo gave him a coin and warned him not to get close to the horses. The ostler, a seasoned horseman understood and promised to keep a watchful

---

16 Dorchester

eye on them. Odo wasn't concerned that anyone would steal his horse, Amica could take care of himself. He just didn't want to see anyone hurt.

Inside, they ordered mead and the reeve asked about lodgings for the night. With tankard in hand, Odo surveyed the dark and gloomy interior of the Inn. Filthy rushes covered the floor and hadn't been replaced for some time. A few solitary men drank alone at roughly-hewn wooden tables while a couple of groups of men were in noisy debate. One or two enterprising women patrolled the room and cast a rapacious eye at the newest patrons. Sadly for them, their lusty advances went ignored. Near them sat another small group of three men, one of whom was distinctly eyeing Odo. He peeled away from his friends and casually walked over.

"Hail, friend," he said clapping Odo on the back.

The man's breath was foul. "Greetings," Odo replied warily, turning his head away.

"Ain't seen yer here b'fore."

"Aye, we're just here for lodging." Odo noticed the man's friends were watching.

"Goin' north are ye?"

"Aye." Odo was becoming more uncomfortable as the man edged closer.

One of the man's friends at the table cursed, and the other man stood quickly and yelled back at him. All heads swivelled to face the drama. With seasoned acuity, the women backed away to a safer vantage point and watched dispassionately.

"Friggin' bammers," said the man as he watched his two friends begin pushing each other. He clapped Odo on the back again and stepped away only to freeze. Reeve Petrus held his wrist in a vice grip.

"Perhaps yer care to give m' friend his purse back," suggested the reeve, his voice low and threatening.

Odo looked down and saw the man held his purse, he'd cut the leather thong that tied his purse to his belt. He never felt a thing.

The thief licked his lips trying to decide what to do.

The reeve squeezed harder.

"Ow! Let me go of me hand!" he yelled.

All commotion in the Inn stopped. The thief's friends looked at each other; suddenly their rehearsed argument held no importance. The women shifted their gaze to a new direction, their blank stares replaced with curiosity.

"Give it back, or I will take it," commanded the reeve. His eyes, mere slits, bored into the thief.

Odo had never seen the reeve appear so intimidating.

Eager for help, the thief turned to his companions. They began to weave between the tables and head towards them. Everyone saw them reach under their tunics and pull long daggers, their intent obvious. People scattered out of their way.

"Hey, knock it off, the lot of ye!" yelled the innkeeper and reached for a club.

The reeve applied more pressure to the wrist, twisting it brutally and pulling the thief's arm that still tightly clutched the stolen purse, upwards. With his other hand, he reached for the thief's elbow, seized the joint, and squeezed. In reflex to pressure from the reeve's grip, the hand opened automatically, and the reeve caught the heavy purse as it fell. The thief howled in pain clutching his elbow as the reeve swung in his seat and stood to face the two men quickly approaching.

Odo slid away from the stool but had nowhere to go except outside through the nearest door towards the stable. The reeve held his ground and cleverly positioned himself so that his staff could swing easily between the tables.

Realising he was exposed, Odo backed away towards the door as the reeve's staff collided with the first man's stomach.

Regaining confidence, the thief turned to Odo and snarled. He took a step closer and with his good arm pulled a dagger from his belt, his sore arm and elbow cradled protectively against his chest.

Reeve Petrus was effectively trapped. Although he'd dealt a painful blow to one man, the other was more circumspect and wisely kept his distance and blocked the reeve's exit as he waited for his friend to recover from the strike to his stomach. The Innkeeper leaned over the counter and took a wild swing with his club at one man and missed.

Seeing Odo was unarmed, the thief approached, his knife scything wildly through the air. Odo kicked the door open and rushed outside with the thief following closely behind.

"Hand over the rest o' yer coin," he hissed.

The ostler was nowhere to be seen.

Odo didn't reply and faced him, backing slowly away from the robber towards Amica. He would pass close to the rear of his horse. He hoped the thief would follow.

"Amica," Odo said quietly.

Amica was tied to a rail and was eating noisily from a wooden feed box. When he heard Odo's voice, his ears twitched. He looked up briefly and continued eating. Odo edged closer, then passed, brushing by his rear, the thief followed paying no attention to the black stallion.

The thief saw he had his victim backed into a corner of the stable. "I knows ye got another purse, gimme!" He held his hand out.

Amica responded quickly, his timing perfect. His left rear leg lifted slightly and he waited for the thief to take another step closer. He didn't have to wait long. The thief took another step towards Odo who was now backed against the stable wall. Amica kicked. His leg shot out with incredible force, his hoof striking the thief high on the thigh. It was a mighty kick delivered by a powerful horse. The thief immediately dropped his knife to clutch his leg and screamed. His leg useless and unable to bear any weight gave out and he collapsed. He was lucky that he fell away from the horse or he would have been kicked again.

Odo ran towards him and picked up the dropped knife.

Reeve Petrus stepped out from the Inn. "What's all the noise 'bout?" He saw Odo standing above the injured thief and laughed. "Tell me, lad, did ye do that?"

Odo glowered at the reeve.

At the Innkeeper's urging, a few patrons followed the reeve outside and picked up the thief, his appeals for compassion falling on deaf ears as he was tossed onto the street to join his two companions.

Odo and the reeve returned inside to receive a stern warning from the innkeeper. "I'll not be havin' anymore shenanigans from the likes of ye." He glared at both Odo and the reeve. "I know ye didn't start it but no more, and I don't care if ye'd be the king hisself, no trouble!"

"Aye, ye'll get no bother from us, as long as yer mead is fresh," smiled the reeve in response.

CHAPTER THIRTY-FIVE

The dry, rutted road cleaved a winding path through low hills, meandering streams and industrious villages. Sometimes they crossed old bridges built from stone in a forgotten era, at less frequent times the road was uniform and they were able to canter for a while and the countryside passed in a blur. It was all new to Odo; he had never been this far away from home and with each passing mile he missed Charlotte more and more.

The weather was warm and favourable, and at every opportunity Reeve Petrus lamented the fact that he wasn't supervising the harvest and felt derelict in his duties. As before, the two mounted riders attracted attention but not the friendly or welcoming kind. Used to the disparaging looks from fearful peasants and suspicious nobles they made good progress and with lengthening late afternoon shadows, saw the seaside town of South Hamtun glimmer in the distance.

"I knows a place we can find a bed," said the reeve once they arrived at the outskirts and slowed to a walk, "Just keep yer purse inside yer tunic."

Odo needed no prompting, having already suffered at the reeve's unending repartee of good-natured taunts for most of the day.

They rode through busy streets admiring the unfamiliarity of it all. Ahead Odo saw the tall spire of a building and pointed it out to the reeve.

"Saint Mary's Church."

"Seems that most buildings here are big," observed Odo.

"Aye, a tad different than Mellester."

As they approached the shore, Odo noticed many smaller boats beached a considerable distance from the ocean. "Why are they all up here? Is something wrong, does a storm approach?"

"Is the tide. Here in South Hamtun the tides are very high. That's why ships are on the river."

Odo nodded as if he understood.

Eventually they veered onto a small street and into a fenced yard and another lean–to stable. They climbed stiffly down from their horses and stretched. An ostler eagerly approached, then stopped when he saw both coursers. He looked at both weary travellers and waited.

Reeve Petrus pointed to empty stalls, "Over there?"

"Aye, that'll be fine," the ostler replied.

"Don't get too close to their legs," warned the reeve.

The ostler nodded and went to fill the feed bins and add fresh water as Odo and the reeve tended to their animals.

"Soon as we see the innkeeper bout a room, we'll wander down and find us a cog on the river."

"Cog?" questioned Odo.

"Aye, a ship that'll take us and the horses."

The first two ships they enquired at were full and had no space available. Someone suggested to the reeve that a newly arrived Frisian cog may have room and to ask for its master, a man named Hilke. For Odo, he didn't know where to look, the chaos, the newness of it all was compelling. He followed a step or two behind as they walked along the river, staring at the moored vessels, the hustle and bustle of frantic activity and men offloading and loading merchandise. It seemed shambolic.

It didn't take long to find the Frisian ship. A man stood on the dock yelling and hurling obscenities as his crew unloaded the squat vessel. The reeve approached confidently.

"I'm lookin' for Hilke, do ye know where I can find him?"

The man removed a clay pipe from his mouth, and with its stem scratched beneath his hat. "I am Hilke." He eyed the reeve carefully.

"My friend and I require passage to Herosfloth along with two horses."

The master nodded, then turned his attention briefly at Odo. "Where are yer horses?" His accent was thick but understandable.

"Stabled, close by."

The master removed his hat and wiped his brow with his sleeve, his eyes constantly roaming over his ship, the dock and the men who scrambled about. "Ye can pay?

"Aye, we can," assured the reeve. He shook a bulging purse.

"We will sail with the morn tide, be here early, as the sun rises," informed the master. "Pay me then."

"In the morn," repeated the reeve, cementing the arrangement.

Odo arranged for Daniel to sleep at his home during his absence, and every evening on completion of her day's work at the Cheese Shoppe, Charlotte would double check with him that everything was in order. She was returning after visiting Daniel and was about to enter her family home through the rear doorway when she heard the muted, nasal voice of Priest Durwin coming from inside. Rather than impolitely intrude, she paused briefly at the door to listen.

"…who, while keeping the outward appearance of Christian religion, she devises or follows false opinions or even for a desire for approval, earthly reward, or worldly pleasures, I cannot say what exactly–"

"How can ye say that?" appealed Cheesemaker Gerald, his voice rising in stress. "Is untrue. Charlotte is a devout Christian and has never spoken ill of the Church."

Priest Durwin sat stiffly in a chair with his hands clasped in his lap. He tried very hard to look sympathetic and shook his head slowly. "Heresy is a contamination, an infection from which true believers have to protect themselves."

Someone gasped. The priest turned to the curtain which separated the sleeping area from where he sat. He knew the Cheesemaker's woman, Agnes, and daughter were there along with their baby.

"T'was Oswald who taught her words, the Latin and the English. He did this so she could help him, and his Church," pleaded Gerald.

"My heart goes out to ye, Cheesemaker Gerald, but canon law, uh, the Church is very clear."

"Nay, nay, ye are mistaken!" Gerald rose from his chair and began pacing.

Charlotte covered her mouth with her hand as she listened in total disbelief from behind the door.

Gerald halted and faced the priest. "Clear on what, do tell?"

"Aye, well ye see, there we have little choice." Priest Durwin tried again to look compassionate.

"What choice, speak?"

"Excommunication."

Both men heard the stifled cry coming from behind the curtain.

"Nay, nay! This cannot be."

"I am but a mere priest and have little say in these matters, I can only do my best to bring ye and yer family closer to God and the Church."

Charlotte almost fell and leaned against the wall for support.

"How's about a donation, then?" asked Gerald.

Priest Durwin tried hard to prevent his smile from showing. "A benefaction? The Church always looks kindly on those who wish to admit fault and seek a pious path to redemption, after all we are all sinners. But heresy is not a trivial charge, Cheesemaker Gerald."

Gerald slumped into his chair. "Then what else can I do to satisfy ye?"

"It is not me who ye seek to please as I am but a poor priest in God's service. It is the will of God and through the Church he speaks." Priest Durwin scratched his chin as if giving the matter thought. "There, uh, might be a way."

Gerald looked up with hope.

"If Charlotte were to enter a convent… Aye, that may be enough along with a moderate bequest, of course."

"A nun! Are ye saying Charlotte enter a convent and become a nun?" Gerald asked incredulously.

Charlotte slid to the floor and buried her face in her hands.

"Do you suggest a convent is not a righteous path for salvation?" Durwin raised his eyebrows. He heard the sound of weeping come from behind the curtain and correctly assumed it was the cheesemaker's wife, Agnes.

"Nay, nay, I misspoke. As a father and an honest proprietor, Charlotte is important to my business. To lose a hard worker would not sit well for my business or for my customers."

"God is aware of the sacrifices we all make," smiled the priest.

"And ye, I mean the Church, wishes for Charlotte to become a nun because the priest, Oswald taught her to read words?"

Priest Durwin found no difficulty in looking disgusted. He nodded with a sour look. "Exeter Nunnery would be a suitable place."

Charlotte silently mouthed Ex-et-er Nun-nery?

"Why is my child and my family made to suffer because of what a priest, who is now dead, taught her?"

Priest Durwin thought carefully for a suitable response.

"She has done no wrong!" Cheesemaker Gerald's voice rose in anger. "I suggest ye spend your time looking fer a way to keep her here, not farm her out to a convent!"

"It is the will of the Church." Priest Durwin eased his lanky frame upright. "I must bid ye farewell, it is late." He walked to the door. "At the month's end, I will take her to the convent." He let himself out as Cheesemaker Gerald stood staring into the fire shaking his head.

Priest Durwin Babcock was quite pleased with himself and thought his visit with the cheesemaker went quite well. He walked back to the priory eminently happy.

"I think we should eat lamb tomorrow, Grace."

"But it isn't Sunday, master," she replied.

"And we need some better wine."

"Have ye cause to celebrate?" asked Grace, somewhat confused.

Priest Durwin turned from the scroll he was reading and looked at her. "Aye, in a manner of speaking, I do. Appears as though Cheesemaker Gerald's daughter will enter a convent."

She looked shocked. "Oh, my goodness! But master, why would she do that?" she asked. "And of poor Odo, does he know of this?"

"This is no business of the herdsman, is a Church affair. I expect you'll be wanting coin for the food?"

"I, I don't understand. Why would Charlotte go to a convent?"

"It isn't of concern of ye, Grace." The priest removed a heavy box from a chest and after unlocking it with the key he kept around his neck, carefully fished out some coins and handed a few to Grace and for good measure put a few more in his own purse.

"That's Oswald's roof box! That coin is for the new roof!" She was visibly upset and her voice had risen.

"I suggest ye keep yer mind on matters of a housekeeper and not let it wander," snapped Priest Durwin.

"Ye can't go usin' that coin for other things. Those coins are from the good folk of Mellester who gave in order to see a new roof for their church," she bit back.

"I will not have ye talk to me like a wench. Show some respect, woman!" He raised his arm as if to strike her, but she held her ground and stared unflinchingly back at him.

"Why is Charlotte going to a convent?" she repeated. Her blood was boiling.

"Get out, leave me," snapped the priest.

As morning broke over Mellester Manor a dark cloud seemed to hang over Cheeseman Gerald's Shoppe. Charlotte and her mother, Agnes cried until their eyes were red, and Gerald was out back stomping around in a fury. Customers weren't treated to the normal cheery banter and instead hurriedly departed the shoppe before harsh words were spoken or feelings bruised.

Grace set out early for the market to purchase food for the priest and decided to visit Charlotte first.

"Mornin' Mother Grace," greeted Charlotte politely with a forced smile.

Grace chewed her lip thoughtfully and looked at the young woman. She leaned forward and spoke quietly. "He told me, he did. Last evening. What happened, Charlotte?"

Charlotte dabbed at her eyes with her apron and shook her head. She'd known Grace her entire life, as long as she'd known Oswald. They'd never been close, the age difference was too great, and Grace, much like Oswald, had always been supportive but never friendly. She was surprised at the change in demeanour.

"I don't know." It was too much for Charlotte and she began to weep again.

"Go inside, dear," said Agnes. She looked at Grace and inclined her head, suggesting Grace go with her.

Once inside their home, Charlotte broke down and wept uncontrollably. Grace did her best to comfort her.

"I'm to go to Exeter Nunnery," she finally said between sobs. "If I don't, then I will be excommunicated."

Grace looked horrified. "What fer? What have yer done, child?"

"Priest Durwin says it's because Oswald taught me to read."

Grace looked up, her expression hardened.

CHAPTER THIRTY-SIX

Odo retched again, his discomfort no longer providing amusement to Reeve Petrus or to the crew of the Frisian cog when they were aboard. The poor young man had spent most of the journey to Herosfloth hanging over the side of the boat and repeatedly emptied his stomach until there was nothing left. The reeve insisted Odo drink water and that like everything else he'd eaten or drank, found its way into the Narrow Sea[17] soon after.

Both men stood in Herosfloth at the dock with their horses. While the voyage for Odo had been traumatic, the reeve and the horses seemed no worse for wear having made the journey by boat numerous times.

"I think I feel less poorly," Odo gasped. He wiped his mouth with his sleeve and accepted the water the reeve offered.

The reeve was looking about. "We should probably find some food," he suggested without thinking.

Odo groaned, then turned away and retched again.

This time the reeve did grin. "But we do need to find Sir Renier, and better sooner than later, eh?"

It was Sir Renier who found them, or rather his sergeant who was sent by the knight to keep watch for newly arrived boats. In consideration of Odo's state of health, it was prudently decided that they would leave for Chaumont-Sur-Epte the following morning. The reeve rented a room at

17   *Narrow Sea – English Channel*

an inn, and after assuring the horses were in good hands, Odo retired to recover.

"How far is it to where the king is, Milord?" asked Odo.

Sir Renier was smiling. After hearing of Odo's first ocean voyage and the suffering he endured, he looked to be in remarkable condition this early morn. The knight put it down to youthful vigour. "Is an easy two-day ride, not far."

Odo looked pensive.

"Somethings wrong?" enquired the knight.

"I want to thank ye for helping me Sir Renier. I, uh, am beholden to ye."

"Is nothing, and there is more to this than just yer ownership of that land. Sir Gweir and Sir Hyde wish that ye keep title, they trust ye, Odo, and know that the Falls Ende mill will fail if the Church takes title on yer land. It was convenient that I had to come here to see the king at this time, *oui*?" He patted Odo on the back and prepared to mount his courser.

The small group left the confines of Herosfloth and began their road journey through Normandy. Sir Renier was accompanied by his sergeant, Thomas Roundtree, the same man who'd given Odo his first archery lesson, and a squire.

Odo noticed he was the only one not armed. Sir Renier wore a full-length suit of chainmail with a plain surcoat worn over the top. A nasal helmet was attached to the saddle and easily accessible if needed, while greaves protected his legs and even his courser wore some barding. Thomas Roundtree was dressed in a similar fashion and also carried a broadsword. In addition, a Welsh longbow was affixed to his saddle, not that dissimilar to the one he now owned. He grimaced at the memory of his recent attempt at using it. Reeve Petrus, as usual, had his staff strapped to his horse and his broadsword swung from his hip. The squire, Steven, a quiet and very serious youth, was also armed with a shorter sword but wore no armour. He led a sturdy hackney packhorse and Sir Renier's war-horse, a large grey destrier. Odo couldn't take his eyes from the massive beast. He didn't stand any taller than Amica, but the horse had a much broader chest and more powerful legs. The grey wore a decorative coat emblazoned with the St George Cross and the de Pierrepont coat of arms.

As the procession headed out, Sir Renier took the lead with Thomas riding on his left side. Behind, rode the reeve and Odo, and lastly, Squire Steven with the two horses trailing behind.

"Why is everyone armed and wearing armour?" Odo asked Reeve Petrus soon as he had opportunity.

"King Louis of Frankia and King Henry aren't seeing eye-to-eye. Louis has attacked places in Normandy that are under King Henry's rule, so there are some angry Franks runnin' 'bout the countryside here."

"Should we be fearful?" asked Odo.

"Aye, that we should, lad," he replied. "Keep yer eyes open."

They rode at a moderate pace heading east and loosely followed the beautiful Seine River. Herosfloth was a long way behind when Sergeant Thomas issued a warning yell. Sir Renier pulled to a stop and twisted in his saddle to look.

From behind, Odo could see a group of horsemen cantering towards them – he tensed.

"King Henry's men!" shouted Sir Renier.

"Ye can relax Odo, nothing to fear," advised the reeve.

As the horsemen drew near, the standard bearing a white background with a red cross of St. George was easily visible. Reeve Petrus explained to Odo that the standard indicated the men who rode with the flag were probably Englishmen, or Franks, most likely from Normandy, who swore fealty to King Henry.

The approaching men rode in a two-abreast column led by four knights and followed by four sergeants. The column split, encircling Sir Renier's small group.

The leader of the group offered a friendly greeting to Sir Renier; it was obvious they knew each other. Odo couldn't understand what was being said as they spoke in unfamiliar French.

As the two knights conversed amicably, Odo saw the remaining knights giving him and the reeve careful scrutiny. A couple of knights pointed to the reeve's staff and laughed.

"It seems the standard bearer has lost Sir Renier's pennant," commented one as he pointed to the reeve's staff with a gauntleted hand. They broke down in laughter at the reeve's expense.

A smile played across the reeve's face but he held his tongue.

"What have we here, two peasants riding stolen horses with Sir Renier?" gibed a knight. "And with a broadsword too, eh, careful ye not injure yerself."

"Perhaps they will sow crops for King Henry after they have conquered King Louis's lands?" suggested the third knight.

Sir Renier looked over his shoulder and gave them a caustic look.

The leader of the group was busy giving Sir Renier directions and ignored the taunts by the men under his command.

"Why do ye grace Sir Renier with yer presence?" one knight asked Odo.

Odo looked in the other direction and feigned disinterest.

"Have ye lost yer tongue? Answer a knight when spoken too, show respect!" the knight bellowed.

Odo slowly turned to face the knight who spoke and held his arrogant stare. "I ride with Sir Renier at his invitation."

Reeve Petrus coughed. Odo's reply wasn't what he expected.

The knight shifted his attention to the reeve. "Have you something to add? Care to tell why Sir Renier is blessed with yer company?"

"Aye, I can," stated the reeve. His smile vanished. "It is because of my wit, charm and dashing good looks that I am able to provide Sir Renier with the finest French women."

Sergeant Thomas couldn't hold back and grinned, trying to cover his mouth with his hand.

"I see ye may have some hardship with woman yerself and probably miss their warmth and touch in yer bed," added the reeve.

"Petrus!" warned Sir Renier.

All heads turned to Sir Renier and Odo saw the slight twitching of his mouth.

"We must continue, *adieu, chevaliers*!" With a wave Sir Renier spurred his horse and quickly rode off.

The knights glowered as the reeve rode past. Within a short time, the small company of knights overtook them, again their column split as men rode either side and galloped ahead into the distance.

Once they were out of sight, Sir Renier pulled his horse to a stop. "I will have ye know, Petrus, I haves no difficulty in inviting *dames* to my bed!" Without waiting for a response, he rode off to the guttural sound of the reeve's easy laughter.

The afternoon was uneventful, and Odo enjoyed viewing the ever-changing countryside and the beautiful Seine from high atop Amica. His courser wasn't difficult to control, wasn't skittish, and seemed very happy with his new master and so the riding was pleasant.

It was late afternoon, not long after they'd stopped to water and rest the horses, when they first encountered trouble. Again, it was the sharp eyes of Sergeant Thomas who saw a group of distant riders approach, only this time they came from ahead, and veered from their path to intersect them.

A small, tattered pennant of King Louis flew from the group.

"Looks like they're spoiling for a skirmish," volunteered Reeve Petrus as he swivelled his head to ensure more French knights weren't coming from behind. His face was grim.

They were outnumbered by armed enemy knights and there was nowhere to run or hide. Sir Renier knew that aggression and confidence on his part could aid and cause their adversaries some measure of doubt. Immediately, he unclasped his nasal helmet and affixed it to his head and gave a curt order to Squire Steven to lead the destrier and packhorse towards a tree and relative safety a short distance away. Odo required no urging and quickly followed the squire.

Reeve Petrus formed up on Sir Renier's right, and Sergeant Thomas remained in position on his master's left. Being right-handed, Sir Renier's vulnerable side while being astride a horse in battle was his left side. To attack an enemy approaching from his left, he would have to lean and twist across his horse to strike with a sword or to defend himself. In this formation, it was the expected duty of the sergeant to protect the weaker side of his master.

All three men had their swords drawn and in a controlled canter bore down on the approaching group.

From their livery, Sir Renier confirmed there were three French knights, accompanied by two sergeants, all feal to King Louis. It didn't take a sage to realise five against three weren't good odds.

The quickly moving French knights spread out slightly and their sergeants followed a short distance behind. Their intent was obvious; they intended to meet in battle with the Englishmen.

As the two small forces advanced towards each other, Sir Renier automatically searched for weakness. It wasn't difficult to see a splash of crimson across one knight's chest and he noticed both sergeants were also slightly wounded. Although the Frenchmen appeared to have only minor wounds, he felt the odds improved somewhat. Because of the blood, he assumed they already fought earlier and hoped they were tired.

He quickly indicated to Sergeant Thomas to engage the wounded knight on the left, then continue through to the wounded sergeants. He hoped the two French sergeants who trailed would flee and Thomas could quickly return and focus on the injured knight. He instructed the reeve to attack the French knight on the right while he contended with the knight commander in the centre.

Odo and Squire Steven remained mounted and watched silently as both groups met in a clash of whirling steel. Sir Renier was a master, his sword flashed and arced in the late afternoon sun and yet every stroke was countered and parried expertly by the French knight.

Meanwhile, Thomas Roundtree slashed and hacked his way past the injured knight and with a primal scream, bore down on the two sergeants. As Sir Renier correctly guessed, they had no appetite for a fight and decided to turn and trot away before the frenzied English sergeant could approach. Thomas quickly turned his courser and sought the wounded knight who was about to join the attack on Sir Renier from his vulnerable left side.

Reeve Petrus was no knight; he'd been trained for many years as a sergeant and about to take his oath of fealty to become a knight when he'd been savagely kicked by a horse. As far as swordsmanship is concerned, Petrus had extraordinary skills, but fighting on horseback, he was seriously disadvantaged. As the French knight and the reeve met, their swords clanged and they slashed and hacked at each other. Their horses, shoulder to shoulder, collided and jostled while their masters fought for their lives. They circled each other probing for weakness or advantage, and it didn't take the French knight long to realise the Englishman had no strength in his left leg. With no leg power the reeve could block, but he found it difficult to attack with any results when his opponent was on his right. The reeve was unable to push down on the stirrup and obtain any leverage with his damaged leg. The French knight sought to profit from his opponent's failings and was merciless as he continued his onslaught on the reeve's right side.

The two injured French sergeants regained their courage and decided to enter the fray just as Thomas slipped his sword past the defences of the wounded knight and drove his point through a gap in his torn chainmail and into his upper chest. The knight fell from his horse with a cry. Without pause Thomas turned his attention back to the sergeants and began to earnestly chase them down.

It was a frightful experience for Odo to watch men fighting in battle amongst the frenzy and noise of clashing steel. Sir Renier was fighting valiantly, but his opponent was equally skilled. Each knight met the other, blow for blow.

Odo could see the reeve was beginning to struggle, he was tiring and the younger, agile Frenchman continued to take advantage of the reeve's weak leg. Seeing an opening in the reeve's defences, the Frenchman suddenly lunged forward and slashed at the reeve's neck. Petrus didn't expect the move and was a little slow to defend it, his feeble leg causing him some difficulty. He instinctively brought his sword up to deflect the blow. At the last moment the knight changed his swing and his broadsword glanced off the reeve's shoulder. Wounded and temporarily stunned, Petrus slumped in the saddle. His courser stepped past the knight and spun agilely to face the Frenchman again.

The French knight knew he had the advantage and was determined to quickly end the fight with the Englishman; he turned his horse to face him. What he didn't expect was to see a staff appear in the weakened Englishman's hands.

Separated by only a horse length, Reeve Petrus squeezed the flanks on his courser and it shot forward. With his staff extended, its end struck the knight centre chest, much like a lance. The blow caught the knight unprepared. In pain and winded, he fell from the saddle onto the ground.

The Reeve quickly pulled to a stop and in his unorthodox style, lifted his right, off-side leg, swung it forward over the saddle's pommel and slid from his horse. In a fluid, practiced move, he dropped the staff, unsheathed his sword and in the preferred familiarity of fighting on his feet, adopted his peculiar upright stance. Before the knight could defend himself, the reeve's blade struck him savagely in an unprotected area near his armpit. The French knight toppled backwards in a gush of blood. Reeve Petrus sank to the ground breathing heavily and bleeding. He was thankful and fortunate to be alive.

Odo saw that Sergeant Thomas was in a fight for his life with one of the French sergeants.

Seeing his master was beginning to tire and struggle, the other remaining French sergeant headed back to the fight to come to his support, it would be two against one. Sir Renier was in danger. Odo bristled at the thought and Reeve Petrus was hurt and too far away to assist him.

Without thinking, Odo leaned forward and Amica surged away, his high step in marked contrast to the other coursers. Only Reeve Petrus saw the powerful black horse, with Odo lying flat across his neck, barrelling down towards the last two remaining knights still in combat. Unable to see the approaching French sergeant, the reeve watched in stunned silence, confused by Odo's reckless behaviour.

Sir Renier was beginning to feel confident. Though his opponent was skilled and determined, he knew he would best him soon. The other knight was flagging, and his strikes and blows were slower and struck with less skill and force. Sir Renier sensed victory.

"Behind!" shouted Reeve Petrus in warning as he finally saw the quickly moving French sergeant.

With sword raised, the French sergeant advanced on Sir Renier from his blind vulnerable side where he could strike a fatal blow. He knew if he failed, his master would die.

From his peripheral vision, Sir Renier saw the flash of steel from the French sergeant and knew his life was over. There was nothing he could do to defend himself.

The French sergeant never saw the mighty black courser.

Once Odo guided Amica onto a converging path, the horse instinctively knew what to do. Amica's chest impacted against the shoulder of the slightly smaller French horse that was in full stride and knocked it clean off its feet. Both the Frenchman and horse went flying. While the French horse awkwardly regained its feet and shook itself, its rider landed clumsily in a heap and didn't move. Unhurt, the French steed trotted away.

The last remaining French knight, distracted by what he saw, fleetingly let his guard down. It was enough for Sir Renier, and he slashed downwards, driving his sword through the chainmail and deep into the knight's abdomen. The knight dropped his sword and slumped forward. With one hand he gallantly remained on his horse by holding on to the saddle's high pommel, and with the other, clasped his stomach as his horse walked away.

Odo pulled Amica to a stop. His own heart thundered in his chest. He saw the last remaining French sergeant turn tail and gallop away and was relieved to see Sergeant Thomas unharmed. The brief, violent battle was over, and Odo quickly headed for Reeve Petrus.

Squire Steven rode over and began to treat the reeve. Sir Renier had bandages and other basic equipment stored away on the pack horse and before long the reeve was cursing loudly as Steven began to sew the wound closed. Sergeant Thomas was already cleaning and sharpening Sir Renier's sword.

"Ye risked yer life for me. It was a foolish and brave thing yer did, Odo," said Sir Renier.

"If I hadn't, that sergeant would have killed yer."

"I too, am now in yer debt. Do yer make a habit of saving the lives of knights?"

Odo laughed, "Aye, it seems that way, Milord."

"I will not forget this. *Merci beaucoup.*" Sir Renier dipped his head in respect as the reeve unleased another tirade of profanity.

The sun was low against the distant hills when Sir Renier and his small group slowly headed towards Wellebou, on the River Seine, a short distance away. What they encountered shocked them.

CHAPTER THIRTY-SEVEN

"Papa, if I don't go, the priest will have me excommunicated. This will affect everyone in our family, no one will do business with you ever again, we'll be shunned." It was an ongoing discussion lasting two days, ever since the priest departed their home.

"I'll see the death o' him," growled Gerald as he clenched and unclenched his fists.

"I wish Odo were here," Charlotte sobbed.

Agnes stepped up and held her tightly.

"Tomorrow I will go to Sir Gweir, he may be able to help," Cheesemaker Gerald added.

"He's gone to Ridgley Manor to see Sir Hyde," Charlotte offered. "Something about the Irish that concerns the lords.

Gerald stared into the dancing flames of the fire. "When will he return, do ye know?"

Charlotte shook her head. "Nay."

"If I go to this convent, then ye and Odo can find a way to get me out." She unwrapped herself from her mother and went to her father and hugged him. "Papa, we'll find a way, don't worry."

Priest Durwin Babcock leaned back in his chair inside the priory. He placed both hands behind his head and stared at the far wall. He'd just completed the preparations for his next Mass on the subject of devotion, aptly titled *Quod devotio. Officium annuntiandi veritatem de Maria verum est de defendere Jesu Christi*[18]. This he knew would only lend support to the decision by Cheesemaker Gerald to have his daughter enter a convent and remind his parish of their devotional responsibilities.

He felt the presence of someone watching him. "What is it, woman?"

"I has a question about Charlotte?" Grace asked.

Durwin sighed and rolled his eyes.

"Why it be important to ye she enter a convent? She done ye no wrong and ye know she is betrothed to Herdsman Odo. Charlotte's a good girl–"

"Ye are talking beyond yer standing. Be good of ye to keep that in mind," he snapped.

"I'd been with Oswald for nigh on a score and the some years. I helped him when he was poorly and couldn't work. I learned a little about the Church, I did, and I knows what ye are doing ain't right."

Durwin launched himself upright from the chair and spun to face her. "How dare ye talk to me like this! Ye are nothing but a lowly wench who seeks the warmth of a fire and a bed for your hand in cooking." He pointed his finger at her face. "And to satisfy the needs of a pious cleric. Not to preach!" he spat. His cheeks reddened, and his eyes burned into her.

"What will ye do about the church roof? Buy more wine and fine food, or see the tailor for new vestments with the roof coin? Will ye despoil this church just like ye robbed Odo Read of a wife?"

Grace didn't cower or back away. She'd devoted a good portion of her adult life to an honest priest who cared, no, Oswald loved his parish, she

---

18   *Devotion. Proclaiming the truth about Mary is to defend the truth about Jesus Christ.*

corrected herself. With devoutness he brought God into the lives of the people of Mellester and acted honourably. And this young upstart before her had nothing but blind ambition in his misguided sights. He distorted the tenets of the Church to line his pockets and those of Bishop Immers. She felt ashamed. She couldn't walk away from this ungodly man. There was nowhere to go but in Oswald's memory she wouldn't back down.

Priest Durwin looked at the face of his hearth wife and saw open defiance – he felt revulsion. He raised his hand and struck her firmly.

Grace felt the stinging blow and fought to remain standing. Her eyes watered but she held his gaze.

He struck her again. This time she fell to her knees and maintained eye contact.

In disgust Priest Durwin Babcock walked away.

Sir Renier raised his hand and his small group stopped. Then, one by one each man rode up and paused beside the knight. In a feeding frenzy flies buzzed relentlessly and fed on the corpses of both French and English knights that littered the ground. Pools of congealing blood lay beneath bodies and snaked in rivulets into the long and dry grasses of the French countryside. One horse was dead, all the others were nowhere to be seen.

Sergeant Thomas, ever vigilant, moved a step or two further and pointed. "Look, one lives!"

Lying propped against the side of a ditch a knight barely breathed. The only indication he lived was the shallow rise of his chest and the irregular blinking of his eyes. Sir Renier spurred his horse and rode towards the fatally wounded knight. He dismounted and bent down and recognised the man immediately. "These are the men we spoke to earlier!" he yelled over his shoulder.

"Who did this?" Odo asked in a whisper.

"I'd say it was that miserable lot that fought us b'fore," replied the reeve in a hoarse whisper.

Thomas dismounted and handed the reins of his horse to the squire and walked from corpse to corpse. All but one had perished in battle. "Seven Englishmen dead and only one lives," he told Sir Renier. "Three French knights and four sergeants were killed."

Sir Renier tried to communicate to the injured knight, but he couldn't respond. Already his skin was turning blue and he took short, rasping gurgling breaths, an indication he may have suffered a punctured lung. He clasped the fallen knight's hand, lowered his head and prayed for his brother in arms.

The English knight gave a final, long drawn out breath and lay still. His life was over. Sir Renier stood and crossed himself. "We will bury these *vaillant* men in two graves. One here, one there." He pointed to where he wanted them dug.

Squire Steven retrieved two spades from the packhorse and as dusk began to approach he and Thomas dug into the hard-packed earth. Odo dragged the bodies to each grave while Sir Renier began to collect fallen weapons. The reeve, with his injured shoulder tried to help as best he could but he was just in the way.

Both the French and English would be buried honourably in their own graves and each with their own weapons. No one spoke unnecessarily, they worked silently, lost to the reminder that life was temporary and ephemeral, and cruelly reminded that death awaited them at any moment.

Reeve Petrus felt a little guilt; these dead men were the same men he had verbally sparred with earlier in the day.

Odo spelled Sergeant Thomas and dug furiously; he wouldn't relinquish the spade until the grave was wide and deep enough, and then went to help Squire Steven until they were finished.

It was dark when Sir Renier offered a few words in both French and English and concluded with prayer. It was a sombre evening as five exhausted men again set out for Wellebou.

The horror Odo witnessed disturbed him. He'd never witnessed men fight with such ferocity, desperation and skill. There was a beauty in the way they fought, but there was no beauty in the way they died. Sir Renier spoke of honour, but where was the honour in dying?

A commoner had a natural fear and dislike of knights. Knights flaunted their wealth, were outspoken, and enjoyed their revelry, frequently to excess. After seeing men die in battle this afternoon he thought he understood them a little more. These were brave men who could die at any time, while a long life and death by natural causes wasn't expected. No wonder they acted as they did.

What he'd learned was that an enemy might be feared in battle, but they were respected, even in death. There was no distinction In death, they were all the same.

He remained silent and thoughtful as they slowly entered the environs of Wellebou. Beyond anything else, he felt fortunate to be alive.

CHAPTER THIRTY-EIGHT

Sir Gweir didn't anticipate any disquiet in Mellester during the absence of his reeve. Since there always seemed to be varying degrees of bother when Odo Read was near, he calculated Mellester would be without any serious disturbances while the gregarious herdsman visited Frankia.

Under the watchful eye of his old friend, Petrus, he naturally assumed the reeve would ensure Odo didn't get himself into another pickle. They could probably enjoy a pleasant journey through Normandy while Mellester basked in a productive and uneventful harvest. In the absence of Reeve Petrus Bodkin, Sir Gweir assigned his marshal to deal with the pillory and any other problems with lawbreakers and miscreants.

The sun had yet to rise when Sir Gweir's marshal, accompanied by four men-at-arms, quietly led repentant brothers Samuel and Tedric Brooker from the gaol behind Mellester's Manor and down the carriageway towards the village. A few curious onlookers met the group along the way and were soon joined by a growing crowd. The priest, Durwin, led the procession after eagerly joining the throng at the bottom of the hill.

Priest Durwin surmised that a populist approach would best serve the Church and keep himself in good stead, and with such a mindset went about invoking God's name in retribution for the heinous crimes of which the brothers were judged guilty.

There were many in Mellester who viewed the Brooker brothers with some pity. While they had kidnapped Charlotte, which nearly led to her death at the hand of Lady Constance, the brothers were genuinely remorseful and contrite. Word soon spread of their sorrowful disposition and under the circumstances, no one disagreed that the punishment was unfair. They would just ensure the brothers didn't find their time in the pillory too uncomfortable.

The priest's view was remarkably different. By using fear and the wrath of the Church, he began to turn sympathetic and curious observers into a hateful mob intent on drawing blood. As he incited more and more people into hysteria, the more nervous the marshal became. He began to feel sorry for the brothers and with kind words tried to soothe their growing panic.

A few impatient villagers began hurling clods of earth at the brothers before they'd even been secured in the pillory, some striking the men-at-arms and one well-aimed lump struck the marshal on his chest. In the darkness, it was difficult to see who the culprit was, but the marshal could hear the unmistakeable raised voice of the priest fomenting the villagers.

Charlotte and her father stood in the entranceway of their shoppe and watched the noisy procession move past them towards the pillory. She shuddered at the recent memory of seeing Odo locked in the device all day. He'd never been the same since. The scars he bore from the horrid experience weren't physical, and only now did it dawn on her the role Oswald played in restoring him to lucidity. Oswald stood resolutely and watched his son suffer unfairly and most cruelly in the pillory. He could do little to help Odo; his presence and scowl the only way he could assist. It was the quiescent love a father had for his son. How could she not have seen it earlier?

She felt her father's anger as they easily heard Priest Durwin's shrill voice reciting scripture and condemning the guilty men to an eternal, miserable life in a fiery deep pit in hell. Gerald turned away. "I'll kill the sod, I will."

Charlotte encouraged him to return to work lest someone hear his comments. She knew his ire was directed at the priest and not the Brooker brothers. In barely contained resentment he stepped across the threshold and entered the shoppe to begin his day.

Charlotte watched a little while longer and in the grey of dawn she saw Grace standing to the side watching the priest. She gave Charlotte a friendly wave.

In the growing light of a new morning the Brooker brothers were positioned in the pillory. The marshal spoke to each of them and wished them luck. It would be a long day and judging by the hostility of the onlookers, he didn't have much faith the brothers would be spared any serious injury. With his duties completed, the marshal gathered his men and stepped away as debris immediately began hurtling towards the two pilloried men.

Typically, some overripe fruit and vegetables, rotten eggs and clods of earth would be thrown. A favourite amongst the young were cow pats. However, herdsmen never let the dung remain in pastures long and so only fresh ones were available to enterprising youths. There was some risk associated with this. Firstly, they didn't want to be caught stealing valuable manure, and secondly, fresh pats were hard to throw without disintegrating and showering them with dung as much as their intended target.

With onlookers wound up in a frenzied mania, the priest stood a short distance away and observed with fascination. In fact, he was revelling in the joy he experienced at having incited the crowd. He felt no guilt nor apprehension for what he'd done. As far as he was concerned the two men had been found guilty of a crime by the Lord of the Manor and deserved to be severely punished. It was the law and unequivocally endorsed by the Church.

The first stone thrown struck the horizontal support with a clunk and bounced harmlessly away. A few people yelled in protest that someone actually dared hurl a rock. The sound of the priest's shrill laughter could be heard by everyone and further encouraged them. A short time later a second rock found its mark and hit the archer in the centre of his head. It opened a savage wound and immediately his head lulled, never to regain consciousness. While the priest continued to urge spectators into a blood lust, the archer, unnoticed by anyone, died.

Priest Durwin thought it appropriate to pray for the dead man and intoned a short but satisfactory invocation after someone brave enough approached the pillory to discover why one of the brothers hadn't moved in a quite some time. After his brief prayer, he continued to observe the torture for a while and offered inspiring words to the participants when they lost interest or needed motivation. He was feeling quite proud of himself and felt he was finally being accepted into the community.

Iedric also watched; not the villagers who he could barely see, but Priest Durwin. If he twisted his head, he could just discern the priest standing off to the side, out of harm's way, and safe from any errant missiles or splash. He heard the cajoling and laughter as his older brother suffered and died. His own simmering anger smouldered in a maelstrom of loathing and hatred and was directed silently at only one person, Mellester's priest.

Out of Priest Durwin's field of vision, Grace watched. Not because she was interested in the proceedings. Her anger was directed at the duplicity of the new priest. She remained undetected by him and kept her own simmering rage barely under control.

Not far away, Cheesemaker Gerald also fumed. Mellester's new priest wasn't endearing himself to the community as much as he believed.

Hunger was the primary reason Priest Durwin eventually left the pillory. He didn't care one way or another if the lone brother survived, and not long after witnessing the violent death of Samuel Brooker, he returned to the priory.

Durwin Babcock had plenty of time to think, and in light of the surly, disrespectful demeanour of his hearth wife, he decided she must go. He'd had enough of her.

When he delivered the cheesemaker's daughter to the convent at the end of the month, he would speak to the Mother Superior about having one of her nuns replace Grace. Priest Durwin was under no illusion that the Mother Superior would be less than enthusiastic about the idea, but when he told her of his plans to build a nunnery in Mellester he was sure she would be more than obliging. He found a number of nuns at the convent particularly pleasing to the eye and regardless of who the Mother Superior assigned to serve him, he was sure she'd be suitably subservient, respectful and obedient.

Mellester was a thriving, developing parish and was an ideal location for a nunnery. Durwin was positive that Bishop Immers would also be impressed when he learned of his plans. In addition to obtaining title on the herdsman's land, including the Falls Ende mill, Mellester Manor would provide a steady stream of revenue for the Church and undoubtedly increase its influence over the new lord.

He arrived at the priory quite elated.

It was approaching darkness when the marshal returned to the pillory and he was surprised to see Tedric, the younger brother still alive. On being released from the abhorrent device, Tedric collapsed into the accumulated filth and lay unmoving.

Quickly Grace rushed to the man and appealed to the Marshall to have his men carry Tedric to the priory. There, she would clean him, dress his numerous wounds and help him as best she could so he had the strength to eventually leave Mellester as required.

Priest Durwin was beside himself with anger when he saw the men-at-arms carry Tedric Brooker into his residence.

They'd encountered more and more of King Henry's men as the small group of horsemen approached Chaumont-sur-Epte, and for the most part they were ignored. A few small groups of knights passed them, some waved, and some just rode by, showing no interest in them at all.

Sir Renier was in surprisingly good humour, but the reeve was in agony, and understandably quiet. Sergeant Thomas was his normal dry self, and the hardworking squire was dependable to a fault. He demonstrated a natural affinity for horses and even Amica let him stand close to stroke him.

They departed Wellebou in the grey of dawn on the final stage of their journey. The weather was sunny and cool and it was a perfect day to ride. During early afternoon Sir Renier called Odo to ride alongside him while Sergeant Thomas dropped back.

He was in jovial spirits and wanted to talk. They spoke of Mellester, Falls Ende, and to Odo's surprise, even Sir Gweir, a man for whom Sir Renier had much respect and admiration. He asked about Charlotte and wanted to know about their wedding and their plans after they were married. At first Odo was a little reticent about sharing. He didn't believe nobility were interested in the mundane life of a herdsman.

"I hopes that ye will invite me to yer wedding," grinned Sir Renier as he looked over at him.

Odo was surprised, and it must have showed.

"Ye think I jest?" he laughed.

"Is just … well … but why, I am but a herdsman, why would a knight wish to come to the wedding of a commoner?" he asked.

"Ahhh, I see now," he grinned. "*Juge un homme par son coeur, pas par ses pieds.*"

Odo looked puzzled, and Sir Renier laughed again.

"Judge a man by his heart, not by his feet. And ye, Odo, should do the same." He waved a gloved finger at him.

Odo twisted to look at the knight. The knight's words resonated with him. Godwin had espoused similar thoughts.

They rode in silence, the only sound the creak of leather, the jangle of metal and the clip–clop of hooves on hard packed dirt.

Sir Renier raised a hand and pointed to their destination, a sprawling castle draped over a low hill. "Chaumont-sur-Epte is a castle that Louis of Frankia uses to store weapons," he explained. "King Henry decided to assault the castle in retaliation for Louis's encroachment and attacks on his land."

"Where is King Henry now?" Odo asked.

"*Certainement*, he is in a tent discussing strategy."

"I hope such a busy king has time to listen to me."

Sir Renier didn't reply. Privately he hoped the same.

They rode on silently, each thinking about their future.

King Henry lay siege on Chaumont-sur-Epte. Men of all descriptions wandered everywhere. Sir Renier pointed out knights, men-at-arms, sappers, engineers, archers, smithies and clerics. Each man had something to do and somewhere to be. Odo didn't know where to look; never had he seen such disorder.

Row upon row of tents sprouted from grassy fields like mushrooms, and roped pastures kept horses secured. There were stables, and sweaty blacksmiths who hammered away, their tireless clanging dissolving into the background noise of merchants, hawkers, and bards. Coarse women plied their trade and Odo thought the atmosphere was almost festive.

Sir Renier asked a lone, passing knight where he would find King Henry's stables, and the friendly knight pointed to where they should go. The group fought their way through busy streets until they reached their destination. On arriving, Sir Renier sent Squire Steven to confirm where they could stable the horses and pitch their tents.

As Sergeant Thomas and Squire Steven began pitching Sir Renier's large tent, the knight went to inform King Henry's secretary he had arrived and to arrange a suitable time when he would take his oath. Odo was told to wait and until he returned before he set out to seek an audience with the king.

CHAPTER THIRTY-NINE

Odo threaded his way through knights in shiny chainmail. Some were dirtied and bloodied and could barely walk, while others looked like they'd never seen battle and never would. The closer he came to the guarded area occupied by King Henry, the busier it became.

Messengers sprinted from tents carrying missives and orders for commanders. Others ran in the opposite direction, bringing word of developments and some of disaster. With caution, Odo approached the cluster of tents that Sir Renier said was where he would find the king.

A man-at-arms blocked his path. "Can't go in there, laddie."

"I wish an audience with King Henry and need to inform the king's secretary," stated Odo confidently using the rehearsed words Sir Renier gave him.

The man-at-arms spared Odo a casual look. "Ye do, eh?"

Men pushed past Odo and entered the compound without so much as a glance by the two men-at-arms who stood guard. "Is this not where I find him?"

"Ye have business with the king?" the guard queried.

"Aye."

The guard gave Odo further scrutiny and finally nodded his approval. "Very well." He pointed to a tent off to the side. "That is where ye need to be."

Odo nodded his thanks and slowly walked over to the tent the guard pointed to. Men of all occupations queued in a long line that snaked outside. Some held scrolls, others looked like learned book men like Steward Alard. No one spoke. He joined the line and waited patiently.

The line moved quickly and so it didn't take long before Odo stepped inside the tent. It was larger than he expected and was uncomfortably warm. Scribes sat at work benches and scratched away copying documents or writing orders while a harried clerk indicated with a flick of his fingers for Odo to step forward.

"What yer need?" he asked without looking up.

"I wish an audience with King Henry."

The clerk finally looked up and saw Odo's clothes. He frowned. "What fer?"

"I uh, I need King Henry to pass judgement and overrule the Church. They have made an unfair claim on my land," Odo said, repeating the lines he'd rehearsed.

"Ye have land?"

"Aye, I do."

"Where is this land?"

"Mellester Manor. I have this title—"

"Name?"

Odo held out the scroll for the clerk "Herdsman Odo Read. I have a document to prove—"

The clerk gave Odo another look, his distaste evident as he smirked. He didn't even look at the scroll.

"Who is Lord of Mellester Manor?"

"Sir Gweir."

"Sir Gweir?" asked the clerk.

"Aye."

The clerk chewed his lip for a moment. "Ye need to go to that tent on the right where ye'll see King Henry's coat of arms flying near the entrance.

"Thank ye."

The clerk flicked his fingers for the man behind to step forward. Odo walked outside into the cool air and immediately saw the tent the clerk spoke of. This tent had a man-at arms standing outside. He walked over and expected to be questioned or warned away, but thankfully he was ignored. Odo stepped past him and saw people standing in another smaller line. He attached himself to the end and resigned himself to wait.

The line barely moved, men shuffled their feet, inspected their fingernails and looked about. Some talked to others, and they all waited. One by one each man eventually approached a clerk and answered questions. Some men became angry and even yelled. The man before Odo was finally called to the clerk and after a few minutes the conversation became heated and then escalated. He began screaming at the clerk and then leaned over, grabbed him by the neck and tried to throttle him. The man-at-arms entered the tent, grasped the man by the collar and tossed him outside.

After order was restored, the red-faced clerk beckoned Odo with his fingers and he eagerly stepped forward.

"I hope ye will show more respect," said the clerk still suffering from the embarrassment of a public molestation. He adjusted his clothing.

Odo smiled.

"Yer want to see the king?" the clerk finally asked, feeling composed again.

"Aye, that I do."

"King Henry is a busy man, why is it yer need audience?"

"The Church has unfairly claimed title on my land."

"Is that so?" stated the clerk.

Odo repeated everything he told the previous clerk. This time he demanded to see Odo's title and he handed over the scroll that Steward Alard gave him. As the clerk unrolled the scroll, Odo pointed, "See, this how I am called, Odo Read."

"Ye know words, ye can read and write?" asked the clerk.

"Aye, a little."

The clerk grimaced and re-read the scroll. "What reason did the Church give ye for wanting yer land? Did ye not meet yer tithes?

"Oh no, I paid, I ain't indebted to anyone," Odo said eagerly, "They claimed dereliction."

The clerk rubbed his chin. "Why?"

Odo explained as quickly as possible the relationship he had with Godwin and Oswald, and the viewpoint of the Church.

"Come back on the morrow, be here early at dawn. I will keep this title."

"Nay, ye may not, is the only one I have, and what happens if ye lost or damage it?" Odo said. "Is best for me to hold it and I can show it to ye again if needed."

The clerk looked at the young man and sighed. "Aye, very well," and handed the scroll back. "On the morrow, be here early!"

"Aye, thank ye."

The clerk summoned the next man in line.

As required Odo reported to the clerk the following morning and was told to wait outside.

"We will call for ye," informed the clerk after assuring Odo carried his title scroll.

Odo waited outside in the morning gloom. As the sun rose, he moved to stand in the shade of the tent. By midday, he was under the shelter of the tent's entranceway and they had yet to call him. By late afternoon the other side of the tent offered him protection from the sun and still he'd not been summoned. Every now and then he'd stick his head inside the tent as a gentle reminder that he still waited, and with a casual flick of his hand and a frown, the clerk waved him off and he dejectedly returned outside to while away the remainder of the day. Sometimes he spoke a few words to the man-at-arms who stood outside the tent and appeared as weary as himself.

It was difficult for a young man to stand idle and do nothing for an entire day when he'd spent his entire life working six days a week from sunrise to sunset. He was bored, listless and anxious - and still no word came from the clerks. Finally, they doused their candles signalling the end of a day, and with armfuls of scrolls, and no explanation, hurriedly departed the tent.

Odo walked disconsolately back to his small campsite and found Reeve Petrus being attended to by a rather peculiar fellow.

It was Sir Renier who located the man. He was essentially a camp follower and trailed an army from battle to battle with no allegiance to any particular side. He did, however, have an extraordinary reputation for curing the injured and ill. Known only by the name Cathal, Sergeant Thomas told Odo the man was an Irish seer, a Fili[19], who was gifted at healing. Sir Renier had business to attend to, and accompanied by Squire Steven, left Sergeant Thomas to ensure the Irish seer saw to the reeve's wound and ensure trouble didn't find Odo.

Cathal's nose was presently buried in a goblet filled with the reeve's urine. He sniffed rather loudly a few times, then removed his nose and dipped his finger into the warm liquid and swirled it around before pulling it out to assiduously study it for colour and texture. In a language unfamiliar to Odo the seer muttered to himself, then slowly emptied the goblet by pouring its contents onto the fire.

The linen used to wrap the reeve's injury was carefully removed and with the goblet discarded, Cathal bent low to investigate all aspects of the sword wound that Squire Steven previously sewed together. Using firelight, he poked, prodded and mumbled in his peculiar language while the reeve resisted the temptation to push the man away.

Reeve Petrus was in pain and the injury he received looked ghastly and corrupt. Concerned for his health, and on a recommendation from an acquaintance, Sir Renier and Thomas went off earlier in search of the mysterious healer they'd heard about. They found him easily enough wandering the narrow streets of Chaumont-sur-Epte with a bulky, leather bag slung over his shoulder. For a meagre tribute, he agreed to follow the

19   *Fili. An ancient Irish seer. Thought to be enigmatic poets who foretold the future in rhyme or riddle.*

knight back to camp to look at the patient.

Finally the Irish seer stood, looked up at the stars and in his peculiar parlance uttered a few unintelligible sentences, then looked to the ground, searching for something.

The reeve caught Odo's attention and raised his eyebrows in question. Odo shrugged, he knew nothing about what the Irish Fili was doing.

At Mellester Manor, Oswald usually cared for the sick. Occasionally he called for a barber when a patient needed cutting open but over the last few years that happened less frequently as Oswald believed barbers were unrefined and brutal and frequently caused additional complications through haste and hurry. To Odo, the Fili's behaviour was vexing. With patience he studied all aspects of the wound, whereas barbers were fast and appeared efficient. In spite of the obvious and urgent need to focus on the reeve's wound, the Irishman took his time. Coming to a decision, he dove into his bag, extracted a large bowl and without a word of explanation, loped away, his robes flapping against his bony legs as he disappeared into the night. Despite the pain from his injury Reeve Petrus began to laugh, and Thomas urged the reeve to be more respectful and keep quiet lest the seer overhear.

"He'd be a wizard," whispered Thomas.

Cathal eventually returned with his precious wooden bowl full of mysterious objects. He sat on the ground near the fire, arranged his robe and began to sing. It started as monotonous whine, transformed into humming, and soon his leg pumped in time to a rather beautifully sung ballad.

At first, Odo, Thomas and the reeve looked at each other in consternation and wondered if the Irishman were suffering some kind of malaise.

Scepticism turned to curiosity as the Fili crooned. He sung in English, the words clear and understandable and told of lost love and romance. Curiosity soon gave way to wonder and everyone stopped to listen. Odo was captivated by the lilting melody and the beautiful words, predictably his thoughts turned to Charlotte.

Cathal sung of fair-headed maidens and eyes that sparkled blue. He described the touch of a woman and the moist softness of eager lips.

Before long a small crowd gathered as people came from neighbouring campsites to listen. While he sung, and seemingly oblivious to the audience he'd attracted, Cathal pulverised the items he collected with a mortar and pestle until it formed into a thick paste. Even the mechanical sound of the mortar grinding into the pestle added to the musical rhythm. Odo took a step closer to better listen and watch as the Fili pounded and ground. The ballad was enchanting and melodious, other than the rhythmic grinding and the Fili's soothing voice, not a soul dared make a sound.

Reeve Petrus laid on the ground propped against his saddle with his eyes closed. Odo could see the singing relaxed Reeve Petrus and he almost looked to be dozing.

Sadly, the song ended. Cathal eased to his feet, unconcerned at the presence of thirty or so men who stood waiting for more. A few eyes were moist. Many missed their women and families and Cathal's beautifully sung ballad tugged emotionally at their heartstrings, a cruel reminder that their king waged war on Frankia and kept them from home. Odo cleared his throat and turned away briefly.

The Fili stepped to the reeve and squatted on his haunches. After tasting the concoction and noisily smacking his lips, he seemed satisfied and began packing the paste into and around the reeve's rather savage inflamed wound. One by one, the audience quietly disappeared, they'd seen enough festering wounds to know the danger it posed to even the sturdiest of men.

The reeve's jaw was tightly clamped shut. A vein throbbed in his neck as he fought to stop from screaming at the pain caused by Cathal packing his smelly concoction over the injury.

When no more paste remained Cathal wiped his hands on his robe and spoke to his patient in a clear surprisingly light voice. "Be not alarmed," he assured, "for Mother Earth gives back as much as she takes. Worry not, you will see many, many more days before you are claimed."

Thomas handed Cathal a good length of linen and he tightly bound the reeve's shoulder, then without a word, he gathered his utensils and implements, placed them in his bag and wandered off muttering to himself.

Thomas was cleaning and polishing Sir Renier's armour in preparation for his visit to King Henry the following evening. He looked up as the seer disappeared. "He'll be back," Thomas said knowingly.

"How do ye know? It looked like he finished," asked Odo. Curious as to how the sergeant was privy to such knowledge.

"He hasn't been paid." Thomas grinned.

Odo felt foolish. "He's a strange one."

"Aye, that he is."

The reeve was already asleep.

The following morning Odo reported to the clerk, as instructed, and asked a few questions about the continued delay. The unresponsive clerk pointed to the area outside the tent and again he found himself idle.

When he left the campsite, the reeve was still sleeping and Sir Renier and the squire had not returned. Thomas wasn't concerned and explained it was a normal occurrence when visiting other knights, and frequently an evening spent socialising often turned into revelry.

Odo was worried about the reeve, and confessed his apprehension to Thomas but the optimistic sergeant suggested Odo's worry was for nought and instead should focus on his mission to see the king.

Odo didn't even know what the king looked like. He hadn't seen anyone who looked majestic or regal other than a few important looking men who shouldered their way past anxious clerks to disappear hurriedly into the profundity of protocol and leather clad tents. Resigned to wait, Odo rehearsed, over and over again how he would plead his argument to the king, and as it normally did, his mind eventually drifted to more pleasant things like his own fair-headed maiden and their future together.

When Odo arrived at the tent earlier the clerks were just beginning their day. They told him to wait, and again he found himself seated outside on dead grass resigned to another day of tedium. People came and went, and it seemed everyone had a reason to be heard by his majesty. Was their need greater than his own?

"Odo Read, from Mellester!" called the clerk. "Odo Read, from Mellester!" he repeated.

Odo stood quickly and with excitement rushed around the side of the tent and entered. The man-at-arms on guard at the entrance gave Odo a wink as he passed.

On seeing Odo enter, the clerk beckoned with his hand and Odo approached.

He looked up at Odo. "I regret to inform ye that His Majesty, King Henry is unable to hear yer plea."

Odo was dumbfounded, "But, but, why? I must see him, if I don't I will lose everything.

The clerk shook his head.

"Can ye ask again, tell him it is of utmost importance. I have the title that Steward Alard gave me," Odo appealed, waving the scroll at the clerk.

"The king's word is final." The clerk looked away. "Next!"

"Ye don't understand, I must see the king. If I don't, everything is lost!"

The clerk turned back to Odo. "You must leave."

"I can't leave, I must speak to the king!" In frustration Odo's voice rose and people began to stare. He felt a hand clamp firmly onto his arm. It was the man-at-arms.

"Be off with yer," added the clerk.

"Best to leave, Odo," suggested the guard. "If yer don't, there'll be trouble, mark my words."

Odo looked at the guard with his mouth open. He didn't know what to say or do. The guard gently pulled him away. He was shocked and helpless. There was nothing more he could do. His land, his animals would be taken away from him. He felt Charlotte slipping from his grasp. Cheesemaker Gerald always said he would allow his daughter to marry as long as he could provide for her. And now? What did he have? He had nothing.

Odo wandered around the village in a daze, his mind reeling from the king's rejection. He spoke to no one and wasn't aware of the time. It was getting dark, and he remembered that the reeve was ill. With a heavy heart he returned to camp.

CHAPTER FORTY

Priest Durwin wasn't at all happy. The man he eschewed at the pillory was now convalescing in the priory under his roof and in the care of that despicable woman, Grace. How the previous priest, Oswald, put up with her sullen moods and nettlesome attitude, he didn't know. What he did know was that he couldn't turn him away; the Church was obliged to offer care, but he wouldn't lift a finger to assist the godless, wretched creature regardless of how remorseful and repentant he appeared.

In fact, Tedric Brooker had not demonstrated any remorse or sought forgiveness since his release from the pillory. Grace nursed him, tended to his numerous wounds, and offered him care and sympathy; both unfamiliar to a man unused to the nurturing side of women. The physical pain he felt was real; he had deep wounds on his head, severe bruising and a number of broken bones in his left hand.

The pain in his head was accompanied by giddiness and a blurring of vision and it wasn't the first time he'd experienced this. His older brother, Burt, the smart one who always had answers, told him rest and sleep would remedy a hard knock to the noggin.

Tedric didn't have the intellect to self-analyse his emotions. He knew he hurt, that was a reality, and as he'd always done, he would just endure and not dwell upon it. His most consuming thought was for the priest and revenge.

He'd heard him goading the villagers when he was in the pillory. He'd wound them into a violent fervour. Even now as he recovered in the priory, the priest's laughter echoed in his head. When the rock struck his brother, he'd heard the sickening thud and immediately the priest clapped his hands in joy and haw-hawed in delight.

It rankled Priest Durwin to no end that Grace was caring for the man, but as soon as there was a sign of improvement, he would turn the outlaw out. Mellester's lord decreed that if the brothers survived, then they must leave Mellester, never to return as soon as they were able. Soon after, he would turn her out when he returned from his visit with Bishop Immers.

He needed instructions on how to deal with Mellester's lord and the tenant herdsman at the end of the month and rather than invoke the ire of the bishop by angering the lord, he would seek counsel to ensure the process was performed to the Church's satisfaction. During his absence he would also visit with a tailor and order new vestments. It was important that a priest of a developing manor appeared suitably attired; after all, if he was going to solicit the support from the Mother Superior for the new convent, then it was crucial that his parish appear prosperous.

He unlocked the chest and removed the box that contained the coin for the new church roof. For a brief moment he paused and stared at the coins and reaffirmed all the reasons why he had the right to use them. They belonged to Mellester's parish and he, Durwin Babcock, was the parish priest. Part of his responsibility was to ensure the money was spent wisely. After all, the tithes all went to the bishop, and the bishop had no clue these coins even existed so they wouldn't be missed. Taking them wasn't depriving the bishop or the Church. He nodded, smiled, and without a thought to the church roof or the villagers who gave so generously, removed a good handful of coins, and just in case, a few more. He returned the near-empty box back inside the chest and locked it.

Grace edged away from the door and returned to her washing. She'd heard the unmistakeable creak of the chest and guessed the priest was again helping himself to Oswald's roof fund. She knew where the key to the chest was hidden, and although the priest carried the key to the small box that held the coin, she could tell how much was left by giving the box a shake.

Priest Durwin stood in the open doorway and looked at his hearth wife. He thought he'd heard movement outside the door when he put the box away, but she looked busy and engrossed in her work. Perhaps he was mistaken.

Sensing the presence of someone, she turned and saw him watching her. It gave her a start.

"See to it that outlaw is gone from here by the time I return in three days."

In reflex, her hand went automatically to the bruise on her cheek. "Aye, master," she replied.

He waited a moment longer, deciding if he should tell her to leave too. Without a word he spun and returned to his room to prepare for his departure. If she left, then he'd have no one to take care of his domestic duties. It would have to wait, he reasoned.

Grace was hanging clothes out to dry. Tedric was nearby, laying in the shade of a tree where he preferred, and she felt a measure of sympathy for him. His face was still a mess and his hand gave him pain. She knew he could have left already, but she didn't want him to go. He was a sweet man and if she admitted to herself, perhaps her sympathy extended to more of an attraction for him. He wasn't unpleasant to look at. Although he had a wild streak, she felt given time, he could be tamed and turn his wanton ways into something more productive.

Tedric's thoughts couldn't have been more dissimilar. As Grace pondered salvation for the outlaw, he contemplated revenge. He watched her hanging clothes to dry on the washing line. She turned and saw him and smiled.

Odo walked morosely back to their campsite to find Reeve Petrus lying against his saddle. As Sergeant Thomas predicted, the Irish seer, Cathal, did return and was seated close by. Both men turned to him in question.

"Why so glum?" asked the reeve.

Reeve Petrus didn't look much better than the previous evening. "Where are the others?" Odo asked ignoring the reeve's question.

"Sir Renier is swearing fealty to King Henry this evening. Thomas and Steven are required to be with him.

At the mention of the king, Odo's face clouded over.

"Have ye something to say, Herdsman Odo?" asked the reeve. His normal affable smile replaced by a stern, no nonsense look.

Cathal inclined his head slightly but remained silent.

Odo sat down and faced both men. He looked down at the dead grass and fidgeted a moment before replying. "King Henry refused to see me," he finally said.

The reeve stroked his beard. "I see – this isn't good is it?"

Odo shrugged. There was nothing he could say or do that would change anything.

"What happens now, can ye appeal?" Reeve Petrus asked.

"According to the clerk, the king's decision is final, and I have to accept that."

A small murder of crows flapped noisily past. They travelled from left to right, and the Irish seer looked up, took note and watched them fly away. He nodded his head as if privately acknowledging something.

"And what will yer do now? Give up?" pushed the reeve.

"What can I do, Reeve Petrus? Nothing! I am but a herdsman! I have no influence, I do not have the king's ear, I am powerless to do anything. All is lost."

Cathal reached behind for his bag and fumbled around for something. Odo watched distractedly as the seer found what he sought and pulled out a small cloth bag and looked skyward towards the heavens for a moment. Although it wasn't yet dark enough to see stars, he must have found what he wanted because he untied the string that secured the pouch and tipped out its contents. Small bones tumbled from the bag and fell onto the dead grass. Cathal bent low to study them.

Odo risked a quick glance at the reeve who returned his own quizzical look. He shrugged, uncertain to the antics of the seer. They watched for a moment longer.

"What will you do now?" repeated the reeve with emphasis.

"I'm going to find somewhere where I can drink my sorrow away and bid my dreams and my life farewell." Odo stood, and faced the reeve defiantly, challenging him.

"Nay, ye will not," spoke Cathal for the first time, his voice clear, articulate and authoritative.

Odo was surprised at the outburst. In question, the reeve's head spun to face the seer.

"Time is the essence. Ye are rash and impatient and ye cannot hurry time, ye must wait. Time is irrelevant in the heavens, and here mortal man is subject to the laws of the earth. Yer time approaches like the wind, it is coming, leave the campsite now and yer time will pass ye by. Remain here, clean and present yerself with dignity. Go now, and yer drinking will be justified, and all will be lost." Cathal scooped up his bones and poured them back into his pouch. He looked up and made eye contact with Odo.

"What is this, what do ye speak of?"

Cathal sighed, a long drawn-out exhalation. "Ye have a choice, leave this camp to drink and give way to yer sorrow … but once you do, all is lost. Ye can't give away yer sorrow without giving away another part of ye. Ye lose a bit of who ye are. Each time ye do this, ye lose more and more." Cathal paused to let his advice sink in. His eyes bored into Odo's. The seer pointed at him and spoke slowly with emphasis, "Ye, Odo, have nothing left to give, but yer word."

Odo swallowed thickly, he'd heard those words before, he'd said those very same words to Sir William all those years ago in Mellester's great hall. They were the words taught, their meaning instilled into him by Godwin, his father. They were words he should never forget, and he had forgotten. He'd given his word to Charlotte, and others. He'd told her he wouldn't give up. He felt ashamed. Cathal was right, he couldn't give up, that wasn't who he was. He blinked away a tear. "What do ye know of this and what I seek?" he cried.

Cathal's expression softened. He smiled at the distressed young man who stood before him. "I know yer time has yet to come and ye must have faith in the conviction of yer belief. Opportunity is like a dark cave. Ye never know what ye will find when yer enter, walk past it, and ye will never know." The seer spread his arms wide. "This camp is yer cave, yer opportunity lays here, not in the village at the bottom of a tankard of mead."

"But why stay here?" Odo asked. He turned and looked at Reeve Petrus for help, but the reeve had his mouth open staring at the seer.

"If ye don't stay, ye'll never find out." The seer stood and grabbed his bag and walked away.

Odo wiped his eyes, he felt terrible. The seer was correct, he had given up.

"What was all that about?" croaked the reeve.

"I wish I knew," breathed Odo.

Odo recounted to the reeve all that happened to him earlier at the tent with the clerk.

There were no words of encouragement he could offer to make Odo feel better other than to tell him to take the peculiar advice of the Fili and remain here at the camp.

His reaction to the seer was unusual, thought the reeve. Never before had he seen the young man react so emotionally and quickly to just a few words. Whatever those words meant to him, they had certainly rung his bell.

The reeve fell asleep. Odo lay on his blanket and stared into the flames of the fire and digested the Fili's words and advice. He felt a measure of guilt for wanting to give up so easily, and the seer accurately reminded him of those haunting words he spoke with such pride. How did the Fili know? Thomas called him a wizard, but wizards were characters in stories told to children, they simply didn't exist. How could Cathal have known what he said, unless it was just a coincidence?

What would he have to do to receive an audience with King Henry? Odo's eyelids grew heavy as he contemplated his next move.

"Odo! Odo!"

Odo sat up as Squire Steven ran into the camp.

"Odo, you must come, quickly, Sir Renier calls for ye," demanded the squire.

"What happened?" Reeve Petrus sat up rubbing his eyes.

"Nothing has happened, Reeve Petrus. Is Odo, he is needed."

"Good, keep the noise down, I need my sleep," grumbled the reeve as he lay back down.

Odo stood. "Why the urgency?"

"Ye need to look more presentable, Odo," the squire suggested as he brushed grass and dust from Odo's clothes. "Come, we must go."

Squire Steven began to run back to the village.

CHAPTER FORTY-ONE

In the absence of wind, pennants, standards and flags drooped dejectedly from tents and flag poles. Occasionally, a small breeze brought them to life and they'd flap proudly for a short time before they fell still and silent, as if in brief homage to the souls of men who'd perished in their shadows. Adding to the ambience, an impressive display of shields emblazoned with a variety of coat-of-arms, badges and symbols, either hung or rested on the ground and proudly affirmed loyalty and steadfast allegiance to mighty lords and a powerful English monarch.

Inside the great tent, food was served at long tables, whereas, outside, in a fenced off area, fuelled by fraternity and alcohol, knights gathered and talked loudly, boasting of ability, belittling adversaries and bragging of conquests. Vigilant guards patrolled the exterior perimeter and kept the unwelcome away.

Squire Steven led Odo towards a crowd of villagers standing near the entrance to the great tent guarded by a hand-full of stern faced, impatient men-at-arms.

"Where are we going, Steven?" asked Odo nervously as the squire elbowed his way through a group of civilian onlookers.

A man-at arms paused to block their access, then recognized Squire Steven and stepped aside. He gave Odo a curious look and said nothing allowing both men to pass. Once inside the tent, Steven stopped to look around.

"Do ye see Sir Renier?" he asked.

Knights and noblemen were everywhere. Some bore evidence of past injuries, others' wounds still appeared fresh. Most were resplendent in their finest armour, cleaned and gleaming by hardworking sergeants who now stood hovering in the background, but within easy hailing distance of their masters. Young squires stood in small groups near the perimeter and made eyes at servant girls who flirted in return as they swished by.

Odo saw at least three large boar carefully spit-roasting over huge fires; a master cook was berating one of them for laziness and struck the man about the head and shoulders. In one corner, a group of *jongleurs* performed with skill, but no one was paying them much attention. He couldn't see Sir Renier anywhere.

It was noisy and loud, and Odo was becoming more nervous by the second. He was out of place and had no business being here amongst these people who he shared so little in common. He questioned again, why am I here?

He felt a tug on his arm and Steven headed off, weaving skilfully around knights, tables and servants. Odo cautiously followed and eventually saw their destination. Outside, within the fenced off area and away from the noise, stood Sir Renier amongst a group of knights and noblemen. Sir Renier turned, saw Odo and smiled broadly.

"Odo, wheres haves ye been?" He yelled above the din and beckoned him closer.

Steven stepped away to stand with a group of squires, leaving Odo alone.

As he approached Sir Renier, who was clearly drunk, reached out and put his arm around his shoulder and drew him into the centre of the group of men. "This is the herdsman, Odo Read, that I told ye about."

One man laughed loudly, his face turning red from the exertion. He gave Odo an up-and-down appraisal before he spoke. "Tell me young man, is it true you've saved the lives of three knights on separate occasions? Or does Sir Renier jest? I must know. There is a considerable wager at stake and only ye can settle it." His grey eyes never left Odo's face as he took a lengthy pull from his goblet.

Odo studied the red-haired man. Clearly, he wasn't dressed as a knight, and wore rather extravagant clothing that masked a solid muscular build. Obviously a noble of some distinction, thought Odo. With uncertainty, he looked at Sir Renier. "Are ye sure, sire?"

"Go on, Odo," urged the knight.

Odo turned back to the noble. "Only two, Milord."

The noble bellowed in laughter, as did a few other knights in the group. Some looked serious and just watched, as their eyes roamed everywhere.

Sir Renier looked surprised. "I thought there were three," he said.

"Ye have saved the life of two knights?" the noble asked incredulously.

"Aye, only two," Odo replied. "But my father also saved the life of a lord."

The noble turned to the other knights. "How many freemen do ye know who have saved the life of a knight, let alone two?" The knights shook their heads. "Who were these distinguished knights you saved, young man?"

"The first was Sir Gweir. He was about to be stabbed and I was able to knock the knife away, Milord."

The nobleman's smile disappeared.

"Who was it that tried to stab Sir Gweir?" the nobleman asked.

Odo recognised the serious tone. "It was Lady Constance, Milord."

A few knights behind the nobleman began to speak excitedly. As they spoke in French, Odo couldn't understand the conversation.

"I see, carry on," instructed the noble after some moments.

Odo turned to Sir Renier.

He nodded, urging him to continue.

"And the other?" asked the noble.

"It was only a week ago and it was Sir Renier."

The noble looked to the knight. "What in God's name happened where you put yourself in such danger? All ye did was travel from England to Frankia," asked the nobleman.

Odo couldn't understand Sir Renier's reply as spoke in French.

The noble was silent and listened intently as Sir Renier detailed the quick but lethal fight near Wellebou.

The other knights all congratulated Sir Renier on his small victory.

"Ye are a brave and resourceful young man," added the nobleman. His smile returned.

"Thank ye." Odo didn't elaborate. "It was my duty, Milord."

"Duty? Duty? What does a herdsman know of duty?"

Odo turned to Sir Renier for help, but the knight wasn't watching him. "Are knights the only ones to learn of duty?" He gave the nobleman a steely look of his own. "Duty is doing something because it's the right thing to do, not because we want to."

All conversation around them stopped and Odo wondered if he spoke out of turn and caused offense.

The noble nodded and appeared not to have misinterpreted Odo's words. "I agree, well said. Now, who was this lord your father saved?"

"Sir William, of Mellester, Milord." Odo was pleased the noble was smiling, but he was becoming increasingly nervous, the man frightened him.

"I do recall something about that, did he nearly drown?"

"Aye, he fell into Falls Ende."

The noble opened his mouth to speak, then stopped and thought a moment before continuing. "Wait a moment," he commanded. He looked over his shoulder and made eye contact with someone. Within moments a man appeared, and they spoke. Odo couldn't hear the conversation but the noble pointed to him. "Herdsman Odo Read?" he asked.

"Aye." Odo confirmed.

The other man, dressed as a clerk, turned, looked at him, then faced the noble, nodded, bowed and backed away.

Sir Renier and the other knights looked on, but no one commented or said a word.

"Come and see me on the morrow, at midday. I wish to ask ye a few questions, and I will not do so here, understood?"

"Of course, Milord, but where will I find ye, I know not yer name?" asked Odo.

The red-headed noble laughed, his face again flushed with the effort. Others joined in, and soon everyone was laughing at his expense. When the noble was again composed, he turned to Sir Renier and spoke. Again, it was in French, and Odo realised it was a language he must learn.

Odo could see Sir Renier shaking his head and wondered what was being said.

Finally, Sir Renier turned to Odo, "I have been rude, *oui*? Please excuse my unacceptable behaviour, I apologise." He bent low at the waist and swept his arm theatrically across his body towards the noble. Herdsman Odo Read, may I introduce to ye, His Majesty, King Henry II."

Odo felt his knees tremble and his hands began to shake. He looked at King Henry, then bowed at the waist. "I am sorry, Yer Majesty, I, I had no idea it was ye I was speaking to. I mean, I thought–"

"Is quite alright, I am to blame too. However, I will enjoy a chat with you on the morrow."

"Aye, Yer Majesty."

"Very well, ye may enjoy some food and drink."

He was dismissed. He repeated what the clerk had done and bowed low and backed away.

Odo saw the wide grin on Sir Renier's face.

The men standing behind the king weren't all guests, many were guards, it all made sense now.

His heart pounded, and he felt lightheaded, and couldn't believe what just happened. What a fool he made of himself. In a daze, he threaded around people and walked towards the exit. Staring at him from beyond the perimeter was Cathal. He nodded at Odo, then he was gone.

When Odo returned to their camp, Reeve Petrus was asleep, and the fire was almost out. After quickly throwing wood on the embers, he woke the reeve only to suffer a stream of profanity. When the reeve paused for breath, Odo took the opportunity and told him all that happened.

When he was finished, the reeve broke down in a fit of laughter. "Odo, lad, ye've done it again. Ye always find a way to provide me with great merriment, and ye haven't disappointed me this time. And now yer to meet the king on the morrow. Why does he want to talk with yer?"

Odo shook his head, "I have no idea."

"Then ye can ask him about yer land?"

"Oh aye, I have every intention."

Reeve Petrus was alone when Odo headed out to meet with the king. The reeve claimed he felt no worse and believed Cathal's healing remedies were potent and effective. Sir Renier, Sergeant Thomas and Squire Steven had not returned the previous night, and Odo walked nervously towards the same tent where he'd spent so much time waiting.

The men-at-arms allowed him to enter without question and Odo walked towards the tent where the clerk had been less than civil to him. The solitary man-at-arms gave Odo a questioning look as if to ask 'what are you doing back here?' Odo gave him a friendly nod and stood in line and prepared himself for a long wait. The same nasty clerk recognised him immediately and frowned disapprovingly before ignoring him.

Another clerk he'd never seen before approached. "Herdsman Odo Read?" he asked.

"Aye," Odo replied.

"This way, follow me, please."

Odo followed the clerk as he navigated through one tent, out another and then finally approached a large heavily guarded tent separated from the others. One of the men-at-arms stepped in front of him. "Your weapons!"

"I have none," replied Odo.

The guard gave Odo carefully scrutiny, allowed him to pass and fell into step behind them as they pushed aside a tent flap to reveal King Henry II in the middle of a heated argument with a handful of important looking men. He almost turned and fled, such were the state of his nerves.

"Remain here," insisted the clerk. He went to stand behind the king and whispered in his ear.

"Out, get out, I've had enough," yelled King Henry to the group of men who surrounded him.

As they filed out a rear exit, England's monarch sat down at a table before a plate of fruit, bread and cheese. He spared Odo a quick glance but said nothing. The clerk took a step back and sat at a desk very similar to the one Steward Alard used. Odo understood now; the man wasn't a clerk, he was a steward or secretary.

King Henry nibbled at some fruit, then pushed the plate away and looked again at Odo. The man-at arms gave Odo a gentle nudge, a hint to step forward.

"Leave us," he said to the guard.

The guard dipped his head and retreated out of the tent. It was only the secretary, the king and himself in the tent.

CHAPTER FORTY-TWO

"When you look at me, what do ye see?" asked the king when Odo stood before him.

"I see a king, Yer Majesty."

"Do yer know, what I see when I look at myself?"

Odo shook his head.

"I see a man," he replied. "Do yer see the challenge I face with that?"

Odo gave the matter some thought. "You suffer as any man does?"

"Aye, I do."

King Henry pointed to a chair. "Sit." He waited until Odo dragged the heavy chair closer, across the thick rug and was seated before continuing. "I fall victim to the words of men as any man does." He waved his hand in the direction of the scholars, counsellors and advisors who just departed. "The fidelity, the deceit ... being king does not give me power to know if a man lies or tells me the truth when I ask a question." He cut a sliver of cheese, held it his mouth then changed his mind and put it down. "Those fools do not want me to deal with the growing crisis in Ireland. What do scholars know of life?"

Odo was puzzled and had no idea where this conversation was headed.

The king came directly to the point. "I received word that Sir Wystan was ambushed and slain, then Lady Constance was brutally murdered."

Odo opened his mouth to speak, but King Henry raised a hand to silence him.

"Let me finish."

The Secretary was leaning across his desk watching and listening intently.

"Sir William was an outstanding lord and a trusted friend, and I miss his counsel and friendship. Of course, I always had a soft spot for Lady Constance; she, too, was a fine and beautiful woman. I have sought answers from many people on how their son, and the good lady were killed, and now that I am acquainted with the details, I have formed my own conclusions. What I require is confirmation." He maintained eye contact with Odo. "If there was foul play, then I will find out and the guilty will be severely punished." King Henry reached for a goblet and took a hefty gulp.

"I was advised not to speak to ye, Odo. Ye are without noble birthright, and because of that ye can't swear fealty to me, or to anyone for that matter, and by that way of thinking, as my trusted advisors tell me, therefore, ye cannot be trusted. Ye are only a herdsman." He placed the goblet firmly back on the table and leaned forward to look at Odo, his expression hardened. "How did Sir Wystan and Lady Constance die? The truth!"

Odo held the king's quizzical gaze and considered his reply. This, he knew was a defining moment, and knew his own future, and perhaps even his life hinged on what he said. "Yer Majesty, I was always taught to act honourably and be truthful. Ye are correct, I have not sworn fealty or oaths, and I know nothing of them. I am as ye say, just a herdsman. But I have something equally as important that I hold dear to me."

King Henry remained unmoving and continued to look at Odo.

Cathal's recent words rung in his head. They pealed like a bell, not of warning, but of guidance. "The man who raised me as his own son, Godwin

Read, taught me that when a man has lost everything, he still retains the most important thing of all – his word. I have lost everything Yer Majesty. All I can offer ye is my word. It's all I have that remains and it means more to me than anything."

The king nodded for him to continue.

"If I fail in that duty, then I will lose Charlotte too. If I lose Charlotte, then my word means nothing." Odo swallowed.

"Charlotte?"

"I will explain," Odo replied.

"Bring wine!" ordered King Henry.

"Yer Majesty, Sir Wystan was troubled and blamed his misfortunes on me."

A servant brought a fine, jewel-encrusted goblet filled with wine for Odo and refilled the king's. Odo recounted to the king all he remembered from when he was a boy and when Godwin saved the life of Sir William and the trouble that ensued. He continued to explain the level of animosity and anger felt by Sir Wystan towards him, and more recently how Charlotte, his betrothed, had been captured. The king listened carefully as Odo detailed how the Brooker brothers sought revenge against Sir Wystan for killing their brother, and he recounted his role and what he witnessed during the death of Lady Constance.

When he was finished, the king remained quiet and leaned back in his chair. Odo was nervous and began to fidget. The silence was deafening.

"Ye have yet to tell me why ye came to Frankia. Why is it that a herdsman rides with a knight?" He finally asked. "Is this all related in some way?"

"Aye in a manner, it is." Odo told the king of Priest Durwin's discovery of Oswald's letter and the Church's desire to obtain his land, based on their claim of dereliction.

"Is Sir Hyde aware ye came here?"

"Nay, Yer Majesty, I do not think so. He said ye had more important things on yer mind."

"And Sir Gweir?"

"I believe Sir Gweir does know."

The king laughed. "Sir Gweir is a crafty fellow. However, Sir Hyde is correct, I have more than enough to deal with here, and as my proxy, Sir Hyde is more than capable of resolving problems such as yours in my name with my gratitude and blessing."

Odo felt deflated, this wasn't going as he'd hoped. He took a healthy swallow of wine.

King Henry turned over his shoulder to the secretary. "Fetch Sir Renier, quickly."

The secretary stood. *"Comme vous le commandez, votre Majesté."* He quickly exited the tent.

"Now then… I have heard a few varying accounts of what happened to Sir Wystan and Lady Constance. It appears there are some who harbour resentment against Mellester's new lord. I believe what you told me, Odo, and I think yer do speak the truth. I still have a couple of unanswered question for Sir Renier before I am completely satisfied. Then I can put to rest the false claims made by scoundrels who wish to tarnish the good name of my fine lords and friends."

The Secretary returned. *"Il sera ici momentanément votre Majesté."*

King Henry raised a hand in acknowledgment. "But we still have an issue with the Church's claim on yer land, do we not?"

Odo looked with renewed hope at the king.

Again, the king retreated into silence as he deliberated. With each passing moment Odo felt despair.

"Ye spoke of Charlotte … ye wish to marry her, and her family is in agreement?" he asked suddenly.

"Aye, Yer Majesty, we were to be married this summer, but it wasn't to be."

The occasional distant voice drifted into the tent from outside, otherwise it was silent and insulated from the world around. Is this the life of a king? wondered Odo. Protected, out of touch and alone?

King Henry sighed. "I cannot and will not interfere with any decision that the Church has made. There has been more than enough discordance with them and I want to see it come to an end."

Odo was dispirited; he saw his land and Charlotte slipping through his fingers.

"Any action I take against the Church will be looked on unfavourably by the pope, and neither he nor I want to see this friction continue. I'm sorry Odo, I'm unable to help ye in that regard. I cannot be seen to interfere."

Odo looked at his feet wondering what he would say to Charlotte.

"However, I do have an important request to make of ye."

Odo looked up.

"Ye will not speak about this meeting, ye will not discuss it with anyone other than Sir Hyde, Sir Renier, and Sir Gweir. This meeting never happened. I need yer word, Odo Read."

"Is all I have left to give, Yer Majesty, of course. I will not speak of this meeting to anyone as ye ask."

King Henry leaned forward. "Ye will return here on the morrow. I have a missive that I will have ye carry to England for me. Then ye will give it to Sir Renier so he can personally deliver to Sir Hyde. Ye will ensure he receives this letter. If something befalls Sir Renier, then I task ye with yer life, make sure Sir Hyde acquires it. Will ye promise me this Odo?" King Henry's eyes were firmly fixed on him.

"I give ye my word, Yer Majesty."

"And I believe ye. Yer a good man Odo, and I have one last request. When yer return to Mellester, send me some cheese."

"Sir Renier has arrived yer Majesty," informed the secretary.

King Henry rose from his seat. "Thank ye fer yer honesty, Odo Read."

Odo stood and respectfully bowed his head. *Cheese*?

"Remember, after rain comes sunshine," offered the king. "While dark clouds approach, they will pass, and your world will be bathed in glorious sunlight."

The king turned rapidly and strode to his secretary.

The meeting with the King Henry was over.

It was a long slow walk back to camp. He wandered out of the village and took a circuitous route, delayed only by a lengthy rest under a tree. When all seemed lost with nowhere to turn, he heard Cathal's words. He couldn't shake himself free of them. The more he tried to discount them as deranged ravings of a muddled man, the more sense they made. The harder he pushed to resist, the louder he heard them. When he finally approached the campsite, he felt energised and had a measure of 'hope.' The king's parting advice seemed appropriate. From where and what direction 'hope' came from, he had no idea, but he promised himself he would take Cathal's advice, he would not walk past a cave without venturing in.

Odo was tired when he returned to the camp, and already the sun dipped below distant hills and in the gloom of dusk, he found Sergeant Thomas busy packing things away.

"We shall return home on the morrow, Odo. At dawn we depart Chaumont-sur-epte. Ridgley Manor is our destination," offered the sergeant with a grin. It was obvious he was pleased to be returning home.

"Well, lad, what did His Majesty have to say to yer?" Reeve Petrus asked.

"He asked me not to share with anyone what we discussed."

"Did he now." He looked serious. "As yer not leaping fer joy, then I expect it didn't go well."

Odo turned to the reeve and shook his head.

They rode as before. Sir Renier up front, with Sergeant Thomas on his left. Reeve Petrus rode behind the sergeant and Odo behind the knight. Squire Steven trailed with a packhorse and the large destrier in tow. It felt good to be astride Amica again, he'd missed his company, even though he visited him every day to feed him and rub him down. Well rested, Amica had a spring in his step and Odo felt the horse was pleased to be underway again.

When pressed to speak of his meeting with King Henry, Odo was resolute and informed everyone he wasn't able to discuss it. Sir Renier, also kept quiet and offered nothing about his private meeting with the king.

Earlier that morning, Odo woke from his sleep, and as the king instructed, made his way back to the surly clerks inside the tent. Without having to wait in line, he was handed a fine, leather-bound, tubular case which contained a scroll. He was to hand it to Sir Renier at the appropriate time and make sure the missive was delivered to Sir Hyde Fortescue, Lord of Ridgley Manor. For the meantime, Odo felt the weight and responsibility of the leather tube as it hung from around his neck and nestled comfortably against his back.

It never occurred to him to question what the letter contained, and he assumed it was matters pertaining to Sir Hyde's role as the king's proxy.

More talkative now that his wound was healing, Reeve Petrus was tenacious and asked a few times what had happened when he met with the king. Odo told him he was bound by his word not to divulge anything. He'd looked in question at the leather tube a few times but held his tongue and said nothing about it.

As usual, it was Sergeant Thomas who spotted the rider approaching from the rear. "Someone approaches, Milord."

All heads craned to look, and it soon became evident the rider was known to them all.

"It's Cathal," stated Sir Renier. "Did he not check yer wound last night and kiss yer goodnight?" he teased.

"Perhaps ye forgot to pay him," replied the reeve with equal wit.

The small group pulled to a stop and they waited for the Irish Fili to ride up.

Cathal rode past everyone and pulled alongside the knight where they talked. Finally, Sir Renier spoke. "Cathal will join us to England. He wishes to accompany us to Ridgley Manor, and then to Mellester where he intends to make his home."

Strangely, Odo found the Fili's presence reassuring, and was secretly pleased. The reeve had no issue whatsoever with him. Now numbering six, the group rode for Wellebou and the seer drifted back and rode in solitude a few horse lengths behind the squire.

And so began their journey back to England.

CHAPTER FORTY-THREE

Priest Durwin met with Bishop Immers. It was a rather brusque meeting and the bishop was less than kindly to him. Eventually he made it clear to Durwin not to antagonise Lord Mellester, but to use tact and be delicate when communicating to him. Durwin didn't feel it important to inform the busy bishop about the young peasant woman who would join the convent, nor did he feel it appropriate, given the bishop's present frame of mind, to engage him in a conversation about building a convent at Mellester Manor.

In another eight days, it would be the end of the month, and the bishop would return to Ridgely Manor and inform Sir Hyde of the Church's intentions and what they expected of their tenants on their newly acquired land. So said, Durwin's meeting with the bishop was over and perfunctory at best.

To improve his mood, Priest Durwin sought the tailor who specialised in making clothes for the clergy and selected some fine quality fabric. He was measured and told to return at the end of the following day where his new vestments would be ready. Durwin returned to Mellester Manor proudly wearing his new clothes and feeling considerably better.

The look he received from Grace was less than he hoped for when he arrived at the priory, and the first words out of her mouth were not respectful.

"Ye used church coin to pay for them!" she pointed accusingly at his finely-tailored habiliments. "Yer a thief, and I want no part of ye, I will make sure the lord hears of what yer done, and he'll tell the bishop, he will."

It took but a blink of an eye for the priest to calculate the damage her irresponsible behaviour could cause, and he gave her a hard push. "Yer will keep yer mouth shut, do yer hear me?" Spittle few from his mouth, such was his anger. He took a step closer.

"I knows how many coin were in Oswald's box, and now it's almost empty. That was for the ro–"

He struck her hard. The force of the blow knocked her off balance and she stumbled backwards and fell awkwardly, bouncing off the table and landing hard on the floor. As he'd hoped, it shut her up. He stood over her, glowering, daring her to continue with her verbal tripe.

She was dazed and rubbing her head when Tedric took matters into his own hands.

Tedric had been listening from behind the door. Although not fully recovered, the broken bones in his hand would take a few more weeks before he was completely healed, his face was almost back to normal, so when he heard Grace yell at the priest his blood began to boil.

He heard the crash of her fall and he snapped. Tedric kicked the door open and strode towards the priest just as he bent over her.

If revenge was the primary reason Tedric loathed the priest, then now his hatred erupted from another cause. Tedric and Grace had become intimate; his newfound feelings extended far beyond anything he previously experienced. His rage was primal and borne from the need to protect and nurture.

His sentiments weren't one-sided. Grace willingly shared her feelings towards him and dutifully expressed concern about his lifestyle choices and wayward tendencies. In turn, he solemnly promised to become a better person, go to church, work hard and provide for her. If it were to be believed, Tedric and Grace were madly in love. And the love of his life now lay prone and hurt on the floor.

Without thought, Tedric stomped towards the priest and extracted a dangerous, narrow-bladed dagger from his belt. Before Durwin was fully aware of what was happening, Tedric had the blade pressed firmly into his brand new and very expensive vestments. With surprising one-handed strength, he drove it all the way in to its hilt. With a surprised expression, Priest Durwin collapsed to the floor, his last thoughts not of judgement and eternal life, but of the awful stain on his pristine and extremely costly clothes.

Grace sat up and stared vacantly at the body of Priest Durwin. "Oh no, dear God, what have ye done, Tedric?" she cried after collecting her senses.

"I'll not see anyone take a hand to my woman," he said as he bent down to lift her from the floor. A trickle of blood ran down her face where she'd hit the table.

"Oh Tedric, what will we do?"

Unused to making decisions, he shrugged, "Should we leave?"

It was evening when Tedric and Grace, each carrying a bag, quietly left the priory of Mellester's church and walked away into the darkness. No one saw them leave, and no one was aware that the body of Priest Durwin Babcock now lay on the priory floor, covered by a blanket.

It was with some relief that Odo was again traveling on land in a southerly direction towards familiar country, after spending most of the return voyage to England hanging over the side of the unstable and leaky boat. The journey from Herosfloth to South Hamtun had been unkind to Odo, although the ship's master maintained the weather was perfect, the sea conditions ideal, and the winds blew from where they should. Odo asserted the vessel was unseaworthy and not suitable to convey beasts, let alone men across the vast open expanse of a tumultuous ocean. Of course, Reeve Petrus and Sir Renier each took turns mimicking Odo's onboard antics, much to the delight of Thomas and Steven. Cathal seemed unaffected by the voyage and by humour. His generous offer of ginger root was politely refused by Odo, and he saw no reason to make light of another's discomfort.

The injury to the reeve's shoulder continued to heal and the change in his attitude was remarkable as each day saw improvement. The reeve expressed his gratitude to Cathal at every opportunity, but the Irishman was deaf to compliments or thanks.

At one time he had looked at the reeve and asked him a question. "Why should I receive yer gratefulness fer doing what anyone should do? If it were unexpected, then perhaps, but thank me not because I know ye would have done the same, as would anyone here."

Reeve Petrus couldn't argue with that logic and silently allowed Cathal to treat his wound whenever the Irishman found it necessary.

After Odo ran out of disparaging comments about the sea journey, he began to think in earnest about how to overcome the problem of holding on to his land. No matter how he thought the problem through, he arrived at the same conclusion – selling Amica was the only logical solution. He knew the courser would fetch a handsome price, perhaps considerably more than what his land was worth. If the Bishop decided to add back rent to the sale price, then he may not have enough money, even combined with his meagre savings. It pained him to even think of it.

Once home, he would discuss selling Amica with Sir Gweir. He may even know of a knight willing to buy the courser. He was saddened by the thought but there were no other alternatives.

Since their departure from Mellester all those days ago, the beautiful, black courser and he developed an even stronger bond and his affection for the stallion grew daily. If there was only another way.

Sir Renier suggested to Odo that they would first visit Sir Hyde at Ridgely Manor, deliver the letter as the king demanded, then leave for Mellester the following day. Odo was happy. He wanted to see Charlotte as soon as possible, he couldn't wait.

The six men approached the familiar countryside of Ridgley Manor, They were all tired after their journey and each looked forward to rest and food. Cathal had never been to this part of England before and he took in the sights, the people and Ridgley's prosperous village as they rode through.

Reeve Petrus greeted those he knew with a wave of his good arm. Even Odo knew a few villagers and they smiled in surprise as they recognised him atop the black stallion. The heavy iron gates of Sir Hyde's manor were ahead, and they were warmly welcomed.

As required, Odo handed the king's leather tube to Sir Renier, while Sergeant Thomas and Squire Steven saw to the horses, Odo tended to Amica and then, unbidden, gave the reeve's courser a rubdown and water. Cathal mysteriously vanished.

The reeve and Sir Renier had been gone for some time, and Odo was wondering what he should do when a man-at-arms came to the stables and said Sir Hyde called for him.

This was the moment Odo feared. Sir Hyde didn't know he had gone to Frankia and surely the lord would require him to explain his actions. He followed the man-at-arms through a maze of passageways and stairs and saw Steward Baldric, with his arms full of scrolls, quills and inkpots, leaving the chamber they were about to enter. He greeted the steward warmly, asked after his daughter Ivy, and entered the room.

Sir Hyde and Sir Renier were the only occupants of the large comfortably furnished room.

"Come," waved Sir Hyde.

Odo respectfully dipped his head, "Hail, Sir Hyde," and entered after making eye contact with Sir Renier.

There were a few comfortable looking chairs surrounding a great ornate table where both knights sat. Sir Hyde indicated for Odo to sit. On the table lay the leather tube beside a few scrolls, presumably from the king.

At about the same time Odo was seated, two armed messengers prepared to leave Ridgley Manor and head towards Mellester Manor with an important message for its lord.

"Ye look tired, have ye had refreshments and food?" asked Sir Hyde

"Nay, Milord, I was going to get something later from the village."

"I will see ye get a room and food, ye will be staying here."

This was an unexpected turn. "Thank ye, Milord."

"Don't thank me yet!" came the terse reply. Ridgley Manor's lord kept his eyes firmly affixed on Odo. "Now then, why is that whenever there is trouble, the name Odo Read is always associated with it?"

Odo turned to Sir Renier for moral support – none was forthcoming. He opened his mouth to reply.

"Nay, don't answer, it will only make me feel sorry fer yer."

Sir Renier laughed.

Sir Hyde's face hardened, and his steel grey eyes bored into Odo's. "Do ye know what King Henry wrote in this letter?"

"Nay, Milord."

"Good. That is how it's meant to be."

Odo was puzzled and didn't know what to say or think.

Sir Hyde leaned forward on the table. "Odo, according to the orders from King Henry, I'm to keep ye here. Ye are not to leave Ridgley Manor, or for that matter leave yer chamber."

"But, Milord–"

"I will not explain his reasons yet, but all will be made clear to ye soon. Fer now, ye are my guest."

Odo turned to Sir Renier for answers, but the knight remained silent.

A heavy thump on the door interrupted any further protestations.

"Come!" yelled Sir Hyde.

A man-at-arms entered.

Sir Hyde commanded the soldier to wait.

"Ye will be taken care of, Odo, but I need yer word ye will not disobey King Henry or me, and attempt to leave yer chamber, is that understood?"

"I'm to be a prisoner?"

"Odo!" snapped Sir Hyde.

Odo was fuming and fought to control his tongue.

"Odo?" Sir Renier repeated.

"Aye, Milord, yer have my word, but forgive me, I, I–"

"Everything will be fine, Odo, have trust and faith," Sir Hyde replied in a softer voice. He gave the man-at-arms a quick look and nodded.

The man-at-arms walked over and touched Odo on the shoulder. "Come with me please."

He stood, and looked at Sir Renier, then Sir Hyde before he left the room.

A dozen heartbeats after the door was closed and both knights were alone, Sir Hyde breathed out a long drawn out sigh. "Poor Odo."

Sir Gweir was pacing backwards and forwards in Mellester's great hall after learning about the death of Priest Durwin Babcock. It troubled him that a man was murdered within his manor, but when he thought about it, he couldn't see that it was all that bad. Since his arrival at Mellester, Priest Durwin brought nothing but complaint and now he was dead. It certainly changed a few things, admitted the lord, and he knew that Sir Hyde needed to be informed immediately. Before he could plan anything, his musings were interrupted by a guard escorting two armed men into the hall.

Steward Alard rose from his seat. "Who do ye seek?"

"We was sent by Sir Hyde, with a message for Sir Gweir."

"Bring it here," Sir Gweir ordered.

He broke the seal and read the lengthy missive before handing it to Steward Alard who curiously waited.

"Go to the kitchen and receive food, I will send for ye soon with a reply," Sir Gweir told both men.

He waited for both men to leave, then turned to the Steward. "Odo and Petrus have returned, but Odo is being held by Sir Hyde? What is this, Alard?"

"I am pleased Odo and the reeve are safe, Milord, but I cannot think to what Sir Hyde is doing. I find this odd," replied the steward. And of these other people..." He ran his finger down a list of names. "I know nothing of this nor have I seen anything like it before."

"We are to collect these villagers and escort them to Ridgley Manor on the morrow? Has Sir Hyde received a blow to his head?" Sir Gweir stated.

Steward Alard shook his head in wonderment.

"Very well, as his vassals, we must do as the lord asks of us," Sir Gweir replied with a heavy sigh. "Alard, see to it these people are informed, and that they must accompany us to Ridgley Manor, no excuses. No one will decline, by order of Lord Mellester. We leave at dawn."

"As ye wish, Milord," said Steward Alard.

Needless to say, the steward's name was also on the list, and this bothered him greatly. He recognised Steward Baldric's fine script and knew he wrote it, a fine man as there ever was. That offered him some consolation, but whatever was happening was peculiar indeed.

CHAPTER FORTY-FOUR

The bed chamber given to Odo was spacious and comfortable, better than at any inn he'd slept in. He was given water and if he wanted food all he had to do was ask. Of concern, someone was outside the door at all times. He slept well, although understandably he woke disturbed. Later a woman entered and looked him up and down and expressed her displeasure at his filthy clothes. She departed tut-tutting and a short time later a servant brought a bucket with warm water, soap and a cloth. Odo expected she wanted him to clean himself. He saw no harm, and as he had nothing else to do, so he took advantage and scraped and wiped away the grime and even washed his hair.

He slept, ate and listened to the sounds of the manor. There was a lot of activity; people were moving around, he heard yelling, and at one time thought he heard a bard. Whatever was going on was unusual. Sir Hyde had been truthful; he'd not been mistreated but was none the wiser as to what was going on and he became increasingly anxious for his own wellbeing.

The same woman returned later in the day and gave him another curious look over. She still wasn't happy and exited the chamber grizzling.

A small parade of wagons and knights left Mellester Manor. Sir Gweir rode at the head and of the procession and he was irritated. Behind, in the wagons that followed, a number of villagers were ordered to accompany him to Ridgley Manor. They'd argued and bitterly complained, but their protestations fell on deaf ears. He'd quickly tired of their complaints and endless questions and reminded them that Sir Hyde Fortescue specifically instructed they arrive at Ridgley Manor this morn and all would be explained.

Sir Gweir's journey to Ridgley Manor wasn't an inconvenience; he'd intended to visit Sir Hyde to discuss the death of Priest Durwin anyway. His marshal informed him that Grace and Tedric Brooker were nowhere to be found, and it seemed entirely possible that Tedric murdered the priest and held Grace as a hostage. There were no other explanations.

Additionally, and on further investigation, the marshal discovered in the priory a small locked box containing a handful of coins inside a chest. That in itself wasn't alarming, however a detailed written tally of the funds was also found inside the chest and according to Steward Alard, it indicated the box of coins was intended to pay for much needed renovations to Mellester's church. Oswald's meticulous reckoning indicated to Steward Alard that two pounds and three shillings were missing.

It didn't take a wise man to quickly deduce that Priest Durwin had been spending extravagantly of late. He'd recently purchased many bottles of expensive wine, high-priced food and he'd travelled extensively in a recently acquired wagon and horse. Certainly not the approved lifestyle of a devout parish priest. Even in death he wore costly new vestments and carried a great deal of coin in his purse. Curiously, the coin had not been stolen by Tedric Brooker. This would be another matter to discuss with Sir Hyde.

Sir Gweir spared a look over his shoulder and into the wagons. Steward Alard was in deep conversation with Cheesemaker Gerald. Huntsman Seth was in the rear wagon talking to Mother Rosa and Farrier Rudd. Charlotte looked very unhappy and demonstrated her displeasure at being dragged away from Mellester by folding her arms and stamping her feet. Luckily, Agnes calmed her down and other than a few scathing looks, it appeared as though she wouldn't cause any more trouble. He didn't take offense at their unhappiness, and as much as the people he brought with him, he also wanted answers.

Charlotte was convinced that the reason she'd been dragged from her home was tied to the death of that nasty priest. She believed she was being taken to see the bishop and then to be carted off to Exeter Nunnery. When her father questioned why all the other people were coming with them, she had no answer. Weakly, she suggested it was because they were all her friends.

Cheesemaker Gerald asked to speak to Sir Gweir over an important matter and was politely told it would have to wait until they returned to Mellester. He wasn't happy about leaving his cheese shoppe, but he knew there was little he could do to change the mind of the lord.

Everyone in the wagon was downcast except for Huntsman Seth who saw it as a bit of an adventure. In turn, the others each protested to the lord, and the response they all received was the same.

The second morning saw Odo more agitated, and as time passed the feeling of unease persisted. He realised he was no longer in charge of his own destiny; his life was in the hands of others. For the first time he considered escaping. But on guilty reflection, recalled he had expressly given his word not to leave.

The bad-tempered woman reappeared and told him his filthy rags needed to be laundered; she left an armful of replacement clothes and told him to change while she waited outside. When she returned he asked her if she knew why he was being held captive. She wouldn't answer him and silently walked out of the room carrying his soiled clothes.

He was surprised. The garments she left him appeared new and were of exceptional quality and fitted him quite well. He had never owned such fine clothes as these.

His self-reflection was interrupted by a knock and Sir Hyde Fortescue entered. A clean full-length surcoat draped over gleaming chainmail and a mighty broadsword swung from a wide belt, and before he could ask the Lord why he was imprisoned the knight held up a hand.

"I know what ye want answers, Odo and ye will have them. First, I want to ask ye a few questions to satisfy my own curiosity."

Odo opened his mouth to speak.

"Sit down!"

Odo sat, his anger simmered. But he knew Sir Hyde was deadly serious. "I apologise, Milord."

"What in God's name did you speak of to King Henry?"

"Milord, he was concerned for the truth, and wanted to know how Sir Wystan and Lady Constance were killed."

"Did he give a reason?" asked Sir Hyde.

"Only that there were some who wished to see his fine lords and friends tarnished and he doubted the honesty of the reports made to him about their deaths."

Sir Hyde nodded and scratched at his beard. "Hmmm, makes sense.

And what else? You obviously spoke of Falls Ende and the Church's claim on yer land?"

"Aye, and he said he could not go against the wishes of the Church and couldn't be seen to interfere. That is why he couldn't help me, he said you were correct, he had more important matters to deal with and you were capable and trusted as his proxy."

Why Sir Hyde smiled, Odo couldn't fathom, he couldn't see what amused the lord.

"King Henry is a wise and clever man, Odo. Do not doubt him, or his wisdom."

"But Milord–"

"Today is the last day of the month, do ye know what that means?"

Odo felt the hopelessness of his situation overwhelm him. He struggled to remain composed. "Aye, is the day I lose everything."

The lord paused a moment. "I will see ye soon." He spun to exit the room. "Oh, yer have some visitors." The door remained open as Sir Hyde departed and Reeve Petrus and Sir Renier strode in, both men smiled broadly.

"What are ye looking so down 'bout?" asked the reeve. "I'd a thought ye would have been happy to see us."

Odo looked to them both. He couldn't speak.

"We have to take yer now, Odo," said Sir Renier. "But ye must put this on, oui?"

Reeve Petrus held a black cloth.

"A blindfold? What will happen to me?"

"Trust us, Odo," replied the reeve.

Odo heard the reeve's voice as he whispered close to his ear. "Be brave lad, be brave."

He should have heard the sound of men, servants or even horses. He didn't hear the sounds associated with a manor. It was the absence of sound that brought the chill of fear into his consciousness. He sensed rather than heard movement beside him. He tilted his head to listen. There were noises, he could hear them but couldn't picture what was out there.

"Are ye ready?" asked a voice, just beyond a whisper and some distance away.

Again, he sensed movement.

"Now is yer time, Odo," said Sir Renier quietly. It came as a whisper. He felt hands on his head and the blindfold was removed.

Bishop Immers woke to a beautifully sunny and warm morning. He lay in bed for a while as he thought of what this day would bring. There was good reason to feel optimistic, he rolled over and stared at the ceiling. "*Et tibi quaecumque petieritis in oratione credentes, accipietis si non credunt,*" he said quietly.

"What was that?" asked the young servant girl who lay beside him.

"Matthew 21:22. And whatever you ask in prayer, you will receive if you have faith," Bishop Immers answered.

"Oh, does that mean if I pray for a guinea, ye'll give me a guinea?" she asked.

"Certainly not!" he barked, "Ye'll get tuppence." He pushed her roughly towards the edge of the mattress. "Get dressed and be off with ye."

She slid from the bed and the bishop watched as she dressed.

"Where's me coin?" she asked when clothed.

Bishop Immers rolled from the bed and found his purse. He fished for tuppence, then out of the goodness of his munificent and ardent heart, gave her an extra penny. "Don't come beggin' fer more, on yer way."

She muttered something unintelligible that didn't sound entirely gracious and quickly left the small room.

The bishop sat on the edge of the bed and rehearsed what he would say to Lord Ridgley when he went to see him a little later in the day. He expected a little coolness from the lord, but ultimately what he sought was some supplication. He had no personal feelings of animosity for either Lord Ridgely or the new lord of Mellester. They were simple, uneducated men with little or no understanding of a bishop's role as successor to the apostles. What do fighting men know of such things? The Church needed funds and Falls Ende would provide a steady stream. Bishop Immers laughed, he would somehow use those words when he talked to Lord Ridgley and made his demands known. Once dressed, he would break his fast before heading off to Ridgley Manor. He didn't like traveling on an empty stomach.

Sir Renier took the cloth and tied it around Odo's head, covering his eyes. Odo stood and each man held an arm and led him from the chamber. He had no sense of direction and had no idea where they were taking him. They didn't speak, and Odo's pleas for answers were ignored.

Eventually he felt the warmth of sunshine on his head and he guessed they were in an open space, possibly the courtyard. It was still, too still. Something was horribly wrong.

There was a flash of brightness and in reflex Odo brought his hands to his face and covered his eyes. At the same time, he heard the unmistakeable sound of people applauding. He heard his name mentioned a few times. Then he felt a touch on his shoulder and he lowered his hands and stared, blinking into the beautiful face of Charlotte. She threw herself at him and squeezed him tightly. This further encouraged people and the clapping turned into cheers.

He was speechless. Never had he seen Charlotte look this way, she was striking and dressed in a blue dress made of satin. It almost shimmered, a ring of reeds sat upon her head and her golden hair shone. What was happening? He fully expected to face death, and now … and here was his Charlotte and all these people, his friends. His mouth opened and his head swivelled from side to side.

In front of him stood Cheesemaker Gerald and Agnes clutching the baby. Odilia, Charlotte's younger sister stood beside them. There was Huntsman Seth, clapping and hooting as only a larrikin could. Beside him stood Mother Rosa, proudly beaming from ear to ear. Why? He didn't know. There were others, his friends and even familiar faces from Ridgley Manor. Off to the side stood a group of knights, their armour dazzled and sparkled. They stood proudly and each of them smiled warmly. Sir Hyde, Sir Gweir, Sir Renier, even Sir Dwain still nursing his injury, and perhaps the man with the biggest grin of all came from Reeve Petrus. There were other knights he had met and knew, and each of them beamed. He saw Sergeant Thomas and Squire Steven. Slightly off to the side stood Steward Alard, Steward Baldric and his little girl, Ivy. She was wearing a blue dress, a small version of what Charlotte wore. In the background, standing alone, he saw the unmistakeable form of Cathal. As they made eye contact the seer nodded.

Sir Hyde stepped from the group and walked over to them. As he approached, Charlotte reluctantly released her chokehold, and stepped to the side.

"What is this, Charlotte?" he squeaked. His voice had still to return.

"Wait, Odo," she said wiping tears from her eyes.

The imposing figure of Sir Hyde stopped in front of them. His steel grey eyes shifted from Odo to Charlotte and back again. Silence descended over Ridgley Manor as Sir Hyde paused. Odo held Charlotte's hand tightly, he was scared.

"Shut yer gob, Odo," someone yelled.

He obediently closed his mouth and held the knight's gaze.

"Yer can thank King Henry for this, it was all his idea," said the knight softly with a wink.

"I, I, don't understand," Odo croaked.

He felt Charlotte reassuringly squeeze his hand.

Sir Hyde cleared his throat and turned to face the group of people. His head swivelled from side to side, his powerful presence demanding quiet. "Is there a person among ye here who have reason not to see Odo Read and Charlotte Cheeseman wed? His voice rung loud and authoritatively.

Odo's head whipped around and he looked at Charlotte. Tears streamed down her cheeks as she returned his gaze. "We're to be married?" he whispered.

Overcome, she could only nod and smile.

"Speak now… has any person reason not to see Odo Read and Charlotte Cheeseman wed?" repeated Lord Ridgley.

"No? No? So be it!" he yelled and raised his fist to the air. Everyone cheered.

The lord gave a small wave and Priest Kirby approached. Ridgley Manor's old priest slowly shuffled towards Odo and Charlotte as Sir Hyde returned to stand sentinel amongst the gathered knights.

Odo's eyes welled and he blinked. He couldn't believe what was happening and didn't understand why. Why had King Henry wanted to see him wed Charlotte, and why were Sir Hyde and Sir Gweir so involved in the marriage of peasants? It didn't make sense. All he knew was that he had never been so frightened in all his life, and then to have that fear evaporate into pure joy… He was finally going to marry Charlotte! He wiped his eyes.

Priest Kirby stood close, he looked in turn from Charlotte to Odo. He leaned in a little closer. "I knew yer father, Oswald, or Odo. He told me ye were his son. If he'd been here today, he'd be very proud of ye, as would Godwin. Both men loved ye, don't judge either of them harshly, they did only what they thought was best."

Odo could barely contain himself. The stress and pressure of the last fortnight were overwhelming and to find himself thrust into this was almost too much to bear. He struggled to remain composed.

Charlotte reached up and wiped away his tears.

CHAPTER FORTY-FIVE

The ceremony was typically brief. Priest Kirby didn't dilly-dally, and the biggest surprise came when he produced two gleaming gold rings. Both Odo and Charlotte's eyes widened, they had no idea from where they came. While they didn't fit snugly, Odo had no problem sliding it onto the third finger of her right hand. Sir Hyde offered to have them altered to fit later.

Perhaps the strangest moment came when Priest Kirby announced that Odo and Charlotte Read were now husband and wife. At that moment when everyone cheered and applauded, Sir Hyde again stepped forward and announced, "Let it be so recorded!"

Stewards Baldric and Alard stepped aside to reveal a small table that contained a hefty book. Odo and Charlotte followed Priest Kirby to the table, where he sat and began to scribble away with a quill. It took only moments before he invited Odo and then Charlotte to each sign their names into the parish register he'd created and assiduously maintained. Sir Hyde hovered nearby and watched the unusual process. Most people could not read or write, but Charlotte and Odo were taught by Oswald, and without understanding why, the couple diligently signed their names where the priest indicated.

Odo knew there was an explanation, marriages were never recorded, but for some reason Sir Hyde, and presumably even King Henry wanted this to happen.

Sir Hyde bent over to look, and saw the names recorded as Odo Read and Charlotte Read. He gave Sir Gweir a private look of relief. Stewards Alard and Baldric visibly relaxed.

Immediately a troupe of minstrels began to perform and servants began bringing food and refreshments to the parched guests.

The happy couple greeted and thanked everyone for attending, although Odo was unaware his guests had no choice in the matter. Sir Hyde invited them inside the great hall of Ridgley Manor where he would explain it all to Odo.

Sir Gweir, Sir Renier and Sir Hyde were the only ones in the hall when Odo and Charlotte entered. They all sat at a table garnished with five goblets of wine.

Sir Hyde raised a goblet. "To Odo and Charlotte Read, may ye both find the happiness ye both truly deserve and may ye both have many healthy children!"

"*Je lève mon gobelet aux mariés,*" quickly added Sir Renier.

Odo looked puzzled.

"I raise my goblet to the bride and groom," laughed Sir Gweir.

All goblets were emptied.

"I apologise to ye Odo fer all ye went through, it was the only way. King Henry thought of a solution where he could help without appearing to go against the wishes of the Church. Ultimately, I will bear the brunt of the Church's anger, but in the end, we will have solved the problem of Falls Ende, and keeping title on yer land."

Odo's eyes widened in disbelief.

A servant entered and refilled all the goblets.

"How, Milord?" he asked finally finding his voice once the servant exited the hall.

"I'm ashamed I never thought of it." Sir Hyde laughed and took another drink of wine. "When ye signed yer name in the parish register, yer signed yer name as Odo Read. In fact, by doing so, the Church accepts yer name as being legitimate. I asked if any man objected to Odo Read marrying Charlotte Cheeseman. There were no objections and yer name was recorded as such."

Sir Gweir began to laugh, soon everyone joined in.

"But Milord, the Church could still lay claim to dereliction, yeah?"

"Aye, I expect Bishop Immers to arrive sometime soon. Let Sir Gweir and I speak with him, ye have no need to involve yerself." Again, Sir Hyde's steely look was a subtle warning to Odo.

"Aye Milord." Odo looked thoughtful and turned to Charlotte who was not at ease in the presence of lords. "What reason was given to the guests who came here?"

"When they arrived, it was explained to them that the wedding was to be a surprise," added Sir Hyde. "King Henry requested that I inform Charlotte of all the details." He smiled at her. "And m'dear, you truly look beautiful, ye make a fine bride."

Charlotte blushed.

Odo turned back to Sir Hyde. "I have one more question."

Sir Hyde nodded.

"How will ye prevent the bishop from going to the pope and complaining about what ye did."

"Ah yes, that is a bit tricky, but it seems we had some divine intervention."

Odo and Charlotte looked at each other, puzzled.

"Priest Durwin was killed. We think it was Tedric Brooker. He has since vanished and taken Grace with him, probably as a hostage," offered Sir Gweir.

"And, with our plan, we are extremely confident that the bishop will celebrate this happy day with us," finished Sir Hyde.

This time it was Sir Gweir who offered the toast. "*Je lève mon gobelet aux mariés.*"

"*Je lève mon gobelet aux mariés,*" they all repeated.

Odo stood and looked uncomfortable, "I've never done this before uh, lords, but I wish to offer good health to King Henry."

Everyone stood.

"To His Majesty, King Henry!" cried Odo with his goblet raised in the air.

"King Henry!" they repeated in chorus.

It wasn't long after Odo and Charlotte returned to their guests and festivities that Bishop Immers arrived. He was rather surprised to find a feast in progress with minstrels singing and people celebrating. Certainly, he found a group of distinguished knights amongst peasants, sharing in song and revelry a bit disconcerting. Initially he believed the festivities were in honour of his anticipated arrival but soon changed his mind when he was escorted into Ridgley Manor's great hall to face not one, but three powerful lords. Although he'd never met Sir Renier, his reputation and distinguished family name were enough to give him pause. His three assistants, all clerics, seemed a little nervous. Priest Durwin was nowhere to be seen.

Stewards Baldric and Alard were also in the hall and as expected were near the steward's desk.

"Hail Yer Grace, how wonderful to see you this day," said Sir Hyde, rising from his seat at the front of the hall. Sir Gweir and Sir Renier each stood at his side.

Bishop Immers smiled warmly and as protocol demanded, held out his right hand. Beginning with Sir Hyde, each knight stepped forward and kissed the episcopal ring.

"Sir Hyde, it is a pleasure to see ye again."

"I'm sure yer visit will be brief, and ye'll be anxious to be on yer way again, so I won't hold yer from yer from the important and tireless work yer perform fer the Church."

No offer of food, refreshments or a bed, thought the Bishop. "Ye are most kind and thoughtful, Milord."

"Now, what brings ye to our little hamlet?"

"It was that trifling matter we spoke of about Falls Ende and the land it sits on. We spoke on it a month past, I believe."

"Of course, have ye changed yer mind, Yer Grace?" asked Sir Hyde.

"Nay, it would appear the Church is willing to accept the burden of derelict land, Milord. And so stated, the Church will regretfully take ownership from this day on."

"Then the Church believes this land was derelict? Sir Hyde adopted an expression of puzzlement.

"It seems so," sighed Bishop Immers.

Sir Hyde frowned. "In order for the Church to obtain title, the land would have been deemed derelict, am I right in thinking this?"

"Yes, Milord, exactly."

"Then I hate to disappoint ye, Bishop Immers. It appears yer trip here was for nought. I do apologise."

Now it was the bishops turn to look surprised.

"Ye see, church records clearly state that Herdsman Odo Read is bound by that name. Therefore, Falls Ende has been legally owned since the death of Godwin Read."

"That can't be, the Church questions the legality of the name. Odo was no son of Godwin Read."

Steward Baldric, could ye find Priest Kirby and have him bring the register here?"

"Aye as ye wish, Milord."

Steward Baldric departed through a doorway where Priest Kirby waited with the register. "Just wait a bit," Steward Baldric advised the priest. After sufficient time passed, the steward again spoke. "When I leave, say a prayer, then enter the hall."

"Very well, Steward," replied the priest.

As rehearsed, Steward Baldric re-entered the hall. "He is on his way, Milord."

Sir Hyde smiled at the bishop and in return the bishop smiled at the lord, and they waited. The priest had yet to show himself. Sir Hyde gave the steward a look and Baldric shrugged his shoulders.

It must have been a long prayer, thought Steward Baldric.

Finally, Priest Kirby appeared, much to every one's relief.

"Kirby, what have ye?" The bishop snapped at him.

"I have a church register, Yer Grace."

"A what?"

"Is a book where I record all parish birth, deaths and marriages, Yer Grace.

"Bring it here," he commanded.

The priest brought the register and opened it to the last page where Odo and Charlotte recently signed.

On seeing the entry, the bishop wasn't happy. "This, this, is a wedding!" The bishop waved his arms madly about.

"Aye, that it is. Yer see, Yer Grace, the Church always recognised Godwin Read as being the legal father of Odo Read. If the Church had not, then there would have been problems with his tithes, and many other things, as ye can see, there is no problem. The Church accepted his name, even today at conclusion of his marriage. So ye can't tell me the land is derelict. Can ye?"

Bishop Immers, called for one of his assistants and they whispered. "Milords, this is a matter I must take up with the pope, it is too important to ignore."

"I'm afraid I have some rather distressing news fer yer, Bishop Immers. Apparently, Priest Durwin Babcock was found slain, three nights ago. We believe it was one of the Brooker brothers who survived the pillory. He has taken Priest Oswald's hearth wife as hostage. There is no knowledge of his whereabouts."

"Wh, wh, what is this?" stammered the bishop as he looked from face to face.

"Aye, very tragic," Sir Hyde looked sad. "We also found something out that was very interesting." He cocked an eyebrow. "Were ye aware that Durwin Babcock was stealing money from the Church to pay for things beyond his means?"

"What do ye say, explain yerself." The bishop turned to look at each lord in turn for answers.

"Priest Durwin was a thief! He stole money from a fund intended to pay for the renovation of Mellester's church. He used that coin he purloined to purchase extravagant clothes and other items of vanity he coveted. It seems peculiar ye have a priest with these faults in a parish stealing from villagers, bishop. My advisors tell me that I must bring this to the attention of King Henry, he would need to be told. Such are the unpleasant tasks I must perform to keep His Majesty apprised."

Bishop Immers needed no reminding that King Henry was rather sensitive to clergy stealing from parishioners. He had made his views quite well known on this, which contributed to the much-publicised friction between the pope and himself. Relations both men were now trying to publicly mend. The last thing he wanted was to be caught between any further tensions between his holiness, the pope and King Henry.

"And is there proof of Durwin's, uh, indiscretions?"

"Oh yes, Steward Baldric was about to formally list them. Ah, Steward, have ye begun to create the list as I asked ye?" Sir Hyde asked.

"Nay, Milord. I've only calculated the amount of coin that is missing."

Sir Hyde frowned.

The bishop rubbed his chin. "And, how much was the difference?"

Sir Hyde turned to Steward Baldric in question.

"Milord, Steward Alard and I believe that it was slightly over three pounds. But we can't be certain until I begin detailing everything properly."

Sir Hyde raised an eyebrow as he stared at the bishop waiting for a response.

"If the, um, full amount were to be recovered, or better yet, found … perhaps the coin were accidently misplaced, then there would be no reason to send a communication to the king, am I correct, Sir Hyde?"

"My thoughts exactly, Bishop Immers. Where should we begin to look for the lost coin?"

The bishop turned to one of his assistants and spoke to him. There was much head shaking and nodding.

"Milords, I believe we may be able to assist. Amongst us, we may have some ideas where the coin could be found. If we were to be successful and locate it, then it could be sent to you, at Mellester Manor. Is this acceptable, Milords?" asked the bishop.

Sir Gweir nodded. "It would be most fortunate to find the coin, and the parishioners, as ye would expect, would welcome that, Yer Grace."

"And of yer visit here today, Bishop Immers?" asked Sir Hyde.

"As I stated when I arrived, it was only a trivial matter, and for the life of me, I, I, cannot recall what the reason was. But I wonder if I could intrude on the festivities and congratulate the bride and groom on their special day, Milord. I'd take pleasure in finally meeting Odo Read."

The knights followed Bishop Immers and Priest Kirby into the courtyard. Reeve Petrus walked over to stand beside his lord. They spoke briefly and then watched as Bishop Immers was introduced to the newly married couple by the old priest. As the bishop warmly congratulated

Charlotte on her holy union and remarked on her beauty, Odo looked up and saw Sir Hyde, Sir Gweir, Sir Renier and Reeve Petrus – all four men were smiling broadly.

Odo felt Charlotte slide her arm through his.

"Ye are indeed a special man, Odo," she said quietly.

He turned away from the knights and Reeve Petrus and looked at her. His beautiful Charlotte. Before he could reply, he felt the presence of another.

"Be warned, Odo, the holy man bears resentment. His loathing and hatred extends beyond gathered nobles and festers even now." Cathal turned his head towards the bishop. "While he smiles and jests with yer guests, he plans of vengeance."

Stunned, both Odo and Charlotte could only watch as the Irishman walked away toward the minstrels. He began to sing. The laughter and chatter died away as Cathal sung of innocent love and unsung heroes.

to be continued...

Other books by
Paul W Feenstra
Published by Mellester Press

Boundary

The Breath of God (Book 1 in Moana Rangitira series)
For Want of a Shilling (Book 2 in Moana Rangitira series)

Falls Ende – Primus (Book 1)
Falls Ende – Secundus (Book 2)
Falls Ende – Tertium (Book 3)
Falls Ende – Quartus (Book 4)
Falls Ende – Quintus (Book 5)
Falls Ende – Sextus (Book 6)

Gunpowder Green (New Zealand Short Stories)

Leonard hardy Series
A Sinister Consequence
A Questionable Virtue

Into the Shade

A Gentleman at heart